On The Way To Alice

By

Pug Greenwood

Heron Oaks

Murrells Inlet, South Carolina

ISBN-13:978-0692914175
ISBN-10:069291417X

Other books as Pug Greenwood:

Bim and Them – ISBN: 0692569561

Tooey's Crossroads – ISBN: 0692566198

Tooey's Crossroads II – 0692628134

Books as Robert F. Lackey:

Pulaski's Canal ISBN: 0692625267

Blood on the Chesapeake – ISBN 0692688676

Raven's Risk – ISBN: 0692831320

Kingdoms in the Marsh – ISBN: 0692831355

Brazen Deceit – ISBN: 0692063145

ON THE WAY TO ALICE

DEDICATION

To my Father,
Earl Lee Lackey, 1922-1992,
North Carolinian, Navy Pilot and Rascal,
who kept my mother shaking her head
all those years.

ACKNOWLEDGMENTS

No book can make its way to print without the hard work of many people.

I wish to acknowledge the valuable assistance of stalwart beta readers and thank each of them for their contributions.

Judee Cooper of Edgewood, Maryland,

Angela Corrieri of Columbia, Maryland,

Marie Feeley of Westland, Michigan,

Debra Gapa-Davidson of Grosse Ile, Michigan,

Mary J Summers of Waterford, Michigan,

John Tighe of Myrtle Beach, South Carolina,

Beta Readers Australia,

Robyn, Jason and Patrick

of Brisbane, Queensland, Australia,

who aided significantly in finalizing this manuscript.

i

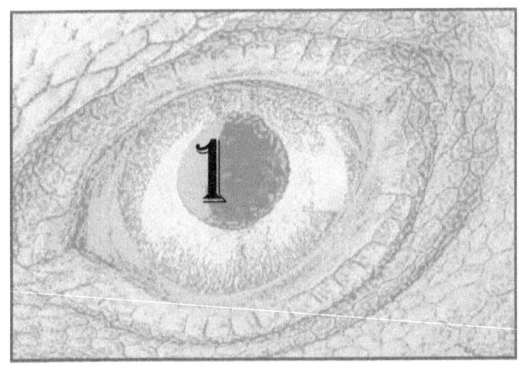

#132 – If this plane crashes, I'm really going to be pissed.

Malcolm Ironwater tapped the period onto the end of the numbered entry into his journal, then flipped it closed and slid his pen back into his shirt pocket. He felt his pen tap against the little bottle of antipsychotic pills resting near his heart, and patted the bottle affectionately. After several failed attempts to sail to Australia aboard tramp steamers that kept putting him off at remote islands to be shed of him, he was finally on his way to the Red Center to set his people free. He was not actually physiologically an Aborigine, but he knew in his heart that he was one of them, and he also knew that even though they did not know him yet, their souls cried out for him to save them. He snatched up his pen again and clicked the tip down.

#133 – I am not Maliqroische Indian.

He knew he wasn't Aborigine, just as he knew that he wasn't really Maliqroische Indian, the name that had come to him in a drug-induced episode; the tribe he used to think he led and had described to all the friendly people who worked at the sanitarium. When he looked into the polished stainless steel mirror in his room (they weren't allowed glass ones) he just saw the same pale Caucasian face that had always stared back at him, maybe with a hint of the Indian his father always told him was part of his ancestry. No, he knew he wasn't

1

Maliqroische Indian. He really knew that now, and he didn't think that anymore. He was pretty sure that he didn't.

#134 – Convincing the swell people at the sanitarium that I am not Maliqroische Indian, is why the kindly nurses, doctors and therapists signed the papers to let me go home again. It was a good thing not to tell them that I am Aborigine. I am sorry I lied to Odie.

They packed him off to home with the little blue and white striped happy-white-people pills he was to be taking, which he didn't always take, and had now stopped taking altogether. Still, he carried them inside the amber plastic bottle tucked snugly into his shirt pocket, as company and camouflage for the tiny speck-sized seeds of a powerful blue flower. The flower only grew within a granite boulder ring known as Indian Rocks, a low-lying rocky ridge back in southern Finton County. It was the home of the little blue flower, but not Malcolm's home. He didn't have one. And, well, he didn't really go home again. He just went back to where he came from last.

Back in Finton County where his sister Odie lived, he told her he was better and had a new job waiting for him in Tulsa. She and her husband Ivy gave him money for a fresh start and took him to the airport. He had felt guilty about telling her that lie, and taking the money. When the plane landed in Tulsa, he stayed aboard while it refueled for the second half of its flight to California. He had felt guilty then too, because he never was going to Tulsa.

He tied the loose leather strings on the flap of his journal and then slid it into the pocket of the seat in front of him. Malcolm had left behind three other barely started journals in his room at the sanitarium, wedged behind the radiator. Each journal was started when it seemed that providence would allow him to make his second lifelong wish come true. He wrote all his plans, then shoved the journal back behind the old radiator with the others, when the Patient Review Board said again, "No Malcolm, not yet."

This time he did not even start his journal until he

was actually aboard an Australian airline, in the air, and over the Pacific.

Alice. Alice Springs. The Alice.

The name floated among his thoughts. It was like Camelot to Malcolm. It became the collection of all the things wished. The center of his center.

His seat jumped again. Malcolm sat up and reached for his journal again and pulled his pen back out of his shirt pocket, and made another entry.

#135 – There's a little snot-nosed kid kicking my seat. He's been doing it since we started our taxi down the runway. When the lights are put out and his ugly mother falls asleep, I could strangle the little shit. But, then they will find him and would probably have to turn around and go back to Hawaii. Then, I would never get to Australia. Maybe I can wait until we're more than half way there. Then it would be too far to turn around.

Writing a journal was good therapy, the psychiatrist had said. It was good to get the bad thoughts out of one's head by writing them down.

Although, sometimes writing them down make them more real.

Malcolm smiled as he closed the journal and then placed it back in the seat pocket.

It was just a thought.

He shifted in his seat, trying to get comfortable. He had this little spot on the left side of his lower back that felt like a bruise when it wanted attention. It really was a spot, according to a doctor at the sanitarium. The doctor was visiting from a big medical school in another state and came by once a year to examine the patients, collecting information for another book on crazy people. Malcolm should have told his regular doctor about the bruise, but didn't think about it until after his doctor had retired. So the circuit doctor had to do.

Well, that's what you get for waiting until the last minute to make an appointment. You get the leftovers.

Doctor Dosker had put him through some tests, and then told him he had a "spot" on his kidney back there, and said he wanted to do a biopsy so he could look at a piece of it under a microscope. Afterward he said something else had to be done about it within the next five or six weeks, so they might be able to stop other spots from showing up and maybe even get rid of that one altogether. That's when Malcolm decided to fool everybody, make his head well, and go to Australia. Then he'd work on that kidney spot thing right after that.

Malcolm clicked his pen over his journal, and made another entry.

#136 – So here it is, day two of week three and I am in an aluminum tube shooting through one of the – spheres (atmo-?, tropo?-, whatever), like a bat out of hell, and still have ten more hours before I can land in Sydney and go to a real bathroom with porcelain and room for my knees. Ten more hours, unless, of course, I kill that little snot-dripping-seat-kicker behind me before we reach the half way point.

Keep it up, kid. You only have three point one hours to live.

At last the cabin attendant came by to ask Malcolm if he would like a drink.

"Tennessee whiskey, cola and lime, please."

He handed Malcolm a can of cola, a small square plastic bottle of whiskey with a miniature black label, and a short plastic glass of ice with a wedge of lime in it, before moving to the row behind.

"Anything for you, Ma'am? Young man, please do not kick the back of the seat, there. Someone is sitting in front of you who is likely to be bothered by it."

Malcolm smiled into his drink.

I love Australia. Kid, you listen to Crocodile Dundee there, and you just might make it to Australia on the INSIDE of this friggin plane.

The woman spoke, "Oh, he's not my son."

Dundee faked a smile and asked the kid, "Where's your mother, young man?"

As the attendant looked where the little boy pointed, a large woman waddled up the aisle, plowing back the outer corners of each seat on either side as she came, like thumbing through a deck of cards.

"Jeffrey. Jeffrey. You can come back with us now,

4

Akisha found another seat for you close to us."

Malcolm sipped on his drink.

Things are looking up! The fat woman has taken the little shit away. Maybe things will get quiet then and I can sleep a while.

No sooner had that hope floated up to the witch of perversity that frequently followed him around, than a disheveled young couple came forward, scanning the seats along both aisles. Malcolm looked up at them, and then quickly looked away, avoiding eye contact.

They had lavender tee shirts over torn and faded jeans. Hers had an orange arrow on front pointing to her left, and below the arrow was the word "his" in large orange letters. His was the counter of hers bearing the word "hers" above an arrow pointing to the right.

Oh, cute! As long as they stick to the correct sides of each other, they're a couple. If not, maybe they'd be sleeping with strangers!

The young woman spoke to the flight attendant and pointed a reluctant malnourished finger at the large mother side-stepping back down the aisle, dragging Jeffrey behind her like a reluctant outside dog being taken in for a bath.

"Sir, that woman told us there were other seats up front here where we could sit together."

Malcolm looked away and slipped lower in his seat, adjusting the coat he had laying across the empty seat beside him. He could see the attendant out of the corner of his eye, hovering at the end of his row, but did not look at him.

Oh, give me a break.

"Well, there's one here by this woman, and I think that's another empty seat by that gentleman."

Go away! Go away! Find another row! Great. Now the other cadaver wants to talk.

"We would really like to sit together", the young man said. "We just got married, but had to fly stand-by to afford the ticket."

Tough shit. Next time pay the full price. Shovel coal for six weeks like I did, then get married!

The woman behind him spoke up.

"Here,..."

Oh, Damn,...

"You take my seat and I will move up to the next row."

Oh, Hell NO!

They both groveled their thanks and began the aisle-to-row square dance with the woman, who then appeared at the beginning of Malcolm's row carrying an armload of sweaters, magazines, pocketbook, novel and a water bottle the size of a well fertilized pumpkin.

Aw shit!

"Sir, would you please take these things until I can get resettled?"

Go to Hell!

"Sure, I'd be glad to."

Shit!

"I just couldn't let those two lovebirds sit away from each other."

"Oh, I understand. That was very nice of you."

I'm gonna puke!

Malcolm accepted the items and then held them loosely with just his fingertips until she could reach for them again. He looked at her as he handed her things over. She smiled and he smiled back as she took them, his eyes fixed on her face as she sat down.

"Have you been to Australia before, sir?"

Great, we get to chat.

"No. First time. You?"

Shit! That's a stupid question to ask an Aborigine!!

"Going home for a while."

Malcolm looked at her features more closely. "Oh, you're, um, Aborigine?"

"Anangu. The name of my race is Anangu. I don't care to use 'Aborigine', it's a European term. Actually my family is Pitjantjatjara."

She stuck her hand out to him, and he took it in a loose handshake.

"I'm Itjanu Williamson."

"Itch anew?"

She smiled. "No. It-janoo. It means rain or spring in English – or close to that. In Anangu it refers to the

6

green time when it rains or after the rains

"Oh. I'm Malcolm Ironwater. Ex-Indian, future Aborigine, er Anywho."

She frowned briefly, then tilted her head and gave him a friendly big white toothy open-lipped grin.

"It's pronounced Ana-New. The a's are short. There's a G in there too, but no worries, it's silent. I've been studying the vapor sniffing problem on some of your Indian reservations, for my PhD in Sociology."

"Didn't know we had vapor sniffing problems. What vapors?"

"Gasoline. It gives a cheap high, then turns the brain into broccoli. We have a similar problem in some places out back home."

Malcolm was lost in silence, not listening, staring at the features of her face.

Her smile faded to a pensive pout. "Mmmmh." Was her only response.

That went well. Nap time!

She snapped open her novel to a place holding a folded customs form, and he scrunched down in his seat to pretend it was comfortable and sought out the waiting sleep. He could not find a position that felt comfortable and determined to sit back up and try to read the novel he had bought at one of the numerous airport newsstands before he boarded, but he did not reach for it and fell asleep in spite of knowing he could not.

"Sir. Sir, you have my blanket." The woman poked him in his side. "Sir, you have my blanket."

Malcolm woke to a darkened cabin, with the thin airline blanket wrapped around his neck and bunched up between his chin and his left shoulder. He looked toward the voice through swollen sleep deprived eyes. His own blanket was laying half off his lap and wrapped around one leg, with the rest of it drooped to the floor. He raised his head and felt a sharp pain across the left side of his neck. He had managed to lay this head all the way over onto his shoulder with the meager tuft of cotton blanket serving as pillow, into a painfully unnatural position. Malcolm slowly struggled against his complaining neck muscles, stretched beyond their normal span and

7

punishing him with tooth-ache like shooting pains as he moved. He stretched within the confines of his seat and managed to hand the blanket back to the woman.

"Sorry. I must have dozed off."

"You went into a snoring coma, sir. We even had the attendant try to wake you to stop the noise, but he said he could only do so much."

Malcolm looked at her and spoke through the stale cotton lining the inside of his mouth.

"Sorry."

The woman emitted a barely controlled exasperated sigh and took the blanket. Malcolm leaned forward and fished the bottle of airline water from the seat pocket in front of him and swallowed the rest of it in three large gulps. He arched his back to loosen some of the stiffness and looked around the cabin. Those close by gave stern meaningful stares.

"Sorry."

He repeated the apology to the woman across the aisle with the fiercest stare. He then pushed the button to activate the little color LCD screen in front of him and ran the channel numbers up to 21 where he found the flight progress graphic. It was a low pixel color map of the Pacific Ocean with a red line tracing from Hawaii to their current location denoted by a little black icon in the shape of an airplane. The little black plane sat in the middle of a great blue field, and there was absolutely nothing else on the screen.

"O-o-o-o-o-h crap."

He sighed. The flight was nowhere near its destination. He endured another three movies, only one worth watching, and the entire recorded repertoire of the news, music and comedy audio channels. After breakfast and three trips to the restroom line, the pilot finally announced it was time to tidy up the cabin before landing.

With aching swollen joints that refused to work smoothly and stiff-legged gaits the passengers moved toward the doors. Like zombie creatures from an old black and white horror movie, they joined into the stumbling stampede off the plane. They struggled to collect baggage, snake through customs, and wander out of the international section of Sydney airport. Then they merged with other herds in other lines to climb onto airport buses going to domestic flights in another part of the airport. As Malcolm settled into his seat, a Maliqroische Indian waved from the back of the bus, calling out his name. Malcolm ignored him. After a brief respite on the bus that managed to make a six mile trip out of a half mile distance between the two hubs, Malcolm found himself in another line to another x-ray machine.

Standing in line, Malcolm's attention was drawn to the far side of the cavernous terminal, where a near-naked Indian was frantically waving at him. Wearing a deer-skin loin cloth and carrying a stone- tipped spear, he began to chant Malcolm's name. Soon the Indian was joined by other similar clad warriors who formed a great chanting chorus.

"Mal-colm! Mal-colm! Mal-colm!"

The sound was almost deafening, but no one in the terminal paid them any notice.

The group of Indians swelled, and began to dance in a circle, still chanting Malcolm's name. Malcolm looked among the others in line, but none of them were looking toward the chanting Indians. In fact, no one in the terminal appeared to notice them at all.

I am well. This is not happening. There are no Maliqroische Indians. I am not an Indian Chief. I am Aborigine now.

Malcolm dropped his bags and pulled out the little pill bottle from his shirt pocket. The chanting grew louder and louder. He gently withdrew a single blue and white pill with his fingertips, until it was at the lip of the plastic bottle. He puffed on the pill to free it of the tiny speck-sized seeds mixed among the pills. He popped the pill into his mouth, swallowing it without water and recapped the bottle.

I am well, dammit!

The line began to move again.

"I am well!"

"That's lovely," said the security person who took his

9

ticket folder and passport.

Malcolm looked back across the terminal. There were no Indians. He smiled at the officer, who returned the same empty smile.

With his just claimed baggage tied with yet another set of destination tags, he lined up to pledge to another attendant that he still hadn't let the bag out of his site, or accepted it from a stranger, except the baggage attendant in the international section. He joined another line-up along another mechanical extension walkway to another airliner. He queued up again behind more wrinkly-clothed travelers, also on their way to Adelaide. They stood waiting on a woman sixty rows farther in, who just realized she had to get back into the aisle to remove her jacket and retrieve a book out of her bag, which was, of course, stowed twenty rows back.

Inch by aggravating inch he made it to row 42, looking for seat A. It was two seats away from the aisle, wedged against the window, so he had to beg his way past the occupants of seats C and B to get to it. The passenger in seat B looked up with the same droop dog expression he was wearing when he saw her.

"Hello," Dr. Williamson said without inflection.

Aw shit!

"Looks like we're seat mates again," Malcolm said, trying half-heartedly to sound polite.

Itjanu looked straight ahead without expression.

"Yeah. How lucky can two people get."

---<>---

Getting a cab at the Adelaide airport was easy. Malcolm knew enough from his reading to sit up front to keep from appearing 'pohmie', as the Aussies referred to stuck-up tourist. He was looking forward to immersing himself in the real outback, not the movie version, but the red sand and bright sun of the "Red Centre". Still, he had planned to spoil himself with one more night of American-style middle class pampering, so he had the driver take him straight to the Holiday Inn on South Terrace. He was rewarded with cheerful Aussie greetings, a very clean room, and access to a decent bar where, to his amazement, the bar tender admonished him for leaving too much of a tip.

Now that'll never happen in the States

There was still plenty of daylight left, so he picked up a street map from the pretty tanned blonde at the front desk and made his way up King William Street toward the center market near Victoria Square. On the way, Maliqroische Indians slipped in among the people walking the sidewalks. As Malcolm spotted them, he waved them away. The market was a maze of covered alleys and walkways dividing several acres into shops, souvenir stands, restaurants, stores, services, and cooked food stands of almost every nationality. It was a farmers market, a flea market, a bazaar, a carnival, a fun house, and a shopping mall of dizzying variety. The thought of a sit-down supper faded away to the tastes of several known and some only suspected tidbits of one ethnic style or another. During one sampling of some peppery meat on a stick, he looked up the crowded walkway and momentarily between two broad shouldered men; he spotted Williamson coming in his direction.

"Aw shit!"

He took off through one of the many cross ways that divided the market up into dozens of little blocks. One stall-lined walkway ended at the back entrance to a super market, where Malcolm entered in search of a soft drink to quench the fire of the last whatever-it-was he ate. He grabbed a bottle of an unknown orange drink that looked like something he had tested before and downed its contents. After paying for the drink, he went to find the one Australian food item he most curious to sample: Vegemite. After repeating his request twice to a heavily accented Korean-Aussie, who was good naturedly trying to understand Malcolm's Southern-Yank accent, Malcolm found the little brown jar with the yellow label at the end of the aisle. He went next for a small loaf of bread and a small tub of margarine, so he would have the right fixings for the morning experience the next day.

The next morning was day five of week three. He had lost one of his days crossing over the international date line, somewhere out there over the pacific, but he would get it back on the return flight. The hotel room did not come with a toaster or hot plate, and he hadn't thought to order toast for breakfast. However, the room was equipped with a very nice and clean iron. Malcolm turned the setting on the iron to *Cotton (No Steam)* and propped the iron between two small stacks of folded towels on the counter in the bathroom. It only took a few minutes to have golden brown toast, and off they went for the first delicate spread of margarine by his large pocketknife fished out of his luggage. Next came the Vegemite. It looked like dark roasted peanut butter, and the tiny sample he had placed on the tip of his tongue the night before told him it would be very salty and much like roasted peanuts.

One thing Americans knew was peanut butter, so Malcolm drove the knife blade all the way to the bottom of the little plastic jar. He scooped out a full third of the contents and spread it thickly over the buttered toast, just the way they do in those stateside peanut butter commercials. Then with the toast looking very much like a chocolate covered éclair, Malcolm shoved a generous corner of the toast into his mouth.

The taste of overly roasted peanuts filled Malcolm's mouth with a flood of signals from his tongue. The saltiness of the paste almost overwhelmed those taste buds on his tongue assigned that sensation. Next came the pungent taste from the yeast base that actually made up Vegemite, and it grew exponentially stronger as Malcolm mushed through the outrageous helping of goo slathered on his toast. The vapors of the paste filled his mouth, his nose and his sinuses. It permeated his taste and olfactory sensors the way a strong Limburger expanded through the head – not tasting or smelling like Limburger, but filling all the food related senses in a sweeping fog that drove away every other taste.

Maybe I put on too much.

The brown paste drew all the moisture from his mouth like alum. The growing leathery texture of his mouth worsened as he looked desperately for a water glass. His stomach roiled and his upper esophagus filled with cotton.

Definitely too much!

He ran to the bathroom, intent on running the tap and scooping handfuls of water into his dehydrating mouth. The assault on his senses of taste and smell was quickly becoming far too much for his morning empty stomach. It forced him to turn away from his dash to the sink and throw himself toward the toilet. He snatched up the lid and expelled the remaining dough ball that had formed in his mouth, but his stomach was not ready to do its job here, only to threaten him with heaves. He lunged back toward the sink, gagging on the plaster setting up in his throat, and reeling from the gases billowing though his nose. He managed to turn the spigot on full force and plunged his mouth into the spraying water, pushing in the water with both hands.

He had swallowed a few more mouthfuls of water when the phone rang, but he ignored it. After three more mouthfuls of water, He was able to stand. Malcolm leaned back against the sink counter, gasping air to clear his mouth and nose, and swallowing several more times. The phone rang again just as his stomach received its first full sample of the yeast.

Definitely way too much.

The reflexive surge from his stomach was undeniable and he lunged back toward the toilet just in time for the first of three dives over the little ceramic pool. The phone rang again, but it could not draw Malcolm out from the Vegemite tempest raging in the bathroom.

Malcolm was sitting on the floor with his back against his new ceramic friend when someone knocked on the room door.

"Mr. Ironwater? Mr. Ironwater?"

Malcolm grabbed a towel and forced himself to his feet, to make the six steps to his room door.

The young deskman offered him an energetic smile.

"Sorry to bother you in your room, Sir, but your taxi has been waiting. We rang up three times but there was no answer, so I got worried. You told Wanda last night you had to meet up with your group this morning, so she made a note for me not to let you over sleep."

13

Malcolm stepped back slightly and covered a robust belch with the hand towel.

"You all right sir?"

" 'Scues me.Vegemite."

"Sir?"

"Vege-," but that was all he could say before dashing back into the bathroom, leaving the deskman standing in the open doorway. Concerned, the young man stepped into the room. Malcolm's voice echoed from the toilet. "Thought I'd try some Vegemite this morning, before I left."

The young man smiled discretely to himself as Malcolm bellowed into the commode. The Desk Clerk looked around the room and spotted the partially eaten toast discarded on the counter, with the gargantuan portion of Vegemite slathered across the top.

"Gawd" he said under his breath. "Bit much there, wasn't it, mate?"

"No shit," echoed from within the porcelain seat. "Would you please ask the taxi to wait a while longer?"

"No worries," and then the young Aussie was gone.

It was thirty minutes before a pale faced Malcolm, stepped out onto the sidewalk in front of the hotel, carrying his duffle bag over one shoulder and his back pack over the other. The taxi driver, ruddy complexion and solidly built with his sleeves rolled tightly onto his upper arms, was leaning against the side of his car under the shade of a large red Eucalyptus tree, reading a newspaper spread wide between his arms.

"I guess you're waiting for me. Sorry to keep you waiting."

The driver flashed a wide grin, took the larger bag and stepped around to the trunk of his car.

"You all right, then? Stanley said you were having a bit of trouble this morning, and you were asking me to wait."

Malcolm had flashes of his turkey dance in his hotel room, when his stomach and his colon fought for first rights in the bathroom. "Not the best way to start out on a back pack tour."

14

The trip to Waymouth Street was made in near silence except for the driver's single unanswered question. "How'd you like the vegemite?"

#137 – Stay away from the Vegemite.

The taxi pulled in to the open space in front of a small office, piled high with backpacks on either side of the door. The sidewalk was full of young people, mostly in their early twenties. It was a collage of tanned skin, firm muscular arms and legs, well-worn hiking boots, shorts, and Tee shirts. Under shiny hair, animated conversations mixed among energetic smiles. After setting his duffle bag on the sidewalk near the others, the driver waved away the offered tip and slapped Malcolm on his back as he got back in his cab.

"Have fun, mate."

Malcolm made his way into the office, which was a jumbled interior version of the sidewalk scene, except there was a desk in the back of the room. He could see the top of a red headed woman over the teetering pile of backpacks in front of the desk. She was talking with a meaty looking man with skin the color of light mahogany contrasting the faded khaki bush shorts and T-shirt, his arms and legs covered with blonde hair. The man turned as Malcolm approached the desk. The man flashed a broad toothy grin and arched his eyebrows almost too yellow to be real.

Malcolm handed his reservation papers to the woman. "Good morning." Malcolm offered, "I hope I'm not too late."

"Ahh. You must be m'Yiank," the man said.

"Excuse me?"

The redhead smiled up at Malcolm after reviewing his papers.

"Malcolm, this is Mac Hartwell. He's the driver on your tour."

"Good morning." Malcolm said, accepting Mac's offered hand.

"T. McGregor Hartwell. Call me Mac. I'll be the guide, driver, radio operator, and first aid corpsman if one's needed. Oh, and ya' can't be sayin' that anymore, mate. Now repeat after me: G'die"

"Gu'day"

"Nah. Try'er again, Malcolm"

"G'day."

"Nope. Try'er again."

"G'Die!"

"Close that time, but you'll still need to work on it some."

He flashed another grin, plopped on a well-worn blue mesh hat in the shape of the traditional outback cover, and then headed for the door.

Malcolm looked after the man and then turned back toward the young woman behind the desk. She bestowed another kindly smile on him.

"You might want to follow after him with your kit. Soon as he gets in the bus, he'll be gone. Mac doesn't stay in town one second longer than he has to."

Malcolm grabbed his bags and hurried after Mac, down the sidewalk and around the corner. There he saw a large four-wheel-drive van with the tour company logo painted on the side. Hooked to the rear of the van was a well dented tan trailer nearly half the size of the van. It was sprinkled liberally with red sand, and sported faded remnants of the same logo on the van. Mac opened the rear of the trailer to a small cloud of red dust and took Malcolm's duffle bag. He tossed the bag into the darkness of the trailer with one hand as he slammed the door shut with the other, even before the bag had time to land. He stepped around to the left side of the trailer, but pointed toward the right for Malcolm.

"You'll need to get in on that side, mate. My door only goes to the driver's seat."

Malcolm stepped up into the van on the other side of the engine box, and looked into a collection of expectant faces, who were obviously waiting on his arrival so they could start their trip. The van looked like it could easily hold twenty people, but those already on board were sitting one person to a double seat on the right as Malcolm walked in. The left side held a line of six single seats along the off-centered aisle. The last split row and the back bench seat were empty. Counting as he went back, he noted that there were only eight other people on the van. Malcolm would make nine, and Mac ten. Malcolm had hoped for a small group, anxious that he not get swamped in a sea of American tourists and spend his entire trip listening to some whiner from Maryland or New Jersey wishing for a McDonald's. It appeared he got his wish for group size, although at first blush any one of those faces could still harbor an American McDonald's whiner.

At last! I'm going home to my real people.

He smiled back at the faces, scanning each one as they scanned him.

Now, which ones are the assholes. At least dogs get a chance to sniff each other.

He halted momentarily, half way down the aisle. Sitting on the back bench was another Maliqroische Indian, waving in childish glee. Ignoring him, he threaded along the narrow aisle to the last double seat in front of the back bench, and swung into it as the black woman sitting across the aisle looked up.

Aw shit.

"Good morning... I mean G'day," he said. "Looks like we are sharing the same tour."

Malcolm wondered if he was wearing the same look of weary disappointment as was Itjanu Williamson.

"Looks like it," she said, turning away and speaking to the window, as the storefronts of northeast Adelaide slipped past the van.

My charm works every time.

Malcolm settled into his seat, slid his pack into the empty space next to him and gazed outside, while Mac began his tour-guide chatter. Intent on finding all the differences between Australia and Finton County, Malcolm paid little attention to the cautions, guidance, and suggestions coming from Mac, or the Indian behind him chanting, "Mal-colm, Mal-colm, Mal-colm."

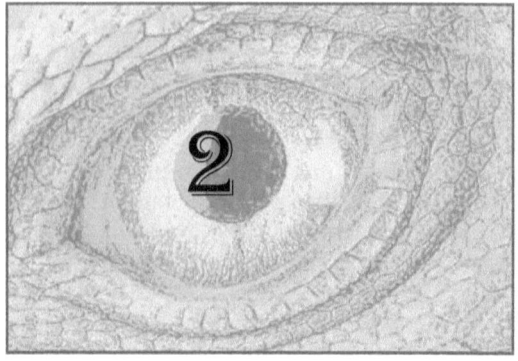

Ninety minutes later the van rolled from the city and into green countryside. The time allowed Malcolm to take a blue and white pill and shoo away the cheering Indian in the back row.

#138 Sometimes Maliqroische Braves can be a super pain in the ass. They are not mine. I am not a Maliqroische Chief, I am Annanew.

Malcolm chatted with the man in the seat in front of him, Hiraht Neemann. Hiraht was not as young as Malcolm firs thought. He was actually a very happy a computer programmer in his early forties from the Netherlands on a month-long holiday.

"What do you hope to see, Malcolm," Hiraht asked.

I can't tell you that.

Malcolm paused for a few seconds. "I have always wanted to see the Outback. I want to spend time with the Anangu."

Itjanu snorted from behind the book she was reading. "Fat chance, that." The comment was made only loud enough for Malcolm's ears.

"What was that, madam," Hiraht asked.

Itjanu lowered the book and merely smiled at him, shaking her head, meaning it was nothing.

"I am curious, though," he continued, peeking over Malcolm's shoulder at her. "Why would a native

Australian take a back pack tour with a bunch of foreigner, like this motley group? Have you never been into the outback?"

She stared at him a moment, then shrugged her shoulders. "Oh, I've been to the outback before, believe me..."

"Then, why?"

She sighed, and set her book down in her lap. "Cheap transportation. Mac goes right into my family's village. Otherwise, I'd have to hire a car, or take a bus and then a long taxi ride. Either way, very expensive."

"Oh. Very smart, um, I didn't hear your name before."

"Itjanu Williamson," she said,

Hirhat raised slightly and slipped a long slender arm across the aisle and offered his hand to Itjanu. "Hiraht Neemann."

She smiled and accepted his hand. Hiraht looked over his shoulder to Malcolm, then turned back toward Itjanu, "So you two have been introduced to each other?"

"Yes. We flew over together from the States," Malcolm said, but before he could say anymore, Itjanu leaned back down in her seat behind her book in cold silence.

Hiraht rolled his eyes back and forth between Itjanu and Malcolm, as he settled back into his own seat. He leaned close to Malcolm with a small smile and whispered. "It did not go well?"

Itjanu spoke from behind her book, "No."

In front of Hiraht was Lyle Woodsford, a recent college graduate from Liverpool, England. In front of Williamson sat a very English woman named Elizabeth Mackenaugh, with pale skin and dark auburn hair who appeared to be in her late thirties. The van occupants divided themselves into two conversational groups. The others were engaged with questioning Mac and exchanging little get-to-know-you conversations. It split the group into two sets of five and that suited Malcolm. Since the Williamson woman no longer actually addressed Malcolm directly, it effectively made his

19

conversational group only four, which suited him all the more.

Just as well.

#139 – I don't think I will save all the ~~Annanew~~ Aborigine.

Minutes later the van to wound its way into the small vineyard town of Clare, the first stop on the tour. Mac found a parking lot big enough for the van and trailer behind the local tourist information building and flipped on the little overhead speakers as he put the van in neutral and cut off the engines.

"There'll be damned few civilized stops for us, ladies and gentlemen. Better make the most of this one."

He gave directions to nearby wineries and shops, and then asked the group to meet back at the van in forty-five minutes.

Malcolm grumbled to himself as he stepped down from the van.

"Hope this doesn't turn into one of those damned if-this-is-Tuesday-this-must-be-Belgium tours."

Malcolm was startled by the pat of Mac's big hand on his shoulder.

How did you get around the bus so friggin quick?

"Nah mate, this is one of those take-too-long-gettin-back-to-the-bus-and-your-ass-gets-left-behind tours."

He chuckled warmly and walked off to a supermarket across the street. Malcolm watched him swagger away and smiled to himself.

Him I like.

The town of Clare was essentially a single main street running north and south with four or five side streets running out into slim rural neighborhoods, or out toward one of the Vineyards that surrounded it. Malcolm waited to see which direction the majority of the group went and then headed in the opposite direction.

The stores along the main street were brick and stucco, nestled in close together, with only one or two of any significant width. The design was more of an old European village than any small town seen in the States.

He crossed the bridge on a narrow walkway next to the road and looked down over a meager stream that crossed under and into the thick woods on the other side.

Just beyond the bridge was a winery that appeared to be an old rust-red painted barn joined to a small outlet store with exposed exterior beams edging faded yellow stucco. The store was faced with an almost old-west style front porch of dark wood set under a generous dark green tin roof. Mounting the three steps to the porch, Malcolm approached the front doors of small paned glass framed over heavy wooden lower halves. The door edges and doorway frames were well rounded from years of traffic.

An old man sitting on the porch withdrew the stem of his pipe as Malcolm passed and gave a friendly nod and toothy Aussie smile. Malcolm returned the smile and went in to the small shop. The winery store offered a good variety of local wines, but mostly their own label, which is what Malcolm wanted most to try. His first choice was two bottles of their shiraz – his guide book told him to be sure to try those first. The young lady behind the counter helped him find a white and a rosé that were not too dry for his not so delicate tongue, but not too sweet.

He tasted the little thimble-sized paper cup sample she gave him. It was too early in the day for him to be in the mood for wine and it only mixed with the still lingering taste of vegemite, so he just smiled as if he agreed with her and bought the bottles. The reminder of his early experience with vegemite gave his stomach a small roll, so he handed over the colorful Australian bills and headed for the door and fresh air. He joined the old man on the bench out front and set the bag between his feet.

The old man eyed the bag as Malcolm set it down and withdrew the stem of his pipe. "You on a wine tour through the valleys here?"

Malcolm shook his head and reached into the generous front pocket of his green twill shorts for his own battered pipe. "No, sir. This is our first stop on the way up the center to Alice Springs."

"Gotta long way to go, mate. That's a real long drive."

"We'll be camping. That's where we're going at the end, but the fun is going to be the camping and visits on the way."

"Camping? Like in tents, like that?"

"Yeah." Malcolm fished out his pouch and filled the bowl and then lit his pipe.

The old man chuckled. "Like flies, do ya?"

"They don't bother me when I'm camping. That's what Deet is for."

The old man chuckled to himself again, but did not say anything else about the flies. "You're a Yank?"

"Yeah."

"I lived up North in my younger days – during the war. We had a station outside Alice. Had a Yank come stay with us for a while. He'd been shot down fightin the Japanese, then came down to the Alice from the hospital while he was healin."

Malcolm nodded his head to the rhythm of the story. Their pipe smoke joined, drifted up within the porch, then slipped from under the eaves and rolled up into the morning sunshine. He smiled toward the Maliqroische Indians dancing along the nearby roof tops.

Wonder how long his story is going to go on.

Two men came around the outer corner from the barn, arguing in tones that spoke of a long acquaintance. One wore a wide brimmed straw hat.

"It was just picked last night, John. Can't be bad!"

The other man was without a hat and carried a clipboard in his right hand. He stopped and turned to the first and tapped the clipboard lightly against his chest.

"Didn't say it was bad, Clyde. I said it was <u>rotten</u>. You musta hooked up the wrong trailer or something, but those grapes are so rotten you can already smell the fermentation!"

"Can't be rotten! Just picked the damn things. We had the machines going all night, down the rows with that trailer," he said, punching the air in front of his trailer with his finger.

22

The man with the clipboard shrugged his shoulders and shook his head.

"Can't use'em, John. That's it."

He turned and walked up the stairs into the store.

Clyde pulled off his hat and slapped it against his pant leg. "Well, shit." He spun around and walked back around the corner.

The old man continued, "When the yank got well, he tried his hand at breakin Brumbies..."

A truck door slammed and an engine roared to life. Gravel jumped across the drive way before the store and a battered Land Rover shot around the corner into view, pulling a trailer with a cargo piled high under a loosely tied plastic cover. Dark juice seeped under the trailer tailgate, dropping little splashes of liquid onto the sandy drive, laying a trail of spoiled grape juice on the road as he drove away.

"And damned if he didn't go and break his ankle," the old man said. "Had to lay up there at the station for another three weeks before he was well enough to go back to the hospital in Darwin."

Malcolm turned back to the old man. "He didn't walk like he was hurt."

"Not him," the old man pointed up the road with the stem of his pipe. "That yank! He come down to get healed up and broke his ankle tryin to be a cowboy. Been seeing a lot of that here lately, too."

Malcolm squinted his eyes at the man. "A lot of broken ankles?"

"No. Rotten grapes. They got machines that pick'em at night so they're fresh, but here lately a bunch of them have come in all spoiled by the next morning. Not all from the same growers either."

Malcolm nodded his head and drew on his pipe as he sorted out the two stories and decided whether either one was worth another question, before he left that scatter-brained old man to himself. "What happened to the Yank?"

"Don't know. Met Maggie at the Boomerang Café, got married to her before some other bloke got any ideas, and came down here in early '43. Started a farm."

"How did your farm do?"

The old man leaned forward and tapped the end of his pipe against the bottles in Malcolm's bag. "Not bad, we think."

The front door opened and the pretty young counter girl leaned out. "Gramma Maggie just called. Said you need to get back up to the house and take your medicine. She asked if you were smoking down here."

"Wha'd ya tell'er?"

Her mouth held a sweet smile within full lips, and her eyelids were crunched completely closed. "Told her I hadn't seen ya doin it."

The old man chuckled and stood, tapping his pipe against one of the porch posts, sending a small cloud of ash out into the parking lot. He stuck his pipe into his shirt pocket and then pointed a thumb back toward the closing door.

"My granddaughter's named Margaret too, after Maggie. She's a right cutie, too."

Malcolm followed the old man down the steps into the lot. The old man headed north up a slight hill toward a group of houses while Malcolm turned South. He stuck his hands in his pockets and smiled to himself as he ambled back toward the center of town. Two blocks down he stopped short and raced back toward the winery to find his bag sitting on the porch where he left it. When he got back to the van everyone else was already on board. They all snickered when Malcolm climbed up and made his way to the back. Mac continued what was obviously an on-going conversation with those already on board.

"Like I said, tell-em forty-five minutes, but plan for an hour and then hope it ain't longer."

Cute.

Malcolm halted in front of his seat and pointed his thumb farther back.

Git!

The Indian laughed and jumped out of Malcolm's seat.

Mac slapped his hands together to gain everyone's attention. "Right, then. Let's mix'em up so everybody gets a chance to meet everybody else."

Uh Oh.

"Those in the back reverse seats with those in the front. Those in the middle two rows, stay where you are but you have to talk with the folks you didn't talk to on the way down to Clare."

Oh Joy. We get to mix and match.

Mac popped in a CD of Aussie Outback music containing a lot of fast guitar riffs and references to Emus and Kangaroos, and then cranked up the volume as the pandemonium of Aussie-musical-van-seats played itself out. Malcolm wound up sitting on the second row, behind Itjanu who fell into a lively conversation with Mac.

The Indian sat crossed-legged on the engine box next to Mac, facing rearward. He repeatedly grabbed at Mac's hat, even though his fingers slipped through the fabric without touching it. Malcolm knew the brave was only doing it to get his attention, so he flashed the Indian a twisted face frown to make him behave. Mac was looking up into the rear view mirror at the same moment. The Indian laughed so loud Malcolm expected everyone in the van to turn toward the Indian, but no one moved.

No more respect for their Chief.

The Indian gave Malcolm a broad smile, and raised his middle finger in belligerent display.

Malcolm was beside Lyle, who was dying to share his last four weeks experiences working as a bartender in Adelaide.

I don't suppose you could fix me a drink now, could you? A double would be nice.

Mac took the van north toward Quorn, which looked weird on the mileage sign, but was pronounced as "Corn". Rather than the obnoxious recount of an adolescent snot, Lyle showed himself to be a good story teller with a decent sense of humor. Much as he tried to dislike the boy, Malcolm finally admitted to himself that he was enjoying the conversation. He managed to trade a few civilized words with Natalia Stoica, the daughter of a

25

Romanian businessman living in Australia, who actually took the tour on a dare and admitted she had never been camping before.

She won't like it.

Peter Atterman and Karina *something-or-other* were in fact a couple. She was a supervisor in an accounting firm in Amsterdam, but nowhere near the appearance or behavior of a stereotypical accountant. She wasn't beautiful, but quite attractive. She emitted an air of sexuality in her body movements and lingering eye contact with all the men in the van. Mac's occasional side glances at her past Williamson, proved Malcolm's observation. Malcolm mentally dubbed Karina the 'Pheromone Queen'. Peter was essentially a beefcake several years younger than her, closer to Lyle's age than Karina's. He worked in the same office and reported to her during the day, but lived with her at night.

Probably reported to her then as well. Strong as an ox and damned near as smart. Male version of the dumb blonde.

The group enjoyed a short stop for a chance to stretch their legs with a walk around the old train station and a quick beer at the corner pub. Mac mixed the seats again as they left town. Not too surprisingly, Karina found herself next to Mac. The Indian remained on the engine box, making vulgar gestures toward Karina and sticking his tongue out of the side of his mouth, whenever Malcolm looked in that direction. Malcolm found himself next to the English woman. In the most British accent, Elizabeth Mackenaugh, quickly milked the basics from Malcolm, and then offered her own blunt history.

"My second husband is shacked up in London with the little whore from his favorite pub. So, I emptied all the accounts and stocks and such, and then booked a holiday here in Australia."

"And you decided to go camping??"

"Well, I've already seen the coasts, the cities and the islands."

"How long have you been here?"

She laughed and clasped her hands together in front of her chin.

26

"Three months, so far. The little creep must be going mad trying to find me."

Malcolm shared her laughter.

"At least my first husband had the decency to die when he was ready to get away from me."

She lifted a plastic stemmed wine glass she had purchased at a winery in Clare and added a few more ounces of red wine. She raised an eyebrow and pointed the near-empty bottle toward Malcolm, but he waved his hand away with a smile.

That explained her chatty disposition.

"Alfred got my twenties, and Steven got my thirties."

She chuckled into her wine glass.

"The next ten or so are going to be mine."

She drained her glass again, refilled it with the last of the bottle, and then used the bottle to slide open the window next to her. She chuckled again and then tossed the wine bottle into the ditch along the road.

The countryside thinned dramatically leaving low grass fields on either side of the road. Mac pulled into an unfenced field, bouncing all the passengers as he made a complete loop in what had recently been cultivated land, and returned to the road through a not too shallow drainage ditch and headed the van in the direction he had come. A few minutes later he brought the van to a halt, locked the brakes and left the van without speaking to anyone. Malcolm traded looks with some of the others, exchanging unspoken questions until the passenger side door slid open. Mac mounted the van with a single step and walked directly back to Elizabeth. As Elizabeth looked up, Mac handed her wine bottle back to her.

"We don't do that here."

"Oh, no, of course not. Excuse me."

"No worries. I'm sure that won't be happening again."

"No. It certainly will not."

He rewarded her with a boyish smile and then returned to close the passenger door and climb the engine box between his seat and Karina. The Indian performed a brief lap dance with Karina while Mac climbed over, and then returned to his perch. The van

27

continued in silence for several minutes while everyone, including Malcolm, gave serious thought to Mac's action, until conversations finally renewed.

Elizabeth slid the bottle back into its bag and then looked at Malcolm.

"Now, where was he when I was twenty? Where?"

She chuckled again with a half smile, the red in her face fading, and followed her own question with a statement to Malcolm.

"And if you are coarse enough to point out that he was probably in diapers then, I shall become your worst enemy."

Malcolm only smiled at her.

I like this one.

He glanced toward the front of the van, but the Indian was not there.

At midday, Mac pulled the van into a roadside park among welcoming trees. He marshaled the people into two groups under the shade of several gum trees. He directed one to prepare the food handed out from the trailer and the other to clean off concrete picnic tables, while he parked the van. Malcolm found himself cutting slices off a large block of white sharp farmer's cheese. Despite his disdain for Mac's 'Rules of the Group', he managed to resist the urge to eat one of the pieces until the others could join in. In his hunger, he was slicing each piece as if it was going to be his own. After several cuts his chore was finished and he turned to head back to the van for his pipe.

Itjanu stood in front of him pointing at the table.

"That's much too thick."

"It's concrete, lady. It comes that way."

"I'm talking about the cheese, uh, um..."

"Malcolm."

"Malcolm. I'm talking about the cheese, Malcolm. You should slice it thin, so people can put it in their sandwiches with the meat and tomatoes."

Malcolm looked at her in mock innocence.

"It's thin enough for me, but show me how thin you like it."

28

She shrugged her shoulders and stepped around him to the table, picked up the knife and began to slice the inch thick cheese slabs into delicate wafers. She cut two of the slabs into deli-thin perfection , then turned around to offer the knife back to Malcolm, but by then he was and stepping up into the van. She stood there a moment longer with the knife handle held out to no one, while she closed her eyes, blew out her breath, and slowly counted to ten.

Mac drifted by, checking the progress of his troops and glanced down at the cheese.

"Still a little thick there."

Itjanu opened her eyes to him and flashed a wide smile. "Yes it is," she said, but her eyes said 'go away', so he did.

Malcolm was last in line when the group queued up to the table, holding a cup of red wine in one hand and fingering a thick slice of fresh multigrain bread with the other. He smelled the honey-nut flavored bread in deep sniffs waiting for his turn at the cheese. When Hiraht stepped away, Malcolm leaned forward to reach for the cheese, but stopped his hand in mid air above the paper dish. He scanned around the table looking for her, figuring she would be watching. Itjanu had seated herself under a young Eucalyptus tree next to Elizabeth and was engaged in an animated conversation, but managed to roll her large eyes in his direction just long enough for their eyes to meet. He smiled and then reached for a spoon, which he used to scoop up the finely chopped cheese and press it into the pocket he formed with his soft slice of bread. He sat in the remaining folding chair pulled from the trailer, and was immediately set upon by dozens of small flies.

Mac spoke from the other side of the table.

"Flies'll get real bothersome once we get out aways."

Malcolm grunted acknowledgement as he slapped the flies away in front of his face with his hand holding the impromptu cheese pocket. This sent little arcs of finely chopped sharp white cheese into the air and onto his lap. Henry Matan began chattering away from the next seat and Malcolm forced himself to appear interested to take his mind away from the ruined cheese and the flies. He smiled at Henry.

Shut up Henry.

Out of the corner of his eye, he could see the Indian leaning forward from the seat behind, conspicuously eating a large slice of white cheese.

"The main library in Quebec has an absolutely astounding collection of mythologies and occult references. I spent months on end of my free time researching the old stories, so by the time I finally got a chance to actually travel to South America, I was almost an expert on the Aztec and Inca legends."

Henry shoved another large portion of his sandwich into his mouth, chewing and speaking around the meat and bread and tomato, and...sliced cheese.

At least you got a slice of cheese, instead of this powder.

Henry rambled on. "You see, it was just as I had suspected, many of the legends of Europe and even Egypt, are repeated under different names in American native lore. And..."

You're eating my cheese, you shit!

"... since most legends have some thread of actual foundation in ancient history, it pointed to the possibility that not only did the legend migrate to the Americas but, and this is REALLY exciting, but also it could have been the very thing in antiquity that spawned the legend. You see, I'm not just tracking the legend, I'm tracking the thing that became the legend."

He punctuated his statement by giving a wide-eyed of-course-you-see-it-don't-you expression and shoving the last full third of his sandwich into his mouth in a single wad, and then managed to swallow it after only two or three chews. Watching the act made Malcolm's neck ache, and also made him notice that Henry did not even have anything to drink after that feat. Henry displayed a victorious smile.

"I'm going to get my water," Henry said.

I should hope to Hell so.

"That's really interesting, Henry," Malcolm called after him.

As Henry headed back to the van for his water, Malcolm slipped away to the sparse stand of trees before Henry could return. After lunch and clean-up, seating in the van was a free-for-all, but all the single seats were quickly taken before Malcolm wandered back from his quiet stroll. Avoiding Williamson in the front double seat, he slid into an empty double, two seats back. Henry watched him from the next row and then moved up next to Malcolm. He nodded and managed a half-hearted but friendly smile to Henry as the man settled in next to him.

Guy, I just want to watch the countryside out this window.

And, as if there had never been a break in their conversation, Henry continued to describe his theories.

"What many people don't understand, Malcolm, is that most myths that have similar versions in different phases of history have a foundation in reality. Common understanding suggests that it comes from something common in farther history, but not something that was real. My studies conclusively show that myths from different countries and even different continents go back to real actions and real beings long before man even knew how to write in hieroglyphics!"

Malcolm nodded in fake understanding while he continued to look out of the window. "Like pre-historic astronauts?"

"No, no, no, Malcolm. Nothing so silly. No, the common source of the myths were beings that already lived here before man evolved. They spread out from Pangaea – the super continent that existed before the earth's plates split and made separate land masses that we know today. They lived on the earth for thousands, maybe even millions of years before the first pre-Neanderthal dropped out of the trees and moved into caves."

Malcolm turned his head to face Henry, and sighed.

"So, where are their bones, and their houses, buildings, whatever they lived in?"

"They have found them, the bones that is. Been finding them for centuries."

31

Malcolm looked closer at Henry, squinting his eyes and raising his eyebrows

"Their bones have been found? When? Where?"

"Oh, all over."

Henry smiled and tilted his head slightly, clearly enjoying the opportunity to explain his theory.

"I guess it's all been kept secret by some international plot by all the governments of the world," Malcolm said.

"Don't be facetious. I'm not one of those conspiracy theory freaks. I'm an academic researcher. I deal in facts, and then scientific theory."

He expelled a lungful of air and turned back in his seat to face fully forward, snapped up a small notebook from his pack and began to study it intently.

Malcolm eyed the little man, reading Henry's clear dissatisfaction with Malcolm's cynicism.

Good. Shut up. Read your notebook. I am not facetious. No, wait. Yes. Yes, I am. I am facetious. You bet your ass I am!

Malcolm cleared his throat and shifted in his seat, still looking at Henry.

No. Don't ask any more questions! Let the shit stew.

"So...," Malcolm let the word out like the slow deflating of an air mattress.

Aw shit, don't encourage him!

"So..." He took in a slow breath. "Where are the bones," Malcolm asked, in spite of himself.

Traitor!!

But, to Malcolm's inner relief Henry continued to study his notebook. Malcolm turned back toward the window. Mack had popped a CD into the van's sound system and an Australian voice filled the air with a light song about a cat named Bill[1].

Malcolm chuckled at the last part of the song.

Henry laid his notebook flat on his lap, and focused his attention on the mottled cover of the notebook. "The scientists find their bones all the time. They just don't know what they are."

---

[1] Many thanks to John Williamson

"Excuse me?"

Excuse us?

The Indian behind them rolled his eyes up and stuck his finger deep in his mouth, in a gagging pantomime.

"The bones are found, but they are misclassified as ancient hominids, or even worse, as pre-historic reptiles."

We liked it better when you were pissed.

Malcolm shot an angry frown at the Indian, "Shut up!"

Henry turned, looking at the empty rear seat, and opened his mouth to speak. The van shuddered with the dull thud of an impact. The rear double wheels lifted off the ground for an instant, followed almost immediately by a single buck of the trailer behind.

"Bloody Hell?!"

Mac slammed on the brakes, sending loose material from the seats onto the floor. The right side front door popped open to bounce against its hinge limits. Malcolm was caught up in the mass curiosity and joined the lemming-dash out of the passenger door and around to the van.

"Blood-dy Hell," Mac said, rubbing his short-cropped blonde hair on top of his head.

He then rested his knuckles against his hips as he stood over the body of a large red Kangaroo lying twisted in a pool of its own blood behind the trailer. Its mouth was crushed into its face with its tongue protruding onto the red dust of the road. The kangaroo had been almost completely eviscerated and its front claws were ripped out.

"Damned thing just ran out in front of me."

Mac rubbed his hand over his head again. He looked at the people gathered around him and the dead animal.

"Just ran out like he wanted to grab at the front of the van. Must have been chasing something and didn't see us. Bloody Hell."

They all stood in silent trance for a moment, staring at the kangaroo, until large numbers of flies began to swarm on the body. Mac snugged his hat back on his head, grabbed the tail with both hands, and began to drag the body off to the side of the road. After only two steps, the big tail separated from the body, long strands of blackened tissue stretched between the parts and a nauseating smell billowed out from the body. Hands flew up to cover noses and mouths. Natalia spun around to the other side of the road gagging and began retching. Henry went to her side and began patting her back while offering his handkerchief.

Mac tossed the tail into the drainage ditch next to the road and brought his arm up to cover his mouth, keeping his hands away from his face.

"Smells like it's been dead a week!"

He stepped across the ditch to the sand and loose dirt between two small clumps of scraggly grass and began rubbing his hands in the sand. He wrinkled his nose as he brought his hands up to smell them and then rubbed them again in the sand. Most of the group moved back toward the front of the van, leaving Malcolm standing in the middle of the road. Mac stepped back to the trailer and flipped open the metal latch holding the door shut. He flung open one of the doors and retrieved a short camping shovel from under the loose packs stacked on the right side. He used the shovel as a wedge to lift and push the body off the road, but the body fell apart in large decaying pieces, leaving trails of falling maggots.

Malcolm shook his head watching Mac. "You must have hit another kangaroo and knocked it off the road. This thing's been dead a good while. It's rotten."

"Didn't you feel us roll over the damned thing?"

"I felt us roll over something. Maybe this was its mate."

"You find the other one and I'll try to believe that. I sure don't want to think something this rotten was just running around."

Malcolm looked along both sides of the road going back a hundred yards, but found nothing. When he returned to the van, everyone else had stepped back inside except for Mac who stood in front of the vehicle.

"Look here and tell me I hit a different 'roo"

Malcolm rounded the front to find Mac pointing at the grill of the van. The grill was moderately damaged and covered with blood across an area the size of a small melon. Just above the grill imbedded in the painted metal were three bony fragments.

"This is where its snout hit, and that there is where its claws jammed into the sheet metal. You saw how that roo's face was pushed in."

Malcolm rolled his hands out and shrugged the universal response.

"I sure as hell can't explain it, but that kangaroo behind the bus has rotted to pieces. It couldn't have been running around."

"Damned if I can explain it either, Malcolm, but this place stinks and we're going on. We'll be at our first camp in another three hours, well, three and a half now.

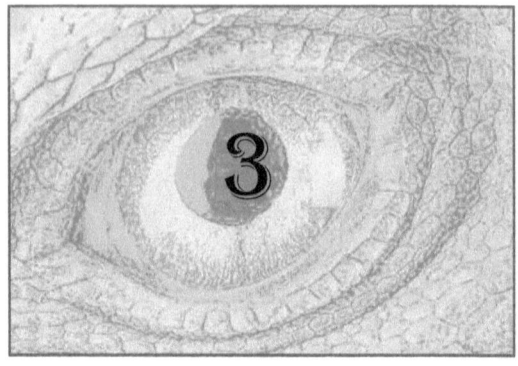

The sun was a burnt orange puddle, low on the horizon beyond Wilpena Pound, stretched out of shape as it slowly compressed through the evening Australian sky. The van pulled into the last site at the end of a road winding through old forest at the edge of grassy fields. Red kangaroos shuffled leisurely through the woods and fields foraging for tidbits among the yellowing stems. Only two kangaroos bothered to rise back-straight still chewing, looking over their shoulders with little interest at still another the passing vehicle train, despite the excitement shared within the van. The campsite was leased to the tour company, evidenced by a much older travel trailer chained to a large eucalyptus tree near a little pavilion at the center of the site. The trailer side displayed a faded match to the logo on the van.

Mac pointed to the trailer. "There's our tents and swags."

His comment broke the group silence, examining their first sleeping destination.

"What are swags," a couple voices asked, joined by other questions from the group.

"Not quite the rustic outback experience your brochure describes."

"Are there bathrooms?"

"Are there showers?"

"Are there decent hiking trails around here?"

36

Mac brought the van to a stop next to the other trailer, turned off the engine and spun around to face his passengers.

"Canvas covers for sleeping bags when you don't use a tent – It'll get that way soon enough – Yes – Yes – and, Yes."

He flashed a big grin.

"Let's get unloaded, get the tents up, and start dinner. I'm starved!"

The fading light slipped into darkness while the group busied themselves with finding and setting up tents from the storage trailer, pulling packs and sleeping bags from the trailer behind the van, and taking part in the shared chores to fix the evening meal. The flies had thinned out to a handful of determined guests that were popped out of existence with the flick of a wet rag by Henry, who had taken on the role of camp exterminator. Dinner was hastily cooked on the camp's fixed gas stove, producing a meal of bland canned spaghetti sauce over boiled noodles. The volume was sufficient, even if not very tasty and provided enough carbohydrates to satisfy everyone's hunger. Mac coaxed flames from gathered sticks collected into the central fire pit, while those who held back from assisting in the cooking earned the right to wash dishes. Folding chairs were taken from the trailer and set up in a circle around the rusted iron ring surrounding the fire.

"The Pound was set up originally by the first settlers as a cattle station and good sized farm," Mac informed the group.

Malcolm was determined to ignore the Maliqroische Indian dancing around the fire, twirling in front of each chair, flipping up the back flap of his breach cloth, mooning each person in turn.

"The valley has a rather small entrance through this gap," Mac continued. "So, it allowed the cattle to roam free enough, and didn't take much fencing to keep'em in. That's why the settlers called it a pound. I imagine Itjanu there can give us a lot more Anangu history than I can."

"Not really," she said. "I didn't pay much attention to those old stories when I was growing up. And my doctorate degrees are in sociology and medicine."

Lyle exhaled his cigarette and turned toward Itjanu. "I've been curious about that. Why is an Aborigine taking a tourist trip to the outback?"

She did not look away from the fire when she answered. "I am Pitjantjatjara and I'm not touring the outback, only going as far as Mutanajulu."

"Visiting your uh, tribe, right?" Malcolm added.

"Believe it or not, Malcolm, not all of us grew up living in red dirt caves, with our bodies painted over in white dots and eating witchity grubs."

"Just thought that your people..."

"My 'people' are academic and scientific researchers. I even sleep inside."

The dancing Indian halted in front of Malcolm and poked a spear through Malcolm's chest, then continued his dance and serial mooning. Malcolm reacted slightly in his chair.

Don't do that!

Mac glanced between Itjanu and Malcolm and cleared his throat.

"Right, then. Henry, what are you hoping to see, here in the outback?"

The Indian looked back at Malcolm as he mooned Lyle, and stuck out his tongue.

Tonight I'm gonna double-pill your ass!

Henry smiled and pointed up toward the sky.

"Among other things, that."

Noses and chins pointed up among a murmur of oohs and aahs. The night sky was filled with bright stars and snaking among them, the undulating translucent curtain of vertical multicolored light from an Aurora above the Pound. Campers stood up from their seats, some chairs falling over into the red sand behind them as everyone moved out away from the fire and the trees to get a better view of the spectacle. People from other sites were already standing in the field. Others were still emerging from the tress, walking sideways like deformed crabs, looking up as they stumbled along.

A dark shape of a man standing nearby, spoke in a thick Aussie accent.

"It's like what I've seen in upper Alaska, but I've never seen it here."

Another voice farther into the field answered back.

"Me too, but this doesn't seem as high, or maybe its smaller and just as far up. Can't tell."

A giggle erupted not far from where Malcolm stood. He could see the face of Henry looking up into the lights, his teeth lit yellow-white by the lights in the sky. Malcolm spoke to him.

"You knew this was going to happen?"

Henry shook his head, but did not move his gaze from the sky. "Something like it. Something. Didn't know it would be this. This is beautiful!"

He crossed his arms, rubbing them slowly, caressing his arms with his hands. "They're coming back."

"What's coming back," Malcolm asked. "The lights?"

Malcolm looked skyward again and back to Henry.

"What's coming back?"

Henry did not respond. His hands had stopped moving and his smile broadened. The Aurora shifted from white to red to green, giving his face first a maniacal then a cadaverous-like hue. He was mesmerized by his vision, and no longer listened to Malcolm's questions.

Dozens of people, strangers to strangers, stood in the field for over an hour watching the display and trading comments, questions, and impromptu theories, until the mosquitoes came. The first few arrivals were heralded by modest pats on neck and arms, but quickly grew to an applaud of slaps as the air filled with the whine of countless biting insects. The insects first drove away the more sensitive, soon followed by a stampede of even the hardiest campers. The group dissolved into a frantic rush to the woods and screened tents. A whine of mosquitoes was joined by a chorus of zippers whizzing around the edges of screen tent flaps and the air hissed from several cans of bug spray fished out from packs to kill the small swarms of mosquitoes trapped within the tents.

Malcolm made his escape to his own tent, but his can of Deet spray clogged, so he stoked his pipe under a fresh match and blew hot tobacco smoke into the dome of his tent where the hungry mosquitoes had collected. Malcolm checked the seams of his own tent assessing that they were still holding. Curses began to drift into the air as rotted tent seams gave way in some of the tents, dissolved by the bug spray. Natalia emerged from her tent shaking her thick head of hair and slapping at the air around her face. She cried as she ran to other tents for safety but only found others facing the same problems. Mac tried to escape the mosquitoes, but soon rose up from his own tent as it collapsed around him. Elizabeth stood up from her own disintegrating tent holding the separated screen over her head as a shawl against the swarming mosquitoes. She ran to intercept Natalia, wrapping them both within the mesh.

Mac waved to others without tents and pointed them toward the campfire. "Get over by the fire!".

He swatted the air around his head as he picked up more dried limbs for the dwindling fire. Then he stepped away to the closest stand of trees and returned to the fire with a eucalyptus branch thick with leaves. He tossed the branch onto the growing fire and the flames leapt among the oily leaves in a blaze of bright yellow light. The flames created a large void in the black swarm of mosquitoes drifting through the campsite.

"If your tent is O.K., stay where you are," Mac said, his voice bellowing throughout the campsite. "If your tent is ripped, then come over by the fire!" He was soon joined by Elizabeth and Natalia, still huddled under the mesh shawl, and then by Hiraht and Itjanu.

Henry walked leisurely over to the fire as well; seemingly oblivious to the mosquitoes, and wearing the mesh head-cover each camper had packed against the flies anticipated in the deeper desert. Designed to be worn over a hat to keep the mesh away from the face, Henry wore it directly over his head looking like a hold-up man. He had slipped on a long sleeve shirt buttoned snuggly around his neck where the mesh had been tucked in, as well as gloves and long camper pants with the lower sections zippered to shorts. Mac looked up from laying another leaf-filled limb onto the fire. The yellow light spread out from the fire pit again shining to the nearby pavilion. Henry stood near Mac.

"Is your tent screwed up as well, Henry?"

"No. I just wanted to be near the fire. I like camp fires."

In the momentary bright light, Mac's face and forearms were shown covered in red welts from dozens of mosquito bites, making him look diseased. Even as the fire drove the mosquitoes away from the pit, Malcolm could still hear the drone of hundreds of mosquitoes crawling over the fabric and mesh of his tent searching for a way in.

The heat of the day finally drifted away and the cool air settled over the camp, but the mosquitoes remained. Small swarms regained the air from resting places on fallen leaves as Mac made several more trips to the stand of trees for more limbs and leaves filled branches to burn. The mosquitoes kept away from the fire but hovered in the air at the edge of its brightest light and laid thick over the remaining occupied tents. Spray cans were offered through barely unzipped slits or retrieved through the cloud of insects of the fallen tents. After two a.m. Mac announced the wood was running low and the remaining tents would need to be shared. He found a solitary usable tent among the dozen or more in the storage trailer. Mac noticed that Malcolm's' tent was actually slightly larger than the rest and could easily hold three people. Learning this, Henry offered his tent to Elizabeth and Natalia, and with Mac and Hiraht agreeing to share a tent, Henry and Itjanu arrived at the front of Malcolm's' tent carrying their sleeping bags. Malcolm pulled his pack away from the tent flap and allowed the two people in while trying to keep out as many mosquitoes as possible. While Malcolm carefully zippered the mesh closed, taking precautions not the stress the seams, the air in the tent filled with acrid insect repellent. Malcolm coughed and rubbed his stinging eyes with the back of his hand.

Itjanu spoke in the darkness.

"That should take care of the ones that came in with us – and kill some of the burning smell in here."

"I LIKE the burning smell – better than that damned

bug spray!"

Malcolm pulled an individual camp cooking set from his pack, feeling the BSA engraving on the bottom of the aluminum pot that served also as kit's container. He disconnected the pot from the set and dropped his pipe into the bottom with a not too subtle metallic clank and then covered the little pot. Itjanu snuggled down into her sleeping bag against the cooling night air and spoke facing away from him.

"Oh, I don't really mind all that much. Go ahead and finish it. If it drives the mosquitoes away, then all the better."

Malcolm reached out and took the lid off the little pot. Before he could withdraw the still smoldering bowl, Henry spoke up.

"Well, I mind,...Please?"

Malcolm withdrew his hand and recovered the lid with a clang.

Shit!

The Indian appeared, sitting on Henry's hip, smoking a large Indian peace pipe, blowing imaginary smoke into Malcolm's face.

Malcolm grit his teeth and snatched his backpack into his lap, yanking out his pill bottle and canteen. He took out one of the blue and white pills, popped it into his mouth and swallowed it with water. He took out another pill, displayed it with exaggerated ceremony in front of the Indian's face, then popped it into his mouth and took a large drink of water. As he swallowed, the Indian showed Malcolm his middle finger again, and then walked out through the tent screen toward the dying campfire.

Sleep came quickly but did not last long. Malcolm woke to a sharp pain in his side. Thinking his kidney was acting up, he thought to search out one of the painkillers he had picked up from the pharmacy, but his thought was interrupted by Henry's voice.

"Malcolm, you were snoring."

"Yeah. Do that when I sleep." He said, and allowed himself to drift back into his sleep.

"Malcolm roll onto your side." It was Itjanu's voice

this time.

"O.K.,", he said, but he did not move off his back and slipped again into sleep.

"Malcolm, roll onto your side."

"I did," he answered through his sleep.

"No, you didn't," Henry spoke this time and punctuated his comment with another skinny elbow into Malcolm's side.

"Aw shit," Malcolm said, mumbling and turning on to this side to avoid another poke.

It felt like only seconds before Mac was tapping his boot against the bulge of Malcolm's head against the tent fabric.

"Flies are up. Got to get moving."

Malcolm rolled onto his back and then sat up letting his sleeping bag fall down to his waist. The day had come with a brightness that hurt his eyes. Henry and Itjanu were busy rolling their sleeping bags. Malcolm looked closely at the mesh and noticed that the mosquitoes were finally gone – and the mesh was now completely covered on the outside by crawling buzzing bush flies.

"Aw shit!"

"Better get out your fly screens, if you didn't already last night," Mac said as he walked from tent to tent. He had hung a large mosquito net from the rafters of the pavilion and draped it over the picnic table. Bleary-eyed campers found tea or instant coffee, grabbed granola bars and slipped under the netting to sit on the wooden benches within the close confines around the table. Mac's cheerful tone was in sharp contrast to his whelp-covered face. The left side of his lower lip was decorated with three red welts and swollen twice normal size, adding a dentist-Novocain "pbuh" to the end of many of his words.

"Don't normally see this kind of fly activity this far south," Mac said. "You'd expect it in the desert, but not usually down here. Never seen this much in the way of mosquitoes here, either."

Natalia placed her hands against the side of her mesh.

"Oh, it was horrible! I don't know if I can stand

43

another night like last night!"

Mac nodded. "We need to move the tents in closer to the fire pit and turn in at first sight of them if it happens again tonight. Can't figure out about the tents, though. Most of them we bought new this season. Used them on my last trip through here a couple weeks ago. They were fine then."

Natalia pointed her granola bar at Mac.

"Maybe you could take some of us back. I can't stand that again."

"Can't rightly go back, Natalia."

Henry joined in the conversation, clearly agitated with Natalia's request.

"No! We can't go back. I came all the way from Canada for this trip."

The general murmur around the table confirmed the group's desire to continue on. Bolstered by the morning light, food and caffeine, talk turned to the hiking possibilities within the Pound. Mac spread a map of the park on the table and explained the trail options. Mac would lead one group up to the mountain crest and a trail that scaled to the highest peak available to trail hiking. A smaller group consisting of Malcolm, Henry, Elizabeth, and Itjanu would hike to the center of the valley to the original homestead and then mount the single central peak to a viewing platform with a commanding view of the internal savannah and bush country.

The trail started through a forest of old trees where the ground cover had been removed for years to allow campers an easy walk. Next, the four passed over a small footbridge across a rambunctious creek filled with head-sized rocks and splashing water. The brush soon filled in between the trees and edged against the narrowing trail, reaching out to stroke the hiker's legs as they passed. Little clouds of flies joined them, collecting on the fronts of the mesh, requiring waving swats described by Mac as the unofficial Australian Salute. Henry carried a noticeably large pack, but quickly outpaced the other three, eager to find his way to the top of the mount, and quickly left his group far behind.

The lay of the ground began to rise. Easy conversation fell away to silence as more attention was paid to climbing steps over ankle-twisting rocks and loose gravel. The trail then dipped down a steep hillside into a ravine next to the tumbling creek, and the trio walked carefully along the flattened logs laid end to end where no ground trail provided footing. Like a line of dizzy orangutans with arms extended, holding walking sticks out for balance, Malcolm and the two ladies wobbled single file along the logs.

The last section of logs crossed over the center of a waist-deep sandy pond fed by the creek. The logs ran twenty feet across without a handhold. Elizabeth went first followed by Malcolm and then Itjanu. Nearing the far bank, Itjanu stumbled and called out in a panic. She spun her arms wildly, trying to correct her failing balance, leaning farther and farther past her center of gravity. In a last desperate act to regain her footing she reached out and grabbed Malcolm's sleeve. Her weight was more than Malcolm could counter.

Like khaki-clad dominoes, Itjanu fell off the log, watching the water rush up to meet her face, as Malcolm followed her. Itjanu went in first, still trying desperately to keep her feet out of the water and so went in head first. Malcolm splashed in above her, flapping his arms as he went in, and immediately kicked by Itjanu, as he sank on top of her. Itjanu had rolled onto her back on the sandy bottom, but Malcolm was above her, blocking her frantic scramble back to the surface. Malcolm's body pressed into hers, pushing her back down to the bottom. He struggled to push her away as she clawed to get him off her. Hands, feet, arms and walking sticks intertwined as each one fought the other to get back to the surface. The surface roiled with their movements as they pushed each other away. Finally they managed to push apart and find the bottom with their feet and came sputtering to the surface coughing and spitting.

"Dammit, woman!"

"You were drowning me, you shit!"

"You pulled me in, you idiot!"

Itjanu swung out with a roundhouse punch that

drove a water dripping fist into Malcolm's cheek. Both fell back into the water, then quickly scrambled to their feet, facing each other with fists up in boxer's poses, spitting water and gasping for breath. They stood facing each other, each accusing the other of stupid acts that made the fall far worse than it should have been.

From the shore of the little pond, Elizabeth squatted down sitting lightly on the heels of her hiking boots and keeping her knees primly together. She cleared her throat loudly. Both water soaked hikers turned to face her.

"Whenever you two children are through playing in the water..."

Itjanu offered up her walking stick to Elizabeth, who pulled her up the bank. Malcolm climbed up from the little pond as Elizabeth and Itjanu walked up the steep trail out of the ravine. Water dripped from the brim of his bush hat and the ends of his shirtsleeves and shorts, running along his arms and legs. Fine-grained red sand turned into rust colored mud on the palms of his hands and his knees as he pushed up to his feet. He rubbed his throbbing cheek where Itjanu had landed a well-practiced punch, applying a thin smudge of Australian rouge to his face.

Crazy damned woman!

"Crazy damned woman," he told the nearby bushes at the edge of the pond.

Slipping off his pack, water poured from the top flap. Sighing and shaking his head, he opened it to assess the damage. He carefully withdrew his camera bag and kissed the vinyl dust proof case that was also waterproof. First aid kit, canteen, and even his lunch sandwich were all packed in waterproof bags this morning and still dry. The only water damage was among the loose-leaf pamphlets he had just bought at the park store giving the history of Wilpena Pound. Remembering his journal, Malcolm flipped the pack around and zipped open the outer pocket cover, but the journal was not inside. He scanned the edge of the pond and peered into the clear water, then remembered he had left the journal back in his tent. His relief was short lived as he stared down at

46

the center of the pond and saw his gnarled Appalachian walking stick lying on the sandy bottom.

'Damn!'

He spit out his breath, blowing water droplets still dripping down his upper lip and stepped back into the water. He stubbed his boot toe on a root running over the sand and fell spread eagled face down into the water, still holding onto his sandwich baggie – which popped open when he slapped into the water.

Malcolm was still standing in the middle of the small pond, swinging his walking stick like a cudgel, beating the surface into froth with its gnarled head when Elizabeth peered down at him from the pathway.

"Really, Malcolm, are you going to spend the day playing in that mud puddle?"

Malcolm did not turn around to face her as he answered.

"Go on ahead. I'll catch up with you."

Elizabeth withdrew her head and Malcolm flung his walking stick up onto the bank then trudged through the water to the shallows two steps away, churning the water into a spray as he climbed out. The splashed water had turned the modest bank into slimy red clay. Malcolm's foot slipped as he stepped up from the pond and he fell face first onto the red mud. Two hundred yards beyond the ravine, Elizabeth and Itjanu stopped on the trail, listening as a staccato string of vulgar curses bellowed up through the trees, sending dozens of gala parrots screeching into the air.

Elizabeth turned toward Itjanu, allowing just the hint of a smile and slightly raised eyebrows. "And Yanks say we British have no sense of humor. Malcolm should really do something about his temper, don't you think?"

Itjanu smiled broadly showing naturally perfect white teeth and watched the flock of galas settle back into the treetops. "Whatever he does, I don't think cool water dips should be part of his regimen."

The two women shared a laugh and then continued on their way toward the old homestead. They had just finished reading the last of the signs arranged in front of the cabin when Malcolm squished past them. He plopped down on the cabin porch and began unlacing his boots. Itjanu looked away, but Elizabeth boldly watched the red blotched creature. Malcolm removed his boots and poured red water from them. Then he slowly stripped off his soggy wool hiking socks from pale archless feet and double- twisted each sock, wringing a small stream of water from each one. Socks that had been snow white when he pulled them from his pack this morning, were now rusty ochre.

The mid morning sun was beginning to punch its way through the treetops and painted the cabin wall and porch floor near Malcolm in a golden hue. He flipped his socks to loosen the weave and draped them over the edge of the porch in the sunshine. Shooing away the little swarm of flies that had found him, he pulled down the fly screen bunched around his hat and covered his face. He laid on his back in the sunshine with his hands behind his head and his feet dangling off the edge of the porch.

The warmth of the sun felt wonderful on his wet clothes. His body relaxed and his eyelids slipped gently over his eyes. Within a minute, he drifted off to a nap heralded by a series of lengthening snores escaping from his open mouth. The snores grew in volume and followed Elizabeth and Itjanu past the bronze Aborigine relief, even to where the steeper trail led them up the rocks toward the viewing platform. It was past noon when Malcolm awoke to the sound of a small Appalachian boy yelling "Hey!", and the burn of intense sunlight on his exposed knees still bent over the edge of the porch.

Malcolm rose up feeling sharp pains in his lower back from sleeping on the hard wooden boards. Something flapped next to him and yelled "Hey!" He turned to find a Magpie staring boldly at him less than two feet away and clutching the remnants of his sandwich bag in its claws. Globs of soggy bread with pecked-apart roast beef and cheddar cheese encircled the bird where it had feasted on the ruined sandwich while Malcolm slept. Malcolm had been determined to eat it anyway when he fished it out of the pond, but now the Magpie had beat him to it. Malcolm waved his arm at the bird.

"Git!"

It hopped back another foot, flapping its wings and yelling at him in defiance, "Hey!" and kept its wings spread wide, in challenge for the prize. Malcolm reached out and snatched the torn bag, receiving a hard peck to the back of his hand from the determined Magpie.

"Oow!" A drop of blood rose on the back of his hand. "Damn you!" He waved his arm again, but the bird did not give ground and called back at him again. It dashed forward and scooped up another piece of cheese, swallowed it then screeched at Malcolm again. Malcolm swirled around and grabbed his walking stick to swing at the bird, but the Magpie read his intent and flapped into the air out of reach.

Malcolm reached for his socks and boots to put himself back together, so he could continue his hike. As he laced his boots, the pushy bird returned to the porch with a few friends, just out of stick range, and they took turns dashing in to peck up more pieces of the sandwich. Satisfied the birds would take care of the remaining crumbs, Malcolm scanned the area to ensure he had picked up all his trash, then headed up the slope to the next trail. He spared a few moments to read the bronze relief and then followed the arrow to the base of the hill.

The hillside was mostly man-sized boulders with small tufts of grass and the occasional bush sprouting here and there. The trail steepened and his knees began to pump hard from one foothold in the rocks to the next. Rising notches of sand and gravel piled up behind rock edges required long strides to mount the next step. Soon his heart pounded, sweat formed inside his hatband and began slithering down in meandering rivulets behind his ears and down his forehead. The flies worked all the harder to get in through the mesh to the coveted beads of moisture.

He had to stop after less than a hundred yards to wipe his face with his red handkerchief and take a sip from his canteen. The months he had spent sitting in the sanitarium and days spent sitting in planes and buses had not helped maintain his stamina.

I worked long days on the farm back in Finton County. This walk shouldn't be so hard.

49

Far up the hill, the Indian danced in the bright sun on top of a boulder, dressed in thick buffalo skins.

I hope you pass out, Tonto.

He looped the canteen strap over his shoulder and wiped the hatband, feeling the baking heat of the Australian sun on the top of his head. The temperature had risen dramatically and the air over the boulders at the far edges of the hillside shimmered in the heat. A blue tailed lizard scampered across the next step seeking shade from the sun as Malcolm stepped past him.

Malcolm stopped again after another hundred yards, feeling the strain in his knees as the trail angled steeper. He had risen above the tree tops back at the cabin and the pond. The hill rose even higher further ahead with an occasional painted arrow visible on rock surfaces pointing first left then right, showing the beginning of a series of switchbacks to mount the next grade. He was disappointed in his own poor physical shape.

I am in no condition to make this climb. And this is supposed to be the easy trail.

He fingered the handhold on his walking stick and looked out at the horizon. Scanning the crests encircling the Pound a few miles away, he saw a string of dots along the ascending ridge to the south.

Must be the other group.

The dots were less than half way up their own steep slope and he was glad Mac had suggested he take the lower climb. Dark clouds were off in the distance to the east, shadowing the land below them and rolling in his direction.

Wouldn't mind a little shade from those things.

After another hundred yards of knee-straining trail, he was beginning to gasp his breaths as he stopped to swat away the little cloud of flies swarming around his head. He looked back down the hill and saw he was barely twenty yards above his last resting spot.

Man, I'm really out of shape!.

A hot wind gusted along the side of the hill tugging hard at the brim of his hat and sweeping away the flies to the other side of his head. He pressed his hat firmly onto his head and faced into the baked air breeze, enjoying the momentary clear view through the mesh without the flies. The dark clouds were now rolling above the ridge of the Pound, huge gray-green masses tumbling over one another, kicked along by driving winds high in the sky.

Wonder if it's cooler up there. A little rain would be nice.

Even though his clothes had dried from his dunking in the pond, the heat on the hillside was almost oppressive, and sweat was replacing the pond water. Within moments, the harsh sunlight was filtered then blocked by the thick clouds, shading the entire expanse of the Pound in a gray-green haze. The wind swirled around Malcolm as he ascended a dozen more switchbacks into the rapidly cooling air. Another Magpie swept by overhead, screeching in distress, flying tail first in the strong wind, beating its wings against the gust in a losing struggle to return to its treetop. The flies were wiped from the hillside, the last few stalwart insects trying in vain to hold on to Malcolm's arm, but were swept away as he watched.

I hope you get smashed into a rock.

His hat brim was flipped by the wind and jerked up to the limit of the face mesh, its lower edge caught by the elastic band under Malcolm's chin. He pushed his hat more firmly on his head and cinched up the chinstrap, then removed the mesh, slipping it into his pocket and happy to be shed of it.

Malcolm mounted another switchback turn and looked up in the direction of the viewing platform, but sight of it was still obscured by a stand of low lying scrub trees below the summit. The sound of rushing wind stilled momentarily, allowing Malcolm to hear shouting from the summit, but could not understand the words.

Williamson's probably taunting me for taking so long.

He stopped at the next turn giving his ragged breath the opportunity to catch up with the growing demand for oxygen from his aching chest, and lifted the pack off his back enough to allow cooling air to brush along the sweat soaked shirt underneath.

A growling thunder rolled within the heavy cloud overhead, the swirling center of the formation seemed to be hovering above the Pound. The haze became a mist as he climbed higher and the clouds drifted lower over the hilltop, flooding the scenery in eerie faint green light. He came to a large boulder in the center of the trail marking a division in its direction. Painted on the rock surface were two arrows pointing in opposite directions. The left arrow angled up above the words *Viewing platform*, while the right pointed upward over the word *Peak*. Rounding the boulder to the left he saw the platform, still a few feet below its level, with a view of the horizon between its support legs. Malcolm saw Itjanu and Elizabeth gathered around Henry near the center, both pulling at his clothes. Lightning flashed out from the cloud overhead, striking one of the scrub trees not far from the platform. Malcolm jerked away from the flash, then looked back at the trio in time to see Henry swing a roundhouse slap, striking Elizabeth full force in the face and sending her down onto the grating of the metal platform.

"What th—"

Malcolm sprinted the last few yards up to the platform ignoring the thumping pain in his chest and mounted the dozen steel steps in three strides. The platform was a shamble of packs, hats, and standing metal poles holding artifacts of some kind on their tips. A taller pole was in the center holding a shining item encased in glass on its pinnacle. Green lightning struck out again through the rushing mist, striking just in front of the platform. The rushing wind filled the air with a roar. Henry was yelling up at the clouds. Elizabeth looked toward Malcolm with blood streaming down from a bloody nose. Blood droplets spewed into the air as she yelled to Malcolm, but he could not understand the words in the tumultuous wind.

Itjanu grabbed at Henry as he started to turn back toward the taller pole. "You Damned Fool! Get down from here before you get killed!"

Lightning struck again, hitting the corner pole and sending a wave of green light rushing across the platform. Malcolm's legs tingled from the high voltage current and Elizabeth frantically pulled her hands up from the metal grating and tried to stand. Malcolm stepped toward Elizabeth as Henry broke free from Itjanu, his sing-song chanting insanely disconnected from his actions. He delivered a driving punch to Itjanu's stomach, bending her over double and sending her to her knees. Another lightning strike found the platform. Malcolm's legs erupted in waves of fierce pinpricks as he turned toward Itjanu. She had regained her feet and was lunging again toward Henry. Henry held on to the pole with his left hand and delivered another savage gut punch into Itjanu with his right. Malcolm instinctively threw himself at Henry, knocking the man to the corner of the platform with a two handed push and then turned to examine Itjanu.

Malcolm was standing in the center of the three poles when the lightning struck again, hitting him square in the chest. Pain shot through his body, green sparks radiated out from his fingertips, the edges of his ears, nose and lips. His hearing was pierced with an incredible high-pitched squeal that went higher and higher and higher as stars exploded in his vision. The squeal went beyond the pitch of human hearing. Everything seemed almost frozen in mid motion. He was overcome by an oppressive silence pressing heavy against his eardrums. Itjanu leaned toward him, hands and fingers outstretched to him, her eyes slowly widening in horror and her mouth gaping.

Henry was up off the platform, flinging himself through the air, floating slowly at Malcolm, his face contorted in a snarl, and a single drop of spittle suspended in the air in front of his face. The bodies moved slower and slower. The sky darkened by shades of gray and green. A thin line of twisting green light formed around the top of Malcolm's head like a crown of sparklers. It descended along Malcolm's body, leaving the surface above it in blackness that had no light. The line moved down to his feet, then expanded from him to the edges of the platform, like a fire line spreading out in a field, leaving everything within it burnt. The green line found its way out to the edge of the platform, the black within it flooded Malcolm's vision and his consciousness. He felt an overwhelming pain spread though his body, and then there was nothing.

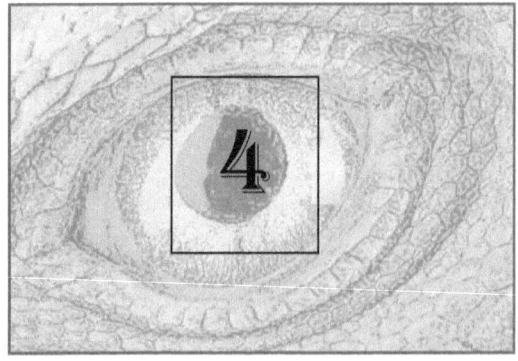

Malcolm frowned and slowly opened his eyes, willing them to focus, but they would not. He turned his head from the gray light swirling in front of his face, but it was everywhere. He was lying on a pad somewhere, could smell the aroma of his own pipe. Knew he was back in his tent. There were hushed voices somewhere nearby, but not too close and he could not understand the words. The spinning whirl grew faster and nausea washed over him. He was momentarily aware of intense pain in the center of his chest, but the sensation was fleeting and he slipped back into the blackness, floating, sinking, until his thoughts stopped. He awoke again, forcing himself to climb up from the black into the grayness above it. His throat was rasping, trying to push the word through the sticky gum coating his tongue and mouth. It was supposed to be a sentence, but only the one word graveled out.

"Water."

It did not sound like his voice, but someone else. Something bit him on his forehead and he moved his hand to swat it away, but his hand only danced feebly by his side and the thing stayed there gnawing into his skin.

"Water."

This time it sounded like his own voice, but it was far away, whispering down a hall, no louder than the whine of the mosquitoes. He heard the zip of an opening tent flap and then it zipped closed. Someone slid next to him on the ground. Hoarse whispers hissed into his ear, but he only understood the occasional word

"...you   experienced...Damn!...What did..interfere!...Damn...wake up!"

Malcolm tried to understand the voice.

"Wha-what? I can' unner..."

His face stung with a slap to his cheek.

"You shouldn't have interfered! You ruined it, you bastard. You weren't ready for it, so you'll probably die anyway, but I'm going to have to find the next place, Damn it!"

"Wat-er..."

"I'll give you water you interfering..."

A hand slid under Malcolm's head raising him up and putting the opened canteen to his lips. The water was from heaven, soaking his parched tongue, adding desperately needed moisture to the inside of his mouth. He swallowed the first trickle and stopped to say thank you, but the trickle became a flood filling his throat and mouth and up into his nose. The gift from heaven turned into a watery assault. He began to cough and gag, but still the water came. Malcolm tried to push the canteen away, to turn his head, but the hand held him and kept pouring in more water that ran down his face and onto his chest. He coughed again, gurgling in the flood of water filling and refilling his mouth between sputters.

The tent fly zipped open again and the water stopped pouring. Malcolm managed to roll onto his side and spit out the mouthful of water and gasp for air. There was another form kneeling beside him, wiping his mouth. The first voice spoke again. Malcolm recognized it as Henry.

"He asked for water, so I gave him some, but he grabbed the canteen and took in too much and started coughing like that."

The very English voice of Elizabeth filled the darkness of the tent.

"Get out, Henry." She turned to Malcolm. Henry left, zipping the tent closed behind him..

"Easy there, my cowboy Yank. Never gulp more than you can swallow, or is it never bite off more than you can chew – whatever. Just spit that out. When you're ready to drink into your stomach and not your lungs, I'll give you some more."

Malcolm tried to speak, but only coughed again, pushing out the water still in his lungs. She patted him gently on his shoulder.

"Welcome back, grumpy."

He could feel her turn away from him and heard her call out. "He's baa-a-ack! Either of you two wizards care to come examine our human lightning rod?"

More bodies entered the tent and a flashlight exploded yellow white light within the tent. The air at the top of the tent came alive with dozens of mosquitoes.

"Ironwater?"

"Y-yeah."

Malcolm rolled onto his back and brought his forearm up over his eyes against the glare of the flashlight.

"Ironwater, I am Doctor Manfred Hydter. My wife and I are on holiday here. Came over to your camp when I heard we'd had a lightning strike among one of the other campers. May I examine you?"

"Yeah, I guess..."

"How do you feel?"

"I feel like shit."

"Feeling like shit is good. Feeling like anything would be acceptable, but feeling like shit is probably two or three notches up from there. You ought to be dead, you know."

"Somebody was just here helping me work on that."

The doctor pulled open Malcolm's shirt and shined the light onto his chest.

"God almighty."

Malcolm coughed again. "Nope, it's just me..."

The doctor chose to ignore Malcolm's irreverence. "All you have is an intense sunburn, and the hair in the middle of your chest is gone – not that anyone was going to have to shear you anyway – you don't really seem to have a lot of body hair. The thing is, well, you see, your chest, it's not really bad. It's just that spot..."

"Don't say 'spot, Doc'. Shit always happen when

someone says 'spot' about my body."

"Yes, well, uhm, your, ah area on your chest appears to be, well, green."

"Green?"

"Green."

"What do you mean, Green? Like I'm infected?"

"No. That would be red."

"So, what's green mean?"

"Usually rot, but – "

"Rot!"

"But not in your case. Actually it looks like some juvenile spray painted the center of your chest with, well, green paint."

"Like a big bruise, Doc? You mean blue green? Or Yellow and blue?"

"No, not really. It's just green. About the size of my fist. Not like a bruise, though."

"Then like a what?"

"Don't really know. Your skin doesn't even appear to be damaged. It's just well,...green. Nice sort of froggy green."

"I've been hit by lightning and my skin has turned froggy green?"

"Well, yes. No. Not your whole body, just apparently that one spot, er area, on your chest."

Malcolm reached up and gently touched the area of his chest where the lightning hit him. The skin did not feel unusual, with only the slightest sensation of a sunburn. He still felt an intense pain deep under the skin that continued to tell him of a horrendous burn. He was relieved to find that his skin was far better than he expected, having green skin was not a relief. He reached out for the flashlight held by the doctor then turned it down toward his chest and raised his head to looked at himself. The pores were perhaps slightly more noticeable, but otherwise, except for the weird color, it did appear normal.

"Have you been taking any unusual medications," Doctor Hydter asked.

"No doc, why?"

"Why, well, we're still trying to figure out why you are

alive. One thought Dr. Williamson and I discussed, was some kind of protective chemistry, perhaps brought about by a combination of drugs..."

"I don't do Drugs."

"I meant prescriptions."

"You and Dr. William..., Itjanu Williamson? You and a sociologist are trying to figure out what happened to me?"

"First, Itjanu interned under me when I was in Sydney. She was on her way toward being an excellent internist when she decided to pursue sociology. Second, we know what happened. You had two witnesses describing the incident in detail. That we know. What we don't know is why the strike didn't kill you."

"Yeah, you keep telling me that."

The tent began to spin as a wave of nausea swept over Malcolm and he lay back down on the sleeping bag.

"What the hell was that fool Henry doing up there anyway," Malcolm asked.

Itjanu's voice joined from behind the light of the flashlight.

"He said he was trying to draw the green lightning."

"Well, the little sonofabitch did it. He was in here a few minutes ago and was trying to drown me, to boot."

The whine of dozens of mosquitoes floated around Malcolm's head and sang to the spinning nausea in his brain. The doctor pointed the flashlight up to the dome of the crowded tent.

"We need to spray in here and then get out a while so this man can rest."

Someone produced a small can of bug spray that the doctor took and then placed his hand over Malcolm's nose and mouth.

"Hold your breath, Fellah."

Malcolm managed to get in a decent breath before hissing and cool chemical vapors filled the upper air within the tent. Elizabeth slipped a thin cotton kerchief into his hand.

"Cover your face with this, cowboy."

She then joined the others in a duck squat exodus out of the tent. Outside the tent, Mac spoke to Henry.

"Things are well under control here, Henry. Why don't you go help keep the wood up for the fire?"

Malcolm kept his eyes closed and placed the kerchief over his face against the toxic insect spray, but welcomed the respite from the drone of mosquitoes. Lying quiet and willing the grogginess at the edge of his consciousness to take him again, he heard the sound of another breath in the tent with him.

"Henry, you sneaky little shit, if you're back in here, I'll..."

"No, it's me," Itjanu said.

She shifted in the darkness to find a more comfortable position. "Thanks for your help up there."

"Ah, you probably would have done the same thing."

"Between you and Henry. I bloody doubt it. I would have just hopped down the stairs and let you two cook."

He chuckled under the kerchief.

"Then why?"

"I'm not really sure. Elizabeth was all fired up to get us out of danger. Henry was doing this crazy chant and had those things up. I don't know, it just didn't seem right. That's a sacred place to my,...group, village, whatever. You wouldn't want someone peeing on your Washington monument, would you? Then he slapped Elizabeth and I just reacted."

"Yeah, me too."

Silence filled the tent between them and Malcolm spoke again.

"You're welcome."

The tent flap zipped down.

"Well, don't get all mushy on me. You're more predictable as your usual shitty self."

Fabric whispered as Itjanu slipped out of the tent and zipped the flap behind her. Malcolm pulled the kerchief from his face and sat up on his sleeping bag to chase after her with another cynical remark, but the thought was swept away by overwhelming nausea and he vomited water into Elizabeth's kerchief. In the light of the blazing campfire coming through the insect netting Malcolm looked down at Elizabeth's western kerchief.

Yippy ti yi yay.

And vomited into it again.

Dawn slipped in under the darkness and pushed the night sky into gray, turning off the stars. Malcolm opened his eyes and rolled over on his sleeping bag. He had been left to sleep alone, either in respect due to his near death experience, or to escape his snoring. He eased himself up to a sitting position waiting for the morning gnawing of his "spot" in his low back or pain from his new one on his chest. He stretched, pushing his arms out and knuckling the tent fabric. He rotated his shoulders and back, left and right to ease the coming knot that joined him each morning, but it did not arrive.

He gingerly opened his shirt and raised his tee shirt to see what had become of his green sunburn. He dropped the edge of his tee shirt and gasped.

"Oh Shit."

He raised his tee shirt again. The skin condition that now spread over his entire chest and down the front of his abdomen. He twisted to one side, then the other and found the edges of the green spreading to his spare tire. He snatched his flashlight from his pack, pulled out on his waistband of his shorts and shined the light down to his groin. He released a ragged breath at finding himself down there to be the usual color. He set down his flashlight and pressed tenderly along his chest and abdomen, searching with his fingertips to discover how much discomfort this change in his skin color heralded. There was none. He pressed firmly at the area in the center of his chest and found no discomfort there, either. He sat in worry for several minutes trying to guess the meaning of the green coloration, but then forced himself to be satisfied with the absence of any new pain. In fact, and he twisted his back again at the thought, in fact he had no pain; not even the usual camping out sleeping on the ground stiffness.

He became aware of a throbbing erection and an almost painful need to empty his bladder. Still in his shirt and shorts from the day before, he abandoned the idea of waiting to put on his shoes, and frantically struggled with the tent flap zipper to make his way out of the tent. He leapt from the tent struggling to contain his urinary urgency and dashed stiff-kneed and wobbling to the closest bush. He relaxed slightly as he neared the bush, unzipping his fly as he came up to it, but then noticed one of the other tents was pitched next to that bush. He looked frantically for another place where he could release the explosion building up in his bladder. Straight legged and waddling, he trotted further away, propelled only by the balls of his feet, making a beeline for a clump of bushes at the edge of the campsite just before the grassy field.

Waddling his hips and rocking his shoulders side to side he unzipped his fly again and began to assume the correct manly position even before he quite arrived. He sailed into the bush using a high-pressure yellow jet of urine ahead of him like a clipper's bowsprit. The stream knocked away leaves, pressed back little limbs within the target area and splashed into the main trunk, sending a misty spray in a corona around the contact point.

"Ah-h-h-h-h-h-h-h..."

He arched forward keeping his knees ahead as much as possible and looked up at the morning sky with satisfaction only a man in the woods knows and cherishes. And still it flowed. Goosebumps ran along his spine and across his abdomen, celebrating this moment of manhood and this ultimate release; relief that harkened back to the first wet diaper and first wetted tree. And still it came. With childish satisfaction and adolescent pride, he released his handhold and let his manhood stand to its duty.

Resting his hands on his hips he turned his attention to the power of the stream itself. He noticed how it bobbed one little limb back and forth in its force, and then began to angle and twist his hips to pick out individual limbs and leaves as targets. He began to hum to himself knocking one little limb then another, then keeping two of them bouncing at once. Having the two limbs swaying in alternating frequency, and tilting his head from side to side in symphony, Malcolm then added a third limb, then a fourth, then four limbs and a leaf.

If only Ivy Broadway was here, I'd put his little

displays behind the barn to shame. To shame!

He raised his arms and snapped his fingers to the rhythm of his hips, singing in a whisper.

"I'm the mas-ter, boom! I'm the mas-ter, boom!"

At last the yellow torrent sagged and began to drizzle onto the red sand in front of his feet. He arched his hips forward and gave forth a mighty internal pelvic squeeze that sent a single short-lived stream to the top of the bush.

"Hoo-ah!"

Then he snapped his fingers one more time, a shiver ran through his shoulders, then he gave an exaggerated nod in self-satisfaction. He turned away from the bush and reached to zip himself up. He stopped, frozen in his one sided hump-shouldered stoop to reach for his fly, and looked directly up at the smiling faces of Elizabeth, Itjanu, Karina, and Natalia.

Malcolm spun around on his heels still in his crouch, and began shooing himself back into his fly and trying to zip it up as fast as possible. The bottom edge of his tee shirt was still sticking out through his fly and jammed the zipper half way up. He grabbed the loop of fabric and tried to pull it free and at the same moment tried with his other hand to free the zipper enough to close it. Neither would budge, so he grabbed the tee shirt with one hand and hit it with his other trying to rip the material free of the zipper.

"Don't punish it for doing what it's supposed to do, Malcolm." Elizabeth's mock sincerity inflamed Malcolm's embarrassment. The three other women turned quickly away, but Elizabeth remained where she was and continued her conversation.

"Maybe my Harold should have been hit by green lightning. No, that wouldn't have helped. He was a horney little devil anyway, just not for me. No, for him white lightning would have been just fine. Just cook him and leave me the money."

Malcolm ignored Elizabeth's rejoinder. He continued the struggle with his zipper as he walked bent-over around to the other side of the bush and came face to face with a full-grown Emu. Malcolm bellowed in his surprise, and the Emu squawked in its own surprise, giving Malcolm a hard peck on his forehead for the trouble, and brought blood.

"Damn you!"

Malcolm growled, and forgetting his zipper, grabbed at the Emu's long soft feathered neck. The Emu struck again at Malcolm's forehead, drawing blood again, and ran out into the field. Focusing all his embarrassment and anger on the big bird, Malcolm made a dash at it again to grab its neck for pecking him. The bird zagged to the left and Malcolm ran after it intending to at least shoo it off even if he couldn't grab the thing. He would wait for his anger to dissipate and his aching muscles to stop him after a few more strides.

To his own amazement, and the Emu's consternation, Malcolm kept pace with the bird until it zigged to the right. It left a gap of ten feet in its turn and then headed back out toward the middle of the field. Stretching his legs from a toe-pushing lunge to a full running span, within twenty paces Malcolm had caught up with the bird again, and again it zagged to the right. Malcolm almost slipped in his socks squishing through a small sampling of Kangaroo droppings, but regained his footing in an arm swinging windmill motion and dashed after the bird again. Twenty-five paces closed the gap, Malcolm figured the bird would zag to the right again, and when it did Malcolm lunged for him grabbing the terrified bird firmly by his leathery throat with both hands.

They both slid to a stop. At first the bird flapped its ragged winglets and tried to kick Malcolm, but the grip he held on its neck brought most movement to a halt. The Emu trembled in Malcolm's grip, its dark beady eyes rolled back in its round head and it began to fall limp within Malcolm's hands. Realizing that not only had he actually caught the Emu, Malcolm was shocked to realize he was about to strangle the poor wretch. He relaxed his grip slightly until the bird tried to stand again and looked at his captor. When he was satisfied that the bird was actually looking at him, he released his grip with one hand, but keeping it firm with the other, balled his fingertips to the palm of his hand forming a knuckles ridge. He then raised his hand slowly over the bird so it could watch the movement, and then 'thunk'- knuckled the bird on the top of its head.

"Now, how do you like it? Huh?"

He then released the bird, letting it crab, flap, and flutter away from him into the tree line. Malcolm nodded after the bird, wiped the blood dripping from his forehead with his hand and then turned to look back toward the campsite at the far side of the field, but only a single man stood watching. The man stood there staring as Malcolm re-crossed the field and as he neared the man held his cup up in salute, slurshing the untouched tea still in his cup.

"Damnedest thing I've ever seen. Never seen a man run down an Emu before." He chuckled nervously. "What with that tuft of cloth hanging out, I thought maybe you were gonna bugger the damned thing!"

Malcolm stopped and looked down at the offending tee shirt tail, still hanging from his jammed zipper. He grabbed the material in a tight fist and yanked with all his strength. The cloth and zipper both followed the resulting rip full up the front of his shorts to his waistband. The man dropped his teacup and hurried away. Still standing at the edge of the field looking straight ahead, Malcolm yanked the ripped pieces of his shorts away from his body and dropping them into the grass. Naked, except for the half ripped away tee shirt and Kangaroo-dung-covered socks, Malcolm marched back to his tent.

Amidst a relentless swarm of desert flies Mac managed to coerce the group through breaking camp, taking the few good tents into the trailer, and cleaning the campsite. Breakfast was a meager meal of granola bars picked up at the park store on the way out. Malcolm swore to the neighborly doctor and to Mac as well, that he was fit to continue the trip. Malcolm managed to avoid another examination and lied that the green area had almost faded away. The park ranger was appeased when Mac explained that they had a doctor among the group that would watch over Malcolm for any adverse reactions. They were sent on their way with nothing more than the receipt from the campsite and a caution to have Malcolm looked at in Oodnadatta.

Despite his sullen mood and obvious resistance to company, Malcolm was joined in the back of the van by the person he least wanted to visit.

"Henry, you need to stay away from me this morning."

"Malcolm, we need to talk."

"No we don't – yes we do. Why'd you try to drown me you little shit?"

"That was an accident, but that's past. We have some important information to discuss for our next ceremony."

"Our...next...ceremony? Are you out of your freaking gourd? I'm not doing anything with you."

"You must. We're bonded now."

"Henry, go sit up front or so help me,..."

"I saw you catch that Emu."

"Big Deal. Go away, Henry."

"Could you have ever imagined doing such a thing? Running down an Emu, I mean?"

"He was probably sick or something, and I was really pissed – like I am now."

"The flies didn't bother you, did they, Malcolm?"

"What the Hell do flies have to do with Emus?"

"Nothing. But, they have something to do with you."

"Henry, if you don't leave me alone, I'm gonna knock the shit out of you!"

Heads turned from the front of the van and Mac looked up through the rear view mirror.

"Everything all right back there?"

Malcolm answered. "Yeah. Henry was just apologizing for trying to drown me last night." He turned his face close to Henry's. "Git."

Henry frantically gathered up his notebooks and moved to another row on the opposite side.

Malcolm turned his attention to the sweeping view of red sand and spinifex tufts, running off miles to the horizon. After staring out the window for several minutes, motion at the corner of his eye focused his attention back inside. The van had brought with it hundreds of flies from the campsite. Hiraht and Elizabeth were actively swatting at the flies with their bush hats, and several windows on the other side of the van were laced at the edges with black flies.

Malcolm's window was free of them. The one lone fly that had caught his eye had flown away. In fact, there were no flies anywhere around him. He leaned forward over the seat in front of his, where the window still hosted twenty or so flies milling about its edges. Malcolm extended his arm slowly toward the window, and the flies quickly flew away toward the front of the bus. He watched the window, waiting for them to return or be replaced by a couple dozen of their cousins, but none returned. He repeated the experiment with the several dozen clustered on the large rear window of the van.

Mac began to swat around his head as he drove. "Bloody hell, these flies are horrible. All right everyone, when I speed up open your windows and shoo these little blighters out."

As the whine of the engine increased, the windows opened washing the inside of the van with hot dusty wind. When most of the flies were gone, Mac yelled back, "That'll do her", and the windows were quickly closed to the symphony of swatting hats and kerchiefs knocking dust from clothes and windows. Malcolm picked up his walking stick from its roost between the seat and the side frame, and then reached it over the intervening seat tops to nudge Henry in the shoulder. Henry spun around in his seat and looked back at Malcolm.

"All right Henry. Come tell me what you think you know about the flies."

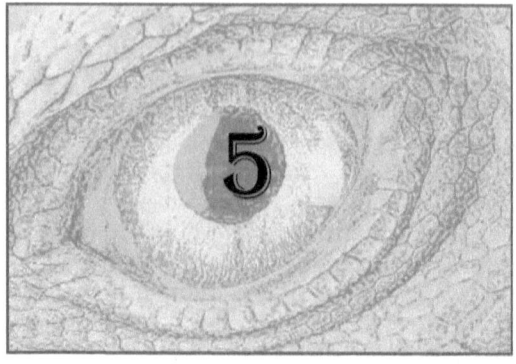

Henry fairly bubbled with excitement as he brought his pack and notebooks back and sat next to Malcolm. "There is just so much to tell you, I am overwhelmed with where to begin..."

"The flies?"

"Well, yes, the files are just an indicator – a verification – of my whole theory. You see, Malcolm, ancient mythology is based on stories that were told long before writing was developed..."

"Wait a minute. I ask you about the flies and you start with a history of the friggin world?"

"Please bear with me. If I don't start with the beginning, it won't make sense..."

"Start with the flies. Give me the thirty-second version."

Henry stopped with his mouth open, his eyes flitting back and forth from side to side in obvious search of what to say next. He closed his mouth. He took in a deep breath and opened his mouth again, but still said nothing. His hands ran up and down the spines of his several notebooks in his lap, finger tapping each in succession. He opened his mouth again and then closed it with a snap, exhaling though his nose. He then screwed up his face, took in another breath and sputtered it out.

"O.K. Flies stay away from you because they are afraid."

Malcolm waited for another statement from Henry, but it did not come.

"Flies run away because they are afraid of anything big that moves, Henry. Then they come back."

"Yes, Malcolm, they come back, except to you."

"All right. Then what about the mosquitoes that bit me last night and that damned Emu that pecked my forehead this morning?"

"They won't do it again."

"Of course they won't do it again, we're a hundred miles from there."

"Use Kilometers, Malcolm. We're in Australia."

Malcolm leaned close to Henry. "Don't push it."

Malcolm straightened back up in his seat. "All right, we're a, um, one hundred and, um, seventy kilometers from there. Whatever. They can't do anything to me again."

"I think during the night you went through a change, Malcolm, Most likely the first of many. You are becoming something different, something more, much more."

"Yeah, the fly killer. So why wasn't the Emu afraid of me?"

"She was. She was probably terrified, but you had triggered an even stronger emotion: Motherhood."

"What?"

"Malcolm, you had just spent almost five whole minutes pissing on her nest. Of course she was, well, hee hee, pissed."

I could really hurt this guy.

The following hour was a monologue in which Henry poured out his theory of mythology and the world in general. It was obvious to Malcolm that Henry either had few opportunities to actually speak with another human being, or shunned them intentionally.

"It's my unifying theory of all folklore. Folklore becomes part of our written history, but it's all jumbled through false memory, misunderstandings and simple omissions. There is a species of beings that have almost always been here on earth. I can't even guess their origins, but they are force beings, energy if you like. On some geologic cycle they need to inhabit living

69

organisms, but it doesn't always work. Sometimes the biologic form can't handle their occupation, like that kangaroo Mac hit. It was already dying long before that. You saw it on the road when Mac tried to pull it off to the side."

"Jesus! Henry, you think I'm going to rot." Malcolm absently rubbed the spreading green under his shirt. "That can't possibly be true..."

"Can and is, Malcolm. Listen to me."

Henry fingered his notebooks again, absently touching individual ones as he peppered Malcolm with his improbable chain of ideas.

"So, let me get this straight, Henry. I've just been hit by green lightning carrying an ancient alien being that is now growing inside of me, and that's why I'm turning green. Is that it?"

I need a drink, and this loony needs to be committed. The good people back in the sanitarium would just love him!

Henry crossed his arms and pressed his lips tightly together. "Trite, but close."

Malcolm exhaled his irritation. "All right."

He slumped down in his seat, leaned his head back and propped his knees against the seatback in front of him. Then he fished a small bag of trail mix from a cargo pocket in his shorts. He popped the seal and offered some to Henry who waved them away with a flicker of his hand.

"All right, Dr. Livingston, tell me more."

"Like I said, the transformation doesn't always work. Not all species and not all individuals within a species are both acceptable and susceptible. Do you understand that concept?"

Malcolm nodded his head, slipping his fingers into the trail mix.

Mmm cashews. I like cashews. What else is in here?

"Go on, Henry, I'm listening."

What are these little white things?

"That's why ancient myths are full of mixed beings: Lions with human heads, humans with jackal heads, hawks, leopards, etc. Now doesn't that make sense with common knowledge about myths in both the Americas and ancient Egypt?"

Malcolm arched his eyebrows and nodded his head.

Ahh, it's little pieces of dried pineapple. Don't usually like pineapple, but this is good.

Malcolm examined another white square from the plastic bag and tilted his head toward Henry as he popped the piece into his mouth. "And...?"

"Well, once they find the right mix, I think maybe it needs refreshing for time to time."

"Like a coke?"

I could use a coke, this stuff is really dry. Where's my canteen?

Malcolm reached down between his legs and pulled his canteen from the upper pouch of his pack. As he brought it up he noticed that his usual pale inner thighs exposed by his bunched up shorts were now pale green. He paused in mid reach and extended two fingers from around his canteen to press repeatedly into the skin. There was no pain or any unusual sensation that indicated a problem, except for the fact that his skin was turning green. Malcolm spoke to his thigh.

"Maybe it's some kind of weird Australian rash. Excuse me, Henry."

Malcolm slipped past Henry into the aisle and moved up three rows toward the front. Itjanu was leaning back against the window reading a novel, her legs resting across the empty seat beside her. Malcolm gently slid her legs off the seat and slipped in next to her.

"Itjanu, er, Dr. Williamson, I need you to feel my thighs."

Itjanu frowned over her book at being disturbed and laid it firmly onto her lap.

"Malcolm Ironwater, even if I was absolutely frantic to feel a man's thighs and everyman in the world was lined up for me..."

"I know, I know. I'd be toward the back of the line."

"Ironwater, you wouldn't be in the line."

Malcolm grabbed the lower hem of his shorts and pulled the edge up exposing almost his entire upper

71

thigh. Itjanu looked at the hand movement and opened her eyes widely at what she saw. "Good grief!"

Elizabeth had watched Malcolm's arrival with interest from her seat in front of Itjanu. With a playful smile on her face she craned her head over the ridge of the seat back. "Are we playing show and tell now, are we? May I peek too?" She looked down at the verdant thigh and gasped. "Good God, Gertrude!"

Itjanu frowned into Malcolm's face. "You said it was going away!"

"Yeah, well, I lied. I was really hoping it would, but just don't want to go to some clinic or hospital just now. It feels all right, though. Just looks weird."

"Do you have a fever?" Itjanu reached up and laid the back of her hand to Malcolm's forehead. "You don't feel warm. Stick out your tongue."

Malcolm did as he was told and then retracted it as Itjanu leaned closer and pressed his eyebrows up to open his eyes farther.

"Your sclera look normal. Is your vision all right?"

Malcolm answered yes to that and the series of questions that followed, until Itjanu stopped asking new ones.

"Well, if Doctor Hydter thought you were going to last until you made it to Oodnadatta, I guess I have that as an assurance that I haven't overlooked something."

Mac flipped on the intercom.

"All right ladies and gents, we'll be in Mutanajulu in about twenty minutes. This is a Pitjantjatjara village. The town council allows us to visit the cultural center, but the folks that live there don't like to be stared at and definitely not photographed. You can shoot inside the center and take outside pictures of the center itself, but no local people in the shots. That's the deal. I need to be real serious about that. One shutter click at the people and we'll have to leave, and then they'll expect me to collect the film in your camera. I don't want to have to do that, but I gave'em my word. Anyone having a problem with that needs to come up here and talk to me."

There was a general murmur of agreement, but Natalia stepped into the aisle and moved up to the seat next to Mac and engaged in a low animated conversation that Malcolm could not hear. Mac shook his head emphatically several times and then Natalia returned to plop down in her seat pouting.

Mac turned off the lone paved road and began the mile drive up a well maintained sandy road, running through another open plain leading to a sparse stand of trees at it end. The van then passed from the spinifex plain into the trees leaving a long reddish cloud in its wake behind the dust covered trailer. Edged by lines of hearty wattle bushes and short Mulga trees they saw a perfectly green rectangle of approximately three acres. The neatly trimmed field would have been a proud front lawn to any expensive mansion, but was fixed at each end by netted goals.

"They've got a real nice soccer field here," Mac said. "The school has taken the regional championships for six years running."

The road turned again bringing the van past a windmill pumping station and a large vinyl water tower decorated with an array of white dots around a red and brown snake outlined in thick black lines. Beyond the water tower was a short block of neat white houses holding low-hanging curved tin porch roofs; cars and small pickup trucks were tucked away on short driveways next to each house. Another turn and another row of houses, less maintained, most without window panes or doors, some with small groups of Anangu lounging on the sand yards under shading tress.

"Some of these folks lived in the desert the way their grandparents did until just a few years ago. They're not all that comfortable being closed up in a house."

A naked child stood by the road waving and giggling through gapped Pearl white baby teeth as the van passed. Elizabeth waved back, but Itjanu was not looking out. The van passed an old man stumbling along the roadside with his nose stuck into an open can.

"Petrol sniffer, that one," Mac spoke out to anyone listening. He looked up through the rear view mirror again. "Itjanu, I guess this is home for you, aye?"

"A destination, Mac. Just a destination."

Mac grinned into the mirror.

"Oh, I thought this is where you grew up. Family and all?"

Itjanu did not answer and Mac made the final turn to the little three-car parking lot beside the cultural center.

The building had once been white cinderblock, but was now painted in a series of overlapping murals depicting desert creatures or red, yellow, black and white dotted designs. Mac turned off the engine and stepped out of the van toward the open front door of the building. He was met by a middle-aged European woman wearing the same loose smock and billowing colorful cotton skirt worn by Anangu women. She skipped out like a bubbly girl and pulled Mac to her in a warm hug. Lean with healthy tanned skin and sliver streaked blond hair, she kissed him on the cheek and pushed the hat from his head to hang behind him by its string, then rubbed his head affectionately. He wrapped his arm around her waist and guided her to the group of campers emerging from the van.

"This is Margaret Mackenaugh Fletcher. She is the center coordinator and will be our guide and lecturer for the Mutanajulu Cultural Center – and gift shop, so have your money ready for some fascinating Anangu artwork."

"Pitjantjatjara," she corrected him. Her eyes fell on Elizabeth.

"Hello Elizabeth."

"Hello Maggie."

"You two know each other," Mac asked in surprise, then tapped his forehead. "Of course. Mackenaugh. I didn't put that together."

The two women hugged and Elizabeth spoke. "She is my husband's sister." Elizabeth turned back toward Margaret. "Has the little weasel contacted you?"

"Yes, he rang up in tizzy at two o'clock in the morning. Never did give any consideration for the time difference. Just rang up asking if you've showed up here and told me you'd ran off with all his money."

"What did you tell him?"

"Told him you were probably in Monte Carlo losing it

74

all at Blanco. He was positively apoplectic."

"Well, don't tell him I'm here. He ran off with his secretary for a fortnight of mattress jousting, so I moved all the accounts and left."

Margaret chuckled. "Good on you! But, I guess you haven't heard then?"

Elizabeth tilted her head and arched her eyebrows in question.

"The little trollop found out his money was gone and dropped him like the smelly old cod he is. He's at home pining away for his money, and you – in that order."

Margaret swept the faces of the others in a beaming smile.

"Sorry to bore you all with family dirties. Let's get you inside to see some wonderful original work. 'Liz and I can gossip later."

The cultural center was a large open room occupying almost the entire building, divided down the middle by wood framed pegboard. The center aisle was lined with stacks of framed paintings leaned against the pegboard on one side, and in unframed piles of canvas on tables along the other. To the right was an open area for craft work in wood carving and painting. Two Anangu women were chattering away in Pitjantjatjara, working over a large canvas being decorated in multicolored dots and design lines around a black and yellow goanna. They looked up and smiled at the visitors and then returned to their work and ongoing conversation.

The left side of the room was structured more like a typical western arts and craft store with a small cubicle in the rear fitted with folding chairs arranged around a VCR and television. Margaret ran a brief tape of traditional Anangu tribal life, portrayed by another village that had set aside the canon against photography. While Hiraht, Karin and Peter watched a follow-on segment; others roamed the gift shop looking at best samples of paint and carved art, and spinifex woven baskets. Elizabeth and Margaret were cloistered around the cluttered desk that had once been Margaret's workspace.

Itjanu walked alone among the crafts fingering work

like she herself had produced as a child in that very village before the cultural center was built. Then it was for use by her family, not for sale. Margaret looked beyond her sister-in-law where Itjanu lingered near the canvas paintings. She excused herself from Elizabeth and joined her Itjanu.

"Itjanu, I thought you would be out visiting relatives, or even chasing down your grandfather about all the excitement your group has been having. You know, he told me long ago about green lights in the sky and something to do with the old Kurpany legend. And now we have this nightly Aurora. Have you seen him yet?"

"You came after I left, but you seem to know a lot about me."

"They've talked about nothing else since the university informed us you were coming. Your grandfather comes in every day to ask if I've heard anything from you."

"You mean in between the hours he spends trying to dissolve his brain with petrol fumes? Yes, I saw him along the road on our way in."

"That started when L-, when your grandmother died, but then I think perhaps you know that. He still hopes to see you."

"If he would even know who he was looking at?"

"I know ya! I know ya better than ya let yaself know ya," the old man said from the doorway.

They turned toward him. His faded shirt and dark pants were ripped and stained from long wear without changing. He looked only at Itjanu."I can't ever decide if you are the blackest white woman I ever knew, or the whitest black woman I ever knew."

Itjanu stood in silence looking at him. The flies buzzed around his head and settled on his cheeks to explore his skin, but he did not swat them away.

"You shoulda come back to say goodbye to her," he said. "You shoulda been here to say her name a last time before she left and we had t'cover it up! It can't be said now, not yet."

"It's been four years. It's time to uncover it." Itjanu pointed to the plaque on the wall near the craft area, naming the founders of the cultural center. One name was still covered in black tape, as was their custom. The old man would not come in to look at the plaque.

He did not enter. He did not go into buildings, and she would not move to the door.

The old man shifted his feet. "The wallabies and the roos are dying out there."

"It's a virus," she said.

"It's that damned light in the night sky."

"You know I don't believe all that."

"Sometimes the people go out into the desert and sometimes they think Liru is just a stick. But it bites them anyway. It doesn't care if the people think it's only a stick. It knows it's a snake and it does what snakes do."

Itjanu did not comment on the old adage, and the old man pointed back outside.

"You come sit by the fire with me after awhile. You gotta help me do something about the light. She can't come back to help, even though I know she wants to, so you gotta help."

The old man turned and walked away. Itjanu looked at the empty doorway and spoke without turning. "I need to get my bags off the van."

"That went well, don't you think," Malcolm said."

Itjanu glanced over her shoulder in his direction.

"Shut up, Malcolm."

She walked out to the van and did not return to the cultural center. She was simply absent when the campers filed back into their seats with bags of souvenirs.

Elizabeth questioned Malcolm. "You spoke to her at the door, Malcolm. Didn't she say anything about coming back or saying good-bye to us?"

"Nah, she just said she was going to get her bags off the van and was gone."

Mac flipped on the intercom with an electrical pop in the overhead speakers.

"Right, then, Ladies and gentlemen it will only take about thirty minutes to get to our next campsite. We'll be staying tonight in Mutana Creek, just on the edge of Anangu land."

77

The air in the van filled with sweet acrid mist. Malcolm turned in his seat to see Natalia emptying a can of air freshener at the ceiling. Several hands waved in front of crinkled noses spiraling the waves of mist drifting down through the low setting sunlight. Natalia stuck up her chin.

"The van smelled like bug spray and body odor, and this smells like..." She stopped spraying long enough to turn the can on its side and read the label. "...a subtle floral aroma."

Elizabeth coughed through the settling haze. "It's not subtle at all, Natalia, it's quite strong. Don't you think, Malcolm?"

"I liked the bug spray smell much better."

My nose feels like it's been raped by a friggin gardenia! And Henry took in a lung full of propellant, alcohol, and probably 7.5% carcinogens.

"I think it smells nice, Natalia," Henry said.

Malcolm shook his head to himself.

With a nose full of book mold, mustard gas would probably be refreshing.

"I've got to open a window."

Hiraht, Elizabeth and Malcolm opened windows and quickly mixed the aroma of a feminine deodorant spray with fine red dust. The damp spot of spray on the ceiling directly over Natalia was instantly outlined in red. The dust in the air thinned as Mac pulled the van onto the main dirt road heading farther north through the plain and geared back up to cruising speed again, to the whine of gears and wheels and the frequent 'thock' of rocks tossed up into the wheel well. No sooner had the sounds become routine than he began to slow again, and then turned onto another side road past to a faded tin government sign proclaiming

Mutana Creek, 5 Km.

Mutana Creek held less than a dozen cracked paint storefronts almost evenly divided on each side of the main dirt road. Tin roofs extended over worn plank sidewalks and most of stores were abandoned. The middle store on the left held two recently cleaned large glass windows, almost filled on the inside with overlapping taped signs offering specials on one commodity or another. A chipped wooden sign saying "Cuthbert's Store" swung lazily under the porch over a central screen door set back between the two windows.

The right side of the street began and ended in large brick and tin buildings set apart from the intervening row of boarded up shops that once offered haircuts, laundry, leatherwork and baked goods. The names were still legible on weather bleached signs hanging above nailed doors or protruding from porch posts. The first large brick building displayed no sign and had no boarded windows, but still held the air of vacancy by allowing the passerby to see through to the back windows of nearly empty rooms. The building at the far end of the street proclaimed in fresh paint on a large sign over the single entrance "Mutana Creek Pub". A rumpled faded blue pickup truck was parked in front of the pub next to a new red and yellow motorcycle.

Mac pulled the van in front of the pub and opened the doors. The easy thump of a bass drum and the faint twang of a guitar floated out into the street from behind the closed pub door. The music was followed by a muffled voice singing to a two-step rhythm, but the words to the song were lost in the buzz of black flies that formed a cloud around the camper's face nets as they emerged. Except Malcolm.

Beyond the pub was a vast expanse of desert, its beginning marked by the remnants of a wire fence at the edge of town. A scraped dirt road ran arrow straight to the horizon. Next to the road was another long scraped rectangular area, marked at one corner by a thirty-foot pole holding a drooping windsock in the faint breath coming in off the desert. Mac stepped toward the pub door, swatted at a trio of flies pirouetting in front of his face and squinted at the still fierce settling sun.

"We can stop in here until 'fly down', for those of us bothered by them," Mac said, looking back toward Malcolm. "And then go set up camp. Cuthbert's looked open, if anyone wants to pick up something extra for tonight."

Mac opened the door to the pub, letting the singing escape into the street after its music and went in. Malcolm looked across the street from the pub. There was a newly fenced in area enclosing several acres of mostly open land with a few small trees spread among several iron fire rings. Near the entrance gate was a row of narrow-doored cubicles that ran along the inside of the fence with small wooden platforms in front of each door. The international blue and white symbols for men and women decorated two of the cubicles; the others were marked "shower."

I guess that's our camp site.

Mac was already shaking hands with the bartender and moving around the bar to pull himself a beer by the time Malcolm made his way in. Mac introduced the operator/bar tender, Bill McLeod, amidst shared jibes and clinking glasses being filled with cold beer, cola and water.

"Might just have this place someday, if Bill there will sell the rights to it," Mac explained as he handed Malcolm a tall draft in a heavy glass mug. Malcolm looked over the top of the glass as he took a long breathless drink from the frosted mug. Bill reached around Mac for another mug.

"Yeah, well he can have it anytime. No one much comes here anymore, 'cept blokes like Mac here, bringing you campers. Been better this last three weeks what with the night lights an all, but it won't last. Then this whole bloody place'll roll up into a dust ball again."

Mac smiled at Bill and winked at Malcolm as he handed Natalia a canned diet cola.

"She'll be right, Malcolm. Little fixing up, advertising with the right folks, maybe a contract with some of the tour groups. This here's what I want after I'm tired of running the roads."

Mac pulled himself a beer and brought it around the bar to sit next to Malcolm. Malcolm had his elbows propped up on the bar top, suspending his mug between drooping hands. He turned his head from his beer toward Mac.

"And when might that be, Mac."

"Any day now, Mate, any day now."

Malcolm grinned as he swallowed the last of the beer and set the mug across the bar to Bill for a refill. He slowly swung around on the bar stool looking at the interior of the little bar. Off to the left was a young man in a black leather riding suit edged in red, stalking around the far side of the pool table with a cue in his hand and a cigarette hanging loosely from the corner of his mouth. The rider bent over to examine the lay of the pool balls, set his cigarette gingerly on the edge of the table near a red and black motorcycle helmet that matched his outfit, and leaned over the table to make his next shot. In the shadows behind the rider stood to an older Anangu man in faded denims, a tattered straw hat pushed back on his head. He was leaning against the back wall, resting his hands on the top of a cue.

The young man smacked the cue ball hard and sent a series of balls charging into the padded edges and churning back across the table, but none found its way into a pocket.

"Shit," he said.

The old man pushed himself off the wall and limped slowly toward the table. Sliding the stick in gnarled black fingers, he tapped the cue ball into a series of gentle runs across the felt tabletop until all of the striped balls were sent almost without noise into their pockets. Without hesitation or comment he sent down the eight ball, and then rested his hands on top of the cue stick again, looking at the young man without expression.

The young man jammed his free hand into his pants pocket and came out with four red bills. He tossed them onto the table top, snatched up his helmet and left the pub. The old man picked up the abandoned cigarette and puffed it back to life.

Bill watched the old man from the far end of the bar. "Now Mica, Annie told me you'd quit."

Mica kept the cigarette in his fingers and walked slowly over to the bar next to Malcolm.

"What's me tab, Bill."

The motorcycle roared to life outside, and a thick cloud of red dust drifted by the narrow front window.

Bill pulled a worn ledger from under the bar and opened it toward the back.

"Forty-eight dollars, Mica."

Mica placed three red twenties on the bar and slid the fourth into his pocket.

"Give me a pack of Players, no wait, Marlboros, I'm on the high end tonight; and a bottle of Carlton for take away."

Bill took the twenties and then placed Mica's order and his change on the bar. "That money won't last long smoking yank cigarettes, mate."

Mica looked into Bill's face. "You don't tell Annie nuthin, O.K.?"

Bill held up his hands, palms facing Mica. "You don't let her ask me. I'm a hell of a lot more scared of her than you!"

Mica chuckled and waved his finger in the air over his shoulder as he limped out of the pub.

Malcolm rounded the stool again looking at all the business cards, foreign currency, pictures, cloth organizational patches, and even a few bras tacked to the walls and ceiling of the pub. One extremely large bra nailed to the ceiling strained its straps against the weight of several coins tossed up into it. There were barely a few square inches of the original knotty pine interior still exposed. Malcolm's eyes rested on a small white wooden sign hung at the forward edge of a shelf of whisky glasses against the back wall, and read out the letters.

"Y.C.W.C.Y.O.G.C.F.R.F.D.S?" He turned to Mac. "What the hell does that stand for?"

Mac did not turn to look at him, but only spoke into his beer mug. "Don't know. Need to ask Bill, I reckon."

Malcolm motioned to Bill, getting his attention and then pointed at the sign. Bill came around in front of Malcolm with his eyebrows arched with an official air.

"You have a question to ask?"

"Yeah, what's that stand for?"

"This sign here? You want to know what these letters stand for? Is that it?"

"Yeah." Malcolm was almost annoyed with the repetition.

"It stands for: Your Curiosity Will Cost You One Gold Coin For the Royal Flying Doctor Service."

Bill and Mac shared a laugh. Bill brought out small plastic replica of a toilet seat from under the bar and raised the lid to the bowl half filled with Australian one and two dollar gold coins.

"You can place your kind contribution in this honored receptacle, or test your jump shot skills at the dainty female under things hanging above your head. Malcolm chose the jump shot and on the third try placed a two-dollar coin rebounding off the ceiling into the left side cup. The group clapped in celebration of his shot and chuckled amongst themselves with the gaiety a few cold beers could bring. A short while later, Mac looked out through little window and noticed the sun setting behind the large spreading red gum tree across the street.

"O.K. folks, let's go set up camp."

Malcolm tipped up his third mug of beer and drained the glass, then twirled around on his bar stool and stepped toward the door as the last in line. Mac started to say something else, but stopped with his mouth open staring at Malcolm. Malcolm watched Mac staring directly at him.

"What?"

Others noticed Mac staring dumbly back toward the bar and began to turn. One by one they turned to look at Malcolm, their eyes wide open. Elizabeth let out a small gasp and brought her hand to her open mouth. Natalia was the last to turn, emitting a trembling

"Ooooh."

"What?!"

Malcolm looked behind him to see what they might be staring at and saw Bill backing away from the bar into the back room. Beside the doorway to the back was a wall mirror and Malcolm could see himself in the reflection and all the others standing behind him at the front door. The skin of his face, his arms and even his hands had turned completely lime green.

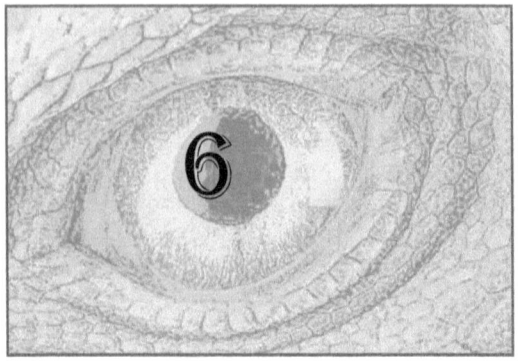

Malcolm walked at the end of the line of campers filing through the entrance gate behind the van and trailer. Peter and Karina tried poorly disguised studies of the areas of the campsite and stealing quick glances back at Malcolm, but Henry and Elizabeth looked boldly back at their green compatriot. Natalia had secreted herself into the van next to Mac and did her best to pretend Malcolm no longer existed. The flies were thinning noticeably, but the first mosquitoes had already arrived and drawn blood from Elizabeth. As with the flies, the mosquitoes avoided the space around Malcolm. Elizabeth slowed her walk to allow the others to move ahead, then jooined Malcolm as he walked by. She hooked her arm under Malcolm's, pulling herself close and walking in step. Malcolm smiled at her.

"You develop a thing for human frogs, have you?"

"I am almost ashamed to say this, Malcolm, but the mosquitoes are driving me mad."

"Yeah, but they seem to have left me alone since the lightning strike back at Wilpena Pound."

"May I share your tent tonight, Malcolm?"

Malcolm stopped and turned to face her fully, his eyes arched high.

"As much as I'd like to believe it's my manly charm that has overwhelmed you, I suspect not."

She looked down, shielding from him with her eyelids.

"Please don't think lowly of me, but I must get away from those damned mosquitoes."

Malcolm laughed loudly.

"So, I'm to be your insect repellent for the night?"

Elizabeth flushed red and nodded to the ground. Malcolm laughed again shaking his head. "Yeah, well, if you can stand my snoring – and you can assure me you'll keep your hands to yourself..."

"Well, of course..."

"I know. I know. I am teasing with you. I figure I'm going to be having a lot of space to myself until we figure out this green thing." He patted her on the shoulder and smiled. "At least I'll have good company."

A small cloud of mosquitoes drifted nearby like so many dandelion tufts caught in the breeze, but then veered away when they came downwind of the pair. Malcolm watched them fly away, and then moved off in the direction of the van.

Mac started a large fire even as others began to set up tents. He looked up as Malcolm approached.

"I had planned for us all to sleep under the stars in swags tonight, Malcolm. The night sky is always beautiful around here."

Squatting between the growing fire and Malcolm, Mac was free of the mosquitoes that had gathered around him since he left the pub. He raised his forearm in front of him to watch the last mosquito take flight and then smiled at Malcolm.

"You're right useful, mate."

Malcolm removed his bush hat and ran his hands across his short hair.

"Yeah, Elizabeth has already figured that out."

He looked up at the nearby trees. Each campsite seemed to have two of them, with everything else cleared away or left as sand.

"Well, at least we have a couple eucalyptus trees for shade in the morning. "

"Call'em Gum, Malcolm. Ozzies call'em gum trees."

"Right. Gum trees."

Malcolm shifted his stance and looked at the small line formed in front of the little restrooms at the far side

85

of the campground. Mac followed his gaze.

"Ah, just use the bushes over there by the fence. It's dark."

As Malcolm turned to walk toward the bushes Mac stood up.

"Guess, I'll join ya, if ya don't mind." Then added in explanation, "Mossies."

Looking beyond the bushes and fence to a nearby tree line, Malcolm spotted a vertical line of white almost glowing in the growing darkness.

"What's that?"

Mac looked in the direction Malcolm pointed.

"Ghost gums. Some of them are so white they're like alabaster. All it takes is a few stars to light'em up."

Malcolm looked up at the first flickering stars, and then down to attend his business and saw something long waver out of his fly. He froze his movement as the thing protruded almost a foot beyond his hands that were protecting himself from the undulating creature.

"Oh my God! Mac, I've got a snake coming out of my fly!"

"Aw, don't brag, Malcolm."

"No really! Look at this thing!"

"Now Malcolm, I'm gonna move away, mosquitoes or not."

"No! Not that. There's something in my clothes. It must have crawled into my shorts somehow! Can you shine a light on it?"

Mac zipped himself up and pulled a small flashlight from his back pocket.

"For your sake, mate, there better sure as hell be something there besides you, or so help me..."

The light burst into the darkness and swooped down to Malcolm's trembling hands. Just below his protective grip a long thin deep green living object twisted and twirled, hanging from the lowest edge of Malcolm's open fly.

"Bloody hell! It looks like a snake!"

Malcolm was becoming frantic.

"A snake! Pull it out. Pull it out!"

"I've never seen a snake that color. Has he bit you?"

"No, I don't think so. Please pull it out."

"All right. All right. Try to calm down. I'll see if I can yank it out."

Malcolm turned to face Mac and Mac kept the light on the thing, holding the flashlight in one hand and slowly extending his other near the snake tail. Mac slowly encircled the snake with his hand, not yet touching it, adjusting his thumb and fingers to get a good grip on it when he grabbed.

"All right, here goes."

Mac quickly closed his grip on the snake, making his fist as tight as he could in one swift motion and yanked on it as hard as his arm and shoulder would allow. Mac's shoulder spun away, his elbow shot out away from his side and he pulled his hand back with all of his considerable strength. The snake came forward, Malcolm yelled out, and his knees and feet came forward following Mac's motion. Malcolm's feet continued up into the air, his waist still following Mac's pull until the momentum was spent. Still moaning a protracted "Oooohhh!" Malcolm slipped through the air to land with a breath-taking thump on the ground in front of Mac.

"It's still there!"

Mac illuminated the spot again and the snake was still lodged in Malcolm's fly.

"Did he bite you?"

Malcolm shifted his hips only slightly.

"N-no. I don't feel anything."

"Better get your shorts off quickly, Malcolm."

Malcolm rolled onto his palms, keeping his legs apart, he stood up and slipped down his shorts and underwear.

"Bloody Hell! It's your ass. I mean its coming off your ass."

"My Ass?? The snake's crawled up my ass??! It's in my ass? Pull it out! Pull it out!"

"No. Bloody Hell! It is your ass, I mean – Bloody Hell – it's your, I mean..."

"What dammit?! What?!"

"You've got a bloody tail. It's coming off the tip of your spine. It's not something hanging ON you, it IS you!"

"What?!"

Malcolm spun to the left trying to look behind himself as the tail spun away from view. He made three complete circles trying to see the thing for himself, without success, and then began turning to the right. Malcolm made three more turns shouting.

"What? What? What?!" with each turn, still unable to see his own tail.

Mac grabbed him by his shoulders to stop his dizzying spins.

"Stand still, mate. Here"

Mac reached down and pulled the tail around Malcolm's hip so he could see it. Malcolm took the tip in his hands as it continued to twist slowly in his grip. He pulled on it and twisted himself half way around again. Then he reached over with both hands and yanked it in the opposite direction. He dug his fingernails into the green tissue for a better grip, then winced and yelled "Ow!" He looked over at Mac in the darkness, the tip of his own tail still held in the center of Mac's flashlight, his labored breath rasping in and out of his lungs.

"Well shit!"

He stood there with his tail in his hands in front of him with his red stained shorts and underwear wrapped around the tops of his hiking boots when several flashlights flared into the darkness, lighting him and Mac like two actors on stage.

"Blood-dy hell?"

"Good God, Gertrude."

"Sh-h-h-h-h-h-h-it."

The meager glare of the flashlights was overwhelmed by the headlights of a rumpled blue pickup truck pulling into the campsite. The old man from the cultural center sat in the pickup bed. The passenger side door opened and Itjanu Williamson stepped into the light, followed cautiously by the two men.

"Mica brought me to say good-bye, but I see your getting along well enough with camp entertainment."

Malcolm's shoulder's drooped and he turned with his back toward the headlights and flipped his tail back and forth, looking at her over his shoulder. Itjanu brought her hands up to her mouth.

"Oh No!"

Behind her, behind Mica, the old man backed away shaking his head.

"Wiya! Wiya!!"

Malcolm pulled his shorts up.

"What the hell else is going to happen?!"

He walked away from the group and out of the gate to the campground. He was heading for the pub, but when he realized it he stopped in his tracks.

No. Don't want to go there. Too many stares.

He turned and began walking up the street, not toward anywhere, just away from where he was. He could feel the pressure of his tail inside his shorts and adjusted himself just to let it hang down through his shorts leg. He walked away from the lights fed by the generators powering the pub and the campground, not wanting to be seen or to look at any part of himself, until he found himself in front of the large vacant building at the other end of the small town. He walked over to sit on the small porch in front of the door, but stood back up after feeling the pressure of his tail and not knowing what to do with it so he could sit down and still keep his shorts up.

"Dammit! Dammit to Hell!!"

The light from the Aurora intensified and the night sky bloomed into a green false dawn. A sharp pain began to burn through his abdomen. He felt as if his spine was on fire and the pain spread around his abdomen and up into his chest. His joints began to ache and throb, and his head felt on fire as well. The fire in his head was joined by the searing pain forcing him to his knees and then down on his hands and he cried out in pain. The pain was severe. Without pause it became worse and worse. Overhead the nightly display of a green tinted Aurora lit up the sky and the pain in his body grew worse. Tears ran down his face and he grabbed at the spasms within his abdomen that doubled him over and pushed his face into the dirt in front of his knees. He retched on the red sand road. He rose up again looking at the lights in the sky and shook his fist.

"Damn! Damn! Damn!"

Mac had built a large wood fire in the center of camp and the group gathered around it to escape the mosquitoes and talk amongst themselves about Malcolm. No one mentioned eating. Elizabeth and Itjanu traded theories between them and with Itjanu's grandfather. Henry was quiet after near two days of almost non-stop chattering with Malcolm, lost in his thoughts and staring into the fire. The others traded comments, questions, and speculations in a buzz of voices that repeated Malcolm's name again and again.

There was a rasping sound in the darkness at the edge of the camp made darker by the loss of night vision from the bright campfire. Silence spread among the group, with Natalia the last to close her mouth. As a group they tilted their heads to listen to the heavy rasping breathing barely discernable above the cracking of the fire. The darkness toward the bushes seemed to lighten faintly and then a form emerged into the edge of the firelight.

It was tall. Something with a big head, or something big on a head. They could see long arms ending in massive hands. The next step brought it farther into the light. Legs and feet like a running lizard, but stretching five feet up from the ground. It had a narrow waist and huge chest, and when it leaned forward, the head came into view showing large fan-like ears extending above the crown of its skull, round yellow cat eyes the size of lemons set far apart on either side of a long dog-like snout barely containing jumbled rows of long pointed teeth. It looked at each of them. Natalia screamed and ran to the van. The old man yelled "Kurpany!", but stood fixed and did not run.

The rest of the group could only sit and stare at the apparition, unable to move or barely breathe. The creature stepped closer to the fire. Expanding its lined yellow chest in a rasping breath, and straightening its body to a full ten feet, it raised its arms showing long clawed fingers, and behind it, enormous bat-like wings fanned out and up with a curved wingspan of at least twenty feet from tip to tip. The creature fixed its eyes directly at Henry.

"This-s-s-s..." it said, curling its forefingers in toward itself, pointing at itself,

"S-S-Sucks-s-s-s-s!!"

The group around the fire exploded into activity knocking over campstools and knocking into each other as the bulk of them dashed like a tight school of fish to the van. Only Henry and Mica remained in their seats. Henry trembled, frozen in terror as the thing neared him. Mica laughed nervously from his seat on the opposite side of the fire. The creature bent down toward Henry, extending its huge head and yellow eyes down in front of Henry's face. The snout of the creature was only inches from Henry's nose, its hot breath rippling the hair on his forehead.

"P-p-please don't kill me," Henry begged, his whole body trembling violently, tears running down his cheeks.

The creature raised upright, placing his three fingered claws onto its hips. "Kill you?"

The he rolled his hands palm up. "Henry, you little shit! You gotta get me outta this!"

Henry swallowed the cotton ball that had formed in his throat. "Malcolm?"

The creature rolled his lemon eyes and bobbed his head, California Valley style. "Well, yeah!"

Mica laughed loudly, flicked his cigarette into the fire as he drank down the rest of his beer, then reached into an opened nearby cooler and pulled out another can. He looked over at the van where faces were plastered against the glass looking back at the creature Malcolm, and waved them back out.

"C'mon out. He ain't gonna eat anybody!"

The van door opened. Mac and Itjanu cautiously stepped down in unison, pressed snuggly together. Elizabeth was close behind them, her forearms folded in tightly in front of her and peeping over Itjanu's shoulder. The trio walked ungainly back toward the fire, like a six-legged body with three heads. They joined Henry and Mica staring at the creature, at Malcolm, as he moved his arms and legs and wings in and out of his own vision looking at what he had become. He shivered and moved closer to the fire, squatting in the sand and reducing his height to a mere six feet. Itjanu walked up to him, her hands twisting her fingertips together closely in front of her.

"Malcolm, is that really you?"

"You want me to show you my tail again?"

She reached out her hand and touched the hobnail skin on his arm. "How do you feel?"

"I feel like shit!"

"That's not very analytical, Malcolm. How do you feel physically?"

He bent his head lower toward her.

"Oh, I feel O.K. I mean, nothing's hurting now. It hurt like hell when this last change started, but there's no pain now. I just don't want to be...THIS."

"Malcolm,..." Itjanu touched his arm. "Stand up and turn around, so I can see what this thing is you've become."

Malcolm rose to his full height again, spreading his wings up over his head and held his arms out. Then he slowly turned in a circle so Itjanu could examine him. She "Mmmm-d" in a doctorly way, then "tssssk-d" a few times, then "Mmmmm-d" again.

Malcolm squatted back down in front of her. "What??"

"Well, you seem to be a reptile, although no species I've ever seen. And um, uh,..."

"What?!"

"Well,... You're androgynous."

"Anne who??"

"You are an-dro-gy-nous." She pointed delicately toward the area below his waist. "Your, uh, 'package' is gone."

"What!!" Malcolm turned facing the firelight and folded his head down to look below his waist, then poked his head back at Itjanu. "It's Gone!! They're gone! I've been neutered! I've been...I've been...decapitated! Oh SHIT!"

Frantically Malcolm flashed his hands in and around his crotch, searching for his manhood, but found nothing but hobnail skin. He plopped down onto the sand, still searching the same areas again and again, looking back up from time to time with pleading yellow eyes. Finally, his shoulders sagged, he stopped searching, and then slammed his fists down on the sand at each side of himself. Still looking between his legs, he yelled.

"Aw-w-w-w-w-w Sh-i-i-i-i-i-i-i-i-i-i-i-i-i-t!!!!!!!!!!!!!!!!!!!" His scream echoed out into the desert and off the hills miles away.

Henry rocketed back to the van. Malcolm shook his massive fist in his direction.

"So much for his mythology investigation! I oughta kill the insect!"

But Malcolm was wrong, thinking Henry had run away out of fear. He returned with his armload of notebooks and pulled a campstool beside Malcolm. "You don't want to be that, right?"

"Well, of course I don't Henry! What madman would..."

"I do!"

"You want to be a giant friggin lizard EUNUCH??"

He almost giggled with excitement. "This is what I came for. Well not exactly that particular body, but... well, it will do!"

The others, except for Natalia, tentatively emerged from the van, but stayed near the door swatting at the mosquitoes. A broad area around Malcolm and the campfire remained insect free. One by one, they edged toward the campfire until they secured campstools only close enough to Malcolm to be outside the reach of the mosquitoes. They stayed almost shoulder-to-shoulder, responding in jerks to Malcolm's slightest movement.

Malcolm looked at the huddled little group. "C'mon people. It's ME. Malcolm. I'm not going to hurt anybody. I just want to get out of this thing!"

Mica casually walked around the fire, closer to Malcolm, carrying his third liberated beer, and slowly fingered the skin on Malcolm's shoulder. He chuckled to himself and shook his head, and then looked over at the old man still standing at the edge of the firelight.

"Get over here, Elea. You're supposed to be the one knows all about Tjukurpa and Kurpany, and all of that.

93

Come help this bloke!"

Elea walked slowly toward Malcolm, his fingers rubbing at the seams of his jeans, leaning forward with his head tilted up, looking into the creature's face. "Don't know what I can do."

Malcolm swiveled his head to look at the old man. "I'm having a real bad day here. So, anything you can do to help..."

Henry slapped his notebooks. "We need to repeat the ceremony at Wilpena Pound."

Malcolm turned his head back, tapping his claw on his knees.

"Repeat?...Oh no you don't, weasel. I'm not getting zapped again!"

Henry pulled the acrylic orb from his pack containing a large opal and held it up toward Malcolm. Malcolm looked at the orb and felt a strong desire to hold it, and reached out a long arm to snatch it from Henry's grip. He held the orb in the firelight staring into the blue and pink flashes reflecting the fire. A sense of satisfaction washed over him and he smiled at the orb, then held it gently to his chest closing his eyes and murmuring to himself. Itjanu watched the effect the opal had over Malcolm, over the creature.

"What is it, Malcolm? What does it make you feel?"

Dreamlike, Malcolm answered without opening his eyes.

"I don't know...peaceful, at home, like an old memory from my childhood, like Christmas morning, coming down the stairs to the tree..."

Henry reached over and took the orb back. Malcolm started with a jerk and twisted on Henry, snarling and showing his teeth, leaning toward the little man with his claws grinding the air in front of him. Henry fell backwards into the sand, digging the heels of his hiking boots into the sand, pushing with his feet to move away from the anger rising from Malcolm. He held the orb back up toward Malcolm,

"H-here, here, take it."

Malcolm blinked and straightened back up.

"Whoa! What was that all about?"

He looked around at large startled eyes from everyone around him.

"It's O.K., It's O.K."

He turned back to Henry.

"Sorry, Fellah. O.K. So you know something about me, this thing, that I don't know. What just happened?"

"I wasn't sure which one would draw you, but it's the opal. Something about it means a lot to...your kind."

Elea spoke. "One desert tribe tells an ancient story that some people can tame the Kurpany. It's not part of the Mala story. It came from the desert people that walked the sand before Coober Pedy came to be, before the camels came. My grandfather told me the western tribe that sent Kurpany to Uluru was maybe from up that way."

Mica walked around in front of Malcolm and helped Henry sit back up in his stool. He gently touched the acrylic orb containing the opal. "Right pretty specimen you got there, Henry." He rubbed the orb with his extended fingertips. "Right pretty specimen."

He chuckled to himself and turned to Itjanu. "Used to mine up that way. Long time ago. When I found them I hated to sell them, even though I needed the money for food and gear."

Mica looked over at Mac. "Met my Annie there. Mean woman, she is."

He chuckled again, shaking his head and righted a campstool next to the cooler. He tossed his empty can into the fire and drew a fresh one from the cooler. He glanced around the group and when no one objected he popped open the can and settled onto the stool, sipping the rising foam on the top of the can.

Malcolm sat there on his haunches, tapping his claw tips on his bent knees with his back to the fire watching Mica sip his beer. He was still unsettled over his reaction to the opal. Even then he felt the strong desire to reach out and grab it again, and that confused him all the more. Burning sap from one of the logs in the fire crackled and popped, sending a small flaming glob in a small arc landing on the skin of Malcolm's right wingtip. The little glob drooped along the vertical surface spreading flammable goo and miniature flames as it ran down the wing, sizzling skin tissue. Malcolm's eyes went wide when his brain got the message.

"Ye-e-e-o-o-o-w-w-w-w-!"

He screamed and jumped to his feet flapping his arms and wings and turning in a circle trying to see the source of his pain.

"Ow! Ow! Ow! Ow! Ow!"

The group scattered once again in terror. Malcolm flapped his wings without control, not sensing the difference between his control of his arms and that of his wings. The backs of his hands banged against the underside of his wings in a confusion of power, bruising both knuckles and wing ribs. Mica could see the burning sap and tried to splash some beer on it, but missed the spot as the wing flapped away. The fire from the sap burned a small hole in the outer layer of skin and then slipped down inside the wound adding to the pain and burning more tissue. Malcolm beat his wings in a reactive frenzy to stop the pain, pushing air against the campfire and fanning it higher. Dust billowed out from the sand beneath his feet and rose into the air as a pink cloud around him. His feet lifted off the ground, dangling loosely several inches above the sand as his wings beat downward keeping him hovering over the spot. Seeing the small burning spot on the tip of Malcolm's wing, and understanding what Mica had tried to do, Mac dove at the flapping tip and grabbed it with both hands to pull it down. Mica watched his jump and followed behind dousing the spot with cold beer that sizzled and foamed as it splashed on the skin.

"Ah-h-h-h-h-h."

Malcolm stopped beating his wings and relaxed in the release of his pain, and fell flat on his face on the ground. Itjanu, Elizabeth and Henry helped Malcolm sit up, while Mac retrieved two beers from the cooler, handing one to Mica as a replacement. "Bloody Hell. This is gonna be me last tour. I swear it."

Mica sipped from his can, then held the label up to the light. "No more Carltons?"

Mac peered over into the empty cooler. "You must'a

poured the last one on ol' Malcolm there."

Malcolm looked at the faces around him. "What the hell else is going to happen to me?! Hunh?"

A bright spotlight sprung to life from the fence line, followed by the sound of a bolt action sliding a bullet into the chamber. A voice bellowed from behind the light.

"Run away from it! I've got'im!! Move back so I can get a clear shot!"

Malcolm's head turned toward the voice, and he whimpered.

"Aw shit."

Just as Malcolm slumped his shoulders and dropped his head in dismay, the gun went off sending a bullet searing through the outer edge of his left ear. The campers began yelling at the shooter.

"No! No! Don't shoot!"

"Ow! Ow! Ow! Ow! Ow!" Malcolm brought his hands up to cover his ears, and his wings instantly beat into action. Red dust swarmed around the group and the campfire, sending a red fog into the bright spotlight, and Malcolm soared straight up into the pale green night sky. Another shot rang out, the yellow flash momentarily lighting up the outline of two men behind the spotlight.

"You people all right?" Mac bellowed and charged stiff-legged toward the spotlight, his hands curled into fists in front of him.

"Bill McLeod, you God Damned Fool! I'm gonna beat ya to a bloody stump! Have ya gone mad?"

Flashlights popped out and several lances of yellow light crisscrossed the darkness toward the men behind the spotlight, as the group of campers followed Mac. As Mac reached the spotlight held by Ian Cuthbert, he slapped it from his hand onto the ground where it sent a white beam into the sky. Bill held his rifle barrel up away from Mac, standing on the other side of the fence, but Mac reached out and grabbed the barrel, yanking the rifle from Bill's hands.

"You trying to kill us?"

"No, Mate. I was trying to save you. I heard the screams, then saw that thing had ya..."

"Oh he didn't HAVE us, he is WITH us."

"What the bloody hell? WITH ya?"

Mica stepped up to the men. "Something happened to one of them campers, Bill."

Elea joined them. "That shape has him, but it's not him. It's that Malcolm."

Mac cleared the rifle to make sure the chamber was empty and handed it back to Bill.

"The green one, Bill."

Bill looked between Mac and Cuthbert, working his jaws trying to say something, but the confusion in his mind would give him no words to speak.

"Can I come down? Is it safe?"

Everyone turned to follow the sound of Malcolm's voice. Silhouetted by the undulating green light in the sky behind him, Malcolm's large ungainly form showed clutching precariously to the highest branch in a ghost gum. Mac turned back to Bill.

"Well, can he come down? Or are you gonna shoot one of my campers?"

Bill let the rifle barrel slide down through his fingers until the stock thumped on the ground.

"I ain't gonna shoot again."

Mac turned back toward the ghost gum and cupped his hands around his mouth, but before he could yell anything to Malcolm, the branch snapped under Malcolm's weight. The dark from sunk below the lights and plummeted down through the unseen branches snapping one after another like the sound of popping corn, ending with a thud and an "Oo-om-mph!"

The large green form landed on its back within the firelight, legs and feet still in the air as it came down, its wings wrapped around it shoulders and folded upward as it fell. A red cloud of dust charged out from the ground impact and settled onto the campstools nearby. Elizabeth was the first to arrive by his side. Malcolm smiled weakly at her and rubbed his ear.

"You still want to sleep in my tent tonight?"

"I don't think so."

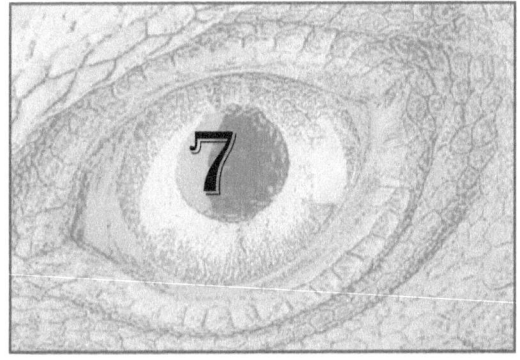

One by one the campers found individual ways to fall into sleep that night. Natalia remained in the van and made her bed on the wide rear seat, but only after she convinced Mac to lock her in and then give her the key through a narrow window slit, then slammed it shut. Elizabeth did indeed sleep in Malcolm's tent, but without Malcolm. Mac pulled the unused swags from the trailer and made a mat and cover large enough for Malcolm's new body. The tents were set up and each had occupants crawl into them and finally drift off to sleep even as they chattered about the strange events.

Mac convinced Bill and Ian to come inside the fence and talk with Malcolm a short while, until they at last believed their homes and families were safe enough to go back to them. Bill made the point of reminding Malcolm he would still keep his rifle loaded and nearby. Itjanu, Elea, Mica and Mac talked late into the night, until the green lights in the night sky finally faded away, discussing ways to help Malcolm. Malcolm had grown up on too many science fiction and horror movies to allow himself to go to a hospital or University for studies.

"They'll want to dissect me!" he had yelled, and the subject was dropped.

Henry stayed by the fire alternating between staring into it or making more notes into his journals, unwilling to discuss options other than his own, until the fire light died down to red and he could no longer read the pages.

He pulled a swag near the glowing red-orange embers and drifted off to sleep.

Malcolm tried to sleep on the padded swags, but could not find a comfortable position. His wings and tail eliminated any possibility of lying on his back, and his new shape did not accept lying on his stomach. He tried lying on his sides for over an hour, but could not relax enough to find sleep. At last he squatted down facing the fire, leaning forward onto his thighs, encircling his knees with his arms and letting his wings and tail relax behind him. He discovered the position was quite comfortable, in fact, suitable. He laid his head on his folded arms and eventually slipped into fitful sleep filled with dreams.

He was flying through warm humid air under a bright night sky. A full silver moon reflected off the surface of a river far below. Wisps of clouds lit by the moon above, no more than feather-brushed cotton strands, slipped by under him and shadowed on the land below. He could feel the slow rhythm of his wings, the modest exercise warming the muscles around his shoulder blades, but not tiring him. A group of dark figures ran on the land from the river shore across the open savannah, heading for a tree line at the edge of a jungle in the distance. His stomach growled from intense hunger as if he had not eaten in days. He lifted his left wing and rolled over to the right in a downward glide toward the dark forms.

As he angled steeper toward the ground, his speed increased and he stretched his wing skin tight, then bent the outer sections back slightly. The easy glide became a speeding descent and he raced down toward the forms, watching them grow in size as he gained on them. The air whistled through his ears and the tips of his wings, the wind buffeted against his open mouth and he reached out his clawed hands. One of the forms turned in terror of the attack and released a great roar as Malcolm swooped down to him. It was a dinosaur, an eight-foot raptor.

He slammed into it claws first, driving the tips deep into its muscles, gripping the bone within the body and then beating his wings again to regain the air even as the force of the impact drove the beast forward. The dinosaur shrieked in pain and horror as it was lifted off the ground and taken away from the group. Malcolm beat his wings in great pushes, grabbing the tropical air in loose wing skin cupped between wing ribs, and pushing himself higher and higher, back above the clouds. The raptor twisted his head around trying to bite its attacker and jerked its body from side to side to free itself, but the claws went deeper, digging into bone for a better grip. Malcolm could feel the warmth of the blood pouring out from the raptor over his wrists and ankles, and he could taste the salty tang of blood mist spewing into the air rushing around the body as he flew back to his lair. He pulled his arms in closer to his chest to bring the beast's neck close to his snout, his tongue dripped, and his lips snarled back to expose long curved dagger teeth.

"Whao!!" Malcolm straightened up with a jerk from his squatted position, looking at his hands and shaking his head, but it was gone, back into the memory from where it had risen.

"Whao!"

Henry was up and standing next to him.

"What is it? Is something else changing?"

"No, it was a dream, I guess. It was so real. I think maybe it was real, like I was remembering a good day at the beach, but that's not what I was doing."

Malcolm described the dream to Henry's vacant smile of rapt attention.

"Yes! That's it! You must be remembering what you, what they experienced."

"Yeah, well, I'm not in to raptor tar-tar."

"MALCOLM wasn't, but YOU may be."

"No. No, Henry, I can't become that. Somehow, I can NOT let that happen. I can't...be...THAT."

"Think about it, Malcolm! If that was a memory of the...thing, then you are connected to a life form that has existed millions of years! My theories are RIGHT!! You are so LUCKY to experience that!"

"Well, YOU can have the experience! I want out of this thing."

"Then let's go back to Wilpena Pound! We'll re-create

the ceremony and transfer the entity between us."

"Now, how would you know how to do that?"

"I've been correct so far, haven't I?"

"Well, yeah, but I think I want to talk to Itjanu about this some more."

"Why Her?"

"Because she's a doctor, and she cares how I feel?"

Malcolm looked up into the night sky. The stars were so many bright lights shining down on the desert. The full moon and the aurora snaking beneath it bathed the camp in silver green light. A gentle breeze slipped through the gum trees bringing the minty smell of eucalyptus with it as it drifted over the campfire, fanning the remaining embers to a momentary orange and then letting them fade back to smoldering red. Malcolm stretched, feeling the breeze tickle the skin of his wings bringing back his dream-memory of flying. He stood and walked to the fence line at the edge of the desert facing into the faint wind that greeted him with a timid gust. He stretched his wings wide, remembering the feeling of his shoulder muscles and slowly waved his wings back and forth into the breeze.

With each push of his wings into the wind he could feel the weight on his heels diminish for an instant and he would rock forward on his toes. He then pushed his wings forward as hard as he could and was rewarded with an excitement, when his feet floated above the ground a few inches, while his body drifted back from the fence like riding an inner tube on a lazy summer river current. When his toes touched the ground again, he pushed his wings down stirring the dust on the ground, his shoulder muscles responded automatically like taking deep breaths after a run. It was instinctive reaction without thought, driving the air beneath him again and again.

Gently, his feet rose slowly over the top of the fence and he floated out toward the desert, farther and farther, higher and higher. He could see his shadow below him; the outline of this thing he had become. His wings moved in and out from the shadow of his torso, and the shadow was unconnected to the ground. He relaxed his arm muscles and leg muscles, letting his wings take his weight. He returned to the sensation of warm shoulder blade muscles working in easy strokes pushing and pulling his wings without thought, the ribs within the wings folding in as he brought them forward the way his foot would automatically bend up enough to pass over obstacles as he walked.

Flying was only a general thought in his mind, no more than the thought given to controlling a leg making a step or an arm reaching for his coat. His shadow became smaller and his vista broadened, the campsite shrinking away from him as he climbed higher into the air over the desert.

The rush of air around his wings as he pushed them down was matched by the wind slipping by his ears, the only sound above that was the quiet folding and unfolding of his wings, sounding like sails catching the wind on a small sailboat. The steady rhythm of the wings became second nature while he gazed down on the desert slipping under him. The desert broke in an undulating line decorated with river gums showing the waterless riverbed. Beyond the riverbed a scrub plain ran out for miles toward the silhouette of a large shape on the horizon. He knew the rock formation, it had a name, but he could not remember it, and trying to remember it was made all the more confused by his brain asking itself how it knew; when did it learn that?

He recognized the lay of the desert below. It was the savannah, and the edge of the jungle well before it became the rocks. It was the scene from his dream, but the river and the savannah and the jungle had been gone for eons. He pushed his wings harder and drove himself toward the rocks. He knew its name now, but he could not speak it, not even in his mind, because it had no word, it was only a thought, a place in the mind that held a memory of a feeling. He had traveled there many times before, but he had not been alone then. There had been several shadows on the ground below as they made their way to...to... He shook his head, unable to reach into his own language and find it a name, knowing that even then it did not have a spoken name. It was a gathering place, but only one of many on this island, and not important enough to have a spoken name. He remembered only one had a spoken name, but he could not remember where that place was, and he pushed himself farther through the air toward the rocks in the closing distance.

Within a few short minutes he touched his feet lightly on the highest rock in the formation, his wings folded snuggly against his back as he continued forward bringing his hands up in front of him. His speed was too great for the slender rocky pinnacle and his arms gave way under the weight of his landing. He slid on his palms then crashed onto his underbelly and plummeted off the side of the outcropping, sliding then tumbling along the sloped far wall of the rock down into the ravine of Mulga trees and scrub bushes.

"O-o-o-oh-oh-oh!"

Several kangaroos that had been napping in the moon shadow next to the rock frantically hopped away in all directions through the scrub plain, followed by the pack of confused dingoes that had been following them. He sat up spitting leaves and sand, and rubbed the palms of his hands and the scratches on his knees.

"That was a crappy landing!"

He rolled over and then came to a squatting position in the ravine, resting his arms on the tops of his thighs with his long hands draped over his knees. Malcolm looked around the ravine and out into the plain beyond. He saw very little among the shadow and the silver light, but as he relaxed after his tumbled landing, the color in his vision shifted to yellow-green and he could even see the horny lizard slowly creeping along the sand a hundred yards away, working its rocking limbs slowly toward its scorpion snack.

"This is great!"

He stood up and walked to the end of the little ravine between the rocks to peer out into the desert landscape with his newly discovered night vision. He could see the kangaroo group he had frightened nibbling among some scrub brush a half a mile away, and the pack of dingoes skulking toward them a few hundred yards beyond. And to his great surprise he could even hear the lead dog panting as he worked his way among the brush. No, they weren't going toward the kangaroos, they were stalking something else. He could see their eyes reflected in the moonlight and they weren't looking at the kangaroos. Curious, he took a few more steps in their direction until he could see around the 'roos. Something metallic glinted in the moonlight, and a dark form shifted position near the metal object.

"What in the world?..."

Malcolm took a few more steps then remembered that he wasn't limited to walking, and began to run, pumping his wings until he lifted off the sand and pushed himself up into the air out toward the dingoes. Within seconds he was gliding in over the object he had seen from the rocks. It was a motorcycle, with the front wheel badly out of shape. Next to the motorcycle, lying on its back in the sand, was the dark shape of a human form. Arranged near the human's right shoulder was a collection of fist size rocks. There was movement on the ground twenty yards out from the motorcycle and Malcolm turned his attention back toward the encircling dingoes, choosing the closest for his first contact.

He knew that feral dogs, whether they were dingoes or wolves, would be vicious pack fighters, and he wasn't entirely sure what he would do. Malcolm glided to a spot just a few yards in front of the dingo, brought his wings forward in a firm push that brought his body upright and set his feet almost silently on the ground. His motion in the bright moonlight immediately caught the attention of the dingo.

The moon was behind him over his shoulder letting him see individual hairs on the dingoes reddish coat. Malcolm spread his wings wide and high, and the dingo halted crouching down with its ears laid back looking at the dark form. Malcolm then leaned his head down and emitted what he hoped would be a long menacing growl, getting close enough to the dingo so it could see his face. The dingo's eyes went wide, it's breathing stopped, and it urinated on the sand between its feet. It then emitted a yelping shriek of terror and began running away from Malcolm, out through the spinifex scrubs as fast as it could run, glancing only once over its shoulder to see if the creature was coming to eat it. The dingo's frenzied escape drew a dust tendril straight across the plain that did not stop until he dropped down into a wadi half a mile away.

The next two dingoes stopped in their tracks, one front paw still in the air showing their indecision; peering at the thing come down from the night sky and watching their leader's reaction. Deciding it was safer to follow their alpha male rather than fight for their expected meal, the two ran for the wadi with rest of the pack scampering after them.

Malcolm smiled to himself at how easy that had been. Knowing the person by the motorcycle was safe from the dingoes, his next concern was injuries the rider might have suffered. He tried to remember his red cross first aid classes, and knew there must be injuries, since the person had remained by the damaged motorcycle and had yet to try to stand. Malcolm whispered to the stranger as he approached.

"It's O.K. The dingoes are gone. I'm going to help you."

The person was wearing a leather-riding suit, black with red piping, and still wore the crash helmet Malcolm had seen him snatch off the pool table in the Mutana Creek Pub. Hopefully there were no serious injuries. He rolled up on one elbow as Malcolm came near him. Malcolm spoke again.

"It's O.K. I'm here to help you."

The man let out a terrified scream, grabbed one of the rocks, and smashed it into Malcolm's snout with all of his strength, hitting the side of Malcolm's nose and cracking two teeth that sent lightning bolts of pain through his nose and eyes and up into his brain. Malcolm jerked back from the attack, his legs giving way and falling, sitting, into the sand behind with a thud.

"A-A-o-o-o-ow-ow-ow!!!"

"Ya-a-a-a-a-a-ah-ah!!!"

The man moved awkwardly, keeping his left leg straight and forcing himself up onto his right knee. He threw the rock against Malcolm's forehead

"Ya-a-a-a-a-a-ah-ah!!!"

"A-A-o-o-o-ow-ow-ow!!!"

"Ya-a-a-a-a-a-ah-ah!!!"

"Get away! Get Away! Get Away! Ya-a-a-a-a-a-ah-ah!!!"

"A-A-o-o-o-ow-ow-ow!!! What the hell did you do that for? I was just trying to help..."

"Ya-a-a...-*a-a*...-*a-ah*...-Hunh?"

"I said, 'what the hell did you do that for?' "

"I...You...I...- this must be a damned nightmare. I must be dreaming."

The man plopped back down onto his rump, and began pressing his straightened leg with both hands, holding its position and grimacing in the moonlight.

"You're NOT dreaming! You just broke my tooth!"

Malcolm sent his long slender tongue along the row of teeth stopping at one then the next.

"You broke TWO! That really hurt!"

"I...I can't wake up."

He slumped back lying out flat.

"I hear your voice, but I keep seeing some monster. Maybe I'm delirious or something. Nothing to drink for hours. Not sure how long. Spit up blood at first – that stopped. Chasing the Roos, then one of'em turned, I swerved. Crashed..."

He slipped into unconsciousness.

Malcolm sucked air through his teeth and grimaced, feeling the cold razor of pain run along the root of one cracked tooth and up into the roof of his mouth and whimpered to himself.

"O-w-w. You didn't have to hit me with a rock, and not in the mouth."

The man said nothing. Malcolm rose up to look at the motorcyclist, but kept his forearm up in front of himself in case the man had another rock for him.

"Hey. You. You all right?"

Malcolm saw the man sprawled on his back in the sand and realized he was unconscious.

"Great."

Malcolm cautiously reached over the man and flipped the rocks away from his reach then turned his attention to his left leg. Pressing gently with his huge hands and being careful not to scratch him with his long claws, Malcolm felt along his thigh, knee and then lower leg. The bones in the man's lower leg gave way to gentle pressure, folding in with a faint grinding sound to Malcolm's keen hearing that sent cold shivers along his spine and made him shudder.

"Yuk. This leg needs to be braced."

Malcolm looked around knowing there were certainly no stick or limbs to be had in this desert. He then looked at the front fork of the motorcycle, leaning his head to the side as he considered the possibilItties. He stepped over to the motorcycle, picking it up as if it were hollow aluminum beach chair instead of a steel frame with a hundred pound engine. Holding the front of the frame in one hand and firmly pulling up on the handle bars with the other, the securing bolts gave way like a beer bottle top and the freed handlebars flew up into the air.

Malcolm arched his eyes and smiled at the result of his strength.

"Cool."

He slipped the fork tongue from the swivel and then plucked the damaged wheel from its bolts, tossing it into the sand and leaving him with what then looked like a large tuning fork in his hands. He carefully laid the tines of the fork on either side of the rider's lower leg and then picked it back up to adjust the width between the prongs and then bent the tongue forward. Malcolm went back to the motorcycle and stripped the leather straps from its saddlebags. He then slipped the tines gently against the man's lower leg until the bent up tongue came snugly against the bottom of his foot, and then wrapped the leather straps around the leg. He leaned back assessing his handiwork and decided it would be satisfactory.

Malcolm slipped his arms under the man's back and under his legs and then stood up. Pumping his wings straight down and driving rust colored dust out away from where he stood he rose into the air, slowly gaining altitude and speed as he swam through the air toward Mutana Creek. His silhouette sailed across the night sky beneath the undulating green light of the strange Aurora.

Dawn was beginning to slip over the horizon from Malcolm's vantage in the overhead sky, but it could not yet be seen from the ground.

"Hey! Hey! We need some help here!! Henry! Wake up Itjanu!"

Malcolm settled lightly on his feet just a few feet away from the dying embers of the camp fire, then walked to the picnic tables and laid the rider out on its surface.

"This guy's got a broken leg! Somebody!"

Mac and Itjanu arrived at the same time from different directions and were followed closely behind by Elea and Mica. Mac pointed his flashlight at the body lying on the table and looked up at Malcolm.

"Who's that? What happened?"

"He was in the pub yesterday evening. I just found him out in the desert. I guess he wrecked out there. He was about to be dingo food. But I ran them off."

Itjanu looked up from the rider.

"Nice leg splint. Anything else hurt? Why is his helmet still on?"

"Thanks. Don't know. Don't know. He favored his leg there before he passed out, but he seemed to be able to move everything else until then."

"He was conscious when you found him? What'd he say?"

"Kind of 'ya-a-a-a-a-a-a-a-a-a-a-!!!!!', then he hit me in the mouth with a rock!"

Itjanu carefully examined the man's body and neck, then removed his riding helmet. His hair was sweat plastered to the side of his head, his face was very pale, and his lips appeared parched. He began to moan and move his legs.

Elizabeth came to the tableside carrying a canteen of water. Itjanu pulled the scarf from Elizabeth's shoulders, poured water from the canteen into it, and then began dabbing the moist cloth onto his lips. Malcolm stepped to the foot of the table. The man raised his head slightly, but Itjanu placed her hand gently on his forehead.

"It's O.K. You're safe now."

"Water, water..."

Itjanu squeezed the cloth and several fat drops of

109

water splashed onto his dry lips and into his mouth. He puckered his lips and swallowed greedily at the water. She squeezed again and he brought hand up and around to pull the cloth down to his lips.

"Oh...Thank you. Thank you. Could I please have more?"

His rasping voice barely carried to the edge of the table. He raised his head off the table, seeing the faces around him and smiling weakly at each of them as Itjanu brought the re-soaked cloth back to his mouth. As she brought it to his lips he looked down toward his feet and saw Malcolm standing there, leaning over the table.

"Ya-a-a-a-a-ah-ah!!!"

And kicked Malcolm fiercely in the bottom jaw with the steel shoe of the brace Malcolm had made for him. Malcolm spun away from the table, spitting out the cracked tooth and its neighbor, and dripping blood.

"Ow-ow-ow-ow-ow!"

Malcolm yelled through his cupped hands wrapped around his snout.

"Damn! Damn! Damn! Damn! Damn!"

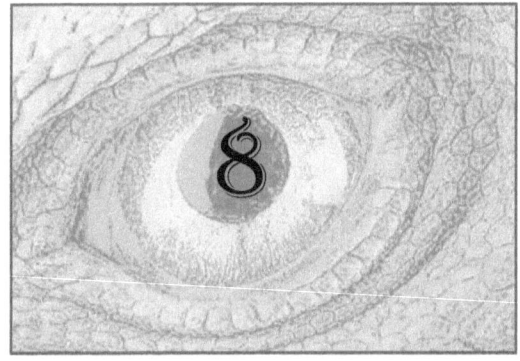

Malcolm opened his eyes and stretched, lying on his mat of swags. The sky was pale blue and cloudless, and the last wisps of the Aurora was fading into the daylight. The sun was creeping over red dunes to the east and the nearby gum trees were casting long shadows across the campsite. He sat up cross-legged, and leaned forward to pop his wings out from underneath him and let them stretch out behind. He stretched his arms and his wings spread out and upward until their tips barely touched five feet above his head. He rubbed his jaw where the motorcyclist had kicked his teeth out, but there was no pain. He felt delicately for the hole his two missing teeth would leave, but there was no gap. His teeth had replaced themselves during the night. He glanced up at his wing tips and saw that the burn hole was gone, filled in by healthy wing skin.

Assuming a leathery wing the color of a ripe limeskin is healthy, then I am in the pink, er, green.

"Malcolm. We need to talk."

Malcolm swiveled his head down from inspecting his wings and to his side where Henry had plopped a camp stool in the sand next to the edge of his swag.

"S-s-s-s-s-s-s!!"

Henry jumped back and fell into the red sand.

"Sorry Henry, morning sinuses, I guess. What do you want?"

Henry returned to his stool.

111

"I want to help you, Malcolm. I want to help you get out of that, that, thing you are. Don't you want that?"

"Well, hell yeah. But, I'm not getting struck by lightning again. That hurt!"

"No. I think you just need to stand by me, and hold the orbs. I will be the one hit by lightning."

"Yeah, right. Go away you little shit. I haven't forgotten you tried to drown me when I was still half conscious!"

Henry scurried off toward the van at the edge of the campground, where most of his other fellow travelers had already gathered and were packing the trailer.

Malcolm looked at the van and sighed.

I can't fit back in that thing.

He rose to his feet and walked to the van. Most of the others scooted around the corner of the van as he approached, leaving Mac, Margaret and Henry facing him.

Malcolm held out his arms with his hands palm up.

"Mac, I guess we need to talk about all this."

Mac swallowed hard, and took in a deep breath. Then, ever the brave Aussie, he stepped forward and reached up to place a firm grip on Malcolm's forearm and guided them toward the nearby gum.

"Let's talk over here, mate. You're still with us y'know and I'll do whatever..."

Malcolm held up his clawed hand.

"No. I can't go on with you, Mac. I appreciate the thought, but I can't fit in the van, and my world doesn't even include a back pack trip anymore. I don't know what it includes – or doesn't – but I sure as hell can't go around looking like this. I don't even know if my mind is going to stay the same. My dreams are so weird, I,...I am afraid I may hurt someone."

He looked at his hands remembering the feel of the raptor in his claws.

"I don't know what I'll do next, but I don't want to hurt anybody."

Mac patted his arm.

"Is there anyone I can call for ya, mate? Anyone or anyplace the company can contact for you."

Malcolm tried to smile, but could not.

"No, it's just me now. And it's just as well it stays that way."

"Well, Malcolm, I've got to tell the company something. I can't just show up one packer shy and hope they don't bloody notice."

"You'll be two shy. Itjanu stayed in Mutanajulu."

"That's right, but she signed a form, ...Oi, you could do that. And say you're staying with her to help her studies, or something. But, mind you, I'm not telling you to do that. We could put you on top of the van if you had any intention of heading on to the Alice. Or even just keep a space for you at the campsites, and let you, er, fly in after we got there. Right?"

"Thanks Mac. I know. But I need to figure this out, if I can. And I need to do it away from people."

Mac nodded his head and placed his hands on his hips, looking around the open desert beyond the camp fences.

"Well the Outback is the proper place t'be, if you want to be away from people, that's for sure."

Mac retrieved a clipboard and a pen from the van and brought them over to Malcolm, but he could not hold the pen within his clawed grip. He dropped the pen and twisted his head toward the van.

"Henry! Henry, come over here and help me please."

Henry hesitated and then fast walked out to the gum tree.

"Henry, I need to sign a form to leave the group and stay here. I figure if anyone in our group could possibly forge a signature, it's probably you."

Mac handed the clipboard to Henry and tapped the pages clipped to the board.

"The back paper there is the sign-in sheet from Adelaide. Malcolm's signature is the last one."

Henry looked briefly at the signature list, then flipped back to the top sheet and signed Malcolm's name as if it was his own. He flipped up that sheet, seeing the form signed by Itjanu Williamson, and smiled a broad smile. Then he flipped to the third sheet, finding a blank departure form and quickly signed it with his own name, and looked back up at Mac, still smiling and handing him the clipboard.

"I'm staying too."

"No!"

Henry folded his arms in front of his frail chest. Malcolm shrugged his shoulders. Mac stared between the two figures, then turned with his back to them, and stomped his foot in the red sand, sending up a small red dust cloud over this boot and white socks. He turned back and pointed his clip board back and forth between the bookworm and the behemoth.

"I'll be back through here in four weeks. If yer not here, leave word with Ol'Bill where ya went, or at least if yer ever coming back. Right?"

"Right."

'Bloo-dy Hell."

Mac walked back to the van and began loading the passengers into the van. Elizabeth was last to get on, waving to Malcolm and Henry over Mac's shoulder as he herded her onto the van. Mac tooted the horn twice as he pulled out of the camp with the trailer surfing the red cloud behind it and headed north, leaving Malcolm standing in the center of the deserted campground, and Henry standing in his shadow.

Malcolm looked down at Henry.

"Well, Henry, you're on your own."

Then he spread his wings and pushed the air down into the sand and lifted above the dust cloud enveloping Henry, and pumped himself higher and higher in to the warm morning air. He looked back seeing Henry become a round dot on the land, and the dot headed slowly to the pub.

Far in the distance the rock formation without a name came into view at the edge of the horizon and Malcolm made a slow graceful turn toward it. The air feather-brushed across his skin and whistled along the edges of his ears. Then he discovered he could fold his ears back like little ribs, like smaller versions of his wings. The whistling stopped, and there was only the sound of the wind being pumped under his wings and the occasional pop of his wing skin like a sail catching the breeze.

The vista below him was painted in hues of rose and amber, pimpled by the occasional mulga tree and speckled by spinifex, and the slow moving dots of small herds of red kangaroo. One group caught his attention, and his stomach growled. He let his urge take him, and folded his wings back in an eagle dive.

Breakfast!

Henry opened the door and shuffled in from the glaring morning sun into the cool dark pub. Bill McLeod was working on a cooler drain behind the bar and heard the door open as the room filled with a flash of light from the outside.

"Not open yet mate. Gimme a couple hours, will ya? Got something clogging up this damned drain."

"No problem. I just need somewhere to sit that's out of the sun."

Bill raised his head over the bar, looking as if the head was all there was to him, his head jerking up from his jawbone on the bar top as he spoke.

"Thought the van already left. Aren't you with the packer tour?"

"WAS with the packer tour. I stayed behind to look after Malcolm."

Bill frowned at the name then wagged his head side to side.

"Oh yeah, he's the, well.., ya' know, the green, ...whatever..."

"Yeah. He's the green whatever."

Bill slid his head off the bar and went back to his cooler drain. Henry listened to the metallic clicking of wrench on iron pipe fittings and looked around the bar room. Bill's voice echoed up from the linoleum floor behind the bar.

"Never seen anything like that. Still not completely sure I shouldn'ta shot at it."

"That was supposed to be me."

"What was supposed to be you? Shootin at it?"

"That,...green whatever. That was supposed to be me."

Bill's head reappeared on the bar.

"How do ya figure that?"

"I came hear for that. That's why I came all the way from Canada to be here for these night lights and what they signify, but that damned Malcolm got in my way."

"Wait a minutes there, mate. You sayin you came all the way here to become a...green,...whatever? You knew it was gonna happen and you came here for it?"

"Not like that. I knew something amazing was going to happen, but I didn't know exactly that. I have been studying myths and legends and finding core truths that led me here."

Bill laid down his wrench and stood up and rested his elbows on the bar.

"Now, how did you come to all that?"

Henry explained his theories as he had to Malcolm. In the quiet that followed Henry's longwinded monologue, Bill whistled through his teeth and looked around the room.

"That's some thinking you been doin. If I hadn't seen that thing last night with me own eyes, I'd think you'd been out in the sun way too long. But, still, I don't know about the rest of that. Past beings, evolution, future beings,... that's all way too much for me. What I got here is a littler mystery about what's cloggin me damned cooler drain."

He knelt down, picked up his wrench, gave the drain coupling a hard twist, and the pipe separated from the drain.

"Bloody Hell! The drains full of slugs and maggots. Don't hardly see a slug around here, but there must be dozens of them wiggling around in there!"

Henry smiled serenely at him.

"It just keeps happening. Things that are not supposed to happen just keep happening. Bugs, animals, the lights in the sky. They're coming, and the green whatever is just their next step."

Bill poured salt into the drain and stood up again.

"Well, I need a drink. Bar's open."

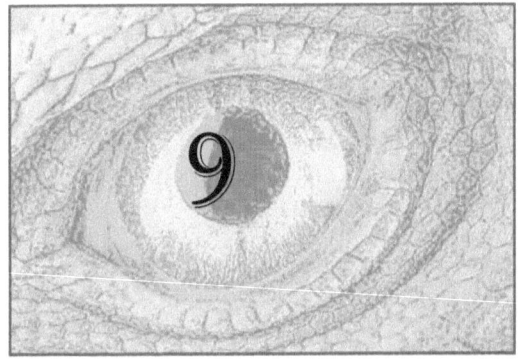

Malcolm stretched his wings and arms, then twisted his back to work out the kinks from his last flight into the next valley. His arms were tired from carrying the huge load of greenery he had picked and brought back to his brood. The big red roo nuzzled under his arm, trying to flip Malcolm's hand up over its head.

"Oh, all right, here."

Malcolm gently scratched behind his ears, and then patted his back, looking at the healing scratches from his grab at the kangaroo several days before.

"I'm really sorry about that, Barney. I didn't mean to hurt you..."

Barney nuzzled his arm again and thumped its big tail into the sand as Malcolm scratched his favorite spot, and a small rose colored cloud drifted up around them until a faint breeze shooed it away.

The rest of the group Barney had been running with were now settled around Malcolm, knowing they were safe from Dingoes with Malcolm, and that Malcolm would look after them. Malcolm munched on some wild fruit that seemed to agree with him and sighed a heavy sigh. Barney rolled his big soft eyes up at Malcolm and melted onto the ground while Malcolm continued to scratch the side of his neck, and Barney's leg began to twitch in synch with the scratches like a happy puppy. Malcolm blew out a breath and gently laid Barney's head down as it dozed off, then he stepped to the edge of the plateau looking down at the valley of red sand and spinifex that ranged for miles below.

"I need some food. Real Food. Hamburgers, hot dogs, chilli cheese fries, potato chips. Yeah, potato chips. I want potato chips,... and beer. COLD beer."

Malcolm placed his huge clawed hands on his hips and addressed the heard of kangaroos around him.

"Guys."

Barney raised his head up and looked around until he found Malcolm in his sleepy vision. Others stopped what they were doing and turned their heads toward him as if they understood him.

"Guys, I'm sorry, but I need to take off for a while. You'll be fine here, but I need some people food and some people to talk to."

Two of the roos looked at each other as if in question.

"Yeah, people. It won't be easy, but I can't stay like this. I mean, it was fun and all, once I decided I couldn't eat you. But, well I need some people food, and some people beer."

Then he lumbered into the cave set back from the edge of their plateau, and came back out with a brilliant opal the size of a golf ball holding it up for the others to see.

"What do you think? This ought to be enough for a beer or two. Right? Besides there are hundreds of these back in there, just piled up."

He frowned and tapped his foot, and then looked down at the opal in his claw.

"We'll, maybe I should take two just in case."

When he came back out of the cave, he spoke over his shoulder to the kangaroos.

"Don't wait up, guys. George, John, Ringo, be sure and turn the TV off before you go to bed."

Then he pumped himself up into the evening air as the kangaroos watched him until he was just a dot skimming along under the few clouds drifting by overhead, and then lost in the undulating green light of the Aurora.

Minutes later he sailed through the evening sky and landed delicately on his feet in the campground across the road from the Mutana Creek Pub. The door was open, and yellow light spilled out onto the dusty hard packed road in front of the pub, turning the greenish light from the Aurora overhead into a sickly lime green. He rolled the two large opals within his hand, and thought about a deep drink of cold Aussie beer, licked his lips and walked across the road. The music box was blaring a lively song with electric guitars and a hard back beat, and his head and hips began to rock to the rhythm of the song as he walked to the door. Laughter floated into the night air, and pool balls clacked against each other from the pool table just inside the door, and a man sitting at the bar back slapped his mate and gave off a lusty belly laugh. Malcolm bent down to get his head under the door frame, and smiled to the crowd holding out one of the opals between the claw tips of his right hand.

"Excuse me. I'd like to buy a beer with this."

No one at the bar turned.

"Excuse me!"

A man leaning across the felt top of the pool table to reach a long ball shot looked up from his cue, staring at Malcolm. Malcolm's huge head, shoulder and right arm were stretched into the room. The man at the pool table dropped the cigarette from his mouth onto the felt. "Holy shit! Holy shit! What the hell is that??" Then he shoved Bill McLeod out of his way as he raced to the back door. The man's pool partner gave a shudder and followed his mate out the door, stepping on his boot heels as he dashed out into the green night.

People at the bar turned to stare at Malcolm, who tried to back out quickly, but hit the back of head on the door frame. "Uh Oh..."

Men reached in all directions for anything hard, emitting a chorus of grunting profanities. "Bloody Hell!"

One man spun on his bar stool bringing out a large revolver and thumbing back the hammer as he brought the barrel around toward Malcolm. Bill rolled his eyes and began slapping down weapons and nearby cue sticks with his bar towel. "No. No! It's that Damned Yank!"

"Yank, Hell," Roared the gunslinger.

Malcolm ducked his head down to clear the door frame just as a shot rang out splitting the skin along the crown of his head. "Yeoooow!!"

Malcolm reflexed up again, hitting the door frame again and cracking the wood, then pushing the ground in front of him for all he was worth, backing out into the street. He swiveled in the green light, pumping his wings with all his might, and rocketed into the air right below the thickest limb of the only large tree in Mutana Creek. He slammed his head into the limb, and then dropped like a dead whale, face first onto the packed sand, sending up clouds of dust exploding in all directions. Everyone with a vehicle rushed to start their engines, while friends and strangers alike jammed inside with them as they shot away from the pub, as fast as their engines would take them. One man flung himself bodily through the air at the bed of the last departing pickup truck and barely made it without being killed.

Bill McLeod walked out of his empty pub and stood in the middle of the road watching all of his customers flee town, put his meaty hands on his hips and sighed.

"A good night's trade shot to hell."

He looked across the road at Malcolm lying unconscious in the sand under the town tree, and walked over toward him.

"Shoulda shot ya when I had the bloody chance."

He kicked a stone lying in the road and watched it roll across the road and into the door of his pub, then reached into his back pocket and took out a small flashlight he kept to read labels in the dim light of his storage room. He shined the light on Malcolm, and saw the gash across the top of his head.

"That had ta' hurt."

Then he nudged Malcolm's shoulder with the tip of his boot.

"You alive Yank?"

Malcolm groaned and rolled onto his back.

Bill nudged him again.

"You'll live. Saw you fall out of this tree before. Now git outta here. You're bad for business!"

He walked back to his pub and closed the door behind him, leaving Malcolm to lie in the green darkness, but the door would not close. The cracked door frame blocked the door from above and the rock inside the door sill blocked it at the bottom.

"Bloody Hell. What next?"

Bill retrieved a hammer from behind the bar and used the claw to pull the old wood door frame down into passable shape to take the door, then reached down to flip the rock out with his finger tips, but froze still in his stoop as he looked closely at the rock.

"What th'..."

Bill picked up the opal and held it up to the light swinging over the pool table. Then he quick-stepped behind the bar where the light was brighter and picked up the magnifying glass he kept behind the bar to read shipping invoices. He turned again putting the light over his shoulder and looking closely at the stone with the magnifying glass.

"Holy Rodney! Biggest Opal I've ever seen outside a museum!"

The door slowly opened and Malcolm leaned into the empty room.

"I'm sorry Bill, I never meant to do that. I just wanted a beer..."

Bill held up the opal toward Malcolm.

"This yours?"

"Yeah. Would you take it? Maybe it'll help pay for the door. If it isn't, there are more out in the desert."

Bill smiled at Malcolm, noticing the gash in his head was almost completely healed, and rolled the opal around in his hand.

"Yeah, it might do. Then again, it might take several,...aw shit, I can't even lie to a bloody Yank monster. It'll more than do."

Malcolm gently tapped the top of his head.

"It heals quickly, but it still hurts like hell. Oh, and there's another one of those out there in the road somewhere."

Bill chuckled to himself, then stepped into the back room to retrieve a four gallon ice bucket. He set it under the lip of the bar and yanked back all three of his draft beer pulls.

"Say when, mate."

They sat there in the silence except for the river of beer flowing down from three spigots until the bucket was three-quarters full, and cool condensation on the outside of the metal bucket matched the height of the beer.

"When."

Bill grunted as he set the bucket on the bar and Malcolm edged himself close from the other side, sitting on the floor and taking the bucket in both hands like a toddler with a milk glass. Bill stepped around the bar and patted Malcolm on his arm as he went toward the front door, turning on his flashlight.

"You just work on that for a minute or so, Yank, while I step outside and rescue that other little lost opal."

Malcolm's reply was lost among the echoes of gulping beer within the bucket.

Malcolm released a reverberating belch as Bill returned to the pub holding both opals in his hand, beaming like a child at Christmas. Malcolm patted his lips and pointed a crooked finger toward the empty bucket set back under the beer pulls.

"May I please have another?"

"Mate, you could drink all my barrels dry and I would still owe ya change from these opals."

Malcolm leaned across the bar and tapped the three beer pulls with his finger claw. He smiled as the yellow liquid fell into its own foam within the bucket. He burped again and looked at Bill over his shoulder.

"How 'bout we start me a tab, then? You tell me when you need more."

Bill held up the two perfectly round opals in front of his eyes, completely filling the outline of his sockets and gave a beefy grin below them.

"Yank, this is more than I make in a year. I'd have to take out a loan just to give you change. If we had a bank in town, and I had any credit in it."

"Malcolm."

Bill lowered the opals.

"What?"

"Malcolm. The name is Malcolm."

Malcolm extended his huge clawed hand slowly in front of the pub owner. Bill placed the opals in his left hand and took the ends of Malcolm's claw in a firm grip.

"Bill McLeod. Pleased ta meet ya Malcolm."

Bill stepped behind the bar, placing the two opals on the bar top between them and drew himself a mug of beer. Then he held it up toward Malcolm.

"Here's to ya, Malcolm"

Malcolm smiled a shark-toothed smile and held his bucket by one hand up to Bill's mug. Bill looked at Malcolm's teeth and shuddered, and then chugged his beer, keeping an eye on Malcolm over the glass rim. They both finished at the same time, setting mug and bucket hard on the bar in a single sound. Bill wiped his mouth with his forearm.

"I'll have another – since you're buyin', Malcolm"

"I'll have another, too, Bill."

The mug went under one spigot, and the bucket under the other two until the mug was filled, then the bucket was moved under the third spigot until it was nearly full. Bill topped off his mug to replace the settled foam, and held it up toward Malcolm, but before Malcolm could hold his bucket up in salute, Bill began gulping his beer. Malcolm snatched up his bucket and began gulping again to match Bill.

After yet another round of beer, Malcolm wiped his forehead with his massive forearm.

"S'hot in here. Le's go outside."

Bill released a manly belch and nodded toward Malcolm.

"Let's top'er off then head out into the cool under the old tree."

As the dark green sky faded away, pushed back by the rising sun, Malcolm and Bill were sitting under the town tree across the packed dirt road from the pub, each holding a half full container of beer in one hand, swaying the beer in front of them as one sang a traditional Aussie standard and the other sang an old Hank Williams song; both out of tune, neither in synch, but both swaying together. Overhead in the branches, the Magpies and galahs twisted their heads between looking down at the humans and each other. All of them were squawking and swaying back and forth in ragged rhythm as Malcolm and Bill sang.

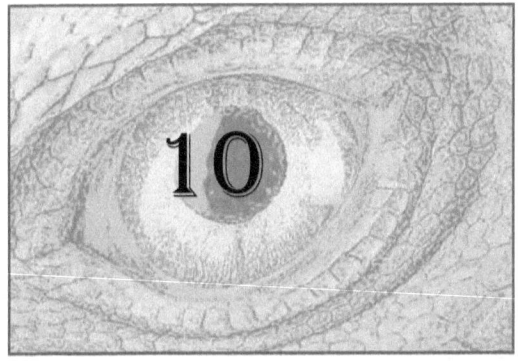

Bill managed to bring out a case of vegetables and fruit from the pub cooler and handed them to Malcolm before he headed for his bed to sleep off the night. He hung a closed sign in the pub window and then locked the front door. Malcolm squinted into the light of the rising sun and pumped his wings into the air, flying at a forty-five degree angle, holding the case of food and sweating profusely in the warm air. A few minutes later Malcolm stumbled onto the plateau, opened the case and set it down for the kangaroos and walked stiff-legged into the coolness of the cave, and then collapsed onto the sand floor.

Throughout the day the kangaroos took turns moving by the opening to the cave and nibbling on the vegetables and fruit, while Malcolm emitted a roaring series of snores and snorts that occasionally loosened rocks from the outside of the cave, sending them galloping down the hillside in little dust trails to the valley floor below. The case of food was only an appetizer for the hungry kangaroos, and one by one they looked back and forth among themselves and over at the cave opening, and then began to meander down the hillside to nibble on sparse vegetation in the valley as they were accustomed.

The sun was low in the west and the plateau deserted when Malcolm drug himself out of the cave into the late afternoon sunlight. He sat on the ledge with his legs hanging in the air above the valley, and licked the dry

125

inside of his mouth. There was one apple remaining in the nearby case, and he pulled the box closer to retrieve it and popped it into his mouth, the way he would have tossed in a grape in the past. He crunched the apple once and swallowed it quickly.

"Well that won't do. Not at all."

The kangaroos were gone. He sighed to himself, looking at the nearby spots some of them had taken for their own during their short visit. He sighed again and listened to the faint wind slipping past the plateau on its way somewhere else. And he sighed again. He pushed himself off the ledge dropping into the open air in front of the cliff face below the plateau, opened his wings to catch the air and swooped out over the valley, looking for the kangaroos, but they were gone. So, he pumped his wings hard against the air and brought himself back to the plateau and went back into the cave to retrieve two more opals. These were slightly larger than the two he had taken the night before, and he started to put them back to find two smaller ones, but the mound of opals contained none smaller, and there were hundreds of them. He strode out of the cave and stepped into the air off the ledge and pumped his wings toward Mutana Creek.

A couple pick-up trucks and an old jeep were parked on the street in front of the pub. Not wanting to create the panic he had yesterday, he sailed around behind the pub and landed softly in the sand next to the trash cans already overflowing with beer cans. He leaned within the shadow of the squat building and gently tapped a claw onto the back door. He could hear the music box playing and voices within the pub, but no one came to the back door. He tapped the door again, slightly louder this time. The door opened from inside as Bill was talking to someone over his shoulder behind him and not looking forward as he stepped out.

"What? Oh Jesus!!" And jerked up, falling back into the doorway.

Malcolm leaned forward to help him back up. Bill regained his footing and quickly closed the door behind him so no one would see his guest and then looked up at Malcolm.

"Sorry Malcolm. Still gettin' used to ya. Was starting ta believe maybe I drank too much last night and imagined it all."

Malcolm carefully pulled Bill's hand forward and dropped the two larger opals into his palm.

"Good Rodney, Malcolm. You tryin to run me off, or just get me killed??"

"Just wanted to stay current with my tab."

"Current?? Hell you're years in advance, probably decades. I haven't had a chance to look into selling the first two, and I'm not sure I want it out that I have the things. I mean, the folks around here are salt of the earth and all, but well, things happen sometimes."

"Oh, I hadn't thought of that. Here, I can take them back for now,..."

Bill shoved the two opals deep into his trouser pockets.

"Nope, I got these. Now mate, I can't tell you how much I appreciate you giving me these, and the beer will never pay you back, so we got to come to terms on how all this works out. You understand what I mean?"

Malcolm scratched his head.

"No."

Bill crossed his arms in front of his chest.

"I ain't taking something for nothing, and I ain't taking a lot of something for doing anything that's not right. I came out here to do things on my own, my way. I'm not out here cause I couldn't do nothing else, like this was left overs. I had to work my arse off to get this lease, and I like it out here."

He put his hands on his hips and looked around at the scrub land behind his pub.

"By God, I DO like it out here; like it the way it is- well, mostly. So, just what is it you expect for these opals. Are you gonna ask for my soul or something?

Malcolm leaned down close to Bill's face, their noses only inches apart.

"There is something that you have that I want?"

127

Bill stepped back, leaning up against the door behind him. Malcolm smiled a big toothy grin.

"Beer."

"You're giving me a fortune, two fortunes, for beer?"

Malcolm held his hands out.

"Look at me Bill, where can I go? Who is gonna have a heart attack and die just because they see me? Who is gonna drive off the road or smash head on into someone else because they see me. Who is gonna try to shoot my ass with a bazooka because they think I'm something from their nightmares or an old horror movie. Where ELSE can I go??"

A tear slipped out of one yellow eye and rolled down the side of his snout.

"Bill, you're the closest thing to a friend I have right now."

Bill looked from side to side then fixed Malcolm in his eyes.

"And what is it you need a friend to do?"

"Just let me come back."

"Just come back? Come around?"

"Yeah,... and beer."

"Just beer?"

"And food."

"What kinda food?"

Malcolm's stomach rolled.

"I have such a tremendous desire for..."

"For what?"

"Fresh fruits and vegetables."

"You're kidding? Don't make fun of me, Malcolm. I'm really trying here."

"Seriously, Bill. That's all I want. I tried meat the other day. Well, I tried to try it, but it just didn't appeal to me. I've been flying around taking fruits and vegetables from gardens and orchards – and I know I shouldn't steal, but I've been so hungry. And now I'm hungry for people."

Bill pressed himself tighter against the door and reached for the door knob.

"You're hungry for People??"

"To-TALK-to, Bill. To-TALK-to!"

Bill blew out his breath and wagged his finger at Malcolm.

"Don't say 'hungry' when you talk about people, Malcolm. Trust me on this!"

"OK, OK. Can I have a beer??"

"Sure mate. I'll get yer bucket"

Malcolm sat on his haunches and twiddled his thumb claws, watching the sky darken and the nightly arrival of the green Aurora. Moments later Bill edged out of the back door empty-handed, pulling it tightly behind him as he came out.

"Er, Malcolm, we need help. I have a part timer that's been helping around the pub at busy times, and I think we need to tell him about you."

"OK, if you're sure..."

"I mean we, er I, need to introduce him to you..."

"Oh,..."

"Yeah, his name is Teddy and he works for a few coins and whiskey. I'm sorta getting him ready ta meet you, if you're willing."

"If you're sure it's OK, I guess we can try. What if he starts yelling and screaming?"

"Well, that's what I'm getting him ready for. I just set him down at a table in the pub with a bottle of Doogan's Rye and a big bowl of salted nuts. We'll let him work on that a few more minutes 'til he's limbered up a bit. I'll get your beer now."

Bill returned to the back door and hefted out Malcolm's bucket of beer, then held his finger up to his lips in quiet, smiled and then closed the door. Malcolm took the bucket and sat in the sand sipping his beer and watching the Aurora snake back and forth in the night sky, painting the pub roof and the top of the scrub trees in faint green light like lime watercolor on black paper. Then he walked to a sandy mound several yards away from the building and sat down with his legs stretched out in front of him and resting on one elbow, holding his beer bucket in his other hand to relax while he waited.

The back door to the pub opened again tossing yellow light into the green night, and two figures edged through the doorway, and then the yellow light was sliced off as the door was quickly closed. One figure came out away from the building in Malcolm's direction, and gave a hoarse whispering whistle.

"Malcolm? 'Zat you?"

Malcolm set his beer down and stood up from the mound, then walked slowly toward the figure. Bill reached out to pull Malcolm by his wrist toward a sitting form next to the trash cans.

"Malcolm, this is Teddy. Teddy, this is Malcolm."

In the green-tinted night light, Malcolm could see as well as most people during the day. Teddy was a bushy faced unshaven man, his once clear white skin covered in red tarnish. His frizzled uncombed hair jutted out from under an old stained ball cap with the team logo long worn off, and his hair merged with his beard in a continuous field of kinks and knots flying in all directions. In smudged khaki shirt and shorts ragged at the edges, he sat on a crate leaning back against the building, a large band-aid across one knee just above a grease stain. He was holding a bottle in one hand and an empty double shot glass in the other, smiling warmly toward Malcolm. Malcolm leaned down close so Teddy could see his face. Teddy's glistening eyes wandered over Malcolm's face and then he smiled sweetly at Malcolm.

"How ya doin, mate?"

Malcolm extended his massive clawed hand in front of Teddy, and Teddy promptly dropped the shot glass into it and dribbled whiskey out of the bottle over Malcolm's hand, missing the glass entirely. Teddy brought a wobbling finger up to the side of his mouth.

"Shh-shh-hh. Bill's gonna introduce us to someone real special,...and mind ya don't make any noise when he gets here."

His head wandered around his shoulders until he found Bill in his view.

"Ain't that right, Bill?"

Then he dropped the bottle into the sand by the crate and plopped his chin onto his chest, slipping off into a deep loud rasping snore. Bill pushed his hand hard against Teddy's shoulder to wake him, but he folded down upon his own lap like a worn out rag doll with his hands dangling over the edge of the crate. Then he resumed his diesel engine snoring between his knees that reverberated off the back wall of the pub. Bill shook his head and shoved his hands onto his hips. "Bloody Hell."

Malcolm looked keenly at Bill. "That's not a Teddy, but I believe you got him limbered up, all right."

Shouts were coming from within the pub, and Bill reached for the door handle.

"Course his name is Teddy. He told me it was Teddy. How 'bout watching him a bit, while I go serve the blokes at the bar?"

"No wait, Bill. This guy isn't a Teddy, he's a..."

As Bill went back into the pub and the yellow light disappeared, Malcolm spoke to the crumpled body stinking of fresh rye and old sweat.

"...he's a Henry."

Malcolm punched the dirty man's shoulder with his finger tip, but he did not move. Then Malcolm finger-flipped his arm with a resounding 'thwap' that made the man moan in his snores and shift away without waking.

"Aren't you, Henry Matan. You sneaky little shit. Why didn't you go with the van??"

Malcolm huffed, then returned to the mound and settled back on one elbow with his beer in his hand, crossing his legs on the sand before him. He sipped his beer and listened to the music escaping from the bar, and the chain saw snoring crawling out from the darkness behind the pub, and was oddly content for the moment. He shook his head at himself in the darkness.

"I guess even weird people are better than no people at all."

There was a brief crash of glass and metal in the darkness behind the pub, so Malcolm went to investigate and found Teddy/Henry with his head and shoulders in the trash can laying on the sand. He pulled Teddy out and sat him up with his back against the wall.

"You O.K. Henry?"

"No worries, Mate. Teddy. Name's Teddy."

"Let's get you away from these trash cans and sit you on the mound over here."

Malcolm carried him to the mound and propped him up in a sitting position, then held his shoulders straight so Henry could see him, and Henry smiled.

"You're a big bloke. You that thing that came here last night?"

"Yes. Are you going to scream?"

"You want me to?"

"No. But, I don't scare you?"

The little man pointed a crooked dirty finger out toward the desert.

"Saw your cousin recently, too. Name's Malcolm. Redneck from,..."

The dirty little man sat bolt upright looking closely at Malcolm's face.

"Malcolm?!"

"Yes."

"Malcolm, I've been looking for you."

"You've been drinking and sleeping in garbage bins, or worse from the smell of you."

Henry scratched under his arm with angry fingers.

"Worse. Ran out of money, but had to do what I could to stay here. Knew you would come back."

"How did you know that?"

"You had to, so I could find you."

Malcolm shook his head.

"Henry, you're still full of shit."

"Some of the locals, the Aborigine, have seen you before we got here."

He pointed out toward the desert.

"Out there years ago."

Malcolm swirled his head around toward Henry's face.

"When?"

"'Bout twenty years ago."

He pointed up at the Aurora

"They say they had a little one of those out there. Only lasted a couple nights. Not big like this one."

With his finger still pointing out beyond the end of his curled hand, Henry yawned and then slumped back onto the soft sand behind him and resumed his snoring. Malcolm nudged him several times with his knuckle, but

132

only managed to roll Henry's head and shoulders back and forth in the sand. After a few minutes, Bill stuck his head out the back door, silhouetted in yellow light, and gave a rasping shout, trying to be quiet and send his voice out into the night at the same time.

"Malcolm! Teddy! You fellas all right?"

Malcolm answered, "I ate him," but Henry's snoring resumed with vigor and filled the quiet between the mound and the pub.

"That's not funny, Malcolm."

Bill's head retracted back into the pub like a box turtle closing his shell, and took the yellow light with him. Seconds later the door popped open again and Bill set a cardboard box on the crate next to the back door, called Malcolm's name, and pulled the door closed again. Malcolm wandered over to the door to investigate the box. He opened it and looked at the contents in the green light. The box contained a generous mix of apples and pears and celery and broccoli. Malcolm smiled as his stomach growled and he spoke to the back door of the pub.

"God love you, Bill McLeod."

Malcolm picked up the box, then yelled over his shoulder as he walked back to the mound.

"Teddy is Henry!!"

Malcolm returned to the mound and plopped down next to Henry and nudged him with his elbow, but the little man slept on. So, Malcolm sat cross-legged with the box in his lap, and plucked out the fruit and vegetables one piece at a time, like a man eating chocolates from a gift box. He washed it down with beer, watching the light show above, listening to Henry snore and ignoring the faint shrill of a thousand frustrated hungry mosquitoes, hovering in a cloud several feet away that could come no closer.

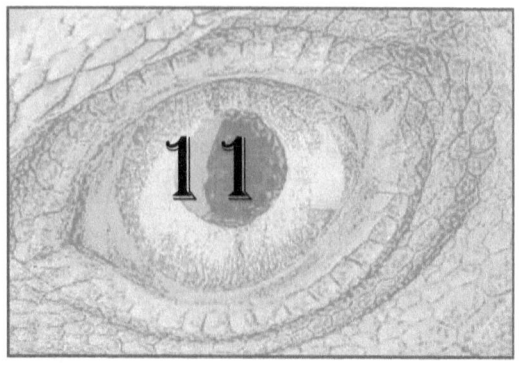

"Malcolm!!"

Itjanu kicked him harder in his side as he lay spread out on the mound, with Henry tucked into his armpit on the other side like a stuffed toy.

"Malcolm!"

Malcolm brought his arm over his eyes to shield them from the merciless sun high overheard. He licked his lips, yawned and then belched.

Itjanu covered her nose and stepped back.

"Malcolm!! Get up. You are disgraceful! Get Up, you slob!"

"What-the--,...What?...What's going on?"

Itjanu stepped back toward him taking a prize soccer swing with her foot and delivering a loud thump to his rib cage.

"Ow!! What's that for?"

He sat up holding his hands against his forehead just where his eyebrows used to be, fingertip-to-fingertip in a dual hand salute, shading his bloodshot yellow eyes from the sun, and squinted through the brightness at the silhouette of his attacker. Itjanu put her hands on her hips and flicked sand at him with the toe of her shoe.

"Is this what you do with your blessing? Legends and myths and even religious history is built around beings such as you have become! And you SQUANDER it getting drunk behind the tavern? You've gone from being a rude self-centered Yank, to a Giant Green rude self-centered Yank! You're DISGUSTING!"

"Whoa. Whao! I didn't ask to become this!" He pointed both inward pointing index fingers at his chest. "Hell, I'm not even sure what THIS is! What SHOULD I be doing here, lady? Can you tell me that, Doctor don't-like-my-own-people-cause-I-wear-shoes Williamson? Hunh? You Tell ME. What should I be doing??"

"Make yourself useful! DO something besides filling your gut with alcohol!"

She spun on her toes and walked away from him toward the road. Dust flew into the air around her as she walked away and a little dark spot formed on the ground just ahead of her. As she walked the spot stayed two feet in front of her and moved with her even as it grew dramatically larger. When it expanded to a size greater than her own noon day shadow she stopped to look at it.

Malcolm landed on his own shadow directly in front of Itjanu with an earth-shaking "Whomp!", sending red plumes of dust in all directions, enveloping himself and Itjanu within an expanding curtain of dust, with only his wings showing above the cloud. His arms were folded across his chest and his chin up.

"What should I be doing? Hunh? YOU tell ME!"

Itjanu coughed within the sand cloud, fanning the dust away from her face.

"Don't DO THAT! You want to KILL me?"

Seeing that her white blouse was now covered in a half inch thick layer of dust like paprika snow, Malcolm leaned down over her and gently flicked her shoulder with a single massive finger, then puffed at her clothes with a tiny oh formed between his lips. She slapped his hand away, then slapped his face if a flurry of both hands.

"Don't touch me!!"

"I'm NOT touching you! What are you doing here anyway? Other than trying to make me feel worse than I already do?"

"My grandfather thinks he can help you."

"Your grandfather?"

"Yes"

"The one that walks around mostly naked, talks to your dead grandmother, and wants you to help him fix the wallabies in the desert?"

"Yes."

"O.K."

"OK? Just like that. OK?"

"Hey, I got turned into a big ass Green whatchamacallit. I'm game for anything."

The dirty little man pulled down on the edge of Malcolm's wing.

"Can I go with you?"

Malcolm shrugged his shoulders.

"OK by me."

He turned back to Itjanu

"Can he come?"

Itjanu looked him over, her upper lip curving slightly and a frown forming on her forehead, and put her hand up to her nose.

"You ride in the back of the truck with Malcolm."

Itjanu stepped out into the unpaved street and waved to a rumpled faded blue pickup truck parked in front of the pub. The engine spat to life and Mica drove it around to the other side of the pub. He got out and flipped an old ratty faded canvas off the truck bed, then motioned to Malcolm and Henry.

"In ya go, gents. Snug as a bug."

Malcolm shook his head and pushed air in front of him with the palms of his hands.

"No way. I'm not getting under that"

Mica looked over to Itjanu. She grabbed onto the tip of Malcolm's closest wing.

"No way are you going to fly into my grandfather's village. The believers will die of fright and the others will make a que down to the only telephone in town. The whole place will turn into a carnival, and your 'big green ass' will stay that way until the day you die, which probably won't be far off!"

Malcolm's eyelids lowered half way and he looked sideways to Itjanu.

"You say the nicest things."

Then he sighed heavily and slowly climbed into the bed of the truck, pushing the truck frame down nearly touching the back tires and curling up like a sleeping hound to fit in the bed, barely leaving room for Henry. After Henry crawled in next to Malcolm, Mica flipped the canvas over them and tied it down at the corners, then went around to the other side to tuck in the tips of Malcolm's wings.

After Mica and Itjanu got into the cab of the truck, Mica chuckled and yelled over his shoulder out his window as he let out the clutch and the truck shuddered forward, "Wagons Ho, Yank!"

The truck was making its way beyond the last building at the edge of Mutana Creek as Bill tiptoed out behind the pub with a box of lunchtime leftovers, flitting among the scrub and spinifex, his head bobbing all around and giving out a hoarse whisper.

"Malcolm? Teddy? Malcolm? Teddy?

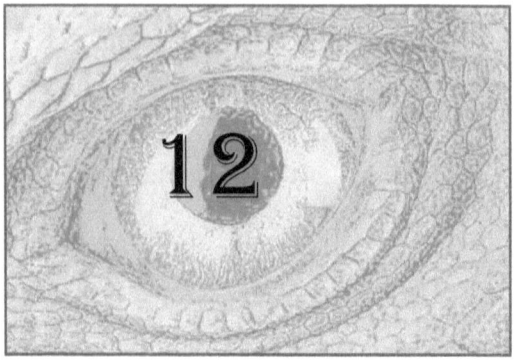

On the opposite end of Mutanajulu from the cultural center, was an abandoned oil company warehouse, closed after the owners reluctantly admitted defeat and moved their drill rigs to another dry well farther west, where they finally went out of business. Modest graffiti decorated one sand-scrubbed outside wall, but otherwise the building had been left alone and unoccupied for years. Mica's pickup truck halted before the double door entrance and the left front fender bobbled to the rhythm of the engine, while Itjanu ran to lift up the short board wedged against one door, serving as latch. The truck rolled slowly onto the concrete floor of the warehouse and parked next to an inside office with its door standing open and its window almost opaque with red dust.

The reverberations of the truck engine within the warehouse ended and all fell into quiet when Mica turned off the ignition. The sun was still high in its arc and bright blades of dust-speckled sunbeams spiked down to the floor from a few holes in the rusting tin roof above. The shade within the baking metal building was almost cool to Malcolm and Henry as Mica flipped off the canvas in a cloud of red powder. Henry slipped off the end of the truck bed coughing and looking around. Malcolm sat up and began stretching his arms and legs and wings to work out the kinks after being curled into a ball for the last hour. Then he sat still a moment with his head in his hands and his elbows resting on his bent up knees.

"Oh, my,...head."

He stared down at his tail lying on the truck bed between his legs and pulled it up, shaking it vigorously and eyeing it as it hung limp in his grasp.

"Damned thing's gone numb. I got erect-tail dysfunction."

Then he reached over the side of the truck bed and finger-flipped Henry's back with the curved top of his claw.

"Oww!"

"23 times, Henry. You farted 23 times on the way here under that nasty tarp!"

Henry frowned over his shoulder.

"I can't help it. Whiskey and peanuts give me gas."

Itjanu walked away from the truck toward a small doorway in an outer wall.

"You gents stay here while I go fetch Grandfather."

She stopped with her hand on the door handle and turned her face back toward Malcolm.

"He's been taking your pills. My Grandfather is a drug addict, and he found your pack with your pills in it, and he took them to get high."

Malcolm raised his head, shaking it from side to side, his eyes open wide.

"They don't get you high."

Itjanu smiled broadly.

"So we found out. I read the label after he started taking them. This is the best he has been in a long time."

She opened the door and turned to go out. Malcolm raised a long clawed finger.

"The seeds. The little seeds! Did he take the seeds too??"

She was already gone and did not hear him, or at least did not answer him.

Mica plopped a dusty backpack next to Malcolm on the truck bed.

"Here ya go, Mate."

And then he dropped a second pack at Henry's feet.

"That driver fella left them behind when you two got off the van and didn't go back on. Said they were yours."

Henry shrieked with Joy.

"My pack! My journals! I thought they had been stolen. I knew I had taken the pack off the van, but then, well, I had a drink in the tavern, and well, lost track of it."

He dropped to his knees next to his pack and lovingly withdrew his notebooks and held them to his chest. Mica stepped away from Henry and fanned the air in front of his face.

"There's a shower in the back the drivers used when this place was still runnin. I got the water on, and you could really use one, mate."

Henry raised his arm and sniffed himself and then jerked his head back with a cough.

"I didn't realize,...I didn't know it was so bad."

Henry placed his notebooks back in the pack and set the pack on the truck bed next to Malcolm and headed for the showers. Mica stepped next to the truck and sniffed the air near Malcolm.

"You're not bad, Malcolm. Thought you might be. Figured the showers would be needed for you more than the little guy."

"No. I think the dust and sand is enough to keep me scrubbed. I don't even sweat – except a little on my forehead the other night."

Malcolm regarded the skin on his arms and abdomen.

"I don't think this was a water-type reptile, and I don't really get hot either."

Mica swatted at the air in front of his face and Malcolm noticed the movement.

"What? Do I smell to you? Most people can't smell themselves, but,..."

"Nah. Flies. They're out and about this afternoon. Buzzin in front of me face like they do. Been much worse than ever since the night light started. After the moisture, you now, but more than I've ever seen before."

He swiped the air in front of his face again and sent a few small black flies twirling higher into the air.

"They call this the Australian Salute out here. Everybody does it. No choice. They don't seem to bother you, though."

Malcolm smiled and reached his hand out toward the closest flies where they spun farther away from him.

"No. Flies and mosquitoes really stay away from me. At least there's that."

"Well there's precious little outside water around here so there's no mosquitoes for us either, but the flies are with us sun up to sun down, unless the wind blows – and then they just pop around to the other side of you."

Mica sat on the open tailgate and automatically brought his hand back up, but then stopped it in mid air, noticing the truck bed was completely devoid of the pesty outback fly. He smiled up at Malcolm.

"You're handy to have around mate. A bit large, but handy even so."

Malcolm gingerly opened his pack and began to delicately move his large clawed fingers among the contents. He lifted out his journal, holding it in his palm, filling no more of his hand than a poker card to the average human. He closed his eyes for a moment and sighed heavily, then let the journal slide back into the pack and continued to stare at the skin of his open hand. He rotated his hand slowly, examining the hand of the thing he had become. Mica watched him.

"She'll be right, mate. No worries. It'll all work out. You just wait and see. It'll all work out."

"I wish I could believe that."

Mica gave him another warm Anangu smile.

"No worries. The old man'll fix you up. You'll see."

Malcolm stared down at Mica's face and sighed.

"When I first met Itjanu, she was the first Anangu I had ever met,...and I'm ashamed to say I thought she was ugly. Now, I'd give anything to be so normal and to be able to give such a kind smile as you or her."

Mica frowned.

"Well Malcolm, you're big and green, and whatever you are, but you're still a bloody Pohm. Itjanu is a beautiful woman, and shame on ya for not being able to see it when ya first met her. And now here you are something between a great big horny toad, a croc with wings, and a dingo's ass. Makes ya think, doesn't it, mate?"

"I suspected the last part was already there when we met on the plane, mister."

Malcolm and Mica turned to see Itjanu with her hands on her hips, a deep frown focused intently on Malcolm, and standing next to her grandfather, Elea. The old man grinned and nodded his head.

"Dingo's ass, are ya? Maybe we be too ugly to help yer lordship, yer green bloody lordship."

Malcolm slipped off the tailgate and squatted on the dusty concrete to keep his head near the height of the old man.

"Yes sir, a dingo's ass. A dingo's ass that is ashamed that he felt that way. A dingo's ass that needs all the help he can get to find a way to be human again."

Elea looked back toward Itjanu and raised his eyebrows, waiting for her response.

"I don't know Grandfather. He seems to behave even more human as he is than as he was. Maybe he should just stay this way"

Malcolm looked down and scratched the top of his head. The sound was like wooden stakes being drug across rumpled leather. Itjanu folded her arms in front of her.

"Well, he did get that way helping us at the Pound. And YOU, you little lizard..."

She pointed at the returning Henry who stopped abruptly.

"You CAUSED all this. You need to help us fix it."

Henry dropped his gaze to the ground and smiled to himself, as Malcolm raised his head in the grimace that was his smile.

"You'll help me?"

Elea turned his face back toward Malcolm. Without turning back toward them he spoke to the other two.

"O.K. Itjanu, you take Mica and go help somebody do something worth doing. I need to talk with Dingo Ass and Little Lizard."

Elea stepped closer to Malcolm and Henry.

"First things first,..."

And with amazing speed he pulled up the walking stick and swung it in an arc landing a cracking blow onto the top of Henry's head.

"That's for pushing my Baby down!"

The stick swooped again in a blur slapping hard against Malcolm's head as well. The echoes of the striking stick bouncing off the tin walls around them.

"And that's for thinking that any woman who is descended from my blessed wife could be anything but beautiful!"

Both Henry and Malcolm crouched with arms over their heads, expecting more blows from the old man's stick. Elea curled his hand against his shoulder again, gripping his walking stick, and brought his right hand to rest lightly on the stick above his left, and then rested his chin on his wrist.

"All right, sit up you two. I'm done for now. And I got some questions. You – Dingo Ass, what are the little blue seeds in with your pills?"

Malcolm raised his eyes.

"You didn't take them did you? Do you still have them?"

"When you get a stick you can ask the questions. Right now only I got a stick, so I'm asking the questions."

Malcolm nodded. Elea grinned.

"So, what's the little seeds in with your pills, which I didn't disturb when I popped two of your pills. Wait, don't answer that yet. What is your name? I mean, besides Dingo Ass."

"Malcolm. Malcolm Ironwater."

"Elea. Elea Williams."

The old man extended his right hand, and Malcolm accepted it carefully with his fingers.

"Fair enough. That's done proper. Now tell me. Malcolm. What are the little seeds?"

"I'm not sure what they are called, but they come from a little bright blue flower that grows within a granite ring of boulders back in the United States in a place called Finton County. It only grows there, as far as I know, and it only grows to be about two inches high, stem and flower. I once put the stem in my mouth and hallucinated for a couple days. And another time I put the flower in my mouth and suffered diarrhea for eleven straight hours."

Elea frowned at Malcolm. "That's dangerous stuff to have. Why'd you bring them ta the Oz?"

"I am, was, going to grow them to help my visions." He drew little patterns in the sand near his feet with the claw of his first finger. "I thought they would help me get to know who I really was. I really wanted to be more than who I was – something different, something special."

Elea snorted. "Well you got that, mate."

Malcolm nodded without looking up, examining his own hand. Elea sighed and straightened his back.

"All right, then. Let's get you fixed."

Malcolm lifted his head, "You'll help me?", then tilted his head and looked into the old man's eyes. "Why?"

"You need fixin'. I need something ta fix." The old man rubbed his chin, then poked Henry gently with the end of his stick. "Little Lizard, you still got the opal charms you used to start all this mess?"

Henry shook his head. "Nope, lost everything except my notebooks."

"Mmm. How big was the opal?"

Henry formed a half-inch circle with his thumb and finger. "That big, and encased in glass, and the base was brass with designs in it like this," and he began to trace patterns in the sand.

Elea held his stick upright with both hands and rested his chin on his knuckles. "Nah. All that don't mean a thing. It's the opal that matters. What color was it?"

"Opal. It was opal colored."

"Just like a Pohmie. Thinks he knows everything, but doesn't know anything about the Oz. Opals got lots of colors, but each opal has a dominant color – speck of color more than the other colors, like hazel eyes."

"Oh, yeah, that's right. It wasn't really much, I don't think, not at all as pretty as opals I had seen before. This one was mostly black, with flecks in it that looked like red and green broken glass..."

Elea sucked air in through his teeth. "A bloody black opal, and with red light in it. A fiery black. Shoulda seen that comin from the start. Now I understand. Black opals very rare. Fiery blacks even more so. Very expensive, very powerful, usually very small, and almost always linked ta trouble. Yep that figures." He frowned at Henry. "How'd you come by a black opal?? You musta paid a fortune for it."

Henry shook his head slowly. "No..., no, my father bought it in a pawn shop for two pounds and had it as a paper weight on his home desk for years. One of the few things he left me. The designs in the brass base are what started my research into ancient cultures."

"The base? The brass base of the opal stand?"

"Yeah,..."

"And ya never thought anything about the value of the stone itself?"

"No,... it wasn't important, just something picked up in a pawn shop for a couple pounds,..."

"Bloody hell. The thing was probably worth a couple THOUSAND pounds – or more!"

Henry stared at the old man, his mouth moving in little jerks, but no sound came from his throat. Finally, he sighed and looked down at the concrete floor.

"Well it's all moot now, because it is gone."

"Would'na helped anyway. Whatever it takes ta do a magic, it'll take more of it to undo it, but that's what we need. And I have no idea where ta look for that."

Malcolm twisted his head around to look at Elea. "We need an opal?"

"What? You gonna squat down on the sand and lay one like an egg?"

"No. There's a cave on a mountain I've been staying in that has a couple hundred opals in a pile."

Elea stared back at Malcolm for a moment. "What size?"

Malcolm shrugged his shoulders. "Finger tip to golf ball."

"In a pile. Opals? Opals just sitting there in a pile?"

Malcolm raised his hand out parallel with the floor and held it about waist high to the old man. " 'Bout that much."

Malcolm looked into his eyes and grinned.

Elea jumped back away from him. "That's the first damned thing we're gonna work on Dingo Ass. You gotta quit grittin your teeth at me!"

"I was smiling."

"You gotta change that, mate. It looks to me like you're getting ready to eat me!"

Malcolm frowned and closed his mouth, then struggled to control his lips. First the middle went up and the edges went down, in jerking motions.

"That ain't it mate. Try'er again"

Malcolm pursed his lips, then pinching them together with this claws, he forced the edges out. With the center of his lips clamped shut and the edges showing teeth, Malcolm muttered, "Meoump miss?"

"What?"

He released his lips and spoke again, "How's this, I mean that – what I did before."

"Looks like you were getting ready to chuck your lunch."

Malcolm clamped the center of his mouth closed with one hand, then used his forefinger and thumb of his other hand to push the edges of his mouth up.

"Mmummws Mnisss?"

Elea shook his head and turned away. "Needs work, mate. Needs a lotta work."

Elea poked Henry as he passed.

"You need work too, Lizard. This is all your fault, and don't think I don't know it."

The old man rubbed his chin then frowned down at Henry.

"What size was the opal in yer glass globe."

"It was about a half to three-quarters inch across."

The old man nodded and turned back to Malcolm.

"Ya say there's a pile of opals in the cave where you were staying? Up in the mountains somewhere?"

"Sure. A bunch. You want some?"

"Find me a black and red one twice the size of the one Lizard had. Go and get it tonight, and some smaller ones, too. We'll need the big ones for a ceremony, and the little ones will buy us gas and food. We're trekkin tomorrow." And then he left the warehouse.

Malcolm turned toward Henry with the claws of his left hand pinching the center of his mouth closed and his other hand pushing his mouth edges up.

"Howmms thimms?"

Henry shuddered and looked away.

As evening swept darkness across Mutanajulu and the bright green Aurora lit the sky again, dark clouds rolled in below it, taking on its color and traded green lightning between the billowing clumps. Thunder boomed across the skies and wind swept sand across the fields and ticked against the side of the corrugated tin walls of the warehouse. Henry peered through the opening of the door as the wind tried to push it closed on him, watching Malcolm struggle into the air, pumping his wings hard to rise into the dust storm, until he was out of sight.

Malcolm strained his wings, fighting the wind and crabbing sideways as he rose, slipping as far to the side as he gained upward. It took ten minutes to finally break free of the dust storm and reach cooler air high in the night sky. The top of the storm was painted bright green to match the Aurora above him. The angry clouds below him threw lightning bolts at one another, in flares of emerald green flashes below. He could see nothing under the clouds for hundreds of miles in all directions, but his sense of direction took him on his path to the mountains far to the west. Occasionally bolts of lightning would shoot up toward him as if the clouds did not want him to pass by, but the bolts would fade into spiraling wisps before they could reach him.

Malcolm steadied his breathing and kept his wings pumping, moving fast in the cool air and flying beyond the edge of the storm, over the valley of his memories and saw the mountain ridges at the horizon. When he recognized the shapes of the peaks and knew he was near his cave, he spread his wings fully and glided to the plateau that overlooked the plain below. Soon his large padded feet touched the rocky clearing and he folded his wings behind him and walked slowly into the cave, letting his big eyes adjust to the darkness. His pupils opened wide and it was as if a light had been turned on in the cave.

Opening the little cloth sack hung around his neck by its string, he knelt before the pile of opals and searched through the collection looking for a black opal. Most of the big ones were common green, and some mixed with pink and blue, but at last he found a large black speckled with points of shiny green and sparkling red. He held in up to his eye and spoke to it.

"There you are sweetie. You are the one that is going to make me human again."

He kissed it and dropped it into the sack, then scooped a hand full of the smaller stones and dropped them into the sack as well.

"That should be enough for gas and food – I guess."

Then he made another scoop and put them in the sack as well. He hefted the sack in his hand, feeling the weight.

"That ought to do it."

Then he worked on his smile a moment until he thought he was getting it right without pinching his mouth.

He stood and walked back out into the light of the Aurora and then stopped, and stepped quickly back to the pile of opals and picked up one more that he held tightly in the palm of his hand.

"And one for good ol'Bill. Just one little bucket of beer can't hurt."

Then he strode to the edge of the plateau and jumped into the air, spreading his wings as he fell, swooping low over the fields below, banking left in a tight turn and pumped his wings toward the Mutana Creek Pub. He was there in just a few minutes, settling his huge feet into the red sand behind the pub, noticing the flaming red torches lined along either side of the runway at the edge of town. He tapped gently on the back door, waited a moment and then tapped harder. Bill flung open the back door and as he did Malcolm put his face into the doorway light close to Bill's face and gave him a new smile.

"Bloody Hell!"

Bill screamed and slammed the door shut. Then seconds later he reopened the door cautiously.

"Malcolm? Malcolm is that you."

Malcolm moved back into the doorway light and Bill poked his finger hard against the big chin.

"Scared the hell out of me, Malcolm. Thought you had left for good – or maybe I had just gotten sober"

"Sorry, Bill. Just thought I'd stop by for a quick beer."

He held the opal out toward the pub keeper.

"You don't have to keep giving me those things for just a beer, mate. I'm feeling guilty over taking the others. Far as I'm concerned, your tab is covered for the next couple years!"

Then he snatched up the opal, gave it a quick look in the light and slid it into his pocket.

"Be just a minute, mate."

He closed the door again. Shortly, he reopened the door and held out a bucket by its handle, straining to lift the weight out to Malcolm. Malcolm took the bucket in one hand and quickly swigged down a third of its content. He held the bucket out toward the airfield.

"What's going out there?"

Bill shook his head and tisked.

"Ah terrible thing Malcolm, terrible. A back packer took a tumble out in the desert. Broke his arm, scorpion bit him, and now he's all poison filled. He musta laid out there a couple days before he could make it in. The Royalies are taking him to Oodnadata, but not sure the bloke's gonna make it. Near dead I hear."

"Royalies?"

"Royal Flying Doctor Corps."

"Oh. Yeah. I heard of them."

Bill poked Malcolm's shoulder.

"You stay outta sight til they're gone, right?"

Malcolm nodded.

"Yeah. Sure." Then he smiled at Bill.

"What'er you smiling about?"

"Is it a smile? I've been working on it."

Bill tilted his head and squinted at him.

"Almost there, mate. Not quite, but it's close. Keep at it. Looks better than before. You stay in the dark. Hear?"

The wind rose and the clouds moved under the Aurora, and the thunder came in with them.

Bill looked out toward the runway.

"The Royalies better get a move on it, if they're gonna stay ahead of this storm."

As if the pilot heard Bill, the engine of the light plane revved, and the light in the cockpit under the single wing went out. The taxi lights came on under the nose, and shone down the oiled dirt runway. The engine revved up to full RPM's and the little plane scooted down the runway, lifting off the ground just a few yards before it ended, and started rising steeply into the air.

Malcolm and Bill watched the plane wobbling into the air. The wind and sand slammed into the plane and began pushing it back down toward the desert beyond town.

"Uh Oh," muttered Bill. "That's trouble."

Malcolm set his beer down in the soft sand, just as the tail of the plane flipped upward.

"Bloody Hell, she's going down!" but Malcolm was no longer there to hear him. He was running and pumping his wings into the wind, soaring for the little plane as it nosed down toward the desert, and then the little plane was lost in the darkness and the sand from the back door of the pub.

Inside the cockpit, the pilot struggled with the controls as the wind pushed the tail of the light plane higher and higher, and he was unable to bring the nose up.

"Come up, Girl. Come up, little darling. You can do it."

He pushed the throttle full power, but the plane floated along in the bully wind like a kite without its string. The nurse in the back held on to the patient strapped in the stretcher with one hand, and held the safety strap above her head with the other. The engine strained, stall lights flashed on the panel, and buzzers wailed. The plane began its slide down toward the hard floor of the desert below.

"Hold on, Jackie! This may be a bit hard."

The plane dived and the rock strewn desert floor rushed up at them.

Jackie, the nurse, let go of the overhead strap and clutched the medallion on her necklace and closed her eyes, never letting go of the patient. The pilot could make out individual boulders ahead of them, still fighting the controls of the plane.

There was a sudden thump against the top of the plane, and the fall stopped. The plane surged forward, still nose down but moving over the rocks in gentle surges, like the small waves of a lake. The nose began to rise. The surges continued, gently rocking the passengers of the little plane, slowly pulling up higher and higher into the air. Jackie patted the pilots shoulder.

"You did it, Stephen! You did it!"

Stephen shook his head.

"Didn't do a bloody thing."

Then he patted the dashboard.

"That's my darling. Bring us up."

Outside the plane Malcolm had his legs wrapped around the thin tail section, and his arms spread far forward and wide, grasping the leading edge of the wing on each side, pumping his wings, straining them up, aching in his shoulders, pumping, pumping, pumping. At last, he was able to bring the plane up over the top of the dust cloud, and could feel the little engine trying to pull the plane ahead. The pilot looked out of the windscreen, and just as Malcolm released the leading edge of the wing Stephen saw the claws slip away in the running lights.

"What the..."

Malcolm released the plane and watched it slowly bank in the light of the Aurora. He turned with it to make sure it was all right. For a few seconds they flew side by side, and the pilot looked out as Jackie checked the patient. Malcolm gave the pilot a wave and a perfectly warm smile. The pilot stared wide-eyed at the vision outside the plane and slowly raised his hand in a half hearted waved. Malcolm sailed back down into the dust clouds. Jackie looked up at the pilot.

"What'er you waving at?"

Stephen brought his hand down to the controls, and spoke to the control panel where all gauges reading normal. "I ain't sayin."

Jackie pulled the little medallion from her neck and kissed it.

Malcolm touched back down behind the pub, but his bucket of beer was now full of red mud. He shook his head, standing in the dusty wind, knowing the same thing would happen if he asked for another bucket, and there was nowhere for him to be inside to drink it. So, he pushed back up into the wind and pumped his way over the dust cloud to find his way back to the warehouse in Mutanajulu.

The dust storm blew in rushes where visibility was impossible, broken by open gaps and then quickly filled. Malcolm was able to find his way back to the warehouse and as he opened the main door to enter, he was joined by a howling red dust cloud that coated the interior in rose colored talc.

"Hey! Watch it," yelled Henry. "Close the damned door!"

He was sitting on the tailgate of the truck eating something from a bowl, and had too late put his hand over the bowl. He frowned down into the red mush that had been kangaroo stew. "It's ruined now, thanks to you!"

Elea, Itjanu and Mica were standing around the front of the truck looking at a map spread across the hood, but looked up as Malcolm entered, Itjanu slapping her hands onto the map to keep it from floating away in the gust.

"Sorry. Sorry, everyone," Malcolm smiled.

Elea squinted in the dim light of the propane lamp hanging above the truck, leaning toward Malcolm. Without taking his eyes off Malcolm he walked toward him, looking closely at his face,

"Do that again."

Malcolm smiled, and the old man leaned forward and slapped the side of his arm.

"That'll do, Dingo Ass. That'll do. You find the opal?"

Malcolm pulled the small sack from his neck and handed it to Elea, who spun on his heels and went to the tailgate to pour out the contents. Henry looked down at the opals.

"Whoa! There's a fortune there!" He looked up wide eyed at Malcolm.

"Can you go get some more??"

Elea slapped his hand as he reached for one."

"Hands off Lizard. These ain't for you."

Itjanu placed her hands on the edge of the truck bed.

"Well done, Malcolm! After we get you switched back to whatever you were before, we'll need to talk about financing a clinic here."

Elea raised the black opal into the light and whistled. Everyone looked up at the stone with eyes wide and open mouthed.

Elea was the first to speak. "That one is a great find." He held it close to Henry.

"Twice the size of the one you used at Wilpena Pound?"

"Yeah, and then some."

Mica stepped closer to the opal.

"That's gotta be worth at least fifty thousand dollars..."

"Or more..." added Itjanu.

Elea shook his head slowly.

"Pity to destroy it."

Everyone else answered in unison

"Destroy it??"

The old man nodded at them. "If the old Kurpany ceremony is the same Henry tried up at the pound, and IF it all works, and IF no one gets killed, this little beauty will vaporize into a puff of dust."

Mica shook his head, staring at the stone.

"Fifty thousand dollars. That's ten times what I can make in a year."

The old man wrapped his hand around the stone and slipped it into his pocket.

"And fifty years, for what I get by on, but it doesn't matter. Malcolm found it and we need to use it to fix him up."

Elea gave Malcolm with a squinting stare.

"Are you worth it, Dingo Ass? Have you done anything in your life to be worth it?

Malcolm looked down and slowly shook his head, but Itjanu stepped to her grandfather and poked a finger in his arm.

"He was born, Grandfather. He is, or was, human. That makes anyone worth it. No matter what they have done to deserve it."

Elea nodded to his granddaughter.

"Your grandmother would have said that." Then he took her hand in his.

Malcolm abruptly raised his head and smiled at the group.

"Hey! I did something. I saved a plane on the way back with the opals. Does that count?"

Once again the group spoke, "What??"

Then Malcolm told them of his stop off at the Mutana Creek Pub, at which point Itjanu snorted and began to walk away. Malcolm described the Royal Flying Doctor's Corps plane, and how he helped it rise above the dust storm."

The group stared at Malcolm in silence. Itjanu turned up to his face.

"Did you really? Is that just beer talk, or did you really?"

Malcolm brought his head down to look Itjanu in her eyes.

"Honestly, I did."

"Why?"

"Because they needed helping and I could help."

Elea placed his hand gently on Malcolm's forearm.

"For service to humankind, and for finding a dandy black opal, you are officially no longer Dingo Ass."

Malcolm smiled again, as Elea spun around and poked Henry in his arm.

"You, however, remain Lizard until we get all your mess undone – and we still ain't settled for you pushing down my Granddaughter."

Malcolm smiled again and stuck his tongue out at Henry, forgetting that his tongue was now almost three feet long and forked, which scared everyone, and Itjanu shrieked. Malcolm let out a ragged sigh as the others recovered from their fright, and walked away to the farthest corner of the warehouse.

Elea turned back to the pile of opals sitting on the tail gate. "So, now we gotta sell'em."

Mica scratched is head. "That may be a bit of a problem. We can sell one or two through the cultural center, but that won't get us any money right away." Mica pointed his thumb toward Malcolm.

"He can fly as he pleases, and eat – well whatever. But if we're drivin to Wilpena Pound, we need petrol and food and places ta stay on the way. That's gonna take cash, and a whole lot more than any of us has. Unless Ittie brought a bag full of dollars in her kit."

She smiled and reached into her purse, pulling out two credit cards.

"It's almost as good as a bag full of dollars, but I'll need money to pay it back."

"Well, we still got the problem of how we're gonna sell'em. One or two here and there is O.K., but that pile is gonna raise a lot of questions."

Elea touched his arm. "Can't you say they came from that old mine of your fathers?"

"Nah. It's been petered out for decades and no one has worked it in years..."

"Then go work it. Scratch it up."

Mica smiled broadly. "Forgot all about that old mine. I need to go home and see if mother still has the permit. It was good for 99 years. Should still be legal. Can't sell a handful of opals without their history and the mine they came from."

Itjanu rubbed the side of her face. "We need to sell them in a place that is used to buying several at a time."

Mica snapped his fingers. "Been a long time since I been there, but I know just the spot. Coober Pedy."

Elea frowned and shook his head. "That's two hundred kilometers in the wrong direction, if we're to go to Wilpena Pound."

Mica pointed to the pile of opals. "If you're going to turn that into good old Ozzie dollars, then we got to go to Coober Pedy first."

Elea shrugged his shoulders. "O.K. then, we go to Coober Pedy."

"Where's that?", Henry asked.

Mica threw his finger out into the darkness beyond the propane lamp. "A long damned way, mate. Out in the middle of the desert. It's a mining town. Famous for Ozzie opals. Almost everybody there works a mine or works a business that sells to miners. That's why we named it Coober Pedy."

Henry frowned. "Why? What does Coober Pedy mean?"

"White man livin in a hole."

"They live in their mines?"

"No. Not mostly, but there are so many played out mines, and its cool in'em, so lotta folks makes their home in the mines. Gets fifty degrees out in the desert sun, Lizard. They take shelter in the cool of the mines."

"Fifty degrees isn't hot, that's chilly."

"Not fifty degrees Fahrenheit, Lizard. Fifty degrees Celsius. That's about a hundred and twenty Fahrenheit!"

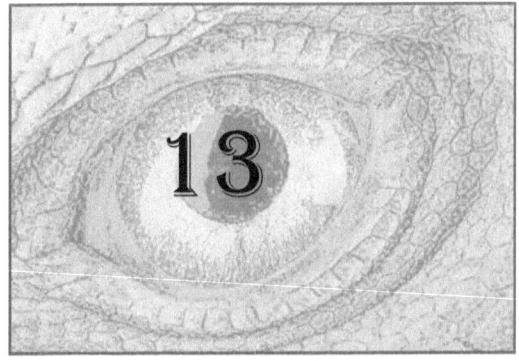

Mica had unfolded and refolded the old stained mine lease contract several times, and each time the buyer had copied the certificate number and then counted out the rumpled bills for the two or three modest opals he pedaled at each brokerage. Too many opals would have required a bank check and too many questions, so Mica had walked the dusty streets of Coober Pedy throughout the long hot day, making a couple hundred dollars at a time. He knew he was getting less than the opals were worth, but he was getting enough to cover expenses and pay off what had been charged to Itjanu's overworked credit cards. He paused at the edge of town and looked out over the desert to the low lying hills shimmering in the distance where Malcolm waited.

Across the street was an inviting tavern with plenty of shade, air conditioning and cold beer, but he still had six more opals and that meant two more buyers before he would let himself stop to rest. Itjanu, Elea and Henry waited at a motel on the far edge of town, where he had left the truck with one bald tire showing threads where tread had once been and going flat, and steam seeping out from the radiator cap seal and still too hot to chance opening.

The metal of the truck engine and the hood had ticked and pinged in the noonday sun when he walked away from the motel in search of his first buyer. He just smiled his empty smile and let the buyers cheat him a little so they wouldn't be too interested in the paperwork, but not too accepting so they wouldn't think he maybe had stole them. He really needed a new tire there on the right front, and the water pump had to be replaced before he could drive the old truck back to Mutanajulu. He had to work this just right, and he held his patience, and walked in the sun between the buildings set far apart along the dusty roads, and looked forward to that cold beer waiting for him after the last opal was sold.

The last buyer was the Dingo Cave Mine on the other side of town. The sign above the glass door to the converted mine proclaimed 'Home of the Monster Opal'. 'The Dingo', as the locals called the jewelry store, was one of the older mines in Coober Pedy, but played out years ago. The owner/operator was happy to have Mica's opals and studied them at length. He pulled the eyepiece away from his eye, pinched the bridge of his nose and blinked several times to focus his gaze on Mica.

"Where'd ya get these?"

"From my mine."

The buyer pulled out a magnifying glass and inspected the lease contract again. He shook his head and pointed a calloused finger toward a huge red speckled opal the size of an orange, that was on proud display behind a thick plate of Lucite and under brilliant light set into pink mottled rock behind the counter.

"Naw. Your opals came from the same place that monster did."

They both stared at the display high on the wall. Mica whistled.

"What's that one worth?"

The buyer reached up and touched the steel frame around the Lucite with his fingertips.

"Assayer told me about twenty years ago it was probably worth fifty thousand. Be double or triple that now."

"Ya oughta have that thing in a safe, mate."

"It's safe enough there. Got all kinds of electronic gadgets around it. This whole place locks down like a bank if the Lucite is so much as cracked. As it is, it's my claim to fame with the tourists. Now, where'd your opals come from?"

Mica pulled his eyes away from the giant opal and looked at the buyer.

"They came from my mine, mate."

"Bullshit. Opals come from clans. The rock they come from makes their color, and the color is different in different spots. Opals that come from the same area all belong to the same clan. I've been looking at opals 50 years, and I know the area where your lease is."

He rolled the opals in his hand under his counter light.

"And these little beauties did not come from that mine. Where'd ya get'em?"

Mica rubbed the back of his head, fingered the edge of his straw western hat, then sighed.

"Won'em in a poker game couple months ago. Been savin'em to have'em mounted for my sweet Annie, but times are tough and I need a new water pump for my truck."

"Something's fishy here." He tapped his fingertips on the glass top counter. "But, I'll give you... two hundred dollars for the three of them."

Mica hesitated, looking out through the glass entry door, seeing the tavern across the street. The man gave a small smile.

"Take it or leave it."

Mica coughed and looked out the door again, then he looked down and slowly shook his head.

"Nah. I think I'll just keep'em and walk across town to that other..."

"All right, all right. I'll give you three hundred."

Mica smiled and held out his hand.

The buyer smirked and counted out the money.

"If you had taken the two hundred, I would've called the constable on you. Do you know where they came from?"

Mica shook his head. "Thought you knew where they were from, where the big'un came from."

"That's just it. I don't have the slightest idea where that big beauty came from. It just showed up here one

159

day about twenty years ago. Aborigine wanted five hundred for it. I gave him two, and then called the law on him as soon as he walked out the door. Figured he'd stole it."

Mica let his smile fade away. "But ya kept the opal."

"I bought it, fair dinkum. A deal was a deal back then. He signed a receipt."

"They catch him?"

"Nah. Disappeared. Back into the bush or the desert, I guess. Never saw him again."

"You got a receipt for me to sign?"

"Sure do." He stabbed a meaty finger on the line at the bottom of the form.

Mica signed it, then the man separated the two copies from the carbon paper and handed the bottom copy to Mica. Mica put on his hat and touched the brim with a finger in salute, then walked out the door. The buyer looked down at the receipt and smiled grimly.

"Thank you... Mr.... Smith, Mr. John Bloody Smith."

Then he picked up the phone on the counter and dialed the police.

Later, Mica finally sat at the bar in the dark shade of a working man's tavern, where red dust trailed from the door and feathered out between the tables and the bar. The window shades were pulled down against the afternoon sun. The only overhead light was over the cash register and reflected in the cracked wall mirror behind the rows of whiskey bottles lined on glass shelves.

Mica pointed at the hundreds of glass whiskey bottles along the upper walls all around the bar and spoke to the bartender, "Nice decorations you got there. Lotta glass and whiskey for someone to knock down."

The bartender flipped a towel onto his shoulder, and pulled a beer bottle from the icewater and set it in front of Mica.

"Anybody try that and they'll get a baseball bat against their head." He looked around the room surveying all the bottles. "Started that about eight years ago, to make sure the Dingo Mine was behaving itself."

"What do the bottles have to do with a mine in another part of town?"

"It's against the law for a mine in the city limits to keep diggin. Breaks up foundations of the buildings above it. Old mines run all under this town. Plenty of opals still down there, but it's too late and too dangerous to mine for'em now. The Dingo tried to go on anyway, and wound up shaking glasses and bottles off my wall. Knocked a hole in my cellar and broke a bunch of wine bottles, so I called the law on'em. They never did pay me for the glasses and whiskey I lost, but at least I made'em patch my cellar. Shoddy job they did of it too. Most of it fell down, so I use the space to store my wine. Least it's cool down there."

The Carlton bottle sat beaded with moisture on the bar in front of Mica, two drops of moisture racing each other down the long brown glass neck. He looked over to the door as it finally opened, spraying the interior with almost blinding light from the setting sun outside. He smiled that generous Anangu smile at Elea and Itjanu, barely recognizing Henry, and scooped up the bottle. The beer was gone and the bottle sitting empty back on the counter by the time they joined him at the bar, and he held up four fingers to the bartender. Elea motioned to Mica, shaking his head, so Mica changed his hand to just three fingers.

Itjanu laid a hand gently on his shoulder. "How'd we do, Mica."

The fresh bottles clinked from the bartender's fingers as he set them down, and Mica leaned close to Itjanu's ear to whisper, "Thirty two hundred, Ittie."

She patted his shoulders and pulled playfully at his ear. "Maybe you could pick up a little something for Annie before we leave town. There's enough for that."

"I'm getting her a new water pump for our truck, at the station next door."

Itjanu slapped him lightly on his back.

"No. I mean something special, just for her alone."

He spoke into his bottle as he began to drink his second beer, "maybe a nice new leather muzzle..."

Itjanu shook her head and sipped her bottle. She looked over at her grandfather, who held up a glass of ice

161

water in salute to her, smiling the old smile she grew up seeing on his face.

The phone rang near the cash register and the bartender answered it, looking at Mica. "Your truck's ready to go. New tire and water pump."

Mica drained his bottle, released a satisfying burp, and spoke across the bar.

"Guess we need ta get something for Dingo Ass. Bartender, you got a cheap bucket I can buy?"

The bartender frowned and looked around behind the bar. "We got an old ice bucket you can have. Just got a new one, and the old one doesn't leak, just has a broken handle. Let you have it for nothing if you buy some take away."

The bartender held up the old bucket and Mica nodded. "All right. Let's have twelve cans of Melbourne."

The bartender shook his head. "That bucket won't hold all those cans. Sure you don't want a box for them."

"Box? Sure. Put the cans in a box, and a couple bags of ice too, but I still need the bucket. Got a mate out there likes ta drink from it."

The bartender locked eyes with Mica and raised his eyebrows. He opened his mouth to speak, but closed it with a little shake of his head, and set the box and the bucket on the counter. "Hope your friend enjoys it."

Thirty minutes later, behind a hillside shading the still hot evening sun, Malcolm sat in the sand at the base of the hill surrounded by a ring of twelve empty beer cans. He held the bucket in front of his face by both hands, like a child gulping a large glass of cold milk, drinking down the last of his beer between gulps and short breaths echoing within the bucket. With a satisfying burp, he lowered the bucket and smiled with a beer foam mustache.

"Thanks. That was just the thing. So, what's next?"

Henry jumped into the bed of the pick-up, and held up the dusty old tarp that had covered them on their truck ride into Mutanajulu. "Wilpena Pound!"

Malcolm shook his head "Not under that – And NOT with you!" He turned to Itjanu and Elea "I'll meet you there. I promise to stay away from folks, but I can do it much easier – and faster – on my own." Then he placed his paw gently on Mica's shoulder. "Thanks for the beer...mate."

Mica smiled. "No worries...mate."

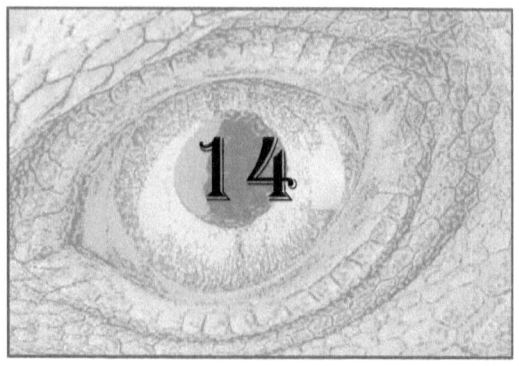

Two days later, Mica drove his old truck into the campgrounds near Wilpena Pound. The group decided to rent two of the little cabins, and were given a map to help them find the cabin locations. On the map, the location of the steel observation tower was crossed out in black marker. Itjanu questioned the park attendant.

"Why is the center viewing platform crossed out?"

She smiled and rolled her eyes. "We had a couple lightning strikes there a while back. Some tourists were injured, I heard. They said it had something to do with Aura Alice –"

"- Aura Alice?"

She smiled again. "Yeah. That's what people have started calling that green nightly Aurora. Anyway, I heard there were some tourists injured – "

Another nearby attendant added, "- one of them was killed by lightning, I heard. Burnt to a crisp, right there on that platform-"

"Not that Sissy, that's just a rumor." She turned back to Itjanu. "So the park officials have roped off the trail to the platform," she pointed up, "and it is off limits until that green thing is gone."

Itjanu frowned. "No one can go up there?"

"No, Miss. Not there nor up on the rim either. The hikers and back packers have been having fits about that, too. That's why things are actually a little slow now –

normally there'd be no chance at a cabin without a reservation made weeks ago-"

"- Months ago!" said Sissy.

Elea and Henry sat on cushions in the back of the truck with their backs against the cab waiting for Itjanu's return. Mica met her walking slowly back to the truck and was with her when she told Elea and Henry the news.

"It must be there. It MUST be there! And, it must be NOW!" Henry flared.

"Keep it down, Mate," Mica warned Henry. "We don't want to attract too much attention."

Henry spoke in a hoarse whisper, "We HAVE to do it HERE and NOW! The Aurora is still strong, but you can tell that it has peaked. It's not a bright as it was. We have to get up there."

Elea smiled and pointed a finger at Itjanu. "You have a cousin on your Grandmother's side, who works around here."

"Who?"

"Can't remember his name. I'll have to think on it a while, until it comes back to me. He's in my memory."

"How could he help us?"

"He used to backpack all around here. Might know trails that aren't marked. Trails that aren't roped off. His name is in my memory. Just have to find it."

"How far back?"

"Not too far. Just need to think about it – he came to a cultural center around here two maybe three years ago. In the Flinders Range for sure, and I think near the Pound. Took some of the things that – your grandmother and others made. Took them to a tourist shop on a highway someplace."

"A highway someplace? Grandfather, that's not very helpful."

Mica looked up in the sky then back at Itjanu and Elea and tilted his head. "You believe Malcolm really helped that Royal Flying Doctor plane?"

Itjanu and Elea both nodded. Henry just shrugged his shoulders and rested his chin in his hand.

Mica beamed. "Then all we gotta do is be in that field tonight, where Malcolm chased down the emu, right after he got hit by the lightning." He turned to Henry. "Lizard. You better have everything needed to do that ceremony, cause we're gonna do it tonight." With that, he walked away toward the campground store. Itjanu called after him.

"What are you going to do?"

He spoke over his shoulder as he went.

"More flashlights. Cheap ones, if they got'em"

The green Aurora reemerged into the evening sky as the sun settled for the night behind St. Mary's Peak. Mica's truck ambled along a packed dirt road at the edge of the grassy field near the campground. Mica and Henry pulled folded chairs from the back of the truck and set them up in front, the same as several other campers who had come to the field to watch the undulating spectacle overhead and sip their evening tea. Mica leaned over toward Itjanu.

"It's fly down, but this group won't be sitting here long. The store clerk said the mozzies have been god awful this season. You're gonna be wantin this pretty soon."

He handed her a small plastic spray bottle of insect repellent, and offered another to Elea who waved it away.

"Don't need that kind of thing. Our people never have."

Mica offered the bottle again. "Mozzies are different this year, Elea. Really mean spirited." Elea only shook his head and looked up at the sky, green light reflecting off his skin. Mica tossed the little bottle near the old man's foot, as a small cloud of insect spray drifted over them from behind. Mica turned in his chair.

"Step away, Lizard. Spray yourself downwind from us."

The swarms came, looking like a gray cloud arising from the tall grasses on the far side of the field where the last of the sun's heat had finally drifted away. The faint hum of the cloud in the growing darkness became shrill buzzes around ears, eyes and mouths as the insects descended for supper. The campers began to slap at themselves, and quickly surrender their spots to the mosquitoes, heading for tent screen and insect spray within the campground, some even leaving their chairs behind in their rush to escape. Henry completed his whole body spray, just as Itjanu and Mica began their own dances with the little bottle in one hand and slapping at the mosquitoes with the other. Even Elea, with an aggravated grump, reached down near his foot and picked up Mica's gift. They were forced closer together by the aggressiveness of the mosquitoes, each person giving the exterior air around them individual spritzes of the repellent, striking back at menacing individual mosquitoes. They were on the verge of retreating to the truck cab, when the air above was brushed by wide dark wings. The mosquito cloud was broken and scattered in dozens of smaller flocks and clumps, spiraling in the backwash of disturbed air.

Malcolm stepped down on to the field in the green darkness in front of them and quickly folded his wings behind. His smile showed as he came close, and the mosquitoes disappeared into the night air.

"I've been watching from the ridge, waiting for a chance to get down to you. Thanks for coming out here to the field. Makes is much easier."

Mica reached out and touched his arm. "Thought this might help".

Malcolm put his paw gently on his shoulder. "Thanks, mate." Then turned to the others. "So, what's the plan? I saw that they've put restricted signs all around the platform. What's that all about?"

"Let's just go," Henry said.

"Wait a minute, fellah." Itjanu held up her hand to Henry, who was starting toward the back of the truck. She turned back to Malcolm. "The park authorities have put the platform off limits until the Aurora is gone."

"To Hell with that. We have to go! Now!" Henry almost shouted.

Itjanu stepped over to Henry and placed a pointed finger in the middle of his chest. "You just wait!" Then she turned to Malcolm and her grandfather. "Do we have everything we need?"

Both shrugged their shoulders. Malcolm looked down at Elea for his answer.

"I'm afraid it's the Lizard's ceremony. We have the larger opal, and I'm sure it will do, but he's the only one that knows what it takes to make the ceremony work."

Henry turned toward Malcolm. "Everything in the back of the truck needs to get up to the platform where we were the first time..."

"- and all the trails are blocked or restricted," Injanu said.

"- and the Aurora is starting to weaken," Henry added.

"- and I have a bloody question," Mica shouted.

Malcolm spun around. "So ask the bloody question!"

"That tale you told us about saving that plane. Was it true?"

Malcolm rolled his palms up and bobbled his head. "Well, yes."

"Then, can you fly us all up there in my truck?"

Malcolm was silent a few moments and looked keenly at the truck. "Yes, I think so."

"Not good enough, mate. Can ya or can't ya?"

Elea nudged Malcolm with his stick. "So, grab ahold of the truck and see if ya can – with no one in it, of course."

Malcolm placed his paws on his hips and looked at Elea. Then he looked at the truck. Then he looked back at Elea. "Don't see any reason why not." Then he looked around the field and in the direction of the campground. "Nobody out watching, and it's pretty dark...all right, I'll do it.

Malcolm stepped up onto the side of the truck bed, forcing the truck springs down as far as they could go on that side, while Mica winced and looked away. Malcolm rested his other foot on the other side, allowing the springs to level out with an inch to spare, then placed his paws on the edges of the roof, with his claws curling inside the window and puncturing the ceiling fabric. Not satisfied with his position, Malcolm searched out better positions for his feet to gain a hold on the truck, shifting his hips closer, then farther back, and then closer to the cab again.

Henry sighed and folded his arms. "Are you going to fly it up or just have sex with it?"

Mica pulled a stem of field grass from his mouth and pointed it at Malcolm, smiling. "Hey, mate. That's a one man truck, and she's bloody well spoken for! A man and his hen house, and all that, you know!"

Itjanu punched Mica lightly with her fist. "Oh shut up, and don't distract him. He's trying to get to the center of gravity."

Mica reached out and tickled Itjanu's nose with the grass. "Thank you, *Doctor*."

Finally Malcolm rotated his foot claws to firmly grab the edges of the truck bed. There was a loud metallic crunch as the metal folded within his grip. He looked back over his shoulder at Mica. "Sorry."

Mica just shook his head and threw his hands up into the air. "Take her up."

Malcolm extended his wings and began to push the air down around the truck, stirring up the sand beneath the grass into a cloud that enveloped him. The others backed away coughing and covering their mouths. Malcolm had to push down harder and harder, trying to lift the truck, blowing winds of dust in all directions, flapping his wings faster and faster, but the truck did not rise. Finally, Malcolm held his wings still and let the dust settle and drift away in the gentle evening breeze floating down the hillside.

Henry kicked at the ground. "Well, that's not going to work."

Malcolm shook his head. "Yeah, it will. Yeah, it will. I don't think I was holding my wings right. I think I need to curve the tips down more- hey, I'm still learning at this!"

Once again Malcolm began to beat his wings, not as fast as before, but with greater downward curvature capturing more air with each pump, blowing more wind and dust out away from the truck each time. Once again the truck was contained in the dust cloud, and with the rush of wind and the beating of the wings, the old springs under the truck began to stretch again. Then with surges of air rushing up under the truck, Malcolm began lifting the truck inches, then feet, then yards into the air. He rose higher and higher into the night sky until the people in the field could no longer see him, until he could see the Flinders Range far to the west, and until he could see the flatlands beyond the ranges. Malcolm tilted to his left to begin his glide back down to the ground, but as he did a pack shifted in the back of the truck and flew against the side of the truck bed, ready to drop out. Quickly Malcolm tilted his wings to the right to correct for the pack and keep it from falling out – but over corrected, and pack shot out of the truck bed propelling toward the surface.

"Uh, Oh!"

Malcolm secured his grip on the truck, the claw tips of his paws actually puncturing the roof to rest against the side of his thumbs. He angled himself and the front of the truck into a steep nose dive, and shot after the falling pack, intent on catching it in the truck bed. Going straight down and pushing the falling wind hard with his wings to make himself go faster and faster, Malcolm rocketed toward the falling pack and the onrushing ground. At less than 100 feet, he swooped under the pack, catching it in the truck bed, then spiraled upward again to slow his plummet. Then he barrel rolled to bring himself and the truck upright again, and smiled proudly to himself at his reflexes and dexterity, as the momentum of his last turn catapulted the entire contents of the truck bed between his legs, over the roof of the cab, into the air in front of the truck, and above his friends in the field below.

"Aw Shit!" Malcolm called out to his friends, "Look out!!", as Mica and Injanu called out from below, "Run!!"

The group ran in all directions from the oncoming supplies shooting down from the sky. Just clearing the people, the bundles of supplies, camping gear, and back packs began to slam down onto the ground, THAK – THAK – THAK, like a string of asteroids hitting the moon. Malcolm followed the bundles, landing the truck with a too heavy thud, microseconds behind the bundles.

Malcolm released his claws from his crushed metal grip areas, his claw tips screeching across the paintless surfaces, and stepped to the ground between the truck and the mangled bundles of supplies. As the dust drifted away in the green light of the Aurora and the group returned from the far edges of the field to inspect the damage to their supplies, Malcolm turned his palms up and shrugged his shoulders, offering a weak haggard smile to his friends. With another screech, the tightly compressed springs of the truck finally pushed back up, bouncing the old truck like an eager puppy.

Henry was the first to return. "Well, I'm damned sure sitting INSIDE the truck!"

Two hours later Mica, Itjanu, Elea and Henry compressed themselves into the truck cab, after Henry finally agreed to the humiliation of sitting on Elea's lap and Malcolm closed the cab door from the outside.

"He better not drop us," Henry whined.

Mica spoke with his shoulder twisted down next to the driver's side door. "Relax Lizard. He's taken this thing up three more times since that first try, and did it perfectly. Anyways, he might drop you, or even one of us blokes, but no way he's gonna drop our Ittie."

Itjanu elbowed Mica in his side. "Oh, shut up, Mica. How could you even imagine something like that?"

"Oow! You still got boney elbows. And you know exactly what I'm sayin. I see the way he looks at you."

Itjanu struggled to turn her shoulders toward Mica. "The way he looks at me? He looks at me like a desert toad looking at a witchity grub! He's a reptile, and reptiles have no emotions."

"Aw Ittie, you know that ain't so. He's no more a reptile than you or me. That's just outside stuff."

Elea squeezed forward to look at Mica. "Well, that's big damned outside stuff. And don't be thinking about that creature and my granddaughter in the same thought. Least not til we get him fixed."

Itjanu jerked her head around giving her grandfather a cold stare. Elea just barely shrugged his shoulders in the cramped darkness. "I was just saying..."

The truck shook as Malcolm settled in the bed behind the cab and fixed his four grips. Then the truck began to rock as Malcolm pumped his wings, and the springs squeaked as their load lightened. The area around the truck was once again engulfed in a cloud of dust, and the cab shuttered with each downbeat of the huge leather wings. The rear of the truck rose a few inches, tilting the passengers in the cab toward the dashboard. Then the front tires lifted off the ground, dangling from the suspension mounts and the steering wheel swiveled eerily free in Mica's hands.

The ground in front of the truck dropped below the hood, and with each surge of Malcolm's wings four stomachs told their owners they were rising higher and higher. They cleared the dust cloud over the ground and the sky was full of the Aurora and stars above it. Even in the darkness they could see the tree lines fall away below them, and they drifted over them surging forward and upward to the rhythm of Malcolm's wings. The surges were no longer desperate, but more like the first upward turn of a circus Ferris wheel, up and out, up and out. The motion was steady and controlled. Malcolm smiled to himself, knowing his strength was nowhere near its maximum, and his friends were safe with him. Farther away from the campground and office lights they sailed up over the trees, through the pass in the mountain range, above the roped off trail and the brook tumbling beside it, and the faint yellow spot of light reflecting off the water.

Below them in the darkness among the trees, crossing the last single plank foot bridge over the brook, two park rangers made their way slowly toward the campground office after checking the platform and ensuring all the safety lines stretched across the platform access trails were secure.

"We shoulda knocked off an hour ago. You know that, don't ya?"

"Ah, no worries. We got torches. We've been along these trails a hundred times. Besides, we had to check that one last line at the base below the viewing platform. Somebody keeps messing with it."

"Could have checked it first thing in the morning. Nobody gonna try these trails at night. Nobody with any sense, at least. Nobody with any more bloody sense, that is, more than me and my corporal..."

"Ah quit your griping, Axel. Sadie will still be there,...course unless Scotty comes back early with his water truck.."

"— that's it! I told you not to bring that up again, Rob. Why the bloody— "

" What was that?"

"You know damned well— "

"No. Look up. What the hell is that— no, turn off your torch."

"Turn off my torch??"

"Turn it off. Now! Look up there. Between those two trees at the crossover rock ahead. See that??"

"What the— "

"Is that a chopper with its lights out?"

"Can't hear it Rob, the gurgling from the brook here won't let us hear much—"

"We'd hear a bloody chopper— "

"Maybe not one of those new quiet ones..."

They stood together and watched the black outline above them sail toward the platform.

"Rob, it's carrying something, something squarish, but I think I get a glimpse of the rotor every now and then. Must be a chopper. One of the quiet ones? Wouldn't that be military?"

"Not in my territory, Axel. A national park is no place for soldiers to be playin their war games. Come on! We're gonna go kick their assess out!"

"Wait a minute, Rob. Hold on! We need to go tell the sergeant. We're two kilometers from the platform, but less than a kilometer from the office. Be there in a jif."

"Be at Sadie's in a jif, you mean. No, by the time the sergeant makes a dozen phone calls and get's told to bugger off by the Army, those blokes in the chopper will play their games, scratch the place up, leave a mess of ration cartons, and be on their way. No way, mate. We're catchin'em and <u>takin' names</u>. Move out, Ranger!" He slapped his shirt pocket as he turned, making sure his notebook and pens were at the ready. Axel sagged and whined.

"Aw hell, it's gonna take us an hour to..."

Ranger Corporal Robert MacAurther was already quick stepping back across the plank footbridge, his knees stiff, his fists pumping back and forth across in front of his shined uniform belt, and his eyes squinting hard above a grimly set jaw. Behind him, falling quickly farther behind, stoop shouldered, shaking his head and muttering to himself, Probationary Ranger Axel Smithers begrudgedly, but obediently, followed in the faint green light.

The foundation of the viewing platform was solidly anchored in the short hard rock ridge, and rose up several meters to allow a good view of the pound. Malcolm gently settled the truck tires straddling the ridge crest, and kept his claws firmly clamped to the edges of the truck body until he was sure it was well settled. The crest slope on the passenger side was far too steep for safe walking, and abruptly ended in a fifty meter drop. So, all the passengers got out from the driver's side and made their way to the closest flat rock slabs where the metal platform steps began. Malcolm began to unload the back of the truck and hand packs and bundles to the others. Henry pushed next to Malcolm and reached in for his own pack.

"I need my pack first! Get my pack for me. There. There! Get it!"

"Hold you horses, Henry. I'm getting it. We need everything out of here, anyway."

"I need my pack, first! I need to check my notes again. We might have to change something this time. Not sure." He snatched his pack from Malcolm's paws and dashed for the platform steps. Mica stepped in front of Henry, blocking his way.

"You need to BE sure, Lizard."

174

Henry looked up at Mica and pushed his glasses back on the bridge of his nose with his finger. "I will. I will. Just get out of my way."

Mica looked over at Elea and shared short wags of their heads at Henry's behavior. Elea shrugged his shoulders. "Lizard's getting feisty."

Henry dashed up the steps to the platform, and settled into a corner with his back against the safety railing. He pulled a small battery light from his pack and stretched its strap around his head, leaving it mounted on his forehead and shining anywhere he turned his head. Then he pulled three of his notebooks from his pack and began to flip through the pages, reading selected passages by his forehead light. He looked up and spoke to Itjanu, his nose and moving mouth appearing suspended below the glare of his light.

"Take the coil of cord from the blue bag, and start cutting lengths about two feet long." Then he pointed at Mica to bring up the metal poles. "Put one of those in each corner and tie them tightly in place with the cord that she is cutting. Leave the longer pole in the middle."

Mica mumbled to himself, "Bossy little bugger..."

Elea brought up another bundle and dropped it heavily next to Henry, then nudged him with his walking stick. "No pushing or hitting my granddaughter this time. You got that? Right, Lizard?"

Henry sighed and looked up at the old man in silence, his lips pressed firmly together. After a short moment he spoke to the old man again.

"Henry."

"What?"

"Henry. My name is Henry, not Lizard. Call me Henry. Say it."

Elea held his stick in both hands and leaned against it. "If this works and no one gets hurt, I will be happy to call you Henry,...Lizard."

Henry shook his head looking at the man, then pushed out a loud sigh, and returned to re-reading the pages in his notebooks. Itjanu stepped next to Elea and placed her hand on his forearm.

"Grandfather, if this works and no one gets hurt, then Malcolm will be human again,...and that little man...will be ten feet tall. Maybe we shouldn't taunt him for now."

Elea turned away to go after another bundle from the truck, mumbling to himself as he walked. "He will still be a small man...and a big flying,... Lizard."

Malcolm landed gently on the platform carrying the rest of the supplies from the truck, and set them in the center of the platform, speaking toward Henry. "OK, professor, what do we do now?"

Henry held up a notebook in Malcolm's direction. " Here. Read through these pages. You will have to chant them when we start the ceremony."

Malcolm took the notebook carefully in his claw tips, and held it up to the Aurora light to read, mumbling as he read. After reading several lines he stopped and looked over at Henry. "This isn't English. Is it Latin? What the hell does all this gibberish mean, anyway."

Henry let out another harsh sigh. "It's far older than Latin, but it doesn't matter what it is or what it means. Just say it! Pretend it means, 'I'm tired of taking up space in this body and I want to give it to Henry'!"

Malcolm raised his head smiling and looked around at the others. "That works for me." His smile lingered as he looked at Itjanu. Mica nudged her with his elbow from behind, and she whirled around and slapped him on his forearm, then pointed her finger at him.

"Don't."

"I was just..."

"—Don't."

Henry stood and walked to one of the metal poles tied in a corner. He slipped an ornate metal cap on the top the pole. The top of the cap ended in a set of prongs resembling slender clawed fingers and thumbs, but with only three fingers. Malcolm watched and looked down at his own hand, recognizing the resemblance. Henry then walked to the middle of the platform carrying the longest pole, pulling Malcolm by his hand with him, and handed the pole to Malcolm.

"Here you take this one, and hold it straight up. Then you stand over here." He pointed to a location at the

176

exact center of the platform. "Wait a minute..." and he ran back to his pack for another prong, which he slipped onto Malcolm's pole. "Hold that pole with one hand and hold your notebook in the other. You'll need to read your lines when I tell you." As Henry walked away, Malcolm looked around the platform and then adjusted his position so the pole was in the exact center. Henry saw the movement.

"No! You stand where I tell you! YOU are in the center and the pole is three feet in front of you."

Malcolm shook his head. "I just don't want to be hit by lightning again. That hurt!"

Henry pointed back to Malcolm's first position. "If you don't stand where I tell you, you WILL get hit by the lightning! It will go wherever the central orb is standing."

Henry turned back to his pack and smiled to himself. *'Oh it will go through you, you idiot. It will go through you and it will hurt like hell – worse than before. Then it will go into me and that will hurt like hell too, but then I will be reborn – and you will die.'*

Still smiling, Henry placed a glass-encased jewel in each of the corner prongs. As he centered each orb, he pressed a small button at the base of the prong and the claw tips snapped tight against the orbs, holding them firmly in place. Henry went to Elea and held out his hand.

"Give it to me."

Elea gently removed the black opal from his waist pouch and handed it to Henry. Then Henry returned to the middle and pulled down on the pole Malcolm was holding, and set the opal into the center of the prongs.

"You hold that straight." He turned to the others. "All of you. Make sure the poles are straight. And don't say anything until we are done!" Henry went to the fourth corner, gripped the remaining pole in one hand and raised his notebook in the other, so he could see it in the yellow beam shining from his forehead. He looked back at Malcolm and pointed to him with his notebook. "I will read a line, then you will read a line. Read it loud, but

177

don't start reading until the echo of my voice is gone. Count to three, then start reading. You got that?"

"Yeah, I got it, Henry."

"All right, this first part is kind of long, so just stand still and shut up until I finish. Then Malcolm, you count to three and start reading your next line. Just the next line. No more. You got that?"

"Yeah, I got it, Henry. I got it."

Malcolm looked around the skyline and overhead. Except for the Aurora and a field of stars, the sky was clear of anything else.

Henry took in a deep breath, and began to read loudly, his tone much like a liturgy, but the words foreign and unrecognizable, some not even sounding like words at all. His voice grew louder and punctuated some of the words. The words were angry, menacing, almost accusatory in their sounds. Louder and louder, Henry's usually frail voice boomed into the night air and echoed off the nearby rocks.

When he had finished his long first passage, all the others were lost in their own thoughts at what they had just heard, lost in the silence that followed. Finally Malcolm shook his head, raised his notebook that had drifted down to his side while listening to Henry, and opened his mouth to read his first line. Henry stomped his foot, vibrating the grid under their feet.

"No! No! No! You MUST come in on the count of three! The timing of each statement is critical!!" He turned and pointed his notebook at Itjanu. "And YOU! Keep that pole STRAIGHT!"

Mica shifted where he stood. "Now, Liz...Now, Henry, we don't wanna—"

"Shut up!" Henry took in a deep breath, held it for a few heartbeats, then blew it out. He spoke through gritted teeth. "Do you people want to help Malcolm or not? He does not want to stay the way he is. You have said that you want to help him, and I have said that I am willing to take on the form, to, to...to save our friend."

The others nodded.

"All right, then. We need to go through this ceremony the way I have described it. Why? Because Malcolm there is proof I know how to do it. So,...let's keep the poles straight, the mouths shut, pay attention, and Malcolm, begin your lines on the count of three after I am finished each time!"

"Got it. Count of three."

Henry adjusted his forehead lamp, took in another deep breath, and began reading the first passage again. At the end of the passage, after three heartbeats, Malcolm read his first line. Three heartbeats after that, Henry read his next line. Line followed line. Both voices grew louder, firmer, more determined to make the sounds known to the night. Line followed line. Incantation followed counter incantation. Call and response. Call and response. Seconds grew to minutes, the minutes stacked upon each other, and the southern cross high above the Aurora began the first degrees of its nightly rotation.

The wind came across the savannah of the pound and slipped gently up the slope below the viewing platform, rustling the clothing of the group as it arrived. The lingering heat of the day baked into the rocks around the platform finally dissipated and the wind pushed it off the crest, and cooler air rushed in to take its place. The wind freshened and shirtsleeve edges rippled, flaps on back packs began a lazy dance on the face of the packs. Then the coolness of the wind tingled the hair on exposed arms and legs, and goose bumps arose to the chill. The force of the wind grew to a noticeable whisper.

Henry and Malcolm threw out their voices louder and stronger, and now the space of time between lines was barely two heartbeats, and the rhythm of the readings were faster. The rhythm of the readings and the wind matched and paced each other. The voices grew in strength to match the wind, and the wind grew in strength to match the incantations. Line followed line. Line followed line.

The wind came in gusts that grew with each couplet. At each corner, feet shifted slightly farther apart to stand firm in the wind, and grips hardened around the poles and the platform railings. Even Malcolm had squatted down and brought his wings in tighter against his back so they would not inadvertently catch the wind and lift him off.

On the lines went, louder and more forceful, but barely finding their way above the sound of the roaring wind whipping around the platform, drawing in clouds from over the tops of the mountain ridges. Both Henry and Malcolm had reached their last page. They were racing through their lines, dashing to the bottom of the page like lemmings charging the edge of a cliff in mad reach for the abyss beyond. The clouds rushed up to the platform, swirling around them with flashes of green lightning racing along the edges of the whirlwind. Four lines left on each page. Call and response. Challenge and counter challenge. Incantation and counter incantations.

Thud! The sound of a heavy hit on the metal grate vibrated throughout the platform. Hearts jerked to the physical impact. Minds raced to comprehend, to anticipate the next phenomena.

"What the bloody hell is going on here, I might ask!"

Another red dust covered Ranger boot stomped on to the grate to reinforce his statement. Ranger Corporal Robert MacAurther had arrived to do his duty.

"Shit!" Henry screamed and shook his notebook violently, as the clouds and the wind, and Malcolm, disappeared.

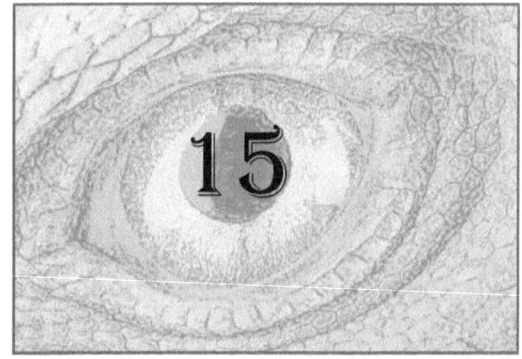

Soaring up and out of sight, only a wisp of Malcolm's tail flipped among the drifting clouds at the edge of Corporal MacAurther's vision, as the Ranger stepped toward the center of the platform. MacAurther placed his hands on his hips and looked around the platform, staring into the eyes of each person.

"This platform is off limits for the rest of the season. There are signs every one hundred meters on every trail coming this way, telling you people that. And there are keep away lines across every trail every two hundred meters. Now – what – the – Hell – are you people doing up here!"

Itjanu stepped closer to the Ranger. "Sir, this is an extremely important ceremony, and we must complete it. We have to..."

"—No!" Screamed Henry. "Tell him nothing!"

The Ranger jabbed an angry finger at Henry, stepping toward him and letting a deep frown settle across his forehead. He opened his mouth to speak to Henry as his vision swept across the platform railing and onto the crest of the adjacent ridge. Seeing the old pickup truck perched across the crest, MacAurther stopped in mid step with his finger still pointing at Henry, but staring opened mouthed at the truck.

A frown settled down across the Ranger's face and he let his hand drift down by his side where his thumb hooked onto his uniform belt. He closed his mouth

181

tightly and tilted his head as he concentrated his thoughts on the old blue truck. Then he spun around with his hands on his hips and gave a crisp military stamp of his boot.

"Right, then. First things first, people. One of you call back your chopper and get that rusty piece of garbage off my mountain! While it's on its way, the rest of you start collecting your mess kits and go put them in the back of the truck."

He swept his eyes across the faces of the small group, still frozen in their places and positions, staring dumbly back at him."Let's snap to it, people! We're cleaning up this little shindig, moving all your gear off my mountain, and then we are going to pay a nice friendly visit to my Sergeant back at the station."

The group looked back at him, slowly shaking their heads, and then one by one let their gazes drift upward.

The Ranger stamped his foot again. "No Aurora worshipping tonight, people. You are coming along as my guests where we can put you under lock and key until we sort all this out. Now, what..."

The eyes of the group slowly drifted back down to the Ranger, as a slight wind puffed from behind him, barely ruffling the fabric of his uniform shirt. A warm moist breath slid down around his head and shoulders, and two huge clawed hands slipped around his arms and waist, gently squeezing into a tender grip. Malcolm brought the Ranger's back tenderly against his chest, and his calm voice vibrated through the man's bones as he spoke.

"I'm sorry officer, but we can't let you do that."

MacAurther hesitated, then forced himself to look up toward the source of the voice, where he met Malcolm's face bending down to him from behind. They stared into each other's eyes, chin to forehead. MacAurther swallowed. The backward arch of his neck made the travel of his adam's apple long and ungainly.

"Good God."

Malcolm smiled. "How ya' doin'?"

MacAurther swallowed again, trying to regain enough moisture in his throat to speak, and then took in a deep breath. "You're under arrest."

Mica slapped his hands together, breaking the trance on the platform. He let out a short chuckle and looked around at the others with a wide grin. "The man's got spunk!"

Henry blinked his eyes, and stepped over to the Ranger in Malcolm's grip. He thumped his pole on the platform and put his other hand on his hip.

"Nobody is ever going to believe you if you tell them what you saw here tonight, so I might as well tell you what is going on. First, we are not worshipping the Aurora, but you're damned close. This is a ceremony to transform the guy behind you from a ten foot flying lizard back into the Yank redneck he was before he stuck his nose where it didn't belong."

Malcolm muttered from above the Ranger's head. "I'm not the lizard. That's you." He added proudly, " I'm Dingo Ass."

Henry grit his teeth and rolled his eyes up into his eyelids, then shook his head. He returned his attention to the Ranger and tapped his finger against the center of the man's chest.

"So, we've got to get you out of our way, so we can complete our ceremony. Now, do you want that alive or dead?"

"Wh-what?"

"Alive or dead? How would you prefer to stay out of the ceremony? Alive or dead?"

MacAurther nodded his head yes several times, his mouth opening and closing, then finally spoke. "Alive. Oh yes, alive. Definitely alive. Definitely."

Malcolm spoke to Henry from above. "Give me a few minutes. I'll be right back."

Henry turned away speaking over his shoulder. "Hurry it up. We don't have much of the night left."

MacAurther looked back and forth between Henry and Malcolm, then snapped his head down as the ground faded away from him. He watched his cap sailing back toward the ground as he soared up into the night sky within Malcolm's grip. "O-o-o-o-o-o-o-h-h-h-h..."

Ten minutes later, Malcolm touched down at a small tourist station, closed for the night, sitting near the highway leading up to Wilpena Pound, and several miles beyond the National Park. MacAurther snatched himself away from Malcolm's loosening grip and whirled around to face his captor. The Ranger jerked out his revolver and pointed it at Malcolm.

"I don't know what the bloody hell is going on, but I'm not going to let some...some..."

Malcolm squatted down with his elbows on his knees and tucked his wings in behind. He snapped the pistol out of the man's hand with his claw tips, and tossed it into the nearby spinifex.

"We mean you no harm, officer. The little man up on that platform told you the truth. All we are trying to do is get me out of this thing I have become, so I can be human again. We will do no harm to the park, nor to anyone else. The first time it happened by accident, and I became this. Now we need to do it again to un-do this." Malcolm pointed to himself, then sighed and offered his palms toward the man. "You have a long walk back, but it's not too far I don't think. Five or ten miles maybe. It shouldn't be difficult. We just need the time." Malcolm stood and turned away, spreading his wings.

MacAurther pointed his finger at Malcolm's back and yelled out, "Yeah..well...next time I see you I'm going to arrest you! Just..you...just you know that."

Malcolm turned back to face him. The Ranger stood there with his arms folded across his chest and his chin up. Malcolm smiled and placed his paw gently on the man's shoulder. "What's your name, officer?"

The officer glared into Malcolm's yellow eyes. "Ranger Corporal Robert Beverly MacAurther."

"You're a good man, Robert Beverly MacAurther." Malcolm flew into the air and out of sight.

Moments later Malcolm settled once again on the viewing platform in Wilpena Pound. Henry pushed his assigned pole and notebook into Malcolm's hands saying, "Finally." Then he took his position beyond

Malcolm. Henry spoke louder so everyone could hear him. "We are going to start from the beginning. Hold the pole straight and still. No one speaks but me and Malcolm." Henry glared at each person around him. Mica returned his eye contact and then spat over the railing. Looking down where he spat he saw the rangers cap lying at the foot of the platform.

Henry sighed, flicked on the switch to his forehead light, opened his notebook and began reading the first segment. When he finished, he looked toward Malcolm, who took his cue and began reading the next segment. Once again, Henry read his next line. Line followed line. Both voices grew louder, firmer, more determined to make the sounds known to the night. Line followed line, this time with better coordination, more force, more intensity. Incantation followed counter incantation. Call and Response. Call and Response.

At last, the wind returned across the savannah of the pound and slipped gently up the slope below the viewing platform, rustling the clothing of the group as it arrived. Again, the wind freshened and shirt sleeve edges rippled, flaps on back packs began a lazy dance on the face of the packs. Then the coolness of the wind carried a heavier chill, the force of the wind grew. Henry and Malcolm threw out their voices louder and stronger, and now the space of time between lines was barely two heartbeats, and the rhythm of the readings were faster.

The rhythm of the readings and the wind matched and paced each other. The voices grew in strength to match the wind, and the wind grew in strength to match the incantations. Line followed line. The wind came in gusts that grew with each couplet. At each corner feet shifted slightly farther apart to stand firm in the wind, and grips hardened around the poles and the platform railings. Malcolm brought his wings in tightly against his back and spread his feet to brace his stance.

On the lines went, louder and more forceful, but barely finding their way above the sound of the roaring wind whipping around the platform, drawing in clouds from over the tops of the mountain ridges. Both Henry and Malcolm had reached their last page. They were racing through their lines, dashing to the bottom of the page. The clouds, fat and dark this time, rushed up to the platform, swirling around them with flashes of green lightning racing along the edges of the whirlwind. Four lines left on each page. Call and Response. Challenge and counter challenge. Incantation and counter incantations.

Malcolm yelled his last line into the roar of the wind and spatter of the rain. An ancient call leapt from Henry's lips, a command shouted in a language no longer spoken by the living. The clouds were a swirling wall around Malcolm and Henry. Lightning flashed within the clouds like green explosions followed immediately by explosion of thunder that shook the platform. High above the tempest, the lower edge of the Aurora flashed bright and pulsated, then sent a near perfectly straight lightning bolt down toward the platform.

In an instant, the beam split just above the platform and struck all four objects gripped at the tips of the poles. The four beams then shot into the opal at the tip of Malcolm's pole, combined once again and fired directly into Malcolm's chest. For a fraction of a second the light connected straight from the Aurora, through the objects, into the great opal and then poured into Malcolm's chest.

Malcolm roared with pain. A green corona ran the length of his body. Tendrils of intense green light snaked out from his body in all directions, creating a sphere of light around him. More energy pulsed into his body. His wings spread and the corona spread along their edges. He flung his arms out, releasing the pole, screaming with the pain. The beam of energy no longer needed the opal or the other objects. It poured straight down from the Aurora directly into Malcolm's chest.

Henry dashed forward and pulled the head off Malcolm's pole. Malcolm roared again, shaking his arms and wings, but unable to move from his spot. Henry pressed the opal against his own chest, squeezed his eyes shut and gritted his teeth. Then he yelled the last command a second time. Green lightning exploded out Malcolm's back and drilled point blank through the opal into Henry's frail chest, driving him against the rail. He screamed a shrill piercing cry of torment.

Electrical veins spread from his hair and ears and off the edges of his teeth. The opal vaporized in an iridescent cloud the size of a human heart in front of his chest. He screamed again, shrill and agonizing. The light pulsed into his body and he was completely engulfed in incandescent green light. Only his scream remained. And he screamed again within the light.

The bolt of lightning severed from the Aurora and continued to flow down to the platform, where it finally passed through Malcolm into Henry's body. Henry slumped to the platform, as the last of the energy ran into him. One by one the others stood up, but Malcolm and Henry lay unconscious. The Aurora faded. The clouds evaporated. The wind sighed and then lay still on the floor of the pound. The stars of the Southern Cross showed brightly in the night sky. Nothing in Wilpena Pound moved or made a sound. Silence wrapped everyone like a heavy wool blanket.

Henry rolled over on to his side gasping for air and retching. Malcolm lay in his naked human body, motionless. Mica and Itjanu ran to him. Mica wrapped him in a blanket and Itjanu felt for a pulse.

"He has no pulse and he's not breathing!" She looked at Mica, "Lay him flat!"

She brought her hands together in a ball and struck his chest, tilted his head back to open his airway and blew into his lungs, then leaned her shoulders up over his and began to compress his chest, again, again and again. Moments slipped by. She blew into his lungs again, and returned to the compressions. Moments slipped into minutes. Her shoulders and arms trembled. Mica pulled at her.

"I know how to do this from the army. Take a rest." He resumed the chest compressions and blew into Malcolm's lungs. More minutes passed. Itjanu returned and relieved Mica. The quiet on the platform with the air still and unmoving, was punctuated only by the muffled grunts of Mica and Itjanu working to make Malcolm's heart beat. After uncounted minutes Itjanu stopped her compressions and looked up to her grandfather.

"He is still in there, Ittie. Bring him out."

Again Mica relieved Itjanu and minutes later she returned to take her turn. As she bent down to blow air into his lungs again, she jerked up back straight, then with all her remaining strength she slapped Malcolm's face.

"O-o-o-ow-w!!!"

"You tongued me! You wicked Yank. I'm trying to save your worthless life and you tongue me?"

He rolled onto his side and held up his hands to deflect another slap. "Thought I was dreaming! Thought I was back before I became this thing!" Then his eyes flew wide open and he sat up, reaching toward Itjanu, "I didn't hurt you, did I?"

Itjanu wiped the back of her hand across her mouth. "Don't flatter yourself Yank. You have nothing to hurt anyone."

Malcolm noticed his hand and arm, and became mesmerized examining it.

"My God. It worked. It worked!"

He pulled the blanket off himself and looked over as much of his body as he could see.

"It worked! I'm Human. I'm human! Look! I'm Human!"

Itjanu turned her head and tossed the blanket back to him, then looked around the platform.

"Where's Henry?"

Henry was gone from the platform. She looked at Mica who shrugged his shoulders to the unasked question.

"I was looking in here."

Then she looked at her Grandfather, who pointed first at the empty ridge where the truck had been and then to the sky.

"Little Lizard ain't so little anymore."

Itjanu and Mica slumped to the platform, resting their backs and shoulders and arms. Malcolm had removed his blanket again and was enjoying looking at his normal flabby body. Elea stood at the far corner of the platform leaning against his stick, looking out over the pound below as the sun began to rise over the far rim.

"Gonna be a hot day, and a long walk."

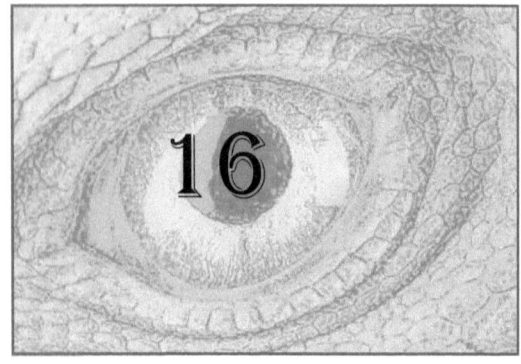

500 miles north west, barely in sight of the Stuart Highway beyond Coober Pedy, a group of red kangaroos were nibbling their breakfast among the sparse vegetation and looked up at the sound of something whistling through the air. Twisting their heads to look at the strange object slipping toward them, they stood mesmerized while an old blue truck plummeted from the sky and crashed into the ground killing two of their group. The surviving reds scrambled off in all directions to avoid similar fates, and a gigantic green flying lizard with bat like wings twenty feet across landed next to the crumpled truck. Pulling the kangaroos out from underneath it by their legs, it ate them both, bones and all.

The heat of the sun had already driven the temperature up fifteen degrees in Wilpena Pound by the time the four people walked down the metal steps of the platform. In Henry's rush to scoop up everything from the platform and rush off with the truck, he had inadvertently left behind Mica's pack, and his own. Mica shared the single water bottle from his pack with the others, in the tradition of the Agnanu. Malcolm, still wrapped in a blanket like an old American television version of an Indian, carried down Henry's notebooks. Mica ambled over to the corner post under the platform support to retrieve the ranger's cap, and then froze, pointing farther under the platform.

"Uh Oh!"

Laying sprawled out on his back in the shade under the platform was Probationary Ranger Axel Smithers. Mica reached down to check the side of his neck for a pulse, then sighed and looked back at the others.

"Can't leave him here. Sun'll be on him in a minute or two."

Itjanu came under the platform and kneeled next to the ranger, patting his face firmly to wake him up. He sat up quickly with his eyes popping wide open.

"Robert, look out!! It's a monster!!" Then he looked around at the faces watching him. "My God! Did it eat him? Did it? Where's Robert?"

Mica nudged the Ranger's leg with his boot toe.

"He's gone. The monster took him away."

The Ranger threw his hands up to cover his face.

"Oh no!! I failed him. I failed Robert!"

Itjanu slapped Mica's leg and faced the Ranger.

"He wasn't eaten. I'm sure he's all right. I think you fainted. Come with us, we're going down from here."

She reached her hand up to Mica who rolled his eyes, shook his head and then slowly handed Itjanu the water bottle. She offered the bottle to the Ranger.

"Here. Take a drink of water. We all need to get down from here."

As soon as she returned the bottle to Mica, she stood and stretched her back from side to side to relieve some of the stiffness and began to walk back down the trail. Elea and Mica slowly followed her. Malcolm flipped open his blanket to the Ranger.

"I'm not a monster. I'm human. See?"

Mica spoke over his shoulder as he rounded the first switchback.

"You gotta quit doing that, bloke."

Axel climbed up the metal stairs to the empty platform, looked around inside the railing and out over the pound, seeing no evidence of Robert. Then he followed the group back down the trail. The sun rose higher and turned the rocks on either side of the trail into an oven, baking the hikers. The sleepless night (except for Axel), the glare of the sun, the radiating heat growing hotter by the minute, drained the strength from their bodies. At each cross tie, they untied and then retied the line across the trail, helping Axel secure the trail.

Two dozen switchbacks later with their meager water long gone, the weary group finally came to the old cabin at the bottom of the trail. They slipped under the welcoming shade among the trees and took advantage of the little cabin porch to rest their feet, until thirst pushed them on. In silence they filed down the trail heading back toward the camp ground. When they came to the little single board foot bridge over the creek, none of them even hesitated before stepping into the cool water and sitting chest deep in it.

"Not really supposed to drink this," Axel said as he scooped mouthful after mouthful of the clear water. They sat in a circle near the center where the sand bottom offered a soft place and clear view of the cool water flowing around them, drinking from their cupped hands, except for Malcolm who simply dunked his face into the water until he had to raise up again to breathe. Occasionally one would look at the other and smile at the wonderful relief of the coolness and the wet and the shade as rivulets of sparkling water ran down their faces and dripped from ears and noses.

"All right, people, get out of my Creek!"

Ranger Robert MacAurther stood on the other side of the creek in rumpled sweat stained khaki shorts and shirt. His socks were down at his dust covered boot tops and his legs showed dozens of scratches from walking miles through baked spiniflex. His hair was plastered to his head, his forehead and cheeks streaked by sweat tracks through red dust. His eyes were puffy from the long sleepless walk back, which had been a grueling eighteen miles rather than a short five or ten Malcolm had estimated. His shoulders sagged and his breath came in the short pant of near exhaustion. The group in the pool could only stare back at him in wordless resignation, and each one unwilling to be the first to quit the delicious pool.

Robert thumbed his holster cover, snapping it shut, and mumbled a barely audible, "Bloody Hell." The he unbuckled his belt and let the revolver settle onto the bush by his leg and stepped into the pool, sitting next to Alex scooping up water. After several gulps he spoke to Axel.

"Nice of you to finally join me."

"I was up there Robert. I saw it."

Robert smiled and took several more gulps of water, then sprang to his feet.

"Right then. Everybody out of the pool. Time to go say hello to the Sergeant!"

As everyone stood up, the Ranger spoke to Malcolm. "Cover yourself, Bloke!"

MacAurther stepped up the bank and recovered his belt and holster, buckling it as the others came out.

"Step lively there. It's only a couple hundred yards to the Ranger Station and we'll sort all this out. You there. Where are your clothes?"

"Lost'em," Malcolm said as he walked by.

"Well, keep that blanket about you, hear?"

As Mica walked by, he handed MacAurther his cap.

"Believe this is yours."

MacAurther examined the cap closely then flipped it onto his head, pulling the bill down tight on his forehead. Herding them with directions from the rear, MacAurther steered them into the station, then had them each sign in. The station had only two lockable rooms for detainees, so he placed Itjanu in one room and the men in the other, except for Malcolm. MacAurther pointed Malcolm to the wooden bench in the little area that served as a waiting room and lobby for the station.

"Not quite sure what to do with you yet. You got a place in the campground? A place where you can get clothes on?"

Malcolm nodded his head yes.

"OK, then I'm going to send Axel there with you so you can get some clothes on and then he will escort you right back here. You understand me? You come right back here with Axel."

Malcolm nodded and walked out with Axel, while MacAurther sat in the Sergeant's office explaining his night. Fifteen minutes later Axel returned with Malcolm and found MacAurther fuming over the paperwork he faced. He told both of them to sit in the two chairs squeezed into the tiny windowless office. He pointed at Axel.

"Is that truck gone from the ridge?"

"I never saw a truck up there, Rob. And there wasn't anything on or around the platform when we left this morning."

MacAurther pressed his lips together and exhaled though his nose.

"Was this guy up there too, or did you just find him in that pool?"

"He was up there when they found me, but I don't know if he was up there last night or came up this morning."

"What do you mean 'when they found' you??"

Axel looked down at his hands and mumbled. Then took in a deep breath, looked into MacAurther's eyes and spoke up.

"I think I fainted last night, Rob. I was under the platform and they were giving me water when I came to. I climbed as fast as I could last night, but couldn't keep up with you. We'd been out there all day in that sun traipsing around the pound."

MacAurther's face was deadpan and his eyelids low over his pupils. He turned toward Malcolm.

"What about you, Nature Boy. What have you got to say for yourself?"

"I think you should just let us all go."

"Yeah, right. I'll just bet you do think that."

"If I can have just two minutes in private, I can really help you with all this. I think you will agree with me."

MacAurther looked at Malcolm's face for a long moment then turned back to Axel.

"Axel, how bout you trotting down to the campground office and fetch us some tea. You might even see how Sadie is doing while you're there."

194

Axel was out of the little office before MacAurther had finished his sentence. MacAurther smiled after the other ranger and gently shook his head. The he fixed his eyes on Malcolm, and crossed his arms in front of his chest.

"You know what, Yank. I was almost in a mood to shoot someone when I came up to that pool, thinking I was going to march right back up that hateful switchback trail and put an end to,... well, something. But,... that little dip in the water brought me back to my senses. So, I'm in the mood to let you ramble away, if for no other reason than to put off the bloody paperwork." He offered the palm of his hand toward Malcolm to speak.

"I was up there last night, Ranger Robert MacAurther. I put my arms around you and took you off that platform. I flew us out and set you down at a closed tourist station about ten miles from here, and you pulled your revolver on me. I knocked the revolver from your hands and then told you that you were a good man."

MacAurther stared at Malcolm for a long minute.

"Are you taking drugs?"

"No. And you know I'm not."

Another long minute passed.

"Twenty miles."

"What?"

"It was twenty miles, you bastard. It took me all bloody night and most of the morning to get back."

"I'm sorry. I didn't realize..."

"You gonna turn into that thing again? At night? Full moon? What?"

"I think it's over for me. It was an accident I became that thing. Some weird ancient ceremony I got in the middle of. Last night we undid it, and I'm free of it."

MacAurther tapped his fingers on the desktop. He spoke in a hushed voice, "What's my middle name? No one outside my family and my service record has that name. What's my middle name?"

"Beverly."

MacAurther scooped up the forms in front of him, wadded them into a ball and tossed them into the trash can.

195

"Bloody Hell. I had no idea how to write all that without having myself put in the looney bin. Only told the Sergeant about the trespassing."

MacAurther took his keys and unlocked both of the detainee rooms. As they filed out into the little lobby, the Sergeant stepped out of his office with a mug of tea in his hand.

"What's this then, Corporal MacAurther?"

"All a misunderstanding, Sergeant. Apparently this involved an ancient ceremony, and they didn't know to get a permit."

The Sergeant nodded his head and rocked back on his heels.

"Right then, next time let's get the proper paperwork. Do you people understand?"

All four murmured they would.

"Very well. All in a day's work. Glad the Ranger Service could assist. Free to go, then." He walked back into his office, and back to his morning newspaper. MacAurther escorted Itjanu, Mica, Elea and Malcolm out the front door and onto the porch to the Ranger Station. MacAurther shook their hands asking them where they were headed next.

Mica rubbed his head. "Well that was my blue truck up there, but don't know where it is now. I guess we need to rent a car to get back to Mutanajulu." He turned to Itjanu, "Sorry, Ittie, I guess we need to use your credit cards again..."

The door to the station flipped open and out stepped the Sergeant and pointed toward Malcolm.

"Say there, uh, Yank, what are your first and last names?"

He spoke back over his shoulder as he was stepping down from the porch, "Malcolm Ironwater."

"Ironwater. Yep. Gotta be you. Country Police found an abandoned pickup truck outside Coober Pedy, with a back pack in having your passport. What Place are you from?"

"Tooey's Crossroads, in Finton County."

"Yep it's yours. How the hell did that happen."

196

Mica stepped forward. "Had my truck stolen last night. Had all our stuff in it. His pack too."

"Whoever stole it must have driven it to pieces, that's a seven hundred kilometer drive from here. I'll tell the Hawker Police down the hill that it's yours, but you'll have to go to Coober Pedy to pick it up – or wait a week or so for them to mail it."

Malcolm had already sat down on the edge of the porch, taking deep breaths, speaking between the legs of the others, "Sorry Sergeant, got a little weak there. Say, I have to go back to Coober Pedy to get my passport?"

"'Fraid so, Yank. You've got to have it with you. Don't want to lose that thing!"

Mica and Elea looked at Itjanu and nodded their heads to her, she looked down at Malcolm. "OK Malcolm, we're going to Coober Pedy. You OK? You're looking a little green..."

"That's NOT funny!"

"...I mean pale, wane, washed out.."

"Yeah, having a little weak spell here. Haven't eaten since yesterday."

MacAurther spread his arms and ushered them all off the porch.

"Then you people need some of Sadie's cooking up at the camp store. Besides, going there may be my only way to retrieve Axel."

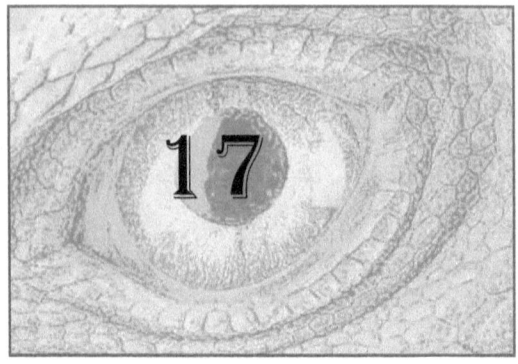

Down in Hawker, Mica found a car rental service within a repair station that offered recent but not new cars, and was able to rent a red van that would allow people to take turns napping. If the old blue truck had not been totally destroyed or the pouch under the driver's seat not discovered by Henry, there were still several small opals that could be sold in Coober Pedy without suspicion.

Mica did almost all the driving to Coober Pedy, so after a very filling evening meal at an Italian restaurant on the edge of town, Itjanu and Elea talked Mica into going to bed early while they walked around town with Malcolm, looking for new places to sell opals. Mica gave them names of places not to go, and places he had not been to before, and then ambled off to the motel room for deep sleep. Itjanu spoke with the clerks, asking about prices and the most popular colors, trying to gauge which shops were likely to pay more.

At the third shop, a narrow little place on a side street not far from the town's community drive-in theater, she noticed a police bulletin through the dusty glass of the clerk's protected booth. She could not read the words printed on the paper posted on the back wall, but even with the poor quality reproduction of a video camera picture, she knew exactly who the warning was about – Mica.

The three left the shop and quickly returned to the motel and met in Itjanu's room.

"That was Mica's picture in the shop clerk's booth. It looked like it was taken when we were here a couple days ago. I'm not sure what it's about, but the large letters I could see said 'Police Warning' and 'Stolen Property'. We cannot let Mica visit any of those shops tomorrow."

Elea shook his head. "Any Black face they don't know trying to sell opals, will cause them to call the police. Without Mica's certificate, we will have no believable way to explain how we have the opals. And we can't have anything to do with Mica and opals while that warning is out there." He poked Malcolm with the tip of a long slender finger. "It's gotta be you. You gotta sell'em."

Malcolm blinked his eyes several times before he spoke with slightly slurred words, "No pro'lem," and sweat ran down his forehead, into his eyes and down his nose dripping onto his shirt. Itjanu reached up a put the back of her fingers against his forehead.

"You're burning up! You have a fever."

"Be aright. Jus need to rest."

With a worry frown on her face she helped her grandfather stand Malcolm up and walk him next door to the other motel room where Mica was already snoring soundly. As she turned to leave for her own room, her grandfather reached out his hand and gently touched her cheek.

"Lettie lives in you, girl. She was always real proud of you."

She pressed his hand against her cheek with her own, and smiled at the realization that they could all use her Grandmother's name again. Back in her room she finally let herself slip into the deep sleep her body craved, and just as she reached the edge of the chasm where the best sleep waited, the wall next to her head vibrated to the sound of three chainsaws binding down in wet wood. She wrapped her head in the motel pillows and struggled into a fitful sleep until two am, when she took the pillows and stomped out of the room to the red van at the far end of the parking lot.

The next morning Malcolm walked stiff legged into the little restaurant operated by the motel and sat next to Elea, across the table from Mica and Itjanu and had morning coffee. He looked up at Itjanu over the rim of his coffee cup saying, "You look as bad as I feel. Couldn't sleep either?"

She looked up from her tea. "Couldn't sleep with the roar of three train engines coming from your room. Can you walk well enough to go in and sell the opals?"

"No worries. Piece a cake."

She reached across the table and felt his forehead.

"You still got a fever."

He drained his cup of coffee, standing as he did and starting to turn away from the table.

"Head's fine. Back hurts though. Forgot all about my spots back there. Guess once I get my passport, I'll need to head back to the good ol'US of A, and see what the docs can do for them."

"We got doctors here, Malcolm."

He smiled and turned back toward her, raising his finger to make a point, and then collapsed to the floor completely unconscious. When he awoke, he was lying in a hospital bed. He looked around to find a pretty standard modern hospital room that could be anywhere.

Sitting on the floor next to the bed was an Indian Warrior.

You got heap big problem, Chief.

I'm not your Chief. I am well.

You bad sick, Chief. Spot getting bigger. Gonna eat you up.

The Indian turned to smoke and drifted out into the hallway.

"Hello?" he called out. "Hello"

There were voices echoing down the hallway, and footsteps that seemed to be coming his way. He raised the white sheet over him and checked his arms, legs and abdomen for color, and smiled to himself.

"No Green."

Clipped to the edge of his folded sheet near his right arm was a call button on a white cord. He pressed it several times and was rewarded with the entrance of a young neat well scrubbed young man with a ready smile.

"Welcome back, Mister Ironwater. You've had quite the little nap."

Malcolm could only whisper "Thirsty" through his sand dry throat.

"Bet you are. Between the dehydration and the fearsome snoring you've been blessing us with day and night, I imagine your throat feels like parchment. Here suck on this." He handed Malcolm a glycerin lollypop without any noticeable flavor. "Let's get your throat limbered up for moisture before I start pouring water down the gullet. Can't have you drowning on my watch. You just give that a sucko while I get the charge nurse."

Malcolm watched the young man leave, working his tongue and throat on the lollypop like an infant frantically working a pacifier. He was still looking around the room trying to identify where he was and popping his lollypop, when the charge nurse entered the room.

"Well, welcome back to the waking, Mr. Willie, er, I mean, Mr. Ironwater. I am afraid the night nurses have named you Freight Train Willie, and I have caught the habit of using the name. Can't have that going on, can I, Mr. Ironwater? Ready for some water to drink?"

Malcolm yanked the lollypop from his mouth. "Oh Yes. Please."

"Sounds like you can handle a little."

He sat up and she handed him a little four ounce plastic cup, which he downed like a shot glass, and handed back to her. She stood there watching him for a moment, holding the cup.

"OK. That stayed down, let's try another."

He tossed back the second cup of water and asked for more, but she smiled and shook her head no.

"Not just yet, Mr. Ironwater. That was a lot for you. You've been drinking through your veins for the past four days. Give your stomach a chance to push along that much water at once, then we'll try some more." She flicked an IV bag hanging from a pole at the corner of his hospital bed. "You still have that draining in."

He noticed the bag emptied into a tube that ran down to a junction of three other tubes, which in turn fed into a tube that disappeared under the bandage wrapped over the crook in his arm. He spoke to his arm.

"What happened?"

The nurse made a few notes on her clipboard, smiled brightly to him and walked from the room, speaking over her shoulder as she left.

"Doctor will make his rounds this afternoon, and he can tell you everything then."

Malcolm leaned back onto his pillow, then pushed the bed button to raise his head up to a near sitting position. He looked around the room for some clue to where or when he was. There was no television, no calendar, no clock, no book of any kind, and no sign of any kind.

The smoke returned to his room and formed again as an Indian sitting on the floor next to his bed.

Malcolm screamed out at the top of his lungs, "Where the hell am I!!!!!"

The nurse charged to his doorway, and shoved her knuckles onto her hips, but did not see the Indian.

"Room 6!" She spun on her heels and spoke in exasperation, "Now shush!" and marched off.

Malcolm tried to get up, but his tubes would only barely let him turn over, and when he tried to lay on his side, his left side hurt him terribly. He rolled over onto his back again, slapping the bed with both hands in a brief fury, until he was exhausted again.

The Indian faded away again.

"At least I can lay on my back again," he mumbled drifting back to sleep. "Damned spot."

The room was dark when he awoke. Only a faint nightlight glimmered above his head and the lights were turned down low out in the hallway. As the sleep faded from his eyes and he could focus in the dimness, he saw a glorious image on the patient table by his bed: a clear plastic eight ounce glass of crushed ice. There was almost an inch of melted ice water in the bottom of the glass, with beads of chilled moisture tracing lines down the outside.

"How beautiful," he said to the glass, and rolled onto his side reaching for the glass. As his hand neared the glass it rose on its own and floated toward him. Another hand appeared out of the darkness beyond the nightlight holding a straw that it dropped into the ice water. As the glass neared his face his bed began to raise his head and shoulders, a face appeared in the light behind the glass, smiling at him.

"Just a sip, Cowboy", the face said.

Malcolm leaned forward to take the straw in his lips, his dry throat muscles already swallowing, eager for the cold water. He glanced up at the smiling face wondering where he had seen it before, knowing he had, knowing he knew her, and then the wonderful ice water finally slipped up the straw and dripped gently over his tongue. The first swallow was only a coating, but the second was full and heavenly, and he closed his eyes to the magnificence of it. He drew on the straw, but the other end gurgled in the bottom of the glass. His lips tried to pursue the straw as the hand holding it withdrew it back into the darkness, and his head drifted back down into the pillow. He could almost feel that one chilled swallow flow within his entire body, cooling it, and he slipped back down into the well of sleep.

"Not so loud, Mac."

Malcolm had heard a voice before that, but was just waking up and couldn't understand what it had said. He looked at the patient table and the ice in the cup had melted into standing water. He reached for the glass and a beefy hand lifted it and the straw toward him. He sucked down the tepid water, grateful for the moisture and taking all of it out of the glass, down to the gurgle in the bottom at the end of the straw. Satisfied for the moment, he rolled onto his back and felt for the bed control to raise his head and shoulder into a sitting position.

Mac Hartwell and Elizabeth Mackenaugh stood by his bed.

Malcolm looked down at the Indian sitting on the floor and then pointed at him.

The two other visitors looked at the floor and then back at Malcolm.

Mac grinned and said, "Don't worry about shoes yet. Your passport and pack are in the closet there. Mica got most of his stuff from the truck Henry dropped out here. How ya doin, mate? Feeling any better?"

"What are you two doing here – and by the friggin way, where the hell is 'here'?"

Mac beamed and answered, "Room Six." To which Malcolm only let out a long sigh and stared blankly into Mac's face. Mac got the signal and added, "Coober Pedy Hospital, Coober Pedy, South Australia, third planet from the sun."

Elizabeth placed a hand gently on Mac's forearm and leaned toward Malcolm.

"I understand you were unconscious when they brought you here. What do you remember?"

"Standing in a little restaurant at breakfast, and then sundown coming really fast."

Elizabeth allowed a brief smile.

"Malcolm, what have the doctors told you?"

"Nothing. Haven't seen one. Saw a nurse, and an orderly, I guess. The orderly said I'd been snoring for a few days. I guess that was yesterday."

Elizabeth patted his hand saying, "We'll be back shortly". Then they left the room.

Thirty minutes later, the doctor entered the room and introduced himself. He gave Malcolm a detailed description of all that had been done for him, the medications he should be taking, an assessment of his condition, and several other pieces of information and instructions the doctor assured Malcolm was vitally important. Malcolm did not hear most of it. He was thinking that one word over and over again while the doctor spoke. Cancer.

That sucks! I thought I had more time with that spot thing? I guess the travelling doctor visiting the Sanitarium was wrong. That's what you get with leftovers!

Itjanu and Mica entered the room. She beamed when she saw Malcolm sitting up.

"Well, you're looking better. How do you feel?"

Cancer.

"Much better. He said I could get out of here. Probably have to stop by the main hospital in Sydney on my way back."

Mica stepped to the side of the bed.

"What was it?"

Cancer.

"Just dehydration. Well, actually a lot of dehydration, but they've got my oil level topped off and I'm good to go."

Cancer. Gonna eat me up.

Itjanu gave him another smile.

"Did you see Mac and Elizabeth?"

Cancer. Nice smile. Need to tell her that – not like she doesn't know anyway.

"You gotta nice smile."

She shook her head and examined the label on the uppermost IV bag still delivering liquid medication into Malcolm's arm.

"Liquor or drugs. It takes liquor or drugs to make a man poetic."

She lightly slapped Malcolm's forearm, shaking her head and smiling.

Mica pointed a finger at Itjanu.

"I don't think it was an apple that Eve offered Adam in the Garden of Eden. I think it was Apple <u>Jack</u>!" He laughed at his own joke and sat in the corner chair, lifting a magazine off the nearby lamp table and flipping through the pages, oblivious to the Indian on the floor.

Cancer.

"What'er Mac and Elizabeth doing here? Didn't the rest of the group go on to Alice Springs?"

Itjanu answered as she stepped toward the heavy curtains at the wall beyond the foot of Malcolm's bed, "Oh yes. Days ago. Mind if I open these curtains?"

Cancer.

"What? Oh, sure. Didn't know they were curtains."

As Itjanu pulled the curtains to the corners, the room flooded with bright light, and outside stood Elea leaning on his stick looking in. Itjanu smiled and waved to her grandfather. Elea smiled back at her and looked over to Malcolm, who gave a half smile and raised his hand in a wave. Elea started to raise his hand as his eyes found Malcolm's and they looked at each other briefly. Elea dropped his hand and turned away bowing his head, walking out of sight.

He knows.

The Indian stood up next to Mac's chair, then walked out through the window pain, not looking back.

Itjanu returned to Malcolm's bedside and told him about Mac's return to Coober Pedy. There was no return business waiting for him in Alice Springs. Tourists were leaving there as quickly as local airlines could take them. This was the peak of the tourist season, but cancellations, short trips, and early returns were plaguing all businesses that catered to outback tourism. Too many strange things were happening in the Red Centre.

Elizabeth stayed in touch with her sister, who shared tidbits about the goings on, in and around Mutanajulu, which included rumors about green Malcolm. Mac was directed by the home office to bring the van and trailer back to Adelaide, unless he could find some tourist work where he was. A chance meeting at Bojangles pub on Todd Street brought Mac and Elizabeth together for dinner, where she hired him with her husband's hidden money to take her back to Mutanajulu.

"Her sister, Margaret," Itjanu continued, "who knows Mica's Annie, told her we were in Coober Pedy, so they came here looking for us and we ran into them at the petrol station just down the street from here. How amazing! Now we are all going together. Mica has turned the rental van over to a family that needs to get to Port Augusta. Mica called the van owner in Hawker who said he'd meet them there to pick it up. Sometimes things just work out really great, don't they."

"Marvelous, just marvelous," he deadpanned.

The next morning, Malcolm had checked himself out of the hospital, with serious concerns expressed by the staff, but with promises he was going straight to the specialty hospital in Sydney. The medicine they had given him made him feel perfectly healthy. He sat on the little bench under the awning just outside the hospital entrance waiting for Mac to pick him up, still undecided what he would actually do next.

Wide spread cancer.

Someone sat next to him on the bench, but Malcolm did not look at the person.

"What you got, Dingo Ass?"

Elea sat next to him, looking straight ahead with both hands gripping the stick standing up between his knees. Malcolm looked at the old man.

"I thought I had earned my distance away from that name."

"That's when you were green. When you were white you still thought my Ittie was ugly. You gotta start over. You got the Cancer, don't you?"

"Yes."

"Saw it in your eyes. Saw it in Lettie's eyes. Know what it looks like. What are you going to do now?"

"Don't know. They seem to think in there that it has already spread pretty far."

"You got weak after you got white again. Was it in there before you turned green?"

"Yeah."

The Indian was standing next to Elea.

"You turned green and you got strong. You turned white again and you got sick."

"Looks that way."

"You gotta turn green again."

The Indian was wearing war paint on his face and arms. He smiled and nodded his head at Malcolm.

"What?"

"You gotta turn green again."

"How in the hell could I do all that again. That's ridiculous. I don't want to be that thing again."

"You stay white, Dingo Ass, and you probably get sicker. You turn green and you probably live."

"Probably?"

"Maybe. Maybe not. Sometimes you dream. Sometimes your dream comes true. Sometimes it doesn't."

207

"That doesn't make a lot of sense."

"My Lettie did everything that made sense. She did nothing to get it and everything to get rid of it. If she came back as a big green lizard and sat on the sand in the night next to me and talked to me, it would be a dream I wouldn't want to end."

"I wouldn't even know where to begin or what to do..."

"Seems like such a simple choice between green and white to me, Dingo Ass."

The Indian smiled and folded his arms across his chest.

You be Green. You be Great Green Chief.

They sat in Mac's company van in the hospital parking lot with the engine and air conditioning running. Malcolm had shared most of the details about his diagnosis with them, and the conversation he had with Elea. The air in the van was full of almost impossible questions. Would it work again? Could Malcolm tolerate the power surge again? How could they get Henry to go along with it? Where was Henry? Where would they get an opal bigger than the last? How would they be able to recreate the ceremony? How could they get past the Rangers and up to the platform at Wilpena Pound a THIRD TIME??? The voices were a cacophony of sound until Elea tapped the end of his stick against the window near him on the last seat.

"First, Malcolm decides if he wants to do it. Green or white?"

Malcolm sighed and spoke quietly, touching the tips of his fingers with his thumb as he mentioned one point after another, "At first I could only think of all I lost as that creature. So much of it terrified me. After hearing what the doctor told me yesterday, I am not hopeful about my future. I have spent my life convincing myself I was something different from what I am. I do have some good memories of the things I was able to do when I was green."

He looked around at the faces within the van.

"I would be green again to be healthy."

209

Mica slapped him on the shoulder. "Good on ya, mate."

Elea tapped against the window again.

"So, Malcolm chooses to be green. Now, who can help him with his dream?"

One by one each person raised a hand and looked toward Malcolm. Mac slapped his hands together.

"All right then, Let's get going. Wilpena Pound, here we come..."

"No!" Mica held up his hand. "We stay here another night. We need an extremely large fiery black opal, and the biggest one in 'Oz is right here in Coober Pedy."

Itjanu shook her head at Mica.

"I was in there, Mica. I saw that monster opal. It's all encased in Lucite. The sign says it is protected by the most expensive alarms in the world, and the shop is barred and locked up more than the best banks."

Mica smiled at her and looked around at the faces within the van.

"That's the front door. I know where his back door is, and he's left it open. Let's go have a beer, or two."

A few minutes later, the group sat at a table in the dark shade of a working man's tavern, where red dust trailed along the floor at the front and feathered out between the tables and the bar. The window shades were pulled down against the afternoon sun. The only overhead light was above the cash register and reflected in the cracked wall mirror behind the rows of whiskey bottles lined on glass shelves. Mica was over at the bar ordering beers and chatting with the bartender as he pulled the bottles up out of the ice water.

"You ever get paid back by The Dingo Mine for all that glass and whiskey they broke?"

"Not a bloody penny. My lawsuit got tossed out of court. Said I knew the risks when I bought the place."

"How'd ya like ta tweak their noses?"

The bartender smiled and winked his eye.

"I'd love it – long as I don't get blamed for anything, ya'know."

Mica picked up the bottles.

"No worries. Let's talk a little more in a bit."

210

As Mica set the bottles in front of their owners, he smiled saying, "We have a way in . All we gotta do is walk a couple kilometers with torches." He drank down several swallows of beer as he sat next to Malcolm.

"You up to a little hike in the dark tonight."

"I am," Malcolm said after drinking down a third of his bottle.

Itjanu regarded him closely and then flipped her eyebrows. "I guess you're well enough. Your color's good."

Malcolm winked and smiled at her, "Just not the right color, yet."

She showed a small frown and shook her head slightly, then turned toward Margaret and began speaking with her. Mac leaned across the table and tapped Mica's forearm.

"So tell me how all this is gonna work?"

Mica glanced around, then shook his head as a group of four men sat at the table next to them. Margaret finished her beer and spoke to the little group around the table.

"Let's go find steaks. My husband is buying."

They found a wonderful restaurant on Hutchinson Street not far from the motel and then made their way back, where they all gathered in one room to discuss plans. Elizabeth and Itjanu would drop off Mica, Malcolm and Mac at the tavern on Crowder Gulley Road, come back to the motel parking lot and wait in the van for Elea. Elea would walk from the motel down the three blocks to The Dingo and watch for anyone coming or for signals from inside the shop. If anything happened, they would take the van back up to the tavern to whisk away the men there.

Just before closing time Mica, Malcolm and Mac walked into the tavern and went straight to the kitchen and then down the stairs to the basement. As they were going down the stairs, the bartender stuck his head through the door way.

"Remember Mica, nothing comes back on me. Right.?"

Mica turned and waved back up the stairs. "Ya got me word, Harold."

Harold closed the door behind him, and then closed up his Tavern, locking the men inside for the night. In the cellar the three men looked around to find the telltale crumbling concrete where the Dingo Mine had provided a poor patch to the cellar wall. In the very back of the cellar a plastic tarp hung over the wall as if it was blocking a doorway. Mac lifted it and found the entrance to the last mineshaft of The Dingo Mine.

"Lotta wine back here. Beer too. Lotta Beer." He shined the light further along the lateral shaft, illuminating hundreds of cases of beer far down a rough rock hallway fifty yards in the light. "A LOTTA beer. He really buys ahead. Reckon he'd miss a bottle or two?"

Mica patted him on the shoulder. "On the way back, Mac. On the way back. OK, gentlemen, torches on. I'm going to turn off the light in the cellar. Don't want any light shining through a hole somewhere that would make a constable think he's got to contact the owner. We can't draw ANY attention to Harold."

Mica stepped back to the plastic tarp, reached his arm around the edge of the opening and the world went pitch black. The sound of the plastic being pulled back down was followed by the near firework display of Mica's flashlight coming on in the blackness. Two other lights joined Mica's as he brought out his compass. Mac and Malcolm brought out theirs as well and they huddled around the glass faces within the light.

Mac pointed to the edge of his compass. "The mine is west-south-west from here. I have no idea how many cross shafts they cut to wind up here, but let's assume it was a lot. That means even though we're only a kilometer from the Dingo, this will take a while. You guys got water? OK. Let's stick together. None of this independent exploration down here, got me? We stick together. Who brought the chalk?"

Malcolm showed the thick pieces of chalk he had picked up at the store.

Mac said, "Good man. At each intersection, draw an arrow that points back the way we came to it. If we have to double back, make sure the arrow is drawn on both walls of the intersection so we can see it coming back from either direction. OK. Carry the chalk in your back pocket. That way if you trip and fall into water on the floor of the mine, it should keep the chalk dry. Wet chalk is useless, and you are unlikely to intentionally sit down in water."

Malcolm looked intently at Mac. "Sounds like you done something like this before."

"I worked three years in the mines around here right after I got out of the Army. That reminds me, Mica. Did I hear you say you been in the service too?"

"Long time ago. Doesn't matter now."

"What branch?"

"Infantry. Doesn't matter now. Let's move this along. I don't really care for mines."

Mac went ahead, followed by Mica followed by Malcolm. Even past the first fifty yards of stacked beer cases, the shaft was still too narrow to walk other than single file. After another fifty yards they came to a 'T' intersection, with one shaft going due north and one due south. They selected the southern shaft and Malcolm drew a chalk arrow pointing back toward the beer cases, and then wrote 'BEER' over the arrow. He could see the quizzical looks on the other two faces.

"This way we'll know it's the last shaft."

"Great Idea," Mac said. "Let's number all the rest of them."

Twenty minutes later they were back at the beer intersection and Malcolm drew the arrow and wrote 'Beer' on the other wall, and they went due north. Ten minutes later they found a shaft opening on the west wall, drew the arrow pointing south on the shaft they were leaving and followed the next one, which lead to a four-way intersection after twenty or thirty yards.

Trying to get Southwest, they marked their previous shaft and took the one going south. This one was much longer, taking a full twenty minutes to get to another dead end, and then another twenty minutes to return to the intersection they had left forty minutes before. The air was cool but stale. The confines of the shaft were

213

beginning to grate on Malcolm's nerves. Forty minutes later they returned again to the four way intersection after running into another dead end. Mac called a halt to walking for a short break, then gave his thoughts.

"I think they cut due north and due south along the axis of their main shaft, trying to cover as much ground as they could under this section of town. If that's so, we're probably in a grid with a generally eastern shaft with north-south exploratory shafts every twenty five yards. It's an old practice. If you find opals, then you start cutting parallel shafts on either side of the opal shaft. Let's see if we can find another four way intersection by going west."

The other two grunted agreement and the three headed west, finding another four way intersection at about twenty five yards. Malcolm marked the intersection, and they continued west. Moments into the darkness, Malcolm heard scuffing footsteps behind him. When he turned around he saw the Indian there holding a wooden torch.

"Go away," he whispered.

Mac stopped. "What was that, Malcolm? You find something?"

"No, Mac. Just an echo, I guess."

They began walking again with the Indian still close behind Malcolm. Malcolm waved him away frantically.

"Git," he whispered.

Mac and Mica both looked back over their shoulders at Malcolm, but kept walking. Malcolm shook his head, sighed and shrugged his shoulders, then followed them with the Indian close behind him.

After a couple hours and several more intersections, they came to a cave-in where the way forward from the last intersection was blocked only a few feet into a new shaft. Mac shined his light up at the ceiling, which rose several feet above head level.

Malcolm backed up several steps.

"Is this going to fall on us?"

The light shining on the whitish concrete bathed the little area in reflected light. Sweat dripped down Mica's forehead.

"Give me some good news, mate. I really need it."

Mac shook his head no and spoke to the other two.

"Nah. This didn't fall because of structure failure, they tried to go up. Must have found opals in the head space and tried to cut down more rock. Look up there. That's concrete. They caused something up there to collapse into a hole." He looked at the other two and chuckled, "and THAT's why the town outlawed mining in town limits."

Mica stretched to relieve some muscle stress. "So now what? We can't go west anymore."

Malcolm looked at his watch in the light. "It's two thirty in the morning. We've been walking three and half hours. We're not making much progress."

Mac turned off his flashlight and stuck it in his back pocket, then stood in the glow of the other flashlights, punctuating his words with his hands.

"All right. Let's try to think this thing through. They stopped at the tavern because they cut into Harold's cellar. He keeps bottles lined along his wall to see if they are digging any more, and he hasn't seen any evidence for eight years. He is their south eastern limit. This is their north western limit. Their north-south shafts are exploratory,... except the one they cut from their original field into this cross shaft in the first place. So,... one of the southern shafts going from one of the intersections we went through, is their original shaft to this field, which is the shaft back to the opal shop..."

Mica spoke up cutting Mac off, "We really need to get me outta this damned mine. You hear me? I need some air. I need some sky over my head, and I need a bloody beer."

Mac placed his hand on Mica's shoulder, "Easy Trooper. Stay with me."

Mica flipped Mac's hand off his shoulder. "Don't call me trooper. Just get me outta here."

Mac pointed back along the shaft they had used to get to the current intersection.

"Malcolm, draw an X through that arrow. Then we're going to start taking the south shaft only from each intersection, until we work our way down to the main shaft."

The next shaft was far more narrow and shorter then they had encountered. Loose small rocks in the low ceiling only scant inches above Malcolm's head dropped onto their hair like landing bugs. The air became more stale and warm. When a head-size piece of rock dropped in front of Mac, all three men quickly did an about face and scrambled back to the intersection, where Malcolm drew another X, and they all tried to catch their breath in the dusty air. The next two southern shafts were relatively short, compared to the others they had travelled, but the fourth went almost twice the distance of any other. At over one hundred yards they came to a wider intersection of shafts where the ceiling was slightly higher and tools were stored in the shafts on either side. Mac put his hands on his hips and smiled to the others.

"Gents, we're almost there. He checked his compass. We're going south west now. We keep straight on."

Mac, Malcolm and the Indian followed him on.

After several more yards, the width of the shaft doubled, the ceiling increased to nearly seven feet, and the air flowed around the men rushing toward an exhaust fan in the distance. A few yards farther down the main shaft they came under an air vent that allowed fresh air to flow down into the mine, being pulled by an exhaust fan farther in. Mica stopped under the airshaft, facing upward and breathed deeply. Far up the metal airshaft where the cool night air poured into the mine, an outside light reflected into the upper edge of the shaft. After several deep breaths, Mica nodded his head toward Mac.

"Sorry to be rude back there, Mate."

"No worries."

Malcolm looked behind and the Indian was gone.

The three walked briskly farther along the main shaft until they came to a large room with old cutting and polishing tools rusting off to the side. File cabinets were lined along the wall with faded cardboard boxes stacked high on top of the cabinets covered in dust. At the other end of the room was a single service door beside an elevator. The elevator door sat open with an empty dusty rolling table standing in the center. The single door was unlocked and lead to metal stairs going up two stories to a platform in front of a brick wall holding another door. The three men stopped at the top platform and Mica gently gave the door handle a slight turn. There was a minor squeak, the latch withdrew, and the door swung open into a store room. Cautiously they walked across the room to a door with a frosted glass upper half. Reading in reverse from the lights on the other side of the glass, the label on the door said 'Supplies'. Mica found a chair in the corner and sat down gingerly. He held up the palm of his hand in universal 'halt', and the other two nodded, finding chairs for themselves.

The air was cool and the smells of the town drifted around the room mixing with the smell of business office supplies. At the end of a set of standing shelves was an old metal filing cabinet with an upside down beer box on top labeled empties. A small refrigerator sat in the back corner near the door they had just used. Mica stood and crossed the room to the refrigerator. He opened the door, bathing the supply room in yellow light and jiggling two rows of neatly lined brown bottles in the door. Inside the refrigerator itself the shelves were filled with more cold beer.

Mica looked back at Mac and Malcolm with a great smile, like a child at Christmas morning. Mac shook his head no, but Mica swiftly looped his fingers around the necks of three bottles and lifted them from the door. In a single motion he turned around scooping up a bottle opener laying on top of the refrigerator, then walked to Mac popping the first cap off into Mac's lap as he handed him the beer, and then the same to Malcolm.

The third cap sailed off the bottle and beyond Mica's reach, flipped through the air into the middle of the room and with an echoing metallic clink hit the concrete floor, bounced and hit the floor again and again until it came to a wobbling rest. The sound was a nerve-wracking noise to the three men, and seemed to echo off the walls. They froze in mid motion. Eyeballs scooting around their sockets looking for sight, and ears straining for sound, of their discovery. After thirty heartbeats in deathly silence, Mica shrugged his shoulders and began gulping his cold beer. Mac and Malcolm released the tension of their muscles, Mac shaking his head at Mica, then the other two cold brown bottles went bottoms up.

After a few moments of relaxation and a couple satisfied muffled belches, the three stood as one and moved toward the inside door. Mac reached for the door handle, but Mica gently pulled his wrist to the side and whispered, "Let me do this." Mac stepped back and Mica brought his fingertips to the door handle, sliding them over the rounded edges, applying featherweight pressure and rotating it the slightest bit then stopped. He released the handle, then came down close to it, examining it in the light of his flashlight. Then he traced the door jamb below and above the door handle, followed the sill above the door and all down the hinge side until he had examined every inch of the door edge. Next he followed the outer edge of the door jamb frame.

Finally he leaned his head close to Malcolm and Mack. "No wires." He then returned his fingertips to the handle and began to turn it ever so slightly, concentrating on the feeling in his fingertips for anything that might tell him they were in danger of setting off an alarm. After what seemed like hours he finally rotated the handle until the door latch withdrew from the jamb, and the door moved just enough to allow a quarter inch peek into the next room. Then Mica stood straight and allowed the door to swing wide open. The three men stared into the next room in amazement.

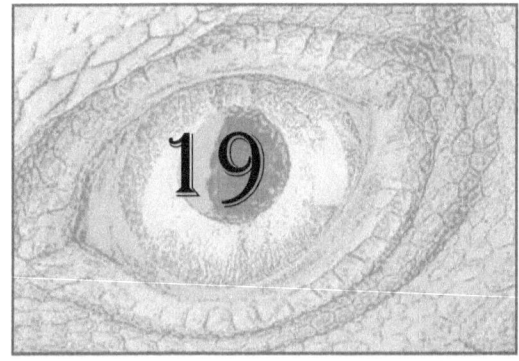

The three men stood packed together shoulder to shoulder in the doorframe, necks craning forward like a three-headed Emu. The room in front of the Supply Room was the protected booth where the owner spent most of his day. Outside the booth in the shop area and around all actual and potential points of entry into the enclosed booth ran dozens of wires to dozens of sensitive burglar alarms, each with its own red light showing it activated. The three men edged daintily into the narrow booth, obviously only designed for one person. Between the three men and the single rolling stool the owner sat in, there was hardly room to move.

Mac inadvertently kicked over the trash can in the booth. The men froze in terror waiting for the hellish wails of the alarms The Dingo boasted, but silence remained. Malcolm began to giggle. Mac tried to shush him, but he continued, pointing to a little gray electrical box mounted on a post to the left of the service window and above the extended empty cash drawer. The men had to shuffle stiff knee'd to rotate all at once to face the little box. Written on the center of the box in india ink marker were the letters 'Bglr Alm'. On the left side of the metal box was a throw switch. At the bottom of the switch's range where the red tipped switch proudly stood, impressed into the metal by the factory, was the word 'ON'. At the top end of the switch range the factory had impressed the word 'OFF'.

Mac shook his head."Naw. Can't be that easy."

Malcolm reached out and put his fingers on the switch. Mica nodded his head 'yes' in the faint light of the booth's nightlights. Malcolm pushed the switch up to the off position, and they waited for the red lights on the alarms around the shop to turn green or go out, but neither happened. After another minute, the three exhaled and Malcolm released the handle and it fell back to the bottom position with a metallic clank. Again they held their collective breath, and again no alarm sounded.

Mica reached to the alarm box and flipped the little handle gently with his finger. The handle just moved up and down to the slightest touch and the pull of gravity. It was obviously broken. Malcolm reached around him and opened the control box. Inside was an old fashioned cylinder fuse with copper ends held in place by copper clamps at each end of the fuse. The fuse clamps were inset slightly, and did not allow enough space for a finger to slip under the fuse to pull it out.

"Wouldn't stick a finger in there, mate. Awfully close to metal contacts," Mica said.

Mac looked around the little booth and noticed an old wooden kitchen spoon hanging by a string loop from a nail in the door jamb leading out of the booth into the shop.

"That's really odd. Bloke's got a wooden spoon hanging in his booth, but the string it hangs by is looped through a hole drilled in the spoon face."

Mica smiled. "So it's not the spoon part he uses. It's the handle."

Mac lifted the spoon loop off the nail and handed it to Mica who handed it to Malcolm.

"See if that fits under the fuse."

Malcolm slipped the flat handle into the slender space under the fuse, and gently pried out the fuse. All the little red lights in the shop turned green, except one. Slowly, the six legged emu crab-walked with knees stiff through the booth door out into the shop. Still together as if they were still in the confined booth, they tip-toed in unison over to the remaining red light and leaned forward as one to examine the hold out. The last red light was at the top of a panel of numbers, and the panel was screwed into the wall near the front door. Mac and Mica looked at each other's faces and then down at the intimate proximity of their bodies then quickly stepped away from each other clearing their throats and adjusting their shirts. Malcolm was left standing in front of the remaining active burglar alarm. He turned his head toward the other two.

"It's the front door alarm. He must set it here just as he leaves."

Mac frowned back at Malcolm. "How can you be sure of that?"

Malcolm pointed at a strip of tan masking tape stuck across the upper face of the panel just above the red light. Written in India ink marker on the masking tape were the words 'front door alarm'.

Mica chuckled. "Not too bright, is he? But good for us. Let's see that Monster Opal."

Facing the booth from the crowded narrow aisle shop area, the framed opal was mounted high on the wall to the right. A bright white light suspended from the ceiling several feet out, shined directly on the opal box. Below the box were several faded newspaper reports about the opal, boxes holding leaflets about opals, The Dingo Mine, and local motels and restaurants with which the shop owner had arrangements. On shelves to the right of that were hundreds of cheap trinkets and souvenirs with 'Coober Pedy, South Australia' printed on them at various angles. Toward the end of the top shelf were several ceramic mock ups of the Monster Opal, in various sizes at various prices. In the back of the top row near the far corner were two inexpensive wood boxes painted to resemble the Monster Opal box, each holding a full size ceramic mock up. Looking at the souvenirs Mica snapped his finger and pointed at them.

"Got an Idea. Let's swap'em."

Mac smiled and went to pull the rolling chair out of the booth, and headed for the space under the Monster Opal display. Just as he was about to mount the chair Mica pulled him down by his shoulders and moved him back under the bright ceiling light. Mounted to the

221

ceiling next to the light was a small video camera pointing directly at the Monster Opal. They spent several minutes looking around the shop, in the booths and back in the storeroom for the recorder that would receive the video images, but could not find it, nor could they find any other cameras. Finally, they decided to just cover the camera lens with one of the cheap alternate Aussie flags, by standing on the rolling chair just underneath it. With the flag in place they unhooked the Monster Opal box from its perch and replaced it with a mock up Mica had covered in floor dust to match.

As Mica stepped down from the chair he looked out over the top of the café curtains the owner had up to block some of the sunlight. Standing in the middle of the parking lot in front of the shop, Elea knew he was being seen by Mica, and he pointed toward the east, then walked away.

"Uh Oh," Mica said as he stepped down, "It's dawn out there. We need to get a move on!"

Quickly the three men worked to replace everything as it had been and returned to the booth and closed the narrow door from the shop. They held their collective breath when Mac reinserted the fuse into the clips – hoping that would not trigger the alarms, and to their relief it did not. Breathing again, they replaced the wooden spoon on its nail, righted the little trash can in the booth, then exited the booth back into the supply room and closed the door behind them. They filed out of the supply room down the metal steps to the old mine, through the mine entrance and down to the first intersection where the roof was high and the shaft still wide.

Mica stopped dead still and snapped his fingers. "Wait here for me." Then he trotted back through the mine entrance and back up to the supply room where he retrieved the three empty beer bottles as well as the three bottle caps and replaced the bottle opener on top of the refrigerator.

While Malcolm waited, he looked to his left and found the Indian standing next to him holding a fiery torch. Malcolm slapped his hand at the apparition. *GO AWAY!!*

Mac and Malcolm were still waiting at the spot he left them when Mica returned with the bottles.

"We can toss'em into one of the side shafts on our way back"

"Good on you," Mac said. "Completely forgot the damned things. All right then, let's follow Malcolm's arrows back to the tavern. You lead out Malcolm."

"No, you two go ahead."

He looked sternly at the Indian.

"I like it better without people following me."

The Indian smiled and Mica took the lead.

Two hours later they emerged from behind the plastic tarp in the Tavern cellar. After Mac turned on the light, Malcolm found a packet of brown take away bags and placed the Monster Opal Box inside while Mica smiled and set a box of Carltons inside next to it , then the trio walked up the stairs.

Malcolm walked first back into the Tavern area with the take away bag in his arms, and into the presence of three police officers standing in the open doorway from the street. Malcolm closed the door behind him with his foot before either Mica or Mac could come out.

"Good morning, Officers," he spoke a little too loudly.

The nearest officer smiled and said, "Here we go, I'll take that heavy load from you," and took the bag from Malcolm's arms. "Can't just let you be out and about with that kind of kit today, now can we?"

The two other officers surrounded Malcolm, standing there smiling with their hands on their revolver belts.

Not knowing what else to day, Malcolm gave them his best "G'Day".

Before the officers or Malcolm could say anything else, Harold spoke from behind the bar as he came out of the kitchen carrying two boxes of beer in his arms. "Not that beer, ya Toad. It's not nearly cold enough. These boys deserve the best of the house. Now you get back down there and finish cleaning my cellar if you want your pay! Get!"

223

Malcolm snatched the bag from the closest policeman and dashed back through the cellar door almost knocking Mica and Mac down the stairs.

Back in the tavern, the police were sharing a hearty laugh at Malcolm's plight and Harold brought out two more boxes of ice cold beer.

"This ought to do you. Just the thing to enjoy after your long night shift."

The smallest officer pulled off his cap and ran his hand through his hair.

"Saturday night in Coober Pedy is always busy. Harold, we appreciate you opening up for us."

Harold wagged his finger at the young officer. "I ain't open, Officer. It's Sunday. I ain't even here, and neither are you."

The first officer slapped Harold on his shoulder and turned to his partners, "Told you my brother-in-law was great, didn't I?" Then he offered money to Harold.

Harold waved it away saying, "Can't sell beer on a Sunday, that's a crime, 'specially since I ain't even here to do it."

They all laughed and the police officers filed out, thanking Harold again, his brother-in-law telling him he would pay him on Monday, winking and smiling as the door closed behind them.

Harold went to the cellar door and yanked it open yelling down the staircase, "Bloody Hell! Your timing is the bloody shits!!" Then he went over to the bar, poured himself a shot of whiskey and tossed it back. "Bloody Hell!"

The three men filed up out of the cellar and into the tavern. Mica started to speak, but Harold waved him away.

"G'wan. I don't want to know anything. Should'nt have let you talk me into anything in the first place. G'wan. If it's anything worth knowin' about, I'll hear it from my brother-in-law."

The travel van was waiting in the sunshine outside the Tavern when the three men came out. Itjanu was driving, Elizabeth sat in the front passenger seat, and Elea sat all the way in the back. They rode in exhausted silence back to the motel and all went into one room. Malcolm set the paper bag on the little round table in the corner. Everyone watched intently as Mica reached in, opened the Carlton box and pulled out a beer. Malcolm then reached into the bag and pulled up the Monster Opal box and set it on the table in front of the bag.

Elizabeth leaned forward from sitting on the edge of the closest bed to get a good look at the Opal.

"Good God. Is that real?"

Mica reached over and tapped the box with his finger.

"Real enough to buy three houses, if we were stupid enough to try to sell it."

The stress of the long night swept in upon them all. Leaving the opal box setting on the table where it was, everyone went to their shared rooms in silence and finding their beds and quickly slipping into deep sleep.

While they slept, the owner operator and only employee of The Dingo Mine opened his shop to a morning of no customers. He had a lunch made by his wife and brought from his home, and taken in solitude in the supply room after locking up for mid day, and washing it down by a couple cold beers taken from the old refrigerator in the back corner. He re-opened at one o'clock and soon received a bus load of teenagers on group holiday to Uluru, who had been brought up to Coober Pedy as a side trip by a haggard driver that knew the Mine owner, and the contents of his refrigerator in the store room.

Two dozen energetic pimply teenagers bustled about the shop for almost more time than the owner could stand, but did wind up buying a fair amount of trinkets, overpriced candy, and far more overpriced sodas. It was too much trouble to take them down into the mine. They bought nothing down there. He had not done that in years, and was no longer up to it. So, he told his stories to the few that actually paid attention to him, pointed up to the Monster Opal, bragged on his alarm system, and warned them not to attempt to reach up to the Opal itself lest they wind up in the hands of the Coober Pedy Police.

Finally the little mob was escorted back out to the bus by a very red faced driver who was handed ten dollars by the owner. Cleaning up the aisles after the teens had gone he found an opened candy pack with bites taken then returned to the shelves. Looking up and down the shelves he noticed one of his two more expensive souvenirs was gone, the life size mock up of the Monster Opal box.

"Damn the little snots!"

He looked up at the original hooked high on the wall next to the booth and saw it still here, then he noticed the flag tied loosely around the video camera. Using a toy spear made in China, with a paper label attached to it saying it was made by Aborigines of the Great Outback, he worked the little flag free of the camera, folded the flag and returned it to its shelf, and locked the front door.

"Damned little snots!"

Then he went through his sales booth into the Supply Room and raised the upside down beer box sitting on the file cabinet next to the refrigerator.

"Damn it all!" he said.

There sitting on top of the video recorder that was wired to the camera in the shop area, was the video cassette he had forgotten to insert the last time he had rewound it. With an exasperated push of his finger, he slid the cassette into its slot for recording and let the old beer box fall back into place.

Later, counting his cash for the day he realized that he had taken in more from the spoiled teenagers than he thought. Even accounting for the thirty dollars he had originally spent on the stolen mock up, which he priced at a hundred fifty, and the ten spot he had given old Jim, he still cleared a hundred fifteen dollars during the day. Then he snapped the burglar alarm fuse into place, punched in his code for the front door and locked himself out for the night, knowing that no one could possibly get into his shop except him.

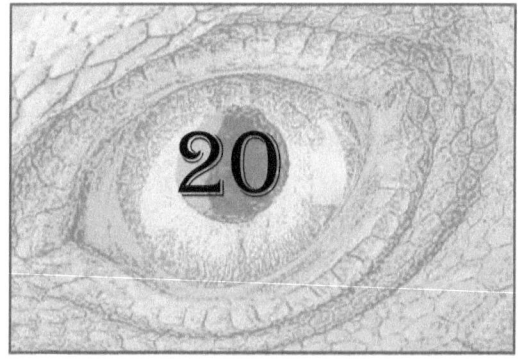

Emerging from the motel as the sun rose behind the hills of Coober Pedy, they stuffed packs into the back of the van in near silence and eased into their seats in the van, speaking in hushed tones. Mica took the driver's seat and Elea sat in front next to him. Itjanu and Malcolm slid into the back seats.

Mica pointed his finger at Elea.

"We gotta go to those plateaus where Malcolm found the other opals."

Elea shook his head.

"It is too dangerous. We have to find another way to lure Big Lizard out."

"No, Elea, it is the best way. We gotta get him to come to us. So we can be ready on our own ground. We don't even know where he is."

Itjanu held up a day-old copy of the Coober Pedy Regional Times. On the cover was an article about strange cattle and kangaroo mutilations near Mutana Creek.

"He's still near where we live."

Elea's head snapped around to face her.

"Where 'we' live? Does that include you, Granddaughter?"

She smiled at Elea. "Well, for now. The point is, it looks like Lizard has stayed around the area, but why. He could find roos and cows almost anywhere, so why is he still in that area?"

Malcolm nodded in agreement.

" Same reason I did. Those plateaus at the edge of the valley. The caves full of opals, all piled up. He is drawn to them, or maybe he is drawn to the place, and that's where the creatures brought their opals."

"And that's where we go and tak'em," Mica said.

"It is far too dangerous, Mica," Elea added. "We aren't even sure where the plateaus actually are, and Malcolm already told us there are no roads up to them."

Mica snapped his fingers as he started the van and said, "We need a chopper."

The other three chuckled, but Mica continued seriously, "Malcolm told us about helping that falling medical plane. I'll bet he would help us."

Malcolm held up his hands.

"How would we convince him that was me? I can barely hold up myself, let alone fly and hold up a plane."

Mica looked up into the rear view mirror, his big brown eyes bright with excitement, looking intently at Malcolm.

"You waved to him. Right? He saw you. Right? No one else saw you. Right? So we go tell him that, and see what he says then."

Itjanu looked between Mica and Malcolm.

"So, where do we go now?"

Mica turned onto the Stuart highway with the rising sun shining into the windows on the right side of the van, and looked back into the rear view mirror at Itjanu.

"Alice."

Malcolm folded his arms and smiled at the mirror.

"Well, at last."

Five hours later, and still three hours south of Alice Springs, where the Lasseter Highway kisses up against the Stuart in the middle of a vast red soil and spinifex plain, they stopped the van at Erldunda . While Mica and Elea bought petrol, water and food, Itjanu and Malcolm found a coin operated telephone to call Bill McLeod at the Mutana Creek Pub. He was able to give them the name of the pilot flying the plane Malcolm once helped.

In the late afternoon sun they came off Stuart Terrace and cruised slowly along Simpson Street to find a parking space near the Royal Flying Doctor Service. Coming out of the RFDS Control Station, a well tanned young pilot with close cropped dark brown hair hurried along examining papers in his hand. Itjanu touched his arm as he walked near them.

"Excuse me. We are looking for Stephen Mallory."

The man was brought up from his concentration and only then noticed the small group on the sidewalk with him. He gave a bright smile in answer to Itjanu's.

"Sorry, ma'am. Stevie's on flight today. He'll be late coming back, too. Probably won't be back here at Control until tomorrow morning. Has his turn at one of the desks starting then. He'll be here by seven."

He smiled again, stepped quickly to his car and was out of the parking lot in seconds.

Malcolm spoke, looking out at the pilot drive off, "Guess we'll need a place to stay. Now that I'm me again and got my pack, I still have some money in it."

Itjanu added, "And I still have room on my credit card..."

Mica chuckled saying, "Here we are with an opal worth maybe half a million dollars, and we're scraping to pay for a motel. Maybe we can find a cheap one..."

"Little cost and good people," Elea said. "It's been a while, but I've been out here with old friends a while back. Stayed out on Undoolya Road and made some new friends. Good people there, and they understand not letting go of outside life."

They soon crossed the bridge over the dry dusty Todd River channel, where water rarely flows. They drove to the edge of town along Undoolya Road to a small motor court with rooms and bungalows arranged around a central stand of gum and palm trees shading a modest swimming pool. The branches of the gum trees also spread over the little horseshoe lane and coved the van in welcomed shade as they entered the court. Elea was first out of the van when they stopped in front of the little office. Even before he was half way from the van to the door of the office, it flew open to the charge of a broad shouldered burly man in his early sixties. His shirtsleeves barely contained the muscles of his upper

229

arms and his wide grin showed like alabaster in the middle of his tanned-leather skin. Before Elea could react, the man scooped him up in a bear hug that lifted Elea off the ground.

"Elea! You old bastard, it's about time you came round to see us!"

He released Elea and turned back toward the office, that was the front room of his own bungalow, and yelled into it."

"Gertie! Get yourself out here! It's Elea! He's come to see us at last!"

Elea held his hand out to the man and tried to introduce him to the others with him, but the excitement of the court owner could not be contained.

"Gertie! Out here, old girl! Come see who's here!"

Just as Elea was about to speak, a trim little woman with touches of gray in her brushed back hair, and a tan only shades lighter than the big man who called her out, came through the front door into the court yard.

"Well, bless my soul! Thought we might never see you again, Elea! Welcome! Welcome!"

She rushed forward and gave him a hug of her own, stood back to look at him, then brought him against her again in a comforting hug. She stepped back with tears in her eyes.

"I was so sorry to hear about... about your wife. Some of your wandering friends came by last year and told us. That broke my heart."

Elea could only nod and speak quietly, "Mine, too. Lettie was one of a kind."

The woman looked back at her husband and smiled, "We can say it, Garner."

The big man patted Elea's shoulder, his eyes glistening with moisture, "Lettie was special. Good on you for releasing her name again." Then he swept his arm over to the three people standing and watching the reunion, "So who are these fine folks, Elea?"

Elea motioned toward each person as he introduced them, "This is my granddaughter Itjanu, my life-long friend Mica, and our new friend Malcolm – he's a Yank, when he ain't something else." Elea allowed a small smile as he said those last words.

Garner and Gertie hugged and shook hands around the group, then Garner put his hands on his hips and nodded toward the chairs near the pool.

"You blokes settle in under the shade while I bring us out some beer from the fridge."

No sooner had each person found a chair, when Garner reemerged with a chest sized green ice cooler held up in front of him with his arms wrapped around it. The ice and the cans shifted around inside the cooler as he set it down, and soon each man had a cold beer in his hand. The two women looked at each other in smiling wonder. Gertie slapped Garner's arm. He quickly snatched up two more beers from the ice and handed them gently to Itjanu and Gertie.

"Soon as we get the beer going down, I'll get the Barbie fired up. I got plenty of Roo, Emu and Beef steaks in the fridge. Mate of mine raises Emu on the other side of the ridge, and I get'em real reasonable."

Gertie spoke to Itjanu, "You favor Lettie a great deal, but I guess you already know that. So, how long are you in the Alice? You'll stay with us, won't you?"

"Just tonight and maybe tomorrow night, we're not too sure, but I have a credit card and..."

"And you just keep that card right where it is, young lady. You're no tourist that we're going to let a room to. Elea is the godfather of my first born son. Not him nor Garner nor me would even be alive this day without what your grandfather did."

Itjanu stared blankly into Gertie's face, and Gertie's eye widened.

"Why that Elea never even told you, did he?"

Itjanu only shrugged her shoulders and shook her head slightly from side to side.

Gertie let out a sigh.

"Well, we were out in the Simpson in Garner's old Land Rover- this was way before you were born- and we took a tumble down a small ravine. It didn't hurt us, but the 'Rover went over'. Landed back on its side, broke something on the carburetor, and split our water tank.

231

We had our old caravan at a spring out there – little bedroom, sink & shower, but we were thirty kilometers out and me in my eighth month with Monty. Garner righted the Rover with a branch, and that's when he found the carburetor was broke. All that time, the water was running out of the water tank and draining onto the sand. By the time we saw it, we didn't have a quart of water left."

Itjanu brought her fingertips up to her lips, and conversation among the others stopped as they listened to Gertie.

"It was far too late in the day by then to try any serious walking, and Garner always has a kit in the back, so we camped there for the night. By dawn we were on our way. At first it was just a comfy stroll. Garner and I had hiked the outback dozens of times and back then I could easily hold my own on any trek. Then the pains started coming. Apparently the rollover had been more troublesome to me than I had suspected. About mid morning Garner made a little sun canopy for me between a couple bushes. The heat had come full on. That's when my water broke."

Itjanu murmured concern, and Garner placed his hand on Gertie's arm. She smiled back at him and continued her story.

"We were in a tough spot. I couldn't go on, we needed help, but there was none coming except what we brought ourselves. We decided for me to stay in the shade and Garner to hoof it back to the campsite for water, a radio and a better tool kit. Then the dingos came round, I guess smelling my water in the sand, and I went into labor."

Garner rubbed Gertie's arm and continued for her.

"That's when Elea showed up. Him and three other bushmen, with nothing but sticks and loin cloths. They guarded us from the dingos, gave us water, and Elea helped deliver Monty, right there under the cover between two bushes in the Simpson. We all stayed there together for three days. They gave us water and we cooked whatever they found over a little fire in the sand. Some of it was one of those dingos, I believe. On the fourth dawn, we all got up and they walked with us back to the campsite. They disappeared back into the desert to finish their pilgrimage. Two days after that a ranger drove into camp saying a bushman had stopped him in the desert and told him of our predicament."

Elea cleared his throat, "Wasn't anything any other man wouldn't have done."

Garner finished his beer and tossed it into a nearby trashcan.

"Well it was you that did that for us...and showed up again to see that the baby was OK, before we went back. Monty still has that little carving you made for him." Garner looked around at the other faces. "My son's full name is Montgomery Elea Atkins, and none of Elea's family ever have to go a night without a roof over their head in Alice Springs, if they want it."

Gertie smiled and patted Garner's arm again.

"And we do have another child,..."

"Jackie's a full grown woman,..." Garner added

"A nurse," Gertie said. "She works with the RFDS. Usually flys with a captain Mallory..."

"Usually my arse," Garner chuckled. "She flys with Stevie every chance she gets. She's sweet on that young man,..."

"Their sweet on each other, Garner, and Stevie's a good man."

"That he is, but I can't make it too easy on'im." Garner smiled looking around the little group. "They'll be over later tonight after they check out from today's trips. You should meet ol'Stevie."

Itjanu smiled at Elea, Mica and Malcolm. Malcolm swallowed another sip of beer and chuckled, "Oh yes, definitely we will look forward to meeting him."

Later, the coals in the grill had reached white hot, as the sun began setting beyond the town to the west. The smell of cooking meat and roasting corn drifted among the trees in the center of the court and people staying at the motor court had joined around the pool, all invited by Gertie and Garner. Mica had taken the van down to the town to refresh Garner's beer supply and had just returned when Nurse Jackie Atkins and RFDS Pilot

Steve Mallory pulled into the courtyard. Garner made introductions all around, ending with Malcolm and Steve shaking hands and sharing beer near the grill.

"After supper, Steve," Malcolm said. "I'd like to talk to you about that close call you had a while back near Mutana Creek." Steve smiled and said he would be glad to, looking curiously at Malcolm.

One of the tourists brought out a portable player and started music everyone enjoyed. Grilled meat and vegetables were pass around until everyone was full of food and beer. In the following quiet most began to drift away from the pool area. Steve was settled comfortably on a lounge chair with his feet propped up when Malcolm settled next to him.

"That was a close call wasn't it, Steve?"

"Uh, Malcolm, Right? Yeah it was. So, what'd you hear about it?"

"Nothing much, but I saw it happen. You were roaring down straight at the boulders."

Steve frowned at Malcolm.

"That was in a bloody thick sand storm. Where were you that you could see any of that."

"I was there."

Steve turned to look straight into Malcolm's eyes.

"You leading up to some kind of joke, mate??"

"The wind had pushed the nose of the plan so far down, you couldn't pull up. Your plane was headed straight into the boulders below like a dart."

Steve chuckled and looked around.

"All right. I get it. Jackie told you, didn't she? I don't much care for..."

"No. I was there. I wrapped my legs around the fuselage, grabbed the leading edges of the wings, and pulled you up out of the dive. It was all I could do to fight against that wind."

Steve stared at Malcolm, a frown deepening in the furrows of his forehead.

"Oh, bullocks..."

"When the plane was settled onto a level course, I let go and flew next to you for a couple hundred yards. I waved and I smiled. And you waved back."

Steve stared in silence for a long moment. He opened his mouth and took in a breath to speak a couple times, but then closed his mouth again and exhaled the breath. He looked away, and then looked back a Malcolm. He gave out a short chuckle.

"Yeah? And what did I see when I supposedly waved out my window? Tell me that, Yank."

Malcolm smiled.

"A big ass green lizard with red eyes, great big ears and twenty foot bat wings."

At that moment Jackie walked up to the lounge chairs, and slid her finger tips though Steve's hair.

"You gentlemen seem to be in serious conversation."

Steve took her hand in his, but did not look away from Malcolm.

"Yeah, seems we've flown together in the past."

Jackie perked up at the comment and looked at Malcolm.

"Oh, are you a pilot, too?"

Malcolm shook his head no.

"Just learning. Saw Steve on one of my early solos. Still haven't earned my wings. I'm trying to get back to that."

She smiled and answered as she walked away, "Maybe Steve can help you.."

Steve kept his gaze on Malcolm.

"Make me believe that was you."

"It all started with a crazy little Canadian named Henry."

As Malcolm spoke in hushed tones so only Steve could hear him, Elea and Mica saw the looks between the two men and came around the pool, settling onto nearby lounge chairs. When Malcolm had told most of the story, Steve looked around and spoke to the others.

"You hearing this?"

Elea and Mica nodded. "It all happened just like he says," Mica said.

Steve slowly shook his head. "Nah, I just can't believe all that..."

Malcolm leaned over and tapped a finger on Steve's arm. "You and Jackie and that patient are alive today

235

because of all that. And now we need your help to keep the Outback from becoming a feeding pen for another one of those things that doesn't have a bone of kindness in him."

Steve finished the last of his beer, tossed the can into the trash barrel, and shook his head slowly.

"I'm sorry, Malcolm, but all that stuff can't be true. Some of it is, and maybe I saw what I thought I saw, or maybe I didn't really. I've got what you Yanks call a 'Bullshit Filter', and a lot of this story just ain't getting through it."

Elea placed his hand on Steve's shoulder.

"There are many strange truths, young fellah. Some stranger than most, but a strange truth is still a truth. There's something out there that's gonna hurt a lot of people, and Malcolm thinks he has a way to stop it. I saw what he was, and saw him come back to what he is now, and I believe him. Sometimes you've got to set aside what you always thought was the only truth, and consider that there might be another one - out there in that desert."

Mica leaned down next to Steve's ear.

"How 'bout a hundred pounds of opals? Would that get through your bullshit filter?"

"Old man, you know we don't use pounds anymore. We use the dollar, and a hundred dollars in opals isn't all that much"

"Steve, I'm not talking about currency. I'm talking about sixteen hundred ounces of prime quality opals!"

Mica traded looks with Malcolm, and Malcolm nodded, saying, "Yeah, there's probably a lot more than a hundred pounds of them in the cave."

Steve cocked his head and smiled, looking among the smiling faces staring down at him.

Mac and Elea sat in the van watching Helicopter AS-005 as it slapped the air climbing above the airport and then nosed down toward the south on its approved heading for Mutanajulu, carrying scheduled medical supplies. RFDS Pilot Stephen Mallory confidently steered the new helicopter recently added to other two 'copters assigned to the Alice Springs unit. Although there was a satisfactory runway near Mutanajulu, the supply run gave Steve his opportunity to acquire the 'copter for required flight hours as well as add a few odd passengers. The run also took the machine to its distance limit on the fuel gauge.

Itjanu sat in the available co-pilot seat watching the red fields below slip quickly under the 'copter, her body pressed firmly against the seat back and her grip on the nearby safety handle squeezing off the blood flow to her fingers. Malcolm sat in the back scanning the horizon for familiar landmarks, yesterday's newspaper laying at his feet showing an article low on page one about recent cattle disappearances.

Steve looked back over his shoulder to Malcolm.

"If this cave is so bloody important to you flying lizards, how do you know this other bloke won't be there?"

"He's up around Alice Springs feeding on cows. He'll have to sleep it off somewhere around there, before he can fly all the way back to the cave."

"How can you be sure of that – oh yeah, you were him. Did you eat many..."

Malcolm shook his head.

"No, mostly fruit and beer."

Itjanu spoke though gritted teeth.

"Mostly beer."

Malcolm leaned forward, pointing at the windshield in front of Steve and raising his voice over the whine of the engine and rotors.

"I think that's it. That's where the cave is."

Steve nodded and pointed in another direction.

"First the medical supplies, then we slip over that way on our way back – unless there is an emergency. Remember, that could scuttle any joy ride. Medical service first and foremost."

Malcolm nodded his understanding and placed his hand on Itjanu's shoulder.

"You doing OK?"

Itjanu flashed him a wide-eyed clenched-teeth grin, and tightened her grip on the safety handle. Malcolm leaned back in his seat rubbing his side to ease the throbbing pain that seemed to match the throbbing of the 'copter.

An hour later the 'copter settled into the dust cloud whipped up by the downdraft of its whirling blades. The hot breath of the nearby desert puffed the dust cloud away, and Steve opened the door to the 'copter. He turned to his passengers.

"You two sit where you are. This is RFDS business."

The local "medical attendant" was a retired emergency service technician who had come home to his family village, and operated out of a back store room provided by the cultural center. A small group of youngsters followed him out to the 'copter like a duck brood, single file and bending low to avoid the still rotating blades high above them. Steve shook hands with the attendant and after a quick chat began handing boxes to the young volunteers. As the boys filed away, the attendant reviewed and signed the supply list, taking the back copy for his own files. Moments later, the 'copter was airborne again and heading toward Malcolm's plateau.

Steve tapped the fuel gauge to ensure the needle was free and pointing at the correct volume in the tanks. He spoke over his shoulder.

"Still not half way down, but not too far from it. This flight isn't supposed to warrant a refuel, so we've got to see to it that one doesn't come up. Malcolm, you've got to get us to the right spot the first time – we only get one chance, then I gotta head straight back to the Alice. You understand?"

Malcolm nodded his head as he had the previous two times Steve had made the warning. After mistaking two other peaks for the ones at his plateau and causing a zig-zag course through the valley, Malcolm spotted his plateau. Thirty Indians in warpaint stood on the lip in front of the cave. He pointed excitedly at the windshield in front of Steve.

"There! That's it! I'm absolutely sure!"

"Better be," Steve frowned.

As the 'copter neared the plateau in front of the cave opening, Steve shook his head and pointed down.

"Ain't enough room to set down there and still have walkin' room. Is there another spot?"

The three of them craned their necks in all directions looking for a better location to land the 'copter. Steve shook his head.

"Sorry mate, I can't..."

"Just set down enough for me to step off, then come back for me."

"I dunno Malcolm..."

"Sure! Piece of cake. I'll step down on the skid and step off as soon as it kisses the ground, then you can lift back up. You can do that, can't you?"

"I can do that Malcolm, but can you step off then get back on?"

"No problem," Malcolm lied. *Maybe my warriors will help me.*

Steve tapped the fuel gauge and quickly examined it, then nodded.

239

"Alright, you get one try. And you get back out of there in three minutes, you hear??"

Malcolm slid the 'copter door open and looked down at the thin skid, and the dizzying distance to the ground far below the plateau. His mouth went dry and his tongue had the taste of brass.

Steve shook his head slightly, but moved the machine sideways to set the skid on Malcolm's side delicately on the hard surface of the plateau. Malcolm placed one foot on the skid, unsnapped his waist harness and stepped onto the plateau. The loss of Malcolm's weight on the skid caused the 'copter to tilt back over the drop off, and Steve corrected the tilt by quickly raising the copter higher into the air. Malcolm turned from the dust cloud and headed toward the cave opening. He noted with relief that there were no recent footprints of his 'roo buddies. Inside, as the blackness of the cave faded to light grays he saw dozens of animal bones gnawed completely of all meat.

Cattle bones. At least not my 'roos. Laying here several days and dried out. So he doesn't come every day...

The shades of gray within the cave grew lighter as his eyes adjusted to the interior, and he moved deeper into the hillside. Near the very end where the cave walls curved down to ground level he found the pile of opals. Much taller now. New ones had been added. Roughly dug.

...but he does come here.

Malcolm withdrew the cloth bag from his pocket and shook it out to make room for the opals.

Never hold all those in this little bag. Barely a tenth. Need to make sure he notices right off that some are gone.

He began searching for the largest and most valuable opals, making a spread out jumble of the once neat pile. When the bag could hold no more and the sound of the returning 'copter echoed through the cave, he turned to leave, then stopped and set the bag down on the ground. He returned to the disturbed pile.

240

Need to really mess these up. Piss him off. Get him looking for me. Piss him off good.

Malcolm smiled at his warriors.

"Join me Braves!"

He unzipped his shorts and peed on as many opals as he could, until his bladder was dry. Voices yelled among the growing sound of the 'copter. Malcolm snatched up the bag on his dash to the opening and the rising red dust cloud roiling into the cave.

Running to the 'copter he tossed the bag to Itjanu, who screeched as she had to release her white knuckle grip on her safety handle to catch the opals. Malcolm barely touched the skid as he dove through the 'copter door. He grabbed anything he could hold on to and managed a serious bear hug around the legs of Ranger Corporal Robert Beverly MacAurther. The Ranger helped Malcolm to sit upright, and patted him on his shoulder, staring intently into his eyes.

"Now ain't you the real traveler. You do get around."

Malcolm stared in surprise at the Ranger, and curious if he too would not see the dozen painted Indian warriors standing on the skids outside the doors.

The 'copter swerved around and nosed down in the cooling evening air, slapping its way back toward Alice Springs, as Steve kept a worried frown shared between the horizon and the fuel gauge.

The sun was setting over Mount Ertwa as Helicopter AS-005 settled onto its landing pad. A hundred miles away, what was once Henry Matineau stepped out from the cave onto the plateau flinging urine soaked opals down into the valley and screeching up into the green lights above. Steve and his passengers waited for the swirling blades to slow as the engine revolutions were gradually reduced. Within seconds the turbine engine sputtered once and gave up any sound except the whirring of the blades, as the last vapor of aviation fuel drifted into the engine. Steve released the grip on the controls and turned to face Malcolm.

"That was too bloody close, Mate. You save my life, then you almost bloody kill me. No more."

Robert leaned forward looking between the two men. "What's this?? Is this for real? Did we just run out of fuel as we landed?? Really??"

Steve looked directly into Robert's eyes. "It never happened, Rob. You hear me?"

Rob nodded to Steve with a small grin. "Never happened. Not at all like the time you..."

"Stuff it, Rob. I don't take chances like that anymore."

"No worries, Stevie. Now, how 'bout telling me why you had to have me ride along on this sight-seeing trip of yours with this whacko Yank I kicked out of Wilpena Pound."

Malcolm and Itjanu walked stiff legged toward the parking area, while Steve and Rob made a beeline to the little operations office in the corner of a nearby hangar.

"Steve, the Yank said he met you when he was, well, in a different state of mind..."

"...and body, Rob. Did you meet him in that state, too?"

"Well, er, maybe. I mean, well, kinda hard to explain without sounding daffy."

"How bout I start it off, Robbie. Does a ten foot flying lizard sound familiar?"

"Jimminey, Steve, what's become of us? Sane blokes can't be seeing that kinda thing, can they?"

"We both seen it, right?"

"Yeah."

"Neither of us were hurt by it, right?"

"I suppose not."

"Well, it saved my life, Jackie's, a patient needing hospital and a damned fine airplane. And 'it' was that Yank we just brought in from the outback."

"Can he change into and outta the thing? Is that him been gobbling up 'roos and cattle out there?"

"No, it takes a special ceremony to make him change and he can't change back without another one. Changing ain't up to him. Then there's this other bloke that took it from him and now 'he's' the lizard thing that's eatin up the outback."

They halted in the growing dark and faced each other.

"It's awfully complicated, Steve – just assuming we ain't both bleeding looney. And what's all this got to do with me now?"

"Well, Rob. We need to change Malcolm there back into the thing, and it's got to happen back at the Pound. You need to help us get in there."

"Naaaahh. I dunno about that..."

"It's got to be there Rob. We've got to be done soon. How many 'roos have you lost from out there in the last month?

"Couple dozen for sure."

"It's that other bloke doing it...and there's another problem."

"What else?"

"I think Malcolm there is deadly sick, and he can't make it as a human any more. He's got to live as the lizard thing, if he's going to live at all. 'Sides, him as the thing is a whole lot safer than the one out there now."

"I must be batty as hell. Some of this is actually making sense to me...say, what was in that bag he brought out of the cave?"

" 'Bout 40 pounds of excellent opals."

"40 POUNDS?! What does he need that for?"

"Bait."

As Rob and Steve entered to operations office, Malcolm and Itjanu sat in the van with Mica and Elea. The bag of opals open and sitting on the floor. Malcolm pulled out two little blue and white pills from the bottle given him in hospital, then gulped them down with bottled water. He leaned his head against the van window, watching the twenty Indian warriors surrounding him vanish, one by one.

Itjanu said, "I think the Ranger is going to help us. They've both seen Malcolm as the Lizard."

Mica twisted his back to ease the stiffness of waiting in the van for their return. "So, what happens next? What else do we need to get to repeat the ceremony?"

Elea held up his finger. "Lot's a fresh meat ta go with them opals."

Malcolm was tired and weak from the trip, and the jump into the 'copter. "Elea, do you still have those little blue seeds you found in my pill bottle?"

Elea shrugged his shoulders, "Well, sorta..."

"What do you mean, '...sorta'? You told me a while back that you didn't take'em, and you didn't throw them away..."

"No, I didn't do either of those things..."

"So?..."

"So, I put'em in the ground."

"WHAT???"

" Lettie use ta keep flowers in a flowerbox outside the bedroom window on the shady side of the house. They all died when she did. Then holding those little seeds in my hand made me think they might grow inta something worth looking at. Something she might have thought of worth looking at. Ain't looked at'em since."

Malcolm frowned into the darkness of the van. "Seed or flower, they could help us catch Henry."

Elea reached out and patted Itjanu on the knee. "Ittie, me and you gonna get a ride back to the village with Garner. Mica and Malcolm go back to Coober Pedy to get our things."

"...and my backpack and passport", said Malcolm

'...and my truck!", said Mica

Elea nodded. "We meet back at Wilpena Pound in 4 days."

In the night sky above them, a blackness, once harbored deep and almost unknown within Henry's mind, had full release within the ten-foot scaled body frantically scouring the countryside for his opals...and fresh blood. The rage in its screech made cattle and kangaroos look up anxiously, and smaller animals in the desert tremble beneath the green glow of the Aurora.

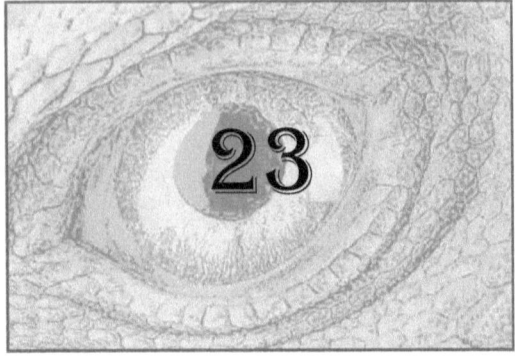

Four days later, three forms stood on the metal platform built on a steep hill in Wilpena Pound. At the base of the rise, Mica's faded blue pickup truck sat in the afternoon soon, waiting patiently for its owner to come back down the hill. Ranger Corporal Robert MacAurther tapped his boot softly on the grating as he looked through binoculars, tracking a dark speck move steadily toward him in the eastern sky above the far tips of Flinders Range. Itjanu and Elea stood at the corner of the platform, leaning against the railing looking in the direction Robert watched, but not yet able to see anything. Elea tilted his head to listen to the whisper of wind in the afternoon air.

"It comes."

Barely above the sound of whispering wind came the steady beating of the air high in the sky. As the sound came closer the beating became louder and faster. All faces turned up toward the figure in the sky, making its way directly toward them; coming on and on. Elea swallowed hard. Itjanu took a step backward away from the rail

"It comes!" Elea shouted.

Robert turned back to Elea, lowering his glasses, "Yes it does, and it's about bloody time."

The steady thumping of the helicopter blades reverberated within the platform as the machine slowed to make its descent.

246

Itjanu folded her arms in front of her, "Tell me how you are able to get the Australian Army to send a helicopter at your beck and call to pick up Mica and Malcolm??"

Robert grinned and returned the glasses to his eyes, speaking under the binoculars, "Not at my beck and call at all, but just this time. This one time. Caught'em up here once doing night training without permission from the park service. The 'copter pilot was supposed to have sent a letter of request, but forgot and thought he could just get through it anyway without telling his major he fell down on the job."

Robert lowered the glasses and turned back to Itjanu. "So he says he'll owe me a big one if I ever need it, as long as I don't put him on report. Seemed like a good bloke and I didn't really intend to put him on report anyway, but a favor from a 'copter pilot could always be of use..." he pointed toward the east, "...and here it is."

Moments later the helicopter settled briefly on the ground at the foot of the hill, then rose in a dust cloud up and over the platform. Hovering over the center of the platform, the 'copter lowered three large boxes by cable. As soon as the cable was retrieved within the 'copter, the ship backed away and settled nose forward at the level of the platform. The pilot and Robert shared thumbs up signs and toothy grins and then waved each other goodbye. Minutes later the copter was well on its way back over St Mary Peak, while Robert wondered what yarn the pilot had spun for the unit leader to cover the flight. Robert, Elea and Itjanu examined the outside of the boxes, but waited until Mica and Malcolm made the climb up the hill before attempting to open any of them.

Mica hopped up the last step to the platform and walked easily toward Elea and Itjanu.

"Still like my truck better."

Unwinded, he withdrew a pack of cigarettes from his shirt pocket and lit one, drawing on it deeply. It was another ten minutes before Malcolm stumbled onto the platform, wheezing and gasping for air.

"All those damned Indians, and do you think just one of them would have helped me? His own Chief? But, no-o-o, they just stood there staring at me. Must have been fifty of them. The bastards."

The others on the platform were unsure what to say.

"Reckon he can still do this thing," Mica asked.

Her face painted in worry, Itjanu brought him a water bottle and let him drink most of it as they sat together on the top step and edge of the platform. Malcolm took three of the blue and white pills with the water.

"Malcolm, are there any side effects to those pills?"

Malcolm chuckled, "Yeah. Depression, and a sense of disconnection from other people."

Mica pointed his cigarette at Malcolm, but spoke to Elea. "I asked him if he needed any help coming up, but he said he'd do it on his own. He ain't looking too good."

Robert examined the heavy plastic boxes, noting the blood seeping from one that was cracked at the bottom corner. "Right then. Malcolm, what do we have here??"

Malcolm coughed, rubbed his side, and pointed back at the boxes with his water bottle. "The two blue ones are insulated boxes full of fresh cut meat. The big wooden box has the bag of opals from the cave, and all the poles and stuff we picked up from the last time here, and some..."

Mica had slipped off his back pack and withdrew the little cedar box so they could all see it. "And here is the Monster Opal, recently 'donated' to the cause..."

"...which will go back as soon as we no longer need it," Itjanu added.

"Right."

Elea reached into the cloth bag hanging from his shoulder. He carefully pulled out three plastic sandwich bags. "And here are those interesting little flowers that became of the tiny blue seeds Malcolm brought from his homeland, Fin-ton County."

Malcolm took the bags and delicately turned them over in his hands. The flowers fragile little blooms were in pristine condition. He smiled at Elea. "You took great care with these. Thank you. Did you taste one?"

"Nah, but I smelled that first bag before I closed it. Fell asleep right after lunch and slept through until after sunup the next day. Had the damndest dreams."

248

Itjanu placed her hands on her hips. "...and he walked around naked on the soccer field talking to himself most of the night.

Elea shrugged his shoulders, "Yeah. That too, I guess."

Malcolm placed the bags on the blue insulated case with the cracked corner. "They're real strong when their fresh. Everyone better wear one of the plastic gloves we brought, before you touch them."

Robert stepped next to Malcolm and gently fingered one of the plastic bags. "So what's the plan Malcolm? How do we make sure that thing comes here and how do we keep it here while ya do your song and dance?"

"We need to set up the poles like it was last time – Itjanu knows how they went. The chants were all written down in Henry's note books, which wound up collected with my pack by the Rangers who found Mica's truck..."

Itjanu nodded in agreement and began taking material out of the wooden crate.

"...then we put opals and some raw meat down at the bottom of the hill – sort of an appetizer for good ol'Henry. We want him thinking about what we got, instead of what we – or he - might do. Then again half way up the hill, and the rest in the center of the platform."

"How can you be sure he'll get focused on that instead of us," Robert asked.

"Well, I did. Opals are a serious draw when you're inside that body and sharing a mind as old as this planet..."

Itjanu spoke over her shoulder as she erected the second pole and tied it to the platform railing. "And the raw meat? Did you...do a lot of that?"

Malcolm shook his head. "No. Not that I didn't have serious cravings for it, but I couldn't bring myself to kill – and then Bill McLeod kept me supplied with fruit and vegetables."

Mica chuckled as he opened the insulated box to get out some of the meat, "And beer as I recall..."

"...and beer. But Henry has a different set of dos and don'ts from me, I guess. Maybe some he didn't even know he had until that thing took him inside..."

"...sounds like he hasn't hesitated to kill anything he wanted, at least not from what I read in the papers." Rob spoke as he was pulling the rest of the poles out of the wooden crate. "What's all this down at the bottom here?"

Well," Malcolm said. "In Finton County that's called logging chain. I got forty feet of it to truss up ol'Henry and help him hold still while we take him out of that Lizard."

Elea chuckled, as he saw the chain. "That oughta do it."

Mica and Malcolm put on plastic gloves and pulled the raw meat out then began cutting deep holes in it with sharp knives. Then Malcolm opened one of the bags of blue flowers and slipped a single flower in each cut hole. Mica opened the large bag of opals and began dropping them by handfuls into the meat bags.

As Mica's hand withdrew another scoop of opals, Malcolm whirled around, his face contorted, dashing at him. Malcolm gripped Mica's hand and forced him to open it. From the loose collection of opals, Malcolm gingerly snatched a black opal sitting in the middle of the rest.

"It's mine," Malcolm snarled. As soon as he placed it in his pocket, his face relaxed and he looked sheepishly at Mica. "Sorry. Don't know what just happened there."

Mica said nothing and went back to his work. Several pounds of doctored meat and a large handful of opals were placed in each of three bags, then Mica took two of the bags and hiked back down to the bottom of the hill below the platform. Malcolm emptied the third bag off the platform and all over the boulder face just below, then dropped the bag to the ground below the boulder. He turned to the rest of the group.

"The rest of the meat and opals we pile in the middle of the platform, just as soon as I push the rest of the flowers in the meat."

Itjanu screamed, "No! No grandfather don't!"

Elea smiled holding a single blue flower in front of his mouth and spoke back to her, "Just a little lick with the tip of the tongue; just enough to know what it tastes like – I won't swallow it!"

Malcolm and Itjanu both jumped toward Elea, but his tongue went out like a snake striking, barely touching the tip of one tiny blue petal. His eyes danced with mischief looking back at Itjanu, "Don't worry granddaughter, it's only a..."

As soon as his tongue passed his lips, his eyes dilated all the way until his irises were almost totally black and he slipped down onto the platform, folding over onto himself like a wet rag dropped loose from its tip. By the time Itjanu and Malcolm got to him, he was looking sternly at the far corner of the platform.

Elea pointed at the corner and yelled out, "Open the pod bay door, HAL!"

Itjanu frowned at Malcolm. "I didn't know he had ever seen that movie."

Then Elea flung himself back like a motorized recliner and rolled his eyes up to his forehead screaming, " My God! It's full of stars!!"

The evening sky reverberated with a raging screech among the few clouds hovering high above, accompanied by the thundering beat of huge leather wings banging tips with each other, shoved together through the air by huge muscles, propelling the beast toward the platform. Toward his opals. Toward the blood.

"Grab him," Robert yelled.

"We need to tie him down," Malcolm yelled. "He won't come out of it for hours – hours we don't have!"

Robert and Malcolm carried Elea to a corner where Robert pulled out his handcuffs and secured Elea around the corner post of the platform.

Henry came on. The thing that had once been Henry. The thing Henry had become, had replaced Henry and taken with it every petty hurt, insult and grievance and added it to its own primal killer instinct. It came. He swooped low at the base of the hill and quickly devoured the raw meat, even taking in the opals with it.

251

Up the hill he flew, scooping up the second stage of bate – raw meat and opals in a single gulp. On to the third bait, barely pausing along the face of the boulder to gorge on every piece of meat, drop of blood and every opal. And then he ascended to the railing of the platform, landing heavily, spreading his wings and showing his chest, tilting his massive head up to the sky and the Aurora glowing brighter than before, and bellowed an ear-splitting roar, driving the people to cover their ears and turn away. His chest was larger than Malcolm's had been and tinged with a red the color of fresh blood, dark dried blood crusted on his claws and heavily on his chin. His eyes had gone from lemon yellow to ruby red with only the pupil still yellow.

He roared again, looking around the platform, claiming the meat and opals for himself, then lunged at the pile in the center of the platform. He covered the pile with his wings, keeping the food for himself. He feasted on huge chunks of meat dripping blood, grinding the beef bones into pulp and swallowing in tremendous gulps. He only occasionally looked around the platform to ensure no one approached him. His glance lingering on Malcolm and his lips at one corner curled into a menacing sneer as blood drooled down.

In his corner, Elea had managed to turn around to watch the monster, smiling at it with misty eyes, then broke into loud song.

"♫ LA-DY OF SPAIN, I A-DORE YOU…"

Henry turned his head toward Elea, but kept chewing and returned to his glutinous feast.

"♫ RIGHT FROM THE NIGHT, I FIRST SAW YOU…"

No one else on the platform dared to move, all looking for any sign the flower-doctored meat might be having an effect on the Henry-Monster.

"♫ MY HEART HAS BEEN YEAR-NING FOR YOU…"

With a final gulp, all the meat and opals were swallowed and the monster whirled around, eyeing each person one at a time, lingering in his eye contact with

252

Malcolm, uttering a gravel voiced whisper from deep in his throat, "Mal-colm."

Once again he spread his gargantuan wings and raised his head toward the Borialis and took in a deep rasping breath, then looked down upon the diminutive people around him, staring, lingering, lost in thought, then looking casually around, tilting his head slowly to one side then the other.

"You hear that," he asked Robert in an almost childlike voice. Then he looked back up in the sky tilting his head again and again. He began to tap his foot ever so slightly.

"There. There it is again," he said to Itjanu. He rocked his shoulders minutely, tilting his head in the opposite directions, then added a rocking motion with his hips.

Malcolm traded looks with the others, a large smile on his face.

Henry raised his hands above his head, his index claw pointing upward, beginning a small dance and humming to himself, but it was not in rhythm with Elea's singing.

"♫ WHAT ELSE COULD AN-NY HEART DO?..."

Just barely making a voice that could be heard, the monster began a musical chant.

"♫ **Nunna-nunna** , nunna-nunna, **nunna-nunna**, nunna-nunna, **munh**-maah..."

Henry began pointing back and forth among the people around him, rocking his shoulders in time and singing slightly louder.

"♫ **NUNNA-nunna** , nunna-nunna, **NUNNA-nunna**, nunna-nunna, **Munh**-maah..."

Louder he sang as he danced in a twirl on his spot, smiling as he danced.

"♫ **NUNNA-nunna** , nunna-nunna, **NUNNA-nunna**, nunna-nunna, **Bat**-maahn..."

"♫ **NUNNA-NUNNA** , NUNNA-NUNNA, **NUNNA-NUNNA**, NUNNA-NUNNA, **BAT**-MAN..."

"♫ LA-DY OF SPAIN, I'M AP-PEALING..."

"♫ **NUNNA-NUNNA** , NUNNA-NUNNA, **NUNNA-NUNNA**, NUNNA-NUNNA, **BAT-MAN**..."

"♫ **NUNNA-NUNNA** , NUNNA-NUNNA, **NUNNA-NUNNA**, NUNNA-NUNNA, **BAT-MAN**..."

Henry stopped abruptly, stood up straight, held his clawed fists as high as he could and screamed out, "I AM **BAT MAN!!**", then fell flat on his face and the whole platform shook violently.

"Roll him over! I'll get the chain. We need to sit him up for the ceremony," yelled Malcolm as he dashed to the wooden box.

"Okie Dokie," mumbled Henry, the end of his snout protruding through the grating below.

Itjanu motioned toward her grandfather and spoke to Mica. "What about him?"

"No worries, He safe where he is – wherever that is."

"♫ WHY SHOULD MY LIPS BE CON-CEA-LING..."

Malcolm, Robert and Mica worked quickly wrapping the heavy chain around Henry's ankles and torso, pinning in his arms, while Henry watched in mild curiosity like a drunk man near the end of his night.

"Little loose there on my right arm," Henry said, then bobble-headed around the platform. "I'm still hungry. Got anything else?"

Selected opals were attached to the poles around the platform. The Monster Opal was attached to the center pole with duct tape, and as the collection was brought close together the dark clouds were already beginning to form. Itjanu looked from the clouds to the glow surrounding each opal atop the poles.

"I don't think the storm was ever coming the first time. It was no lucky chance. The opals are calling it, causing it."

"Must be the power of the black opals," said Mica

Malcolm took up the tallest pole holding the Monster Opal and moved toward the center of the platform. The wind arose and the clouds drew near, lightning beginning to flash within the storm. Malcolm turned back to Itjanu.

"I think you're right." Then Malcolm dropped to one knee, pain in his side spasming through his body. Indians warriors gathered around him in a circle.

Itjanu ran to his side. "Are you sure you want to do this again? CAN you do it?"

Malcolm stood back up with her help. "Got to. No choice."

Mica handed the notebooks to Itjanu and Malcolm. "Guess you gotta read Henry's parts Malcolm, but is it safe for Ittie to read your parts."

Malcolm looked at Henry, then the location of all the other poles. "I think just me and Henry need to be in the center. Don't know if it has to go through me to him or him to me, but no sense in having it go through you too. Might just confuse things or do something to you. It has to be between just me and Henry. Maybe Mica should read the other part?"

Mica pushed his hands up and shook his head NO, then backed away. Itjanu took the other notebook and stepped a few feet away from the center.

Henry rocked his head around to look at Malcolm. "You're a good buddy, Malcolm, but I'm really having fun as I am."

Malcolm sighed and reached over patting Henry's muscular shoulder. 'Yeah, I know, but you just stay sleepy until this is all over."

"♫ ALL THAT MY EYES ARE RE-VEA-LING? ..."

Malcolm looked around the platform. "We are going to start from the beginning. Keep the poles straight and still. No one says anything except me and Itjanu."

Malcolm looked back at Elea, "Hopefully his singing won't interfere with this.

Malcolm pulled on Henry's forehead lamp and switched it on, opened his notebook and began reading the first segment. When he finished, he looked toward Itjanu who began reading the next segment. Malcolm read his next line. Line followed line. Both voices grew louder, firmer, more force, more intensity. Incantation followed counter incantation. Call and Response. Call and Response. The wind surged up from the savannah of the pound and rushed up the slope below the platform.

"♫ LADY OF SPAIN, I LOVE YOU ..."

Malcolm and Itjanu looked around but the wind and the lightning continued, the glow of the opals continued to increase. The wind rippled clothing, and blew away the cloth bags that had held the meat and opals. The temperature dropped significantly. Their breath was a cold fog in front of them as they continued to read and chant. They threw out their voices louder and stronger, and now the space of time between lines was barely two heartbeats, and the rhythm of the readings were faster. The rhythm of the readings and the wind matched and paced each other. The voices grew in strength to match the wind, and the wind grew in strength to match the incantations. Line followed line. The wind came in gusts that grew with each couplet. Their feet shifted slightly farther apart to stand firm in the wind, those at the rails gripped harder.

On the lines went, louder and more forceful, but barely finding their way above the sound of the roaring wind whipping around the platform, drawing in the clouds from over the tops of the mountain ridges. They reached the last page, once again racing through the lines, dashing to the bottom of the page. The dark clouds rushed onto the platform, flashes of green lightning racing along the edges of the whirlwind. The last four lines were read within the whirling storm around them, unheard by the others. Itjanu read her last line. Malcolm read the ancient words, the command shouted in a language no longer spoken by the living.

Green lightning flashed within the clouds overhead, chased by explosions of thunder shaking the platform. The Aurora flashed bright and pulsated, then sent a near perfectly straight lightning bolt down toward the platform. Again, the beam split just above the platform, shooting into the objects offered at the tips of the poles. The four beams then shot into the Monster Opal at the tip of Malcolm's pole held directly in front of Henry and then into Henry's chest. Then the light connected straight from the Aurora, through the objects, into the great opal and poured into Henry's chest.

Henry screamed, "No! No! Don't take it away from me!" He struggled against his chains with all his remaining strength. A green corona ran the length of his body. Tendrils of intense green light snaked out from his body in all directions, creating a sphere of light around him. More energy pulsed into his body. His wings spread and the corona spread along their edges. He flung his arms out, shattering the chains, screaming with the pain. The beam of energy poured straight down from the Aurora directly into Henry's chest. Before Henry could move any more, Malcolm pulled the Monster Opal from the duct tape and pressed it against his own chest, squeezed his eyes shut and gritted his teeth. Then he yelled the last command a second time.

Green lightning exploded from Henry and drilled point blank through the opal into Malcolm. Malcolm screamed. Electrical veins spread from his hair and ears and off the edges of his teeth. An aura of yellow light erupted from his side and merged with the green tendrils of light dancing over his body. He was completely engulfed in incandescent green lightning. He screamed again within the light, and then they were both engulfed within it.

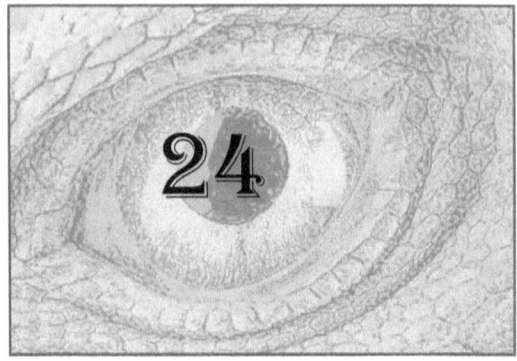

The wind and the rain and the light faded away. Dead silence and darkness blanketed the platform. Vapors rose from the platform like steam off hot metal, but there was no sound. The Aurora faded. The stars of the Southern Cross showed brightly in the night sky. Nothing in Wilpena Pound moved or made a sound. Silence filled the air.

Henry rolled over on to his side naked, gasping for air and retching. Malcolm lay unchanged and motionless. Robert, Mica and Itjanu ran to Malcolm. Mica wrapped them in blankets and Itjanu felt both for a pulse.

"They're both alive with strong pulses."

"♫ NIGHT IN MA-DRID, BLUE AND TEN-DER..."

With that verse sung, Elea's chin settled onto his chest and he fell into a deep sleep. Mica and Itjanu rolled the blankets around Malcolm and Henry, so they would be protected from the evening air coming up through the grating. Mica returned from another trip to the truck a short while later with sleeping bags and blankets. Elea was uncuffed and laid on a blanket, then the covered up in silence to fall asleep as it came to each one.

"You stole it from me! It was mine and you stole it from me, you bastard!!"

Dawn light was bright over the peaks of Flinders Range as Henry stood naked over Malcolm, kicking him with his bare feet. Robert was at him immediately and brought his hands behind his back to secure them with his handcuffs. He threw a blanket around Henry and forced him to sit back down. Shaking his head at Henry, he sat back down on his own blanket.

"Bloody Hell, Henry! I've only had to cuff people two times as long as I've been a Ranger. Elea last night and you this morning. You people have to control yourselves!"

"He stole it from me. Now neither one of us has it. I looked at him. No change. And he took it from me!"

Malcolm sat up on his blanket. "Shut up, Henry. You don't get to fly around at night eating cows and Kangaroos, and I get to die." Malcolm looked at his arms and legs, then opened his shirt. "Nothing."

"Good," spat Henry.

As the others woke and rose up, Itjanu came to Malcolm. "No change at all? Of anything?"

Malcolm only shook his head and looked away.

"All right, people. It's done. We're done. And now it's time to get down off my hill and head back to the campground with you. Far as I'm concerned not having that big nasty thing terrorizing the outback is a good thing, well accomplished. My sorries to you, Malcolm."

Slowly they filed back down the switchback trail to the truck at the bottom of the hill. Henry ran on ahead, eager to find his clothes. After several turns on the trail, Mica reached out to help Malcolm over a steep boulder.

"I'm OK, Mica. At least my side isn't hurting this morning. Maybe my lightning therapy last night was good for something after all. At least for now."

Itjanu reached out from behind him and patted him on the back. Malcolm looked back over his shoulder and traded smiles with her. As he turned his head, a severe cramp struck him high in his left leg and he collapsed down the trail, tumbling several yards and landing face down in the red dirt. Itjanu ran down to him, dropped to her knees beside him and helped him roll over. He had ripped his shorts and torn his shirt and put an ugly gash in his right hand. Before either of them could say anything about the fall or the gash, it completely closed as if it were never there. Her eyes widened and a huge smile spread across Malcolm's face. Then a button snapped off his shirt where it was too tight on his chest, and exposed his upper chest that had become a bright green.

"This is really happening fast, Itjanu!"

One of his shoes split as his foot grew.

"Holy cow! Really fast! And I wanted to tell you..."

"Tell me what, Malcolm?"

"Tell you, but,..."

His shirt sleeve split, and his other shoe split off his foot.

"To let you know,..."

"Know what?"

"That I, I mean we..."

The long green tail reappeared and snaked out the side of his shorts. His shoulders were getting broader, and his torso taller, his shredded shirt slipped to the ground.

"It's so fast, Itjanu, I wanted to..."

"Oh shut up," she said, and kissed him as hard and as long as she could. And as he grew taller and taller, and as his snout began to protrude from his green skin, she had to push him away.

The scales appeared almost immediately. His lemon eyes returned. He sat there looking at his hands, and legs, and sighed heavily as he looked down at Itjanu.

"It's what you need to be, Malcolm."

"I know. It just happened so fast. Too fast."

Elea rounded the trail and came face to face with the fully formed reptile monster. Elea eyed it closely. "So which one are you?"

The monster smiled broadly. "It's me. Dingo Ass."

Elea patted him gently on his knee as he stepped past him. "Well. Let's get you home."

At the bottom of the hill Mica, Itjanu and Elea got into the old faded blue truck. Henry had retrieved his pack and was nowhere to be seen. Mica started the truck and stuck his head out the window, speaking with Malcolm.

"You come to Mutanajulu tonight, Malcolm. We'll have things ready for you in the old warehouse." Then he smacked his hand against the outside of the truck door, laughed and drove away.

Robert offered his hand to Malcolm and took the offered claw in a firm grip. "You're a good man, Malcolm Ironwater. Whatever you are on the outside, you're a good man inside there. Just do me one favor."

"Sure, Rob. What is it?"

"Don't come back to my Park!" Then he laughed, turned smartly on his heels and quick-stepped along the trail back toward the Pound opening through Wilpena creek.

Alone in Wilpena Pound with the midday sun heating the countryside to a shimmering haze, Malcolm raised his wings into the thin heated air and pulled hard with steel spring muscles, darting into the sky so no one could get a detailed look at him. He quickly reached the cooler air at ten thousand feet, where any glimpse of him was a mere dot in the sky and made his way back to the plateau, and the cave, and a solitary existence. He sat at the edge of the plateau, looking down at the valley below, wondering if any of the kangaroos he had befriended had survived Henry, and decided he didn't want to know.

This is it. As a human, I die. As this thing I live. – If I can call this living.

He sat there thinking about that until the sun went down. Then he scooped up his opals in a box he found down in the valley and took them to a creek to wash his pee off of them. When he returned to the plateau he thought about going to Mutanajulu, and he thought a lot about Itjanu, but he decided not to go tonight. He picked up one of the smaller opals and flew to Mutana Creek, where he placed the opal on top of the trash can outback and then hopped up on the metal roof over the kitchen and tapped on it three times. The back door soon opened, but then closed almost immediately with a slam.

Moments later the door opened and out stepped Bill McLeod carrying a box of fresh fruit and vegetables under one arm and a two-gallon bucket of beer with his other hand.

"Malcolm," he whispered hoarsely. "You out here, mate?"

261

Malcolm glided down to the ground a couple yards away from Bill, at the edge of the light thrown out by the back door bulb.

"It's me, Bill. Same ol'me. No reason to be afraid of me."

"Why in the hell would I be afraid of you, Malcolm?"

"Well, there's been another one out there doing a lot of bad things, but that wasn't me..."

"Hell, I knew that. Knew that wasn't you when I first heard about it. 'Sides, Mica called me as soon as he got back in town. Said you might be comin around for a drop or two."

Malcolm plopped down on the edge of the little sand hill where he used to sit, smiling broadly and a little trickle of water sliding down from one eye.

"It's damned good to see you, Bill. It's been a hard couple of weeks."

"And you can take that opal back, you put on my trash can."

"What?..."

"Malcolm, with what you already gave me, I've done paid my 99-year lease all the way to the end of it. Don't you dare give me anything else. Your money (and your opals) aren't any good around here. You don't pay for beer, or apples, or carrots as long as I live. You're always welcome here."

The streams of water flowed from both yellow eyes as Malcolm nodded his head at his friend. "That's real good to know, Bill." And then he began to cry.

Bill came close and reached up to pat him on his back. "What's going on, Malcolm? You hurt?"

"Bill, I grew up always wanting to be someone else, somewhere else, something else, and in the last moment of being me I realized how important that was, and how much I wanted that. But, now I am this from now on."

"Well, you try to eat your veggies and drink that cup of beer and I'll bring you another."

As Bill walked back toward the pub, he stopped and turned around. "Malcolm, I don't go to church any more, haven't been in years. But my sister Pat is an evangelist up in Darwin. She says God don't give you nothing you can't handle and don't put you anywhere you don't need ta be. Maybe you're supposed to be this you. I don't know, but I'll get you that other beer." Then he was gone inside.

As he ate the first apple, Malcolm realized how hungry he was and fell upon the mixed fruit and vegetables with energy, and followed it with serious drinks of beer until the bucket was empty. Soon Bill returned with another bucket of beer. This one was slightly larger than the first.

"Itjanu called and said you could only have two beers. She figured you'd come here since you didn't show up at Mutanajulu. I'm sure she knew they would come in buckets, but I got these new ones in case you came back. This one's three gallons. Ought to do. You don't mind that do you?"

"Mind what?"

"Mind her saying you should only have two beers. Mind her telling you what you should do."

"Don't mind at all." He drank more from the three-gallon bucket, then set it down and looked off at the horizon. "Actually, I like it. I like it a lot."

Malcolm stood up and stretched his arms and then his wings.

"See you later, Bill."

"Where ya'goin'?"

"Mutanajulu."

With a powerful downward sweep of his wings, he sprang into the night sky. Moments later he settled noiselessly onto the ground behind the old warehouse at the edge of Mutanajulu. Pushing gently on the warehouse door he stepped into the light. Empty beer cans and paper plates littered the dusty floor. Party lights had been strung across the crossbeams overhead. Folding tables had been set up in three rows. At the head of the center table, Itjanu sat slumped over with her head resting on her arms folded on the table in front of her. Beyond her table near the back wall were two cases of apples and a keg of beer. She heard him come in, raised her head and looked in his direction, motioning with her hand toward the apples.

"That's for you."

"Already ate."

"Yeah. I heard."

"I also heard I can only have two beers. You said that?"

"Yes."

"What does it matter?"

"It matters what you do with the talents you have. It matters that you don't waste your life. Whatever it is!"

"What do you want me to do? What talents can I share with a world that will be terrified of me?"

She stood up and walked toward him. "Be YOU, Malcolm. Be YOU! Take what you have become and do something special with it!"

"What do you want me to be? What do you want me to do??"

"Be my friend. For now, help me build a medical clinic for Mutanajulu. After that, do what you heart tells you to do."

He stepped in front of her. His head was four and a half feet above hers. He curled the first finger of his clawed hand so the claw would be wrapped safely inside his fist, and delicately touched her cheek with his knuckle.

"O.K."

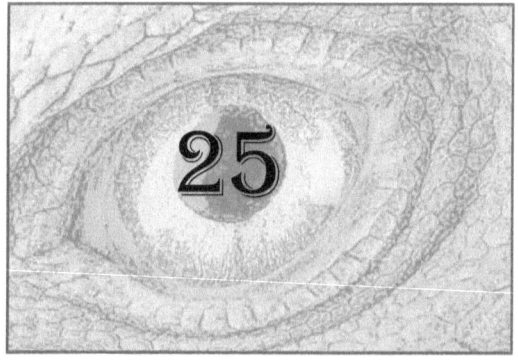

To everyone's surprise, the Monster Opal was not destroyed in the final ceremony. Mica travelled back to the Dingo Cave Mine in Coober Pedy to return the Monster Opal to its owner, who flew into a rage only quelled when Mica gave him the two perfect black opals Malcolm had sent along. The owner also agreed, for a small percentage, to provide an avenue to sell some of the opals Malcolm could bring down from the plateau. The money from the opals helped buy the material to build the clinic, and people from the village helped to build it. Used medical equipment was then purchased in other Asian countries. Mutanajulu Medical Clinic became one of the best village clinics in the outback.

The RFDS established an outpost near the clinic and regularly flew in and out of the nearby runway at Mutana Creek. When weather was difficult or dangerous, or the location of the patient impossible by plane and too far away by helicopter, the clinic's 'special arrangement' made it possible to treat people. Mica found an old abandoned single engine plane, the engine long removed and sold for scrap, but the body sound, and added safety straps for the patients, and lifting points for Malcolm. Malcolm would set the plane down at the far edge of the runway, beyond the bright lights, and patients otherwise unable to receive medical care would be placed on gurneys and rushed to life saving help.

In the rare quiet evenings, Malcolm would sit on his raised platform in the back of the warehouse that had become the clinic. Itjanu would visit him and tell him of her day, and what became of the people he had helped rescue. She would talk about her dreams for the clinic, and he would humor her with stories of befuddled people with quaint names in that place known as Finton County.

"What do you plan to do next, Malcolm? What other amazing things would you like to do?"

"I'm not through here, Ittie. Not just yet. There is more for me to do."

As the months slipped by, the green Aurora that had descended upon Australia faded a little more each night.

Mica had arranged a skylight to be built in the roof above the platform where Malcolm slept. He would look up at the stars and the Aurora as he drifted off to sleep each night. Sometimes he would drift off to sleep watching the morning sky, when he had spent the night flying over the outback helping people; helping the clinic; helping Ittie. Sometimes he would dream, and it was always the same dream. It was the moment before he became the creature again, when he tried to tell her, tried to say it to her while he still could. But she told him to shut up, and she kissed him. That was his best dream.

The Aurora faded more each night until it was at last totally gone. Malcolm was laying on his platform looking up at the clear starry night when he realized it. It was gone. It was the beginning of all that he had experienced since coming to Australia. He came to Australia still in a drug-induced state wanting to free the Aborigine. He laughed to himself.

They should have come to Finton County to free ME.

He laughed again in his half awake state, and drifted off to a deep sleep.

In the morning, he could see the bright blue cloudless Australian sky through his skylight above. He stretched a mighty stretch with his arms high above his head and his thigh muscles thick and tight and ready for anything. He felt alive and fresh and wide awake, and ready for whatever the day would bring him. Someone would have

266

left a box of fruit down on the floor for him, and Ittie would stop by on her way to her office. It was one of his favorite moments of the day – the other was talking with her in the evenings. His platform was five feet off the floor so he could swivel around in the mornings and step on the floor, eager for his day. He spun around, dropping his feet off the platform, and then stood up to stretch again. Only he did not stand up; he fell. He fell and fell and fell until he finally hit the floor.

This must be a blasted dream! I don't fall from my platform. I need to wake up!

His right hip and shoulder and right elbow were all throbbing in pain from the fall. He had dropped to the floor in an awful fall.

What the hell??

He stood up, dazed by his fall and looked up at the ceiling and walls.

This is all crazy!

His shoulders were barely at the level of his sleeping mat. His stool beside the bed was just as high.

What the hell??

To his right was the hallway Ittie usually came through to visit him. Only it wasn't waist-high anymore. It was above his own head.

Gotta be a damned dream!

He stumbled down the hallway, keenly aware of the hot pain in his shoulder, hip and elbow.

This is way too real!!

He went toward the first door and pushed his way in. It was a bathroom – and it was his size. He looked ahead, then knew it was really a dream. There was the face of a black man staring back at him. Anangu. He touched his face and the man in the mirror did the same. He rubbed his forehead and the black man did the same.

Wierdest dream!!

But he stood before the mirror, pushing and pulling and squeezing his face, feeling every move and seeing it all in the face of the black man on the other side of the mirror. He looked down at his own hands and did not see the green; did not see the caucasion; saw the black ebony of the man in the mirror.

267

"No!"

He ran back out into the hallway and flew into Itjanu. She placed her hands on his shoulders.

"Can I help you sir? Do you know where your room is? Let me help you back."

"I am in my room," he said "but that is not me. I'm not black. I'm green."

He ran back toward his room. She ran after him, the farthest part of her brain telling her that was his voice. He rushed back into the bathroom. Stood looking into the mirror. Saw the black man again. Frantic. His eyes following Malcolm's eyes. They both looked into the mirror. Saw her come in. Turned to her. She placed her hands on Malcolm's face. He clasped her hands against his cheeks and turned back toward the mirror over the sink. She stood there. Worry painting her face, looking at him. Her hands in the mirror on the face of the black man in the mirror. The black man in the mirror. Her hands were on the face of Malcolm. She was in the mirror. Malcolm was in the mirror. Malcolm's eyes and the black man's eyes fixed together. Malcolm was the black man in the mirror. He looked at his hands again.

"Oh, Ittie," he said.

She dropped her hands from his face and stared into his eyes.

"Malcolm? – Malcolm. Malcolm, is that you?"

He held her hands in his. Ebony on ebony. Touched her face.

"Malcolm?"

He could say nothing. Had no idea where to begin, what to say. Looked deeply into her eyes.

"Malcolm?"

"Yes."

They sank to the floor, sitting together on the cool tile. Holding hands. Staring at each other in silence.

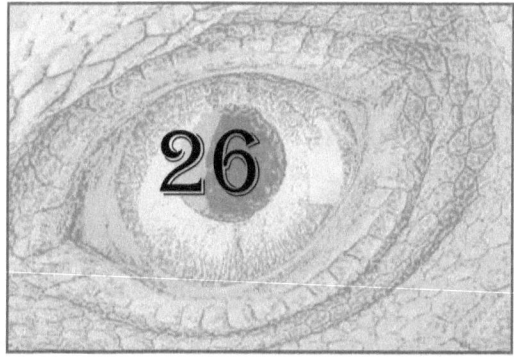

Mica took a sip from the beer can he held and turned back to Malcolm. They were sitting in the Mutana Creek Pub at a table farthest from the bar.

"How'd Bill take it."

"After he thought about it, he just laughed. Said if he could accept that I was the lizard creature why couldn't he accept that I was now Anangu. That was actually easier for him."

"So what's this gonna do between you and Ittie?"

"First I've got to figure what it's going to do between me and me. How long will this last? What comes next? Do I turn into an Eskimo? Chinaman? Maliqroische? Hell, I started with that one!"

The door to the pub flew open and in walked a dozen fresh faced tourists in perfectly pressed khaki shorts and shirts, unmarked new hiking boots, and bringing the noise typical of vacationers. Shooing them in like a hen with her brood came Mac Hartwell. As soon as he found seats for all his charge, he slipped behind the bar to help Bill serve them all.

"Shoutin for Beers here! Beers for the house," he yelled.

Beers were served up to all those at the bar, and the tables nearby, and then Mac brought two frosty mugs to the table where Mica and Malcolm sat.

"Free Beers, Gents. Courtesy of Granby Outback Tours. Mica, how ya' doin mate?"

Mica shook hands with him and asked him to sit. Mac went back to the bar to get his own beer mug and joined the two men in the back of the pub. As he sat down he extended his hand and a toothy smile to Malcolm, "Mac Hartwell. Guide, driver, radio operator, and first aid corpsman – and soon to be: Part owner of this magnificent pub!"

"Malcolm," he said, shaking Mac's hand.

"Now there's a coincidence. Only met two men in my life named Malcolm, and both had beers with me in this very place. The other was a Yank."

Malcolm nodded and smiled his own new toothy grin. Mica leaned in closer to the table so he could be heard over the babble at the bar.

"You buying in here? What about your position with the tours?"

"Given'er up, Mica. This here group is my last. Had enough of it. Lost a Yank and a Canook, and it was just all too difficult on me." He looked at Malcolm. "'Course we found one of them..."

The pub door opened again and in shuffled Henry Matineau, dour faced and searching for a chair far from the bar. He sat at the only remaining table, beside the three men talking.

"Hows'er going Henry," Mac asked. "You ready for a nice cold beer?"

"I guess..."

Mac went off to draw another beer. Mica turned around in his chair to face Henry.

"Henry, you look like shit, mate. You not getting any rest?"

"Mica, the only thing I want to get is me out of Australia."

"Well, I guess it's just as well. Maybe you'll feel better once yer back home in Canada."

Mac set the chilled mug in front of Henry and returned to the table with Mica, then turned back around to face Henry.

"Say Henry, you remember the refined English woman in the group with you and Malcolm?"

Henry gritted his teeth enough that it could be heard at the next table. "Yeah, Elizabeth – something..."

"Well, it'll be Elizabeth Hartwell after she signs the papers with her Ex in Sidney..."

A chorus of yells and shouts arose from the bar as two of the khaki clad tourists began pushing each other.

"Alright! Enough of that, blokes," Mac yelled and went to separate them.

Mica turned back to Malcolm. "Let's walk outside."

They walked around behind the pub and sat on the sand pile where the flying lizard use to sit and drink his beer by the bucketful. They sat on the sand ridge and let their feet dangle above the ground.

Malcolm looked closely at the sandbank. "I used the think this was a little sand hill, just inches above the ground." He shook his head slightly and gave his attention to Mica.

"Malcolm, you gotta hear me all the way through. I'm serious, Mate. Agree?"

"O.K."

"Every hundred years or so, that Aurora comes back over Australia and just sits up there a while. I don't know if it's planned or just happens, but it comes. And when it does sometimes people get turned into those things. I've been told that those things are in between what they were and what they're gonna be. Seems that if it takes, like if a seed falls onto fertile ground it grows into something else, then it moves on to a final condition. It's evolution. It's moving to a higher form of life. It's moving on to a better form of life that doesn't ruin nature, but takes it as it is and lives within it. And it lasts nearly forever.

"Whoa! Lasts forever. Lives forever?"

"Almost..."

"And everybody around you dies off? T'hell with that!"

"You get a choice. It has to do with your opal. The one you're linked to."

"I'm linked to an opal? When does that happen, and what do I do with it – and how the Hell do you know all this stuff is right??"

271

"One thing at a time Malcolm. First, you're already linked to your opal. You found it in the cave out there. It's around your neck right now."

Malcolm fingered the leather line holding the black opal around his neck.

"Oh, that's just a bauble. A souvenir of the time I was the flying Dingo Ass. It's just a trinket"

"Fine. Give it to me and I'll get you another." He reached for Malcolm's opal, but Malcolm grabbed his wrist in a strong grip before he could touch it. "Why did you do that, Malcolm?"

Malcolm looked at his friend's wrist in his grip and then released it, and laughed briefly. "I really don't know."

"I do. You're linked to it. Just like I was to mine. Got mine from the same pile you got yours. Gave it to my Annie, and she wears it every day. She'll be around as long as I am."

"Whoa Hoss! You got yours?? Got yours from the same pile I got mine? What are you saying. Are you saying you were one of those things?"

He smiled.

"For a while. But I didn't have to go through all the trouble you did until it wore off and I evolved."

"Yeah right! And when did all this happen?"

Mica looked him directly in his eyes.

"1842."

Malcolm looked at him and said nothing. Mica's smile warmed.

"I gave my opal to Annie in 1852, after watching her grow from 18 to 28 while I stayed the same."

"How did you know to do that?"

"There's a man lives in the northern part of the Simpson desert. Lives all by himself. Told me he couldn't let go of his opal until his wife lay dying on her bed, but it was too late then. He came before white men ever settled here. He was one of the first Anangu. Saw what happened that became the stories of what the Europeans call the Dream Time. Was there for it. Was part of it. Go see him if you have to, but if you care for Ittie, you give her your opal."

Malcolm stared out into the darkness. "Is Elea evolved?"

"No. But he knows about us. Had his chance once long ago, but decided to let it all run out naturally. You want me to take you to that man out in the desert?"

"Nah. I've been a ten-foot flying lizard with yellow eyes. How could I <u>not</u> believe you."

That night, sitting in Elea's kitchen, Malcolm shared with Itjanu much of what he had learned from Mica.

"So, I will grow old and you will stay the same," she said. Her usual infectious smile had faded to sadness. Malcolm held out his opal.

"Or you can take this, but it may be a curse in the other direction."

She placed her hand gently on his. Malcolm let out a small breath.

"If you accept this opal and stay with me..."

"You mean, if YOU stay here with ME, Malcolm..."

"Yes, as long as we stay together, I will live a little shorter, but you will live as long as I do."

"Then you have to ask for me."

He smiled and sat up straighter. "Itjanu Williamson, will you m-"

"Not me, Malcolm. You have to ask my Grandfather."

Later that night, under a ghost gum tree in a dry creek bed behind the windowless house once shared with Lettie, Elea stood patiently, leaning on his stick. The light from the Southern Cross and attending stars in the night sky above filtered through the limbs and illuminated the tree, as Malcolm fumbled out the words he needed to say. Elea brought his foot up to rest against his other leg as Anangu men had done since before time was counted, waiting for Malcolm to finish.

"Well, Dingo Ass, I guess between the three of you: Mouthy Yank, Ugly Lizard, and Anangu man, Ittie will get the best of the lot. I've seen enough of you to know that you will do right by her. And you've seen enough of me to know how well I can use this here stick."

At the end of the hot dry season, the rains came and the plains turned green with new growth. It is a season called "Itjanu" by the Anangu. Out beyond the paved roads of Alice Springs, a wedding was held in a low lying wadi near a billabong under the shade of an old Coolibah tree. A lovely Pitjantjatjara couple were wed in a traditional ceremony attended by family and very close friends. The groom wore white spots and wandering white lines of the Woma Python. The bride was painted in design to match her groom and was adorned by a magnificent rare black opal. An old man stood near the couple, holding his granddaughter's bouquet of little blue flowers, humming 'Lady of Spain'.

ABOUT THE AUTHOR

"Writing as Pug Greenwood allows the redneck in me to run amok!'

Robert F. Lackey lives with his patient wife, Sandi, in Murrells Inlet, SC

www.rflackeybooks.com